CRIMSON SNOW

CRIMSON
SNOW

THE LAST DESPERATE DAYS
OF IMPERIAL RUSSIA

DAVID SHONE

Cover art: Steve Jones

HOUR GLASS BOOKS

Library of Congress Control Number
2007935459

ISBN
978-0-9798923-0-1

Printed in the United States of America

For Michelle

"History would be an excellent
thing, if only it were true."

Leo Tolstoy

Worthy Reader! Why did I write Crimson Snow?

Blame my Mother. She worked as a housekeeper for a wealthy but aging socialite who possessed a striking resemblance to the late Grace Kelley. Her name was Marilyn Obolensky but I called her Mrs. O.

To me, Mrs. O always reminded me of the sad Miss Havisham figure out of Charles Dickens's Great Expectations. Jilted by time and a lost love, the widow passed her days in her grand but decaying Grosse Pointe Farm home gazing up at a life-size portrait of her dead husband a Russian noble named Prince Serge Obolensky.

Prince Serge wore his imperial Russian uniform well; tall, pencil-thin, he radiated such confidence. Seeing it, I often asked myself what went so wrong in Russia that poor old Serge ended up in a room full of dust.

The answer is Crimson Snow.

Special thanks to Julie Musk.
The greatest gift of all is the gift of time.
You proved it.

Mark R. thanks for the good feedback.

Thank you, Hazel B.
You're a dear neighbor & friend.
Plus, all others whom made *Crimson* better.

And, Bob Atchison's showpiece site:
http://www.alexanderpalace.org/palace/
It truly is an imperial time machine.

For more details on *Champagne Haze*, visit
www.crimson-snow.com

THE CAST LIST

HOUSE OF ROMANOV

Tsar Nicholas II—Emperor of All Russia. His country is entering its third winter of war and the mounting number of casualties is appalling—6 million men wounded or dead. Over a year ago, he personally took command of the army in an effort to slow the bloodletting. This did not have any effect; just more dead line the bottom of the trenches. The huge human cost of the war has made his subjects lose faith in him and his regime. No longer do they ask if there is going to be a revolution. They just ask themselves when. Age 48.

Empress Alexandra—Tsarina of All Russia. She has ruled beside her husband for over twenty years now. Most recently, Nicholas has allowed her to handle the day-to-day operations of his government. With the tsar's attention completely focused on the war, Alexandra feels the need for change. Leaning heavily on the advice of her spiritual counselor Father Rasputin, Alexandra rearranges the tsar's ministers more to her liking. Once a beautiful German princess, Alexandra now resembles a bitterly broken woman struggling to maintain her husband's authority. Age 44.

Tsarevich Alexei—the long awaited heir to the throne. Sadly, the child suffers from hemophilia—a rare blood disease known as the 'royal disease' since it is so prevalent in Europe's Ruling Houses. During one outbreak, he appeared near death until Rasputin performed a miracle, in the eyes of his mother, Empress Alexandra. From that day on, every time the young tsarevich grows ill, the Siberian healer is beckoned to the palace to restore her child to health. Age 12.

Grand Duke Alexander Mikhailovich—Sandro, Nicholas's cousin. He is adventurous to a fault. Previously an Admiral in His Majesty's Navy, but now his heart belongs to the Imperial Air Force and his beloved flying machines. Married to Nicholas's younger sister Xenia. Loves to tell stories, especially ones he features prominently in. Age 50.

Grand Duke Nikolai Mikhailovich—Bimbo, older brother to Sandro. Well-known military historian, celebrated author and scholar. Current President of the Imperial Historical Society and the Russian Geographic Society. Prankster and gambler. Never married. Dislikes the current direction of the war. Age 57.

Grand Duke Paul Alexandrovich—Nicholas's uncle. General of the Cavalry of the Russian Army. His first wife was a Greek princess by the name of Alexandra. She was the love of his life. Alexandra died delivering their second child, Dmitri, in 1889. He never recovered from her loss and allowed his extended family to raise his own children as he escaped everything that reminded him of his old life. Age 56.

Grand Duke Dmitri Pavelovich—the tsar's favorite nephew. An Olympian athlete and model soldier. Currently an officer in His Majesty's Horse Guards, the imperial forces elite. Rumored to be the man Their Majesties wish their eldest daughter Olga to marry. Friend and confidant to Prince Felix. Age 25.

Grand Duke Vladimir Vladimirovich—the tsar's ambitious cousin, nicknamed Vlad. His father Vladimir was the younger brother of Tsar Alexander III, a man many thought in 1894 as a much better choice of tsar in contrast to Alexander's untried son. Nonetheless Alexander chose his own son Nicholas to succeed him, which was his right to do. However, since that day Vladimir has had his eyes fixed squarely on Nicholas's imperfections. Based on Vladimir's first heir who died in childhood. Age 41. Fictional character.

Grand Duke Andrew Vladimirovich—General in His Majesty's Army. Current task is inspecting the worthiness of His Majesty's troops. He does not like what he sees and feels the war has no direction. Loves Mathilda-Marie Kchessinska (prima ballerina) and always has, though knows her heart belongs to the emperor. No matter; twelve years ago the two had a child together, Vova. Andrew wonders what hope there is for Russia. Age 37.

Prince Sergei Platonovich Konstantin—wounded war hero recovering in St. Petersburg. Officer in Her Majesty's Chevalier Guards. Holder of the St. George Cross Russia's highest military honor. Member of the Russian aristocracy's elite. His great grandfather was Tsar Alexander the first— the emperor who defeated Napoleon. His father General Platon Konstantin is a living war hero. His exploits in Manchuria are known throughout all Russia. Sergei feels everyone knows and loves his father but him, a fact he has learned to hate. Age 23. Fictional character.

General Platon Alexandrovich Konstantin—Sergei's father and legendary war hero. His family can trace their proud line back generations. Would prefer to be at army headquarters but the tsar selected him personally for his current role as Head of His Majesty's Secret Police. Close friend to his wife's brother, Grand Duke Alexander. His wife and soul mate passed away before the war. Age 56. Fictional character.

OTHER ROYALS

Kaiser Wilhelm II of Germany—short, wiry with an overly romantic view of war. Grandson of Queen Victoria of England and cousin to Tsar Nicholas and King George. His armies are currently at war with Great Britain, France, and Russia. German casualties are appalling and match those of Russia. It is difficult to take on the world when you are running out of men. For this reason alone, the war needs to be decided soon. His armies on the western front have been at a stalemate for over a year. His forces are winning in the east, at war with Russia. The Kaiser only cares about the front that counts—the west. He needs to break the stalemate before the United States enters into the war. Age 57.

King George V of England—grandson of Queen Victoria of England and cousin to Kaiser Wilhelm and Tsar Nicholas. Enduring his country's third year of war. The British Expeditionary Force too has suffered appalling loses—3 million men wounded or dead, with little gain to justify the growing loss to his people. His monarchy cannot withstand another fruitless year like 1916. That is why he is advising his man in Russia to keep Tsar Nicholas's interest in winning the war. Age 51.

THE POLITICIANS

Senator Vladimir Purishkevich—religious extremist. He considers Tsar Nicholas as 'God's Emissary' to the Russian Orthodox Church, the same church Rasputin is currently making a mockery of with his crude acts of behavior. Famous for his 'dark forces' speech he gave to Parliament in the fall. Age 46.

Alexander Protopopov—Minister of the Interior. Twisted and opportunistic member of Rasputin's inner circle. Former Deputy Speaker of the Duma—Russia's Imperial Parliament—and shrewd businessman. His peers in the Imperial Senate labeled him a traitor for a recent rendezvous he had with a German agent in Stockholm. Age 50.

THE AMBASSADOR

Sir George Buchanan—British Envoy to the Russian Court. Stationed in St. Petersburg for six years now, he is an expert in diplomatic relations, though he is growing tired of his current post. He no longer trusts the Russian Court after Lord Kitchener's ship was sunk in the Baltic Sea. Lord Kitchener was en route to a clandestine meeting with Tsar Nicholas. Only a handful of people knew of this secret mission, including Her Majesty. Sir George holds the German-born empress accountable for Lord Kitchener's death. His only task now is keeping Nicholas and his 15 million men strong army in the war. At least, until the Americans join the fight. Age 62.

THE OTHERS

Father Grigory Rasputin—Siberian priest, yet never ordained. Mystic. Healer. Liar. Drunkard. Womanizer. Despite this, he is fortunate enough to have the empress's ear. He was the only one in the eyes of Their Majesties who was able to save their son Alexei from what seemed to be a certain death. Since then, the 'good father' has been incapable of doing a wrong. Age 47.

Inspector Renko—General Konstantin's second in command in Special Branch, the tsar's Secret Police. General Konstantin's right-hand man. Does most of his dirty work. Has known the general's son Sergei all his life. Sadly, Mikhail, his own son, died last summer in the same battle that wounded Prince Sergei. Age 45. Fictional character.

Mathilda-Marie Kchessinska—Prima Ballerina Assoluta of His Majesty's Imperial Ballet. World famous dancer, now entering the twilight of her professional career. Presently Grand Duke Andrew's mistress. Twelve years ago, Mathilda gave birth to his son, Vova. Never married. Her true love is and always will be Nicholas. They were lovers in their youths. Age 44.

Malachi Jones—Serge's close friend and old roommate from his days at Oxford. Captain of their old rugby team dubbed the Immortals. He was recently temporary assigned to the British Embassy in St. Petersburg for an Allied Conference to be held in January. His job was to help with security. His Father, F.W. Jones, is a millionaire industrialist in Wales. Jones is a product of new money, something he is always reminded of. Age 24. Fictional character.

Prince Felix Yusupov—sole heir to Russia's wealthiest family. Young, bright and extremely good-looking. Was considered to be Europe's most eligible bachelor before his recent marriage to Princess Irina—Grand Duke Alexander's eldest daughter. Rumored homosexual. Felix is a complicated man with complicated tastes. And he makes sure that everyone knows it. Age 29.

St. Petersburg—Petersburg for short, Russia's capital city is dubbed the Venice of the North for its intersecting waterways and breathtaking design. The city's backbone is the Nevsky Prospect, a broad boulevard lined with fine palaces, luxurious hotels and Paris-like shops. Here is the heart of His Majesty's empire and where the story begins.

In the winter of 1916, Imperial Russia was ripe for change. It was Christmas… Russia's third at war. Her capital of St. Petersburg swarmed with war refugees from Poland and the far reaches of Russia's vast empire… these forsaken souls had lost everything because of His Majesty's war with Germany. To make matters worse, the city was facing a food shortage of Russia's own making. In nearby fields, mountains of unpicked wheat simply withered away as bellies lay empty… no one was left to harvest the lands. Russia's youth was at war and they were losing, badly. Germany and her allies were growing bolder. Members of the German High Command had become specialists at the art of warfare and Russia's generals had failed to embrace modern military tactics and paid a costly price … six million Russian men were now dead or wounded. It was a premature end to a generation, yet the tsar's government appeared not to care. Their Majesties's spiritual adviser, a renegade priest named Rasputin, was making a mockery of the imperial cabinet and court as he used his influence over the empress to appoint men to high posts who were willing to do his bidding only. The once god-like tsar looked weak and all too human… a fact recognized by the ambitious men who surrounded him. There was much to lose, there was much to gain, in the land of Crimson Snow.

DAY ONE

CHAPTER 1

Hotel Europe
St. Petersburg, 1916

A heavy hand beating against the door stirred the occupant of a dark room at the Hotel Europe. Underneath his thick bed covers, a sleepy youth yelled his annoyance to the unwanted visitor, "For God's sake leave me alone!" The banging continued as if the hammering fists were fed by his warning. All the young man wished for was to return to the all-healing depths of slumber. Finally, in disgust, he tossed away his sheets. This was no way for the great grandson of a tsar to be awakened.

At twenty-three, Prince Sergei Platonovich Konstantin was a product of the House of Konstantin, a house accustomed to greatness. In that noble household, Russia's most legendary soldiers were born. They were cast like soldiers of lead into hell's inferno, purified, and molded, then sent away to be sharpened to a fine point at some far-off battlefield. For countless generations their military minds had helped transform a backward nation into a great empire that stretched over one-sixth of the globe. But of late, Russia's enemies had grown stronger.

The RAP!—RAP!—RAP! repeated as cold raw air rushed through the room's open windows, causing the tall curtains to bellow and dance.

"Come back later!" His misty breath smoked. "I'm sleeping!" As the pounding stopped, Serge gave a heavy sigh, then, buried his shaggy head below his pillow. He was freezing. His exposed flesh, taut and skinny, was covered with goose bumps. "Why was it so cold," the prince thought? "Oh yes, the windows," he remembered that he wanted to die.

Oddly, Serge's thoughts of suicide kept him somewhat focused and sane. Last night he had opened all the windows. As he was debating which one to leap out of he had passed out. Now, partially awake, he realized his head was throbbing. Damn, he needed a drink. Then, as always, his mind drifted back to the horrors of the war. Remembering the awful stench from that time sickened him. Staring at his bedside clock, he gagged as he saw his medal dangling around an empty bottle. It was given to him for an act of bravery. What foolishness.

Two years earlier, Sergei had eagerly carried on the Konstantin tradition. He had marched toward glory and the empire's western border in an effort to tame the imposing forces of Germany. But the old sword that he carried so proudly could not protect his friends from the German metal that rained down upon them.

With these thoughts twisting about in his mind, the prince heard muffled footsteps from within his suite, "Who's there?"

"It's Renko, Serge." His words poured out into the frigid room like steam from a stopping train.

Regaining his vision, the prince saw the stylish smirk and the square-set jaw of his father's right-hand man, Inspector Renko of His Majesty's Secret Police. Immaculately dressed in a dark suit and overcoat, the inspector strode in, smiling as he replaced a small tool in its leather case. "I was growing tired of knocking, Your Excellency."

"Locks are useless around you."

"Afraid so," Renko replied still sporting a wise crafty grin. The inspector was a short, bald, and somewhat bull-doggish man with an intense and forbidding look about him. Nevertheless, his beefy frame fit perfectly in his fine cut clothes.

The prince attempted to focus on the fuzziness of the inspector's familiar face. He was still somewhat drunk. "What the hell are you doing here at this ungodly hour, the party's over?"

Renko's clean and polished exterior cloaked his true profession as the royal family's trash man. Foregoing the

2

pleasantries, he barked as he paced, "Get up, Serge. We need to talk."

"Later, Inspector. It can wait."

"Not this time." The inspector noticed in the dim light the pile of discarded bottles and turned-over furniture. "Serge, this is your last warning." Unsubtle snores were the reply. The inspector grabbed a silver bucket filled with melted ice and dumped it over the young Russian prince.

As the person under the wet covers screamed, Renko allowed himself a brief chuckle—it had been a long time since he had laughed, and it felt wonderful. As he lit a cigarette, cupping his meaty hands around his gold lighter, he saw the prince sit up. "Do I have your undivided attention now, Your Excellency?"

"I am yours for the moment."

"Good." It tore the inspector's heart to pieces to see Serge like this. Once, the prince had been a bright and strikingly handsome young man, an officer in His Majesty's Chevalier Guards who had distinguished himself in battle. Currently, it appeared he was battling for his soul. His muscular frame was now pencil-thin; dull, hollowed-out eyes gazed out of an uncertain face and his chocolate brown beard was unkempt. He looked more like some poor street beggar than a Russian prince.

The bare-chested prince yawned as he scratched his shrub-like beard and motioned for a cigarette.

The inspector fished out one out from his case. With shaky hands, the prince grasped one in addition to the inspector's lighter. "Sergei, you worry me." Why in the world were the windows wide open in the middle of December? Renko didn't want to know. So, he swiftly crossed the room to close them. "Young Konstantin, you have been drinking too much."

"I drink simply to forget." Looking at a tiny table of spirits, Serge offered Renko back his lighter, "Care for some breakfast?" He wanted to return to the comfort of the dense alcohol fog he had wrapped himself in.

"Don't. It's not even ten yet." For warmth, the inspector rubbed his hairless head. It did not help matters much.

"Ten or two, it makes no difference," Serge said as he poured himself his first drink of the day. "What doesn't kill you makes you stronger, right Renko?"

"Why are you doing this to yourself? Help me understand."

"What is there to understand? I should have died with them."

Through his nose, Renko blew out a small cloud of smoke and replied, "I am truly sorry about Sophia. What happened to her was a tragedy. But—"

"I don't want to talk about it." Before a battle the previous July, Serge had learned of his wife Sophia's death. She had died delivering their first child and the child had died with her. It was a boy. The next day, he had done everything he could to join them and for that they had awarded him a medal.

"Fine my friend. Must I always be the one to remind you that good Russian air still fills those lungs of yours?" The light caught three quarters of the inspector's face. "With such a peaceful view," Renko said, looking out the window that captured the snow-covered square below, "one might find it difficult to imagine that we are at war."

"Nice observation," Serge said, trudging pass him to close the curtains. He never made it that far. From the inspector's expression, he wanted them to remain open. "Why are you here? Is my father growing concerned about the dirt I'm heaping on his noble name?"

"You know that he never in his life relied on his name. Poor young Sergei," the inspector acidly replied. "It's been, what, six months now since your glorious return from the front?"

"Six months, you say, really? Well, time is drudgery. So, tell my dear father that I'm sorry that I'm such a disappointment."

"Yes, your father did send me, today. We are both concerned about you. And, looking at your present condition, we have good cause to worry."

4

"I'm sorry I'm such a burden to you both," Serge said, not daring to face the inspector's eyes. "I would be better off dead."

"Shame on you," the inspector said, shaking his head and thinking of his eldest son, lost in the same battle in which Sergei had been wounded. "What do you know about death?"

"Too much," he replied, covering his face.

"It's normal to grieve. But life somehow goes on, my friend, whether you want it to or not."

"I know. But I can't accept what has happened."

"And you probably never will, so stop trying. But, I must speak to you about another matter."

"Another matter?"

"*Da*, I am afraid so." Renko paused, choosing his words carefully. "I would like to know more about your little gathering of last night."

"Gathering? Why?"

"What were you celebrating?"

"Celebrating?" he said, trying to recall the events of the evening, "Ah … life!"

Renko looked around the trashed room, then at Serge. "You break my heart. Were you celebrating merely life, or was it a dark celebration for someone's death?"

"What are you talking about, Renko? I don't think I'm that drunk yet. Or am I?"

"Her Majesty's spiritual adviser, Father Grigory, is missing and feared dead."

At forty-seven, Father Grigory Rasputin remained many things—a liar, a mystic, a drunkard, a womanizer yet still he was the man the empress leaned on the most for advice in her tight circle of friends. Years ago, Rasputin had been the only one in the eyes of Her Majesty who was able to save her son Alexei from what seemed to be a certain death. Since then, the 'good father' has been incapable of doing a wrong. Though, his close ties to Empress Alexandra enraged the Russian Royal Court.

"Rasputin is dead? Splendid. Now, may I return to bed?"

"Not quite yet, my sad friend." Renko's icy eyes scanned the room. He found it hard to believe that he was in the penthouse suite of the Hotel Europe. The once-luxurious room, like the man slumped over before him, was nearly ruined. "Just answer a few questions and you may return to the ranks of the honored dead."

"Ask away," Serge said, combing his fingertips through his unruly hair.

"Sergei Platonovich—" the use of the formal name told the prince the inspector was serious—"Where were you last night?"

"Renko," he said, shoving his hands deeper into his robe's pockets, as ash fell from his cigarette onto the floor, "please, do you really believe that I'm somehow involved in Father Rasputin's disappearance?"

The inspector hesitated, looking around the room. "*Nyet*, though it appears I missed quite a party."

Serge chuckled. "It was fun, what I recall of it."

"Who attended your small celebration of life?"

"No one of importance; the usual gang of poets, prostitutes, and other degenerates from the Caviar Bar. Now," Serge said as he walked back to his bed, "I needn't waste any more of your precious time."

If he wanted it this way, so be it. "Who was at your little party?" barked the inspector, a man accustomed to having his questions answered, "I need names!"

"Just a handful of people from the downstairs bar. Honestly Renko, must I go through this?"

"Yes. Who was with you last night? Tell me now."

"I told you, no one of importance. I can't even recall everyone. A good friend of mine from my Oxford days arrived on the Moscow train yesterday. It was just he and I and a few regulars from the Caviar Bar."

"Didn't Felix Yusupov graduate from Oxford?" Renko asked in a tone that suggested that he already knew the answer.

"Barely, but that was before me. He graduated the year I began."

"So, your friend is a foreigner then? What is he doing in Petersburg? Is he a British correspondent?"

"No. Good God, Renko. You have been involved in too much intrigue in your life. You are starting to become paranoid."

"Paranoia has kept me alive this long. I still need names. Start with your friend."

"Very well. His name is Malachi Jones, and he works for the British Consulate in Moscow. He's here preparing for the allied conference, to be held in January."

"Odd name," Renko said, recalling it from the list of possible British agents working for the consulate.

"He's an odd man," Serge replied.

"I see. Any of your cousins present? Prince Nikita, or Theodore, or Felix?" The first two were Grand Duke Alexander's two sons and the latter his son-in-law. Serge laughed.

"My cousins? I'm no longer everyone's favorite." Upon returning from the front, he had severed all ties with anyone he had ever loved or who would remind him of his old life.

"So, Felix was not here?"

"Felix? I haven't seen him in ages. Nor do I wish to. We don't exactly travel in the same circles. What's this all about?"

"Rasputin was murdered last night in the Yusupov Palace, Felix's home."

"Murdered? I thought you said he had merely disappeared?"

"*Nyet*. Rasputin was murdered."

"Impossible! Felix is far too gentle a creature to be involved in such madness."

"He told me he did it," Renko said flatly. Gentle was not a term that came to the inspector's mind when he thought of Felix.

"How can you be certain? Felix could be lying. He always does. Rasputin is most likely passed out under some woman's bed. The Siberian is known for two things: his drinking and his womanizing. Normally in that order."

"No, he's dead. We just finished searching his palace, and it's a definite crime scene. There were bloodstains everywhere. Felix showed me and my men the rug they wrapped him up in."

"What?"

"This morning, your *gentle* cousin escorted me and my men to his basement. He showed me where the body had lain. There was a huge bloodstain."

"But why? He could have easily denied it."

"That's what we are trying to find out."

"I don't understand. You tell me that they go through all the trouble and secrecy of killing Rasputin and the first thing they do after disposing of the body is to tell the authorities exactly what they have done?"

"Exactly. That's what troubles me. Your cousin Felix is an odd one, but this crime is even too bizarre for the likes of him."

"Did he tell you where Rasputin's body is now?"

"Not exactly."

"Without the priest's corpse, how can you be certain he's dead? This could all be some childish game."

"I wish it were. But when I asked him where it was, he only replied 'where it belongs.' Believe me, Rasputin is dead. The question is why."

"Why did you earlier tell me he disappeared then?"

"I wanted to see if perhaps you too were involved."

"I see. Damage control. And Nikita and Theodore?"

The inspector looked the other way. "They were there also."

"They're only teenagers."

"I know."

"And Felix," the prince said, already knowing the answer but asking anyway, "Is he currently in custody?"

"He's a prince. What do you think?"

"This is insane."

"I agree. But what is true madness is to strike down the only man the empress thinks can save her dear son."

"What is she going to do?"

"I don't know," Renko replied, shaking his bald head. "All I know is that Protopopov, our new minister of the interior, is currently on route to Tsarskoe to see the empress personally on this matter. Her Imperial Highness wants him to begin an immediate inquiry into the disappearance of her beloved Father Grigory. She wants revenge. I trust the minister will use this situation for his own advantage. According to her, Father Rasputin was not only Alexei's savior but also Russia's. And now, that savior appears to be dead."

Serge started to pace between the tall windows of his penthouse suite with a cigarette clinging perfectly to his lips.

"Remember, Protopopov was personally in charge of Rasputin's own safety, and he failed. He will be looking to avoid the empress's wrath and pin the guilt of Rasputin's death on anyone but himself—most likely, your cousin Felix."

"Renko, there are rumors floating around town that Protopopov is insane."

"He most definitely is, I hear, from the advanced stages of syphilis. But who else would Rasputin—I mean, Her Majesty—choose?"

"Indeed."

"Don't forget, Serge," Renko said, picking his words carefully, "Protopopov is desperate, and desperate people are dangerous. He will have no trouble placing your cousin under arrest."

Serge said, "Renko, what were they thinking in killing Rasputin?"

"I don't know, I suppose your cousin thought he could solve Russia's problems with one single blow."

Serge stopped his pacing. "Then he is a fool. Striking down a Siberian peasant will accomplish nothing. Russia's problems lie deeper than that. These are dark days." Serge stared out of the window, his eyes drifting toward the leafless trees that lined the square and the Nevsky Prospect, the main boulevard of this Venice-inspired city of ice and snow.

As he inspected the icy backdrop below, the words of warning from the poet Gogol came into his ears and he repeated them:

> "Oh, do not trust this Nevsky Prospect, I always wrap myself more tightly in my cloak whenever I walk along it, and I try not to take notice of things I encounter. Everything's an illusion. Everything's a dream. Everything's not what it seems."

Renko was nodding.

After a few moments of shared silence, the prince asked: "Who else was involved?"

"We believe Grand Duke Dmitri also played a part in the plot. His motorcar was seen in the area, shortly after a gendarme reported hearing gunshots coming from the Yusupov Palace."

"I hope you're wrong." Grand Duke Dmitri was Tsar Nicholas's favorite nephew.

"So do I. For everyone's sake."

"Renko, why are you telling me this?"

"Your father wants you away from the capital at once," Renko said, taking another cigarette from his case. "At least, until after the New Year."

"My proud father, the war hero? Why does he even care?"

"Fool, he has always cared about you, even though you give him every opportunity not to."

"You think I should forget about our past?"

The inspector shrugged. "The past is the past. Leave it buried. The future is all that truly matters. My eldest son, and too many of your friends, can no longer say that."

"Nothing matters to me anymore."

"I see that, my son. Nonetheless, you're still alive. And that matters," he said softly, "at least for me."

Serge felt awkward. "Thanks for your concern. But why—"

"Concern?" mocked the inspector, staring at his superior's coddled son, "This isn't a game, Serge. The empress believes the removal of her trusted aide was just the beginning. And, your father thinks she may be right. A mutinous step, by forces targeted against her husband's teetering regime. Every day I hear rumors of the efforts of the imperial family to replace the old regime. Some say Nicholas's days are numbered."

The prince grinned. "Changing of the tsars? Isn't that a little outdated? It's been over a century since that last occurred. Her Majesty is as mad as Protopopov if she believes that."

"Open your eyes, boy," Renko said, not liking the prince's coy manner as he glanced around the grand room. "The imperial family isn't going to allow Nicholas to hand the country to the radicals. They have far too much to lose. Serge, I require only two things of you. First, warn Felix and Dmitri to flee the city at once. Try the yacht club. They often go there."

"All right."

"I don't want them to cause any more trouble. And second, when they leave, go with them. Your father wants you to head south, out of harm's way."

"What?"

"You heard me. Go to your family estate in the south. There, you should be safe."

"Safe from what?"

"No matter, Serge. Just make sure you're on this evening's train. Until then, warn the others and stay out of sight. Grand Duke Alexander's palace would be safe."

"Sandro's?'

"Yes. You should stay there until this evening. Now, promise me you will be on that nine o'clock train."

"I promise."

Renko moved toward the door, truly smiling for the first time since his arrival. "Good. I need to begin my investigation. Your father wants a full report on his desk by this evening. I must somehow attempt to control this chaos before it consumes us all. Your father will personally see you off to the station. Expect him at eight. I recommend you take a bath, and shave that damn beard off."

The mere mention of his father disturbed Serge greatly. To everyone else his father was a national hero, but to him he was only a stranger. "Shave? Why?"

"No matter," Renko said, hugging Serge. Serge followed the inspector to the door. Attempting to find his way back to reality, he asked, "Renko, what is today?"

"It's Saturday, Sergei. The seventeenth of December, a week before Christmas."

"Ah, yes. Well then," he said, adjusting the drawstrings of his robe, "Merry Christmas, Renko."

"Merry Christmas, Your Excellency," the inspector replied, before marching off down the corridor. He had much to do today.

CHAPTER 2

A Private Train
Tracks to Tsarskoe

A cotton-like cloud of blue smoke surrounded a traveler as his train moved south, away from the capital. Rolling his fine cigar through his buttery fingers, the smoker had good reason to be pleased. His old master was dead.

Watching the milky fields pass by, Alexander Protopopov, the new Minister of the Interior, sat quietly. Alexander knew it was only a short ride to Tsarskoe Selo, the imperial village. Over an hour ago, Her Imperial Majesty the Empress Alexandra had summoned him to the Alexander Palace. His task was to inform Her Majesty of the whereabouts of her missing spiritual adviser. That he could easily do with a lie, but she would have to wait a little longer for the truth. As the constant swaying of the carriage soothed and cradled him, he pondered his perfect plan. He gave a small satisfied chuckle to the empty car and to himself; so far, his scheme had gone according to plan. Felix had kept his end of the bargain. Now, it was his turn.

As fields of unbroken snow chugged by, the sleazy politician moved closer to the cabin's window. As he did so, he caught sight of his own wicked reflection of a face creased with age. To him, it was perfection. His fiftieth birthday was in a day but his glassy eyes registered a much older man than fifty. How did he get so old, he asked himself, as he began to play with the pointed tips of his trademark moustache?

"How easily it all slips away," he whispered, "like the fleeting rays of a dying day. You wake up from your short slumber and that glorious day is now gone." He laughed, thinking of infamous parties that turned into orgies, "Time to pay for past sins."

Alexander continued to play with the waxy tips of his moustache. This simple action had always calmed him. His colleagues in the imperial senate claimed he played the game of politics as often as he toyed with its tip. And they were right. Leaning closer to his frosty image, he reflected on how far he had traveled within the government in the last six months. Before, he had been merely a puppet in His Majesty's Duma, the imperial parliament. Now he was the one holding all the strings as he rose to minister. It was astonishing how far an ambitious man could travel with the combined talents of a false tongue and unstable mind.

In his own mind, Protopopov was a great man, and a man who deserved respect from his peers, which he never received. Recently, he had been ordered to meet the German financier Warburg in Stockholm. The meeting was scheduled during his return trip from an allied conference held in Paris. On Her Majesty's orders, he discussed the topic of a possible separate peace with his German counterpart.

When he returned home to Petersburg, the Duma somehow found out about his clandestine mission and labeled him as a traitor. The Empress denied the mission. His good name was ruined and with it any loyalty he once had to the current regime.

The times were changing. The real power in the government lay in the Ministry. Therefore, when the Minister of Interior position became open, he sold his soul to Rasputin. He no longer had anything left to lose. The advanced stages of syphilis preyed daily on his once-brilliant mind. His muscle tremors and hallucinations were increasing at an alarming rate. Soon, he would not be able to hide it anymore. But his final days would be his best. His hands would help form a new regime and a new Russia. He thought of this as he exhaled perfect rings of smoke. What a wonderful legacy. When the train stopped in Tsarskoe Selo, the carriage compartment doors swung open. With them escaped all of the room's warmth, fleeing to play along the frozen fields. By Monday, a new god would claim this town. He laughed, putting on his gloves. "Stain my legacy, and I shall stain yours... with blood."

Shrouded in black, Protopopov stepped down upon the snow-swept platform and adjusted his top hat. Out of habit more than necessity, he played again with his moustache as he gazed over the palatial grounds. He was here to right a wrong, regardless of the consequences. She shouldn't have lied to the Duma. If she hadn't, all of this would not be happening.

CHAPTER 3

Imperial Yacht Club
The Riverfront, St. Petersburg

A weak sun welcomed the arrival of the new weekend, as it ascended over a rough cluster of buildings near the River Neva. The one in the middle looked the oldest and most menacing. It was exactly the image its inhabitants wanted.

The building housed Petersburg's ultra exclusive society the Imperial Yacht Club.

Though its members preferred to simply call it 'the club' it was a political playground for the regime's upper echelon. It was a place where white-gloved servants were beckoned at every member's call. To join this private society took more than money—for anyone could possess that. No, power was the key, in fact a great deal of it. Its members came from the most distinguished families in the empire. Their fathers and grandfathers were the ones who had stretched and shaped Russia's borders to cover over one sixth of the globe. But that was before the war. Now, the chosen few were worried and they had good reason to be. Their empire, which was their inheritance, was vanishing before their very eyes. And so was their power.

Power is a funny thing when it is only perceived. The club's more observant members noticed their white-gloved servants were not as quick to fetch a drink as they used to. And that scared them nearly as bad as the coming year. So with scene set, we pull back the curtain and venture in.

Deep within this imposing residence was a crowded drawing room decorated for the holidays. A strong scent of wood wax mixed with pine attempted to cover up the smell of rot that hung in the air. Here, clustered in a corner, a group of lumpy looking men chatted as they scanned this morning's paper and smoked their cigars. Through a cloud of wandering smoke, they discussed the topic that was on everyone's lips—Rasputin's disappearance.

Serge had arrived in this room ten minutes ago but it seemed more like an hour. He hated this place. It was always filled with fat old men in freshly pressed uniforms. They passed their time stroking their facial hair as often as they stroked one another's egos. Sitting in their cozy chairs, they complained about many things: the senate, the empress, and the tsar—though mostly the tsar.

Dmitri was nowhere in sight.

"I have heard this before," said a general with a pudgy face. "And, the beast always reappears—stronger and closer to the throne." The Russian general sat directly across from young Konstantin. Serge could only wonder why Renko had sent him here.

"But it is true," retorted a man to Serge's right, replying to the general's statement. He was a duke and wore his own regimental colors. His name was Andrew Vladimir, a bookish sort of man, and he hated the tsar more than most of those in the room. So Rasputin's apparent death pleased him. "The dark one is dead." Serge knew the simple logic behind Andrews's hate—the misguided love of a famous ballerina.

Mathilda Kschessinska, his mistress and the love of his life, was in love with another man, Tsar Nicholas. She and Nicholas had been lovers in their youth. Poor Andrew had tried and tried but he could never break the spell Nicholas had placed on her heart. For that alone Andrew hated him.

Serge watched him slurp down some tea with a well-satisfied smile he shared with his eldest brother, Vlad, smoking a big fat cigar, who sat beside him. Their father was Tsar Nicholas's brother.

Serge watched the coils of blue smoke from Vlad's cigar drifting towards the ceiling and thought how opposite the two siblings appeared.

"If it is so, I salute them," Vlad said as he rose. The man was a mountain. A professional soldier, nearly 50 years of age, it was rumored he had broken a man in half once during

Russia's war with Japan. It was only a rumor, but the sheer size of him made the prince wonder if it were indeed true. Broad and tall, Vlad looked like a Russian tsar—big, bold, extremely powerful, and ruthless especially in his regiment's jet-black uniform with tall matching riding boots.

Of course, this didn't stop Serge from asking the obvious. "Salute who?" he said as he entered the discussion. Vlad's massive frame turned slowly towards him.

"The assassins, Prince Sergei" he said, gazing down at him, with a lopsided grin, "of course."

"The emperor may not see it that way, murdering the holy man who nursed his heir back to health," Serge offered.

"Rasputin was an opportunist who played the tsar as a fool," retorted Vladimir.

"Dangerous talk," Serge said without thinking.

Coming to his brother's defense, Andrew continued "Dangerous times, young Konstantin. I see you no longer find it necessary to wear your uniform. Are you still recovering from your war wounds? You look perfectly healthy to me."

"Andrew, what do you know of war?"

"Let's not turn on one another. We are all royalty here," the Grand Duke Vladimir Vladimirovich said. "Our proud fathers and grandfathers fought and spilled their own noble blood to create this mighty kingdom we all see crumbling before us. We must act as one."

"Act as one?" the prince asked as he panned the room for Dmitri. "Against whom?"

"Now, who's speaking dangerously?" Andrew replied.

Serge countered, "I am not here to speak politics. I just want to speak to Dmitri. Have any of you seen him?"

They all looked at one another and slowly shook their heads.

"Try the Bear," Vlad suggested. "He often has lunch there."

"Thank you, Duke Vladimir. I appreciate your help."

"Don't mention it, son. Today is just talk. But we can't be the only ones to see the writing on the wall."

With that, Serge left the parlor feeling worse than when he had entered it. Renko was right. The imperial family was growing bold. In the past, a man—duke or not—would have been cut down for mentioning the tsar in such a tone. What was happening to Russia? Nothing good.

CHAPTER 4

The Firemen's Club
Gambling House

Inspector Renko's motor car snaked its way down one of Petersburg's busy side streets. Peering out of his window, he observed the sight of grimy looking refugees warming their hands over open bonfire wearing patched up coats. All were civilian casualties of the war. Petersburg was swarming with poor, powerless people.

Misery danced like the fiery flames on their drawn faces. It was a depressing sight. These sad companions had already sacrificed all they had for the sake of the empire, and this war: their lands, their homes, their sons, and their pride. Everything that they once cared for was now gone. They were now burnt, beaten, and left for dead.

Renko turned his eyes from the window. He had seen enough. A few minutes later, his car was in front of No.14 Fontanka, the house of Countess Ignateau. Within her fine home was the infamous Firemen's Club, a small but profitable gambling establishment. Typical for a Saturday afternoon, the club was packed, filled with drugged and lifeless faces attempting to escape the atrocity of wartime Petersburg. As a variety of chemicals pulsed through their bodies, men dressed in tuxedos gambled carelessly with their hearts and their souls. What else was there to do? The inspector slowly walked through the club's crowded hallways, looking for the proprietor, Aron Simanovich—a glutton of a man with a pencil-thin moustache, he looked out of sorts wearing a fine-tailored tuxedo.

Aron and Rasputin had known each other a long time. Aron's good sense, knowledge, and foresight had helped create the infamous Father Rasputin. He had cleverly molded

Rasputin, a Siberian peasant from the cold and dreary Arctic, into Russia's most influential man. He had created the Rasputin mystique. The inspector found Aron at the bar, surrounded by thick wreaths of smoke.

"Renko, so it's true?" Aron asked, combing back his thinning hair, "They have murdered my good friend, Grigory."

The club's owner poured the inspector a drink and left the bottle.

Renko paused before he grabbed it. "Yes, I believe our friend is dead."

"He is in a better place than this, then," Simanovich said, raising his glass. "Lucky," Aron said finishing off his drink, "to leave this city of the damned."

Renko polished off his drink. "I need to ask you a few questions."

Aron acted dead drunk. "Rasputin was not the evil monster they all said he was. No, Grigory's eyes were magical. Dark orbs that can peer deeply into the far corners of one's soul."

Renko listened as he refilled his glass.

"Those dark ghostly eyes reflected the ugliness within each man's soul. He could see it all, good and bad, and its constant battle for supremacy within us all. Being a holy man in this fallen city is a dangerous business." Aron poured himself another drink. "We are all sinners here, Renko. Today, the capital will rejoice. The mirror that peered into their unclean souls has been shattered. But I ask you my friend, tomorrow, who will be blamed for all their ugliness?" Aron drained the remaining vodka in his glass with one powerful swig.

With a loud "Ha", he went on, "He could dance all night. One night, we went to see the gypsies at the Villa Rode, thanks to the money you and our government so generously provided."

It was all true, thought Renko. Father Rasputin stumbled into St. Petersburg penniless with only the clothes on his back and became fabulously rich. Besides the large sums of money the imperial family had bestowed on him, he made a fortune selecting the ministers who provided him with protection. Then there were the nice juicy government contracts that Aron and the shrewd priest would sell to the highest bidder.

"There were gypsy dancers and singers whom our friend loved so much, as well as invited 'woman of society,' who fought for Rasputin's attention. He loved to dance the traditional Russian dances. Before going to the Villa, he would fill his pockets with candy, silk scarves, ribbons, powder puffs, and bottles of perfume. These were presents for his dancing partners to 'steal.' He would delightedly announce to his multitude of admirers, 'the gypsies have robbed me!'" Aron burst out with laughter.

Attempting to salvage the discussion, the inspector asked, "When was the last time you spoke to him?"

"I was with him last night until almost midnight. He told me he was going to see 'the youngster,' but he wouldn't tell me who he was."

"What else?"

Aron cleared his throat. "I guess, well, Rasputin was nervous all week. I thought he was going to pace a hole in the carpet, but last night he was perfectly calm. He almost seemed childish with joy. It could have been the Madeira; he drank a lot last night. I told him of the rumors. I told him to stay in last night. Just like Protopopov. All our warnings fell on deaf ears." He chuckled. "Grigory was a stubborn man."

"Yes, he was. You mustn't forget that it took over half of my men to keep him out of trouble. And, at times, that wasn't even enough. Who visited him last night besides Protopopov?"

"The usual admirers. Vyrubova and Glovin."

"What time did Protopopov arrive?" Renko already knew the answer. Aron seemed to sober up.

"I'm not certain. He stopped by to make sure Grigory was in for the evening. He said he had promised the empress that our Friend would be protected this evening. The starets personally showed him to the door."

Renko wondered why Aron was acting more intoxicated than he actually was. "And what else?"

"Nothing, really. Grigory was laughing to himself when he returned. I asked him what he found so funny, and he simply replied: 'The Lord giveth and can just as easily taketh away.'"

"Was he referring to the home minister?"

"I don't know. Grigory was growing tired of the minister, that's no secret."

"What was he getting so tired of?"

"The minister was distancing himself. Rasputin hinted to me that it may be time to say goodbye to him. All it would take would be one brief conversation with the empress at the appropriate time," Aron winked, "and Protopopov would join the long list of egotistical ministers dethroned by a simple-minded peasant."

Was it that easy, Renko wondered?

"It's all bad luck for me."

"How so?"

"Protopopov owes me a great deal of money."

"How's that?" the inspector asked. "He isn't foolish enough to gamble."

"True. But I am. Protopopov is bankrupt. When he asked me to settle his debts, I agreed. I thought it would be good to have the second most powerful man in the empire as a friend."

"Let me guess. He promised to repay you from his department's fat budget?"

"You're good. Now, Grigory is dead, and I no longer hold any leverage over him."

"You said Protopopov stopped at the apartment before you left. Do you remember what time?"

"Not really. But it was after eleven."

"How are you so certain?"

"I looked at my watch at eleven, when one of Grigory's daughters came in to say good night to us. Protopopov stopped by after that."

"Good. And, do you recall, when you left last night, were any of my men outside the apartment?"

"No, but it was cold last night. On cold nights, they normally stay in their cars or off the streets."

"Thanks, Aron. I appreciate your time."

"Don't mention it. Just bring the bastards to justice."

"There will be justice. I assure you," Renko said as he rose from his stool. "Just one more thing. What was Father Rasputin worth?"

"The deceased left very good resources." Aron could not hide his greed.

"How good?" he asked. "I know the two of you made a fortune on the sugar scandal case."

"You knew about that?"

"Yes, Aron. I know a great deal about a number of things." The sugar scandal had involved a wealthy businessman who brokered a deal with the Germans just before the war. At stake was a large shipment of sugar delivered to the German Army. Luckily for the sugar trader, Rasputin was able to use his influence over the empress to make sure the case was dropped.

"Must I ask you again? How good?"

"As much as three hundred thousand rubles," Aron whispered, understating the amount significantly.

"I'm certain his daughters will receive their full inheritance," the inspector said.

"But of course, Renko. What kind of man do you take me for?" With a shallow laugh, Aron finished his drink. "By the way, Burmin is looking for you."

"Where?"

"Guess," Aron said, looking toward the back of the bar.

"The high-stakes table," said Renko as a smile ran across his face.

"The man just got out of prison this morning and now he's robbing me blind. Burmin is no good—a parasite of the war's black market."

"Aron, did you go to Grigory's apartment this morning?"

"No. Why?"

"All his personal letters are missing."

"All the empress's letters to him?"

"You wouldn't know anything about them, would you?"

"No, but I am saddened that I didn't think of it first," Aron said. "Those letters would prove without a doubt that a Siberian peasant and the Empress of All Russia were more than just friends. They would prove that Rasputin personally selected the ministers of our current government. Whoever possesses those letters could be one wealthy man."

"Don't be so certain. Alexandra will not rest until those letters are found and destroyed. The person who holds those letters won't enjoy them for long."

Renko said his farewells and walked toward the high-stakes tables. Peter Burmin was the only son of a wealthy industrialist, and since his birth had been showered with every advantage possible. When his father died, he inherited a small fortune, and the small fortune had grown into sizable wealth during the war. But it was never enough. He increased the odds by entering into secret dealings with anarchists, German sympathizers, and the secret police, playing one against the other and adding to his fortune. Recently, Peter had been playing in the deep pockets of the German Kaiser. At the moment, the Germans were the ones who paid the best.

Peter noticed Renko eyeing his mountain of blue chips. The blonde and beautiful man purred, "Envious?"

"Of you? Pete, the trick is to live long enough to enjoy it," the inspector laughed, embracing the man he had arrested two weeks ago. "Good to see you're in one piece."

"Just a misunderstanding between me and our beloved minister of justice," he said, smiling. "Makarov finds me a traitor."

"You?"

"Imagine, me a German spy?" Peter dryly replied, "It was so good of Grigory to convince the empress to drop these false charges against me."

"Though it still looks like you have a following." A man hiding behind his paper was watching both of them more than his paper. He was one of the intelligence agents Renko knew who was operating out of the British embassy.

Peter paid no attention to him. "I'm a popular man," the gambler said.

"That's one way to think of it. I hear Justice Makarov wasn't too happy to sign the release."

"No—not until he was ordered to do so by the empress herself." He slapped Renko's back. "It is good to have powerful friends."

Knowing that Burmin bought protection through Rasputin, "It seems last night's activities freed up a great deal of your capital," Renko said.

"I wouldn't say a great deal," he replied, laughing.

Burmin was the main channel of German subsidies flowing into Petersburg. His current objective was a speedy reconciliation between Russia and Germany, the sooner the better. The Germans wanted to sign a separate peace treaty by the first of the year. The last two weeks, Peter had spent in his cell, deep within Saints Peter and Paul Fortress.

"What happened? I thought we had a deal?" the gambler asked, not entirely believing him.

"We still do."

"Then why did you allow Makarov's men to arrest me?"

"To keep you safe."

"From whom?" he asked, as he moved towards a cashier.

"Sir George, of course. The British Ambassador wants you dead. And we can't have that, can we?"

"No, we can't." Peter looked over his shoulder.

With a sad look, the cashier counted out Peter's money. "Not if you want me to deliver that letter," he warned Renko

27

as he grabbed Aron's money. "What should I do about the British?"

"Just keep away from your normal haunts this weekend, and, with any luck, they will leave you alone."

"Not good enough."

"What would you like me to do?"

"Having a few of your men around for protection would help matters."

"All right then. Two of my men will stop by later today."

"Good. When do I get the letter?"

"Be prepared to travel on Monday night."

"And the money?" Peter greedily asked.

"Your money will arrive with the letter." Renko placed his arm around him, "Don't worry. I have thought of everything. On Monday, a train will take you to Helsinki. From there, you and the letter will be ferried to Germany."

"A boat? The Baltic isn't exactly the safest of spots."

"Don't worry, Peter. As long as you have the armistice, you will be safe. Just stay in your apartment this weekend. Okay?"

"Sure," Peter agreed. The inspector was crazy if he thought he was going to waste his weekend there. Hell, he had been locked up for the last two weeks. He needed to see the shadier side of the city, enjoy his pre-party to peace. The two exited through the club's back door. "Just think, Renko, by Christmas the war for us will be over."

Walking down a narrow alleyway, the inspector said, "That's His Majesty's wish. And it is my job to make his wishes our reality." With that, their voices drifted apart in the surrounding darkness.

CHAPTER 5

The Bear
Upscale Bistro

Lavishly decorated for the holidays, the Bear Bistro was no stranger to excess. Everyone, especially the lunch crowd, knew it. In this place, their egos were fed along with their appetites. The wealthy clientele would drift out of the narrow doors, and back to the day's bleakness. These once worry-free ones passed each other with a fond sense of regret like two sorry lovers on the morning after. All wanted to remember the better days—the days before the war.

"We're heading for revolution," the ex-president of the Imperial Council declared, as he scooped his remaining peas.

"We're heading for anarchy," said his lunch companion, a financier named Putilov, as he set down his wine glass full of a fine dandelion-colored wine. "The Russian is not a revolutionary; he's an anarchist. There's a world of difference. The revolutionary means to reconstruct; the anarchist thinks only of destroying."

At the other tables, discussion focused on Father Grigory's whereabouts and, from course to course, the story grew.

Earlier, his disappearance was assumed to have been a simple affair of the heart. Everyone just assumed that a jealous husband had shot the adulterous Father. But by noon, the tale that skipped across these white linen tables was that the gypsies had killed him. By one, his death involved the royal family. Rasputin was found to be using the empress and the grand duchesses for his sexual pleasure. When the tsar had found out, he had killed the peasant with his own hands.

The most imaginative and therefore the best received was that Alexandra and Rasputin had been having an affair.

According to the rumor, when Grand Duke Dmitri found out he was furious. So, he asked his good friend Prince Felix to arrange a dinner party in honor of Father Grigory at the Yusupov Palace. After dinner, Dmitri appeared. Entering the drawing room as everyone gathered for drinks, the duke shouted at the priest, "How dare you take advantage of the emperor's trust!" At that moment, he pulled out his service revolver and emptied it into the stunned holy man.

As the bullets pierced his belly, Rasputin could not believe his own eyes, exclaiming, "What have you done to me?" As Alexandra's so-called lover sat in agony on the drawing room floor, the young duke, possessed by an uncontrollable rage, pulled out his dagger and castrated the good father on the spot. The lunch crowd at the Bear Bistro savored the dark symbolism of this version. The truth was that no one knew anything except that Rasputin was still missing, presumed dead. At a small, exquisitely set table, two men with an informed perspective on the disappearance were saying their good-byes over a bottle of fine champagne.

"What happened?" asked Grand Duke Dmitri Pavelovich—the tsar's favorite nephew. A talented equestrian and model soldier, the duke currently served as an officer in His Majesty's Horse Guards, the imperial forces elite, rumored to be the man Their Majesties wish their eldest daughter Olga to marry. He was a friend and confidant to Prince Felix and known hater of Father Rasputin's growing relationship with the royal family.

"I slept until ten o'clock," Prince Felix Yusupov yawned. He was the sole heir to Russia's wealthiest family. Young, bright and extremely good-looking the prince was considered to be Europe's most eligible bachelor before his recent marriage to Princess Irina. Wearing a well-cut cadet uniform of the Imperial Corps of Pages with high Pershing collar and white leather belt, his costume was complete.

He looked almost god-like as he played with the stem of his flute glass. "I had barely opened my eyes when I was told General Grigoriev, the police superintendent of our district, wanted to see me on very important business. I dressed quickly and went into the next room where the general was awaiting for me."

"And?"

"I asked him if his visit was connected with the shots fired in the courtyard of our house last night," Felix said, changing his voice to act out the general's reply, "Exactly. My objective is to ask you for a detailed account of what happened. Wasn't Rasputin among the guests?' I replied Rasputin never comes to my house. The general didn't like my answer. He counters: 'The reason I ask is that the revolver shots that were heard coincided with the disappearance; therefore, the chief commissioner of police has ordered me to send him a report as quickly as possible.'"

"What else?" asked Dmitri.

"I asked the general who told him that Rasputin had disappeared."

"Let me guess. The very same police officer that Purishkevich entrusted with our deed."

"The one and only."

"So, what did you tell him?"

"The truth, of course," he said, combing his fingers through his hair.

Dmitri almost choked on his champagne. "You did what?"

"Relax. I was bound by my oath," he teased. "I told the general that one of the drunken members of my party shot one of my best hounds."

"Did he believe you?"

"Who cares," the prince said as he inspected his glass. Felix reached under the table. "I brought you a farewell gift. It's not much. Though, I hope you like it."

"*Spasibo*, I wish I had brought something for you."

"Rasputin's head was enough."

Unwrapping it, "The compete works of Oscar Wilde," Dmitri said paging through its text. "Your personal hero."

"All I possess is now yours."

Smiling, he said, "I am surprised you haven't already memorized it," knowing the author's influence upon Felix's life.

"Not all of it. At least, not yet," Felix said, refilling his glass, "You know my little secret—I am the fictitious creation of a brilliant man. But, enough of my problems."

Turning to the preface of the book, he noticed Felix's handwriting:

Dmitri,

May I steal a verse from
The Ballad of Reading Goal.

Yet each man kills the thing he loves,
By each let this be heard,
Some do it with a bitter look,
Some with a flattering word,
The coward does it with a kiss,
The brave man with the sword.

Merry Christmas

"*Spasibo,*" the duke said. "I shall cherish it, as I cherish our friendship—forever. But before the senator arrives, I want to discuss what I must say tomorrow night to the tsar. A civil war threatens to tear the empire in two, and we must make certain that he is aware of it."

"We have been down this path before, my dear friend. And now, more than ever, we teeter on the edge of oblivion," Felix said as he looked into his drink, knowing the meeting would never take place because he was involved with other family members in a plan to finish off the tsar. "At least Rasputin is no longer a concern."

"Yes, but other dogs circle, especially Vlad."

"There is no good in Vlad but he is no threat," Felix said as his eyes moved back to his drink.

"Are you blind? Vlad is making it known throughout the imperial family that he wants to be the man to remove Nicholas's crown. And that I can not allow."

It was at that point that the senator arrived. "Gentlemen," he said as he worked his way around the tables, "I apologize for my tardiness. I have had a hell of a morning."

"Sit down senator," the duke ordered as he asked, "What were you thinking when revealed everything to the policeman investigating the gunshots?"

"Your Excellency," the politician replied, "I was caught in the moment."

"Caught in the moment, I would say," Felix said. "You practically bathed in vodka last night."

"You see," the politician admitted, "I normally don't drink."

"As was evident in your poor marksmanship," Dmitri said, his face softening.

This brought a round of laughter to the table. Their dark task was done, and it was time to celebrate before they all went their separate ways. The senator raised his glass and looked at Dmitri as he said, "Splendid shot."

"Senator, where in the world did you learn to shoot so poorly?" the duke said, trying to control his laughter.

The senator laughed as well. "Your Highness, for as much as I drink, I feel fortunate that it was not I that was shot last night." He paused, "Prince Felix, speaking of missed opportunities, and how did you miss that broad beast? The devil himself had his back to you."

"Gentlemen, my well-placed shot hit him squarely in the back, but Rasputin was a stubborn fool. It would take more than one allotment of Russian lead to quiet him, or bring him to the floor." The prince continued. "*Nastrovya!*, my fellow comrades-in-arms. The battle between good and evil has begun. I have full faith that we shall prevail over the powers of darkness!"

"Here, here," the duke said, raising his glass, "For good always conquers evil, and the empress's camarilla lacks its most persuasive member." Felix couldn't resist: "The empress's loss, the River Neva's gain."

"Yes, and hopefully he shall stay in those frozen waters at least until spring," the senator said, "Though I still can't believe the poison did not work."

Felix put down his glass. "Senator, you were not down in the basement with him. Every time he finished his drink and asked for more, I began to wonder whether he was immortal. The only other possible explanation was that the poison was too diluted."

They all agreed. In the daylight, none of it seemed real. But it was. Today, Father Rasputin was at the bottom of the Neva. Felix made one more dig. "Senator Purishkevich, you are a credit to your profession. We go through all this secrecy to quietly slay the beast, and the first chance you get to take credit for our actions, you yell for all the world to hear that we just killed Rasputin." No one at the table laughed. In fact, the prince had chosen the senator for exactly this purpose.

"Yes, that was a mistake," the old man declared. "I was caught in the great moment. With one blow, the affairs of state are returned to the emperor."

"Let him make the most of it," the duke offered.

"Now, gentlemen, speaking of last night, we must focus on our alibis. Are we all agreed?" They nodded yes. So what if the story was a little flimsy and it revolved around one of Felix's guests shooting a dog as a practical joke? It somehow explained all the blood that covered the courtyard, and they were royalty, after all. Father Rasputin was only a peasant. At the end of the day, that was all that mattered.

"From now on," Felix said, "we will leave to others the task of carrying on our work. Pray God that concerted action will be taken and the emperor's eyes will be opened before it is too late. Such an opportunity will never occur again."

"Lord, open the eyes of the tsar to the terrible reality," prayed the duke. "Amen."

"What about Protopopov," asked the senator?

"He has no support now. His creator is dead," the duke said. "I wouldn't worry about him."

Felix added, "Anyway, you will be safely away from the capital by midnight on your hospital train."

"True," the senator agreed. "The front calls. I want to see the morale of our troops first hand."

"As do I," the duke said. "That is why I am returning to army headquarters tomorrow. Someone needs to warn the emperor about Vlad."

"And I leave tonight," the prince offered. "My wife is not well and she has asked me to come down to our Crimean estate for the holidays. I don't want it to look like I'm running away from something." Again, the table burst out with a round of laughter. As soon as they had settled down again, the prince continued: "One last toast—to dead dogs!"

"To dead dogs!" the killers cried as they downed their glasses.

"Godspeed, gentlemen," the senator said, "Until we all meet again."

German High Command

Hunched over a table blanketed by a single outstretched map, a small man braced himself with his good arm, as he inched closer to the map. That's how near he felt he was to his dream of a New Germany; a Kingdom fashioned to his liking, and modeled on the notion of a Germany-dominated Europe. It would be his legacy. And to him, it was beautiful.

"So long ago I dreamt of it," declared His Majesty the Kaiser in a near whisper. "They said I was mad," for insanity was common in his long line of ancestors, "but, insane or not, it is within my grasp."

Still looking at the map, he gazed upon his legions along the Russian front. Soon, over sixty battle-tested divisions would be freed from those bloody fields. The war had lasted longer than anyone had expected. Nonetheless, our enemies are finally weakening, he thought. Before the war, his top strategists had told him his forces would over-power the French armies and capture Paris in the first weeks of the war. They were so confident. He could still recall the staff meeting when one of his generals had said, "Your Majesty, the Schlieffen Plan shall not fail." The officer boldly boasted, as he turned to his peers, "Our armies shall have lunch in Paris and dinner in St. Petersburg." But that did not happen. Lunch took much longer than expected. And at an exorbitant cost to his people; for the last two years his courageous legions had been forced to fight a two-fronted war. Europe had thrown all she could at his military machine.

When the Russian envoy had presented its original terms for a separate peace, he had whole-heartedly agreed. He needed those sixty divisions for the west before the Americans entered the war. It was only a matter of time before they did so. That was why the outcome of Europe must be decided this spring. The Kaiser was famished for victory. And, every month those hunger pains gnawed at him more and more.

He could not endure another summer like the last. The sea battle with Britain at Jutland had been a disaster. His fleet barely limped back into port. And the battle for Verdun had been no better. It was a complete bloodbath. They had lost the crème of their corp. It had been a mistake to listen to Falkenhayen.

Again, he recalled the encouraging words of General Von Falkenhayen before the engagement, "We will bleed the enemy dry!"

That battle had just ended. As a result, his army now stood on the same ground they had held nearly a year ago. The only difference was they had lost over three–quarters of a million men in the process. It was horrible. The war could not go on like this. For one thing, his legions were not limitless. His army had sacrificed too much—a total of six million men not to be the victors. This spring, in the French countryside, the war would be decided. One swift and courageous battle—with all his legions, east and west, finally combined as one.

In Europe, which was the world in the Kaiser's mind, there were only three remaining mighty monarchs left: his two cousins, King George V of England and Tsar Nicholas II of Russia, and himself—His Majesty the Kaiser of Germany. These three Supreme Beings's imperial armies were engaged in a fierce battle being played out in Europe's rural fields. Their actions would decide once and for all the borders of Europe.

The Kaiser let out a heavy sigh. With it came a hard, heavy-set knock on the chamber's door.

Gathering himself he called "Enter," and an oversized general came into the room.

"Your Majesty," bowed the beefy soldier, General Paul von Hindenburg, the Kaiser's new Chief of Staff, "I have just received the revised Russian terms," his eyes returning to the dispatch.

"And, must I read them myself?" demanded the Kaiser as he walked away from the table and towards his trophy room's window. The general thought he was so clever. However, the Kaiser knew that he leaned heavily upon his subordinates's genius—especially that of General Hoffman.

Since his victory at Tannenberg, General Von Hindenburg could do no wrong. To Germany, he was the man solely responsible for the victories against the Russians.

"They want Constantinople and the Balkan Straits," exclaimed the general.

Staring at snow-peppered pines the Kaiser merely retorted, "As expected."

"But your Majesty," pleaded the general, as he crossed the room, "these terms are far too favorable for our enemy."

He continued, "Withdrawing our advancing armies from Poland could be a mistake. Their forces are retreating on all fronts. Their supply-lines are in disarray. Come spring, they will be under our iron heel."

The German High Command no longer tallied the losses of her enemy at the Russian front. All they knew was that they needed to remove the piles of the dead to prepare for next day's butchery. The number of Russians dead was far too many to count. Field Marshal Von Hindenburg knew it. His genius in the art of war had been responsible for the victories in the east, and the high Russian body count.

"Spring, general? It shall all be over by then?" queried the Kaiser.

"Your Majesty, they are near revolution. By spring, our troops will have seized their capital."

Still gazing out of the window, the Kaiser smiled, "You forget who is financing this so-called rebellion. No, by spring our troops will be marching through Paris."

"Your Grace, our troops shall march through the streets of Paris, soon. But first, allow the armies of the east the glory of entering a defeated Moscow. As you have just said, we are deeply invested in Russia; let our forces provide you with true victory in the spring. That's only four short months from now. Surely, you must understand?"

The Kaiser did not reply. He just continued with his back to the general.

Still fighting for Poland and the honor of his men, the general tried again: "We have sacrificed too much German blood liberating that land, to simply abandon it!"

"No, general. If my Russian cousin wants to liberate Constantinople, he can do so," stated the Kaiser as he felt a brief moment of pity for his cousin. Why must you always dream of that city of cities, he pondered? It is of no military importance. But, he already knew the answer. Nicholas was a religious fool. "Let him have his 'Great Church,' for it is entirely irrelevant."

Pleading again, "But, Your Majesty...," cried von Hindenburg as he thought what a tainted legacy this would be for him and his men, "our enemy's back is nearly broken."

"Perhaps this is true." Staring at his own distorted reflection in the window, the Kaiser stopped smiling. As he pulled his withered arm around his body, he turned towards the general. Then calmly the crowned King of Germany proclaimed, "But General Von Hindenburg, we have wasted enough men and time over the Russians. We need those sixty divisions on the front that matters, by early spring at the latest. That means this treaty needs to be signed soon. Have our man in St. Petersburg agree to whatever terms."

"Yes, Your Majesty," the general reluctantly agreed.

Pausing for a moment, the smiling warlord added, "Relax, general, I didn't say Nicholas could keep his crown."

With that, the Kaiser's eyes returned to his map. Poor old Russia, he thought. They would have to pay for their tsar's impractical Byzantine dream of Constantinople. Offering to give up this ancient religious relic of a city was the Kaiser's masterstroke. He knew Nicholas could not resist it. His troops for the last two years had been butchered in a wasted effort to reach the gates of the city of this inconsequential Turkish stronghold.

The Russians weren't the only ones foolish enough to have tried to storm those gates. Last year, hoping to breach the outer defenses at Dardanelle, located only a hundred miles south of the Turkish city, some six hundred thousand British had thrown themselves at this second front. Never establishing a secure beachhead, the invasion had failed miserably. The human cost had been too much and King George had withdrawn his own troops.

Come spring, thanks to Russia's departure from the war, German legions would be able to march over two hundred divisions strong against the weakened fortifications of a war-torn front. With a mere stroke of a pen, it was now almost a mathematical certainty that his combined forces would be victorious. A new German era would engulf Europe; a long-lasting Reich that would lead the world into the twentieth century, a German century. There was no place left for Russia.

"General," barked His Majesty, "On your way out, tell Alfred I need to speak to him. Someone must warn Pasha that the Russians are coming."

The general now realized he had underestimated the Kaiser. It would be a revised version of the Schlieffen Plan. Settling with Russia now would free up the required divisions to end the stalemate in the west. The war would be over before the Americans could even enter it. Then, when the Russian army had amassed near Constantinople, the full German Imperial army would storm through Poland and capture the Russian Bear as it basked in the sun.

"Your Majesty, your strategy is brilliant," the general admitted. "But, will it work?"

"Von Hindenburg," the Kaiser declared as he looked around his trophy room, "Some say I am mad. But I am just a mere man with a dream."

"If I may be so bold, your Majesty, your dream is becoming reality."

Smiling, the Kaiser replied, "That's the idea. By autumn, I shall have the head of a stuffed teddy bear mounted on my wall."

Von Hindenburg added, "Beside your British Lion."

With that, they both laughed. It was a rarity. Kaiser Wilhelm may be crazy, the general thought, but he was no fool.

CHAPTER 6

Dmitri's Palace
Off the River Fontanka

Serge was impressed by the transformation of Grand Duke Dmitri's palace into a hospital. By missing Dmitri at the Bear, it only left here to look. And here could have been any premier facility in Petersburg except for a few tiny differences, such as the chandeliers hanging like huge crystal balls from the sky-colored ceiling.

Since the beginning of the war, the duke had wanted to show his support for the war and his uncle Tsar Nicholas II. So, he had converted his stately home, at least most of it, into a 100-bed hospital, personally financing the staff and equipment. For Dmitri, it was a way to offer a little kindness and care to the men who had sacrificed all for the great cause.

Serge strolled into one of the wards. Caregivers met the soldiers's every need. He could not help thinking that only six short months ago he had been like this broken band of men.

Dressed in a fine-fitting suit, he felt out of place. He could see the soldiers gazing up in envy that quickly turned to hate. He did not belong here, not anymore. When a nurse approached him, he was thankful for the reprieve.

"May I help you?" asked the tired woman with a pretty face as she walked over her dark curls bounced upon her narrow shoulders.

"Yes, you may. I am looking for the grand duke." The woman was Mathilda Kschessinska, prima ballerina of the Imperial Ballet and the woman who had first stolen his heart at the tender age of twelve. Nicholas's father, Tsar Alexander III, had discovered Mathilda at a dance held in his honor. After he had watched her performance, he had praised her:

"Be the glory and adornment of our ballet." And, decades later, at the age of forty-four, she remained just that. She was the only Russian to be crowned with the distinction and rank of prima ballerina absoluta of the Imperial Ballet.

"I just saw him heading toward his private wing. Do you need me to show you?"

"No, thank you. I know it well. Good day—Nurse Kschessinska."

Even in her forties, she could still seduce with a tilt of her head. She had the enchanted look of royalty—a short athletic figure, a very pretty face, and a sharp wit and loose tongue. Her easy laugh quickly disarmed you. Through the years, she had entertained quite a stable of men.

"Young Konstantin, you have grown up, haven't you?" she said, smiling.

"Nice of you to notice," he offered.

She wiped her stained hands with a towel. "I notice a great deal, Sergei. My friends call me Mathilda, but today I would prefer for you to call me ... Marie. Nurse Kschessinska will only make me want to cry."

He wanted to impress her with his charm, but all he could muster was: "Well ... Marie, you do much good here."

She stared into Serge's eyes, and then gave a sad smile. Serge watched her walk away. In her youth, she had been Tsar Nicholas's mistress. That was a long time ago when Nicholas was single and not yet the tsar. Both young and in love, the two of them had shared a house. But it was not to be. The beautiful and talented ballerina was still only a commoner, and Nicholas needed an actual princess. Kschessinska only played the part. But she played it with perfection.

When he reached Dmitri's private apartments, one of the duke's servants recognized him, "Prince Konstantin, what a pleasure to see you again. Are you expected, Your Excellency?"

"No, I am not, Christian," he said as he walked past him. "I would like to surprise him."

"Your Excellency?" replied the servant, shocked by the lack of protocol.

"Christian, no introduction is necessary. Where is he?"

"In the ballroom, sir."

Serge walked down the dark corridor that led to the ballroom. He heard music. Someone was humming and in the corridor it sounded cheery. He entered the light-flooded circular ballroom. The duke's silhouette danced along the polished parquet floors.

"Hello, Serge," the duke said, only then turning from the window. "It has been a long time."

"Dmitri," Serge said, offering him a hug.

The young duke just pulled at his beard. "What's this?" he asked in a scornful manner. "Where is your uniform ... and the Cross of St. George?"

"I—" Sergei had not expected this frontal assault.

"It is our highest honor and is meant to be worn at all times to show your great service to others. Especially here." He paused. "No matter, my friend. It's good to see you again. I'm sure you didn't come for a lecture." He waved his hands. "Do you remember when we were last here, Serge?"

"Yes, I remember."

"It was the last winter gala before the war—an extraordinary day."

"I remember," the prince faintly replied, as he recalled dancing a summer evening away with his dead wife. "Dmitri, why must you stir up the past?"

"Oh, how I long for those days before the war. But we shall soon return to those days. A new spring approaches."

"What if you are wrong?"

"Nonsense. Good will prevail."

"I am not convinced. The empire is falling apart." Serge lit a cigarette.

"Serge, I know you have sacrificed a great deal. But it hurts me to hear a man with the last name of Konstantin speak as you do. Our ancestors have spilled too much blood for it to all vanish before our eyes."

"But the war?"

"I know. It breaks my heart to walk down the wards in my own home. These brave men have also sacrificed a great deal, and that is why we need to bring this conflict to a quick victorious end—for their sakes."

"Dmitri, we are now past that. We need to get out of this war at any price. The cost is too great. I have witnessed too many men butchered. Men like those down the hall forced by gunpoint into the unforgiving marshes, only to step on the remains of yesterday's dead. I have seen with my own eyes how merciless the war can be, to go searching in the bogs for missing friends and only find their helmets and bayonets sticking up through the mud. They are dead because some fool of a commander could not read his damned map!"

"Serge, I know. I have heard such stories, and it sickens me. But, we cannot just give up. In time, His Majesty shall lead us to victory."

"Right now, His Majesty is in a position of weakness. He may find it difficult to save himself, let alone find the support to lead his armies to victory."

"Such treasonous talk, Serge! For your sake, I shall pretend I did not hear it."

"I have heard such talk coming from the imperial family about a possible changing of the tsars."

"Vlad," he spat. "It will never happen. I will not allow it."

"Dmitri, the war has changed the order of things."

"Yes. We are all tired of the war, and I am tired of this topic. Come spring, all will be put right."

"We don't have until spring. The country is ready to explode, and the tsar does nothing."

"His Majesty is leading us to victory."

"I am not so certain. He has many enemies."

"I wouldn't worry about His Majesty. There is a battle that wages, far from the front, to protect the emperor from the vile forces that linger around the throne." Dmitri smiled. "And we are starting to win that battle."

"If you talking about killing Rasputin, I'm afraid his death will change little. The problems of Russia are deeper than one single peasant. So why did you and Felix murder him?"

"Enough!" the duke shouted. "I am tired of this conversation."

"I'm not here to judge you but to warn you," Sergei said. "Your actions of early this morning did not go unnoticed. The empress may already know."

"Nonsense. I am her favorite," he said, but his tone showed his doubt.

"You murdered a man, and no ordinary man. You murdered her close friend and spiritual adviser, not to mention the only person who was able to do anything for the heir apparent."

"He was a traitor." More doubt crept into his voice, "She loves me. She must. The dark one's death was for the greater good of Russia. She will understand. What we did, we did for her own protection."

"She wants to place you and Felix under arrest."

"She wouldn't."

"She will."

"How do you know all of this?"

"Renko."

The duke shoulders slumped. "I see. But, she has no authority. Only the tsar can authorize the arrest of a grand duke."

"Today, she is the tsar and she wants you arrested. You must leave the city at once."

"No. We will not allow this catastrophe to occur. All this has been brought about by the willful and shortsighted obstinacy of a woman. Can you imagine what a degraded and inglorious figure we shall cut in the sight of our allies?"

Serge raised his voice in disgust. "I couldn't care less about our prestige with respect to our allies. My friend, your safety can no longer be guaranteed in Petersburg. You must leave the city at once."

Disgust brewed in Dmitri as he heard this. Coolly, he shook his head, raising his own voice. "Are you insane? And miss this deciding moment in history? Serge, you may discard your uniform and run, but not I."

"Don't be a fool, Dmitri. You're playing a dangerous game, a game you can't win."

"At least I am in the game, my friend. Farewell," he said, storming out of the room.

Disheartened, Serge watched him go. Then, he looked around the room as it grew darker. The faint echo of laughter mixed with chamber music filled his ears. He wasn't the only one haunted by the past.

War Ministry, Overlooking Senate Square

The offices of the War Ministry were extraordinarily busy for a Saturday. General Platon Konstantin's office, which housed the offices of His Majesty's Secret Police, was no exception.

Sitting behind his paper-strewn desk, Platon wearing a heavily starched general's uniform two sizes too big stared into Renko's cool eyes. For the last twenty minutes, the inspector had been filling him in.

A nervous habit he picked up from his father, the general passed his boney fingertips through his heavy slate gray hair. "So, Renko, is everything in order?"

"Yes, I spoke with Burmin earlier at Aron's club."

"Good," Platon said as he moved some papers on his desk. "Saved you a visit."

"Yes, but half the city now knows about his release."

"That's what I'm counting on. He gives the British someone to chase."

Seeing his commander's logic, "He asked for protection. I told him it would be granted."

"That's fine. By providing him protection only legitimates Burmin as our messenger. Plus, it allows us to keep a close eye on him. All good news," the general said before his eyes moved down to a paper before him, "And my son?"

"Not good. He's drinking himself to death."

The general nodded. "That's what I have heard. I don't know what to do. Since his mother passed, I have lost the means of contact with him. We have barely spoken since his wedding."

"He can't come to grips with the loss of Sophia."

"We are all dealing with loss, my friend, some of us worse than others. Now, it is our job to save what is left."

"Yes General."

"Renko, make certain he is on that train. He is all I have left."

"But General, I thought we both were going to escort him to the train."

The general's eyes moved from his friend back to the papers on his desk. "No, I think it is best for my son not to see me. Tell him I will call him when he arrives in the Crimea. Give him this," he said handing Renko an envelope.

"I can not give this to him. He shouldn't find out like this."

Looking up from his desk, the general sighed. "Just give it to him when he is aboard the train. Can you handle that simple request?"

"As you wish sir. He is your son."

"I know he deserves better. But I..." He stopped there. It hurt too much to go any further.

"General?"

"I appreciate your concern, but I know what is best." The general paused. "Besides, I want it this way." Returning to current events, "Are you certain he was not involved in Rasputin's murder?"

"Positive. Through the years, I can tell when he's lying."

"You know my son more than I. That's a sad thing for a father to say."

"General, you have done all you could."

"Have I?" After another heavy pause, "Well, back to matters of state. Fill in all the blanks of Rasputin's disappearance; especially his missing correspondence from the empress. The last thing we need is for those letters to fall into the ambitious hands of the Vladimirs."

"Vlad?"

"Yes, they would not hesitate to make use of them. So, if you find them, destroy them on the spot. You have my full authority."

"Understood. Though, I believe Protopopov currently has them."

"Does he? I shall have to pay him a visit."

"He should be in a good mood. Rumor on the street was Rasputin was growing tired of him."

"That's good to know. Anything else?"

"That's it. Though I will have a complete report on your desk by this evening."

"Thank you, Renko. I appreciate you warning Sergei. That will be all."

"Yes general." And with that, the inspector left the room.

The general walked to the mirror. His uniform was becoming larger and larger, and his once rich head of gray hair was thinning. He moved his eyes to the certificate for bravery he had received from the tsar during Russia's war with Japan.

Serge's father had always been a complicated man. Born a soldier, Prince Platon Konstantin of His Majesty's Imperial Guards had carried on his family's tradition of conquest in the harsh fields of Manchuria. Over a decade ago, Platon and over four hundred thousand Russian troops were sent to battle

Japan. At stake had been the abundant riches of the mysterious Orient. In 1895, after losing the war with Japan, China had agreed to lease the Liao Tung peninsula to the eager Russians. For them, a Russian military base in Manchuria was a grand idea. Of course, China hardly had a choice, especially after the Boxer Rebellion.

It was a short-lived victory.

On February 8th, 1904, Japanese torpedo boats slipped into the Russian stronghold of Port Arthur. With swift, cold precision, the boats struck a decisive blow against the aged and obsolete Russian fleet. To the tsar, the attack presented an opportunity to squash Japan, and he ordered his army east. Thus, like so many others, General Konstantin, only a colonel at the time, left for Port Arthur. He was one of the few to return. Russia's imperial dream turned into a nightmare. The Russian High Command did not take into account the new battleships the Japanese had purchased from Britain. Britain wanted to maintain her dominance in the Orient and gave Japan every weapon she desired.

Konstantin emerged as a national hero. His escapades in Manchuria were legendary. Every small child knew his tale of valor. It took three weeks, but he led his men two hundred miles at incredible odds to Port Arthur—only to learn their commanding general was dead, the tsar's Pacific Fleet was at the bottom of the China Sea, and the city was preparing to surrender.

As all these thoughts swelled and swam through his head, the old warrior got up from his desk, and walked toward the fireplace. Above the mantle was a samurai sword that he had liberated from a fellow warrior some time ago. With aching hands, he reached for his sword. The cold steel felt wonderful against his warm flesh. Grabbing the sword, he muttered to himself, "This is the way a soldier should die, in combat, not slowly and suffering with cancer." With the sword still in his hand, he looked at the wall that captured so many moments of his life—fellow soldiers, family, and friends. Then, his eyes stopped on a photo of a young man in uniform. It could have been him thirty years ago. It was Sergei. He was inspecting the sword's blade when an old friend walked in the door. Platon had summoned Grand Duke Alexander Mikhailovich, his dead wife's brother, here from Kiev two days ago. Nicknamed Sandro since his youth, the dark bearded duke was a tall, lanky warrior with a poet's heart. The general loved this man like a brother.

"Platon," Sandro said, "reliving past glory, my friend?" The duke asked this in his normal good-humored fashion.

"It was anything but glorious," the old soldier said as he returned the sword to its holder. "I am glad the war has not harmed you, Sandro. Are you still wasting your money on those blasted flying machines?"

Seeing Konstantin turn from the fire gave Alexander a better view of his friend. Looking at the gaunt figure before him, Sandro's smile eroded from his face, "You're not looking well. Are you all right?"

"I only have a few months left, my friend," the general admitted with a grin. "So I am trying to make the most of it."

"Are you certain?" The duke didn't know what else to say.

"I am afraid so."

The two warriors embraced, as Sandro laughed awkwardly, to mask the tears he wanted to show.

CHAPTER 7

The Woods
Outside Staff Headquarters

Followed by the watchful eyes of his personal bodyguard, a soldier with large but remote eyes and a flawlessly trimmed red beard, or perhaps it was brown depending on the light, was able to steal a few precious moments from his day, and he spent them with his only son, Alexei. He was thankful for this trek through the woods. The war had engulfed everything, even a father's opportunity to play with his son.

"Only in Russia," the soldier said, enjoying the last drag from his cigarette, "would we pick a town as lovely as this to house an army." It was his army to which he was referring.

Nicholas Alexandrovich Romanov—the Emperor of all Russia—had never asked to be the tsar. In fact, he accepted the title of tsar with as much enthusiasm as one reserves for an unwanted gift. Regardless, the tsar was who he was and for the last twenty years he was growing increasingly tired of it. His reign to this point was pretty much summed by words like: scandal, death, defeat, riot, sunk, burned out, blackened, stampeded or bruised, all in an interchangeable order.

His mark was pathetically less than the Renaissance-style reign he envisioned so long ago. God-like power is a heavy load to bear for any mere man—especially Nicholas. As he exhaled an icy cloud of smoke, Nicholas's deep blue eyes watched the shifting snow dance upon the nearby rooftops.

Nicholas's days were consumed by doing what his staff required and greeting generals and foreign officials. In a long winter's breath, he exhaled his troubles. As his son led the way, he smiled. What a gift God gives you to see the world again through the eyes of a twelve-year-old boy. Alexei's bright smile filled him with joy, and gave him the necessary strength to endure the heavy burden of power. Romanovs had reigned over Russia for three hundred years. One day, Nicholas would hand the crown to his son. At least, that was the plan.

Dwarfed by his guardian angel, "Chekhov," the Tsar said in an elegantly polished tone, "I would prefer to walk alone with my son." His thoughts drifted towards a letter he had received from Father Rasputin the night before.

"As you wish, Your Majesty," said the giant. In the massive man's wake was the picturesque village of Moghilev, a cluster of cobblestone buildings covered in a blanket of new snow.

Tsar Nicholas removed the crumpled letter from his pocket. It was what bore so heavily on his mind.

> *I feel I shall leave life before January 1. I want to make known to the Russian people, to Papa, to the Russian Mother and to the children, to the land of Russia, what they must understand. If I am killed by common assassins, and especially by my brothers the Russian peasants, you, Tsar of Russia, have nothing to fear. Remain on your throne and govern. And you have nothing to fear for your children, they will reign for hundreds of years in Russia. But if I am murdered by boyars, by nobles, if they shed my blood, their hands will remain soiled with blood, for twenty-five years they will not wash their hands of my blood. Brothers will kill their brothers... Tsar of the land of Russia, if you hear the sound of a bell telling you that Grigory has been killed, you must know this: if it was your relations who wrought my death then not one of your family, that is to say none of your children or relations, will remain alive for more than two years. They will be killed by the Russian people. You must reflect and act prudently. Think of your safety and tell your relations that I have sacrificed my own blood. I shall be killed. I am no longer among the living. Pray, pray, be strong, and think of your blessed family.*

The letter was simply signed Grigory.

As young Alexei reached the top of the hill, he yelled, "Catch me if you can!"

"I don't believe anyone can climb this hill faster than you, my son. You're too fast for me!"

The tsarevich had hemophilia, a blood disorder so prevalent in the reigning houses of Europe that it was known as the royal disease. Hemophilia stopped blood cells from clotting naturally; a tiny scrape or fall could be lethal. Nicholas had asked the court physicians: "Is there no specialist in Europe who can cure my son? Let him name his own price; let him stay forever in my palace. Alexei must be saved." But medicine had no cure.

The empress blamed herself for her son's condition. Her bloodline caused his pain. Her grandmother was Queen Victoria of England, and this disease had riddled the queen's descendants.

Since Alexei's birth, an army of Europe's finest physicians had attempted to heal him. But only Rasputin seemed to be able to help; at least, that was what the empress believed. That was why when his meddlesome ministers asked him to send Rasputin away, they didn't realize that, for his wife, the odd-looking Siberian monk represented the only hope for her son. Alexei loved to play like every other twelve-year-old boy. At times, the tsar didn't know whether to laugh or cry. His boy was so frail and thin. There were moments, when the winds gusted that he thought his son would be carried over the hills. What a wonderful sight to see him run. He had waited so long for Alexei. He loved his four daughters, but Alexei held a special place in his heart. At the boy's birth, the court physicians had warned him that might not see his tenth birthday. They were almost right. Then, in a strange twist of fate, Rasputin had entered their lives with his backward ways and mysteriously brought Alexei back from death's door.

Today, father and son played in the newly fallen snow. The emperor was in a chipper mood. Hopefully soon, the war would be over and he would spend more afternoons like this with his only son.

Still shadowed by Chekhov, father and son climbed until they reached the crest. There beneath them was the village of Moghilev. Alexei stared toward the snow-covered hills, while Nicholas gazed down at the town's ancient cathedral. Even in the day, the wintry scene was breathtakingly beautiful. With the cold mountain air burning his cheeks, he knew he was a lucky man.

"Son," swaying his arms from left to right, smiling, "One day, all this beauty and spectacle shall be yours to uphold."

"Papa, you shall reign over this land forever."

The tsar placed his arm around his son. Then they both looked down at the village. This was Russia in the best and purest form, simple and abundant. It was as if goodness flowed freely through its narrow streets and poured down into the passing River Dnieper.

Alexei watched the people wandering the streets. "Papa, they look like ants."

"Ants? No. More like bees. Oh, how they rush through their days. Wouldn't it be lovely if they could rest for a moment, and stand, where I stand, and watch the sheer folly of it all?" His eyes moved to the cathedral spire. His faith grounded him. Right then, Nicholas smiled and produced a shiny red apple from his pocket.

"Is that the apple that Mamma sent you?"

"Yes my observant one."

"It's from the old woman, isn't it, the one who smells so bad and wears those cast iron chains?"

"The mystic Marie. And, I agree she does carry a strong scent."

The name Marie shifted his thoughts to the Marie of his youth. She was a pretty ballerina who stole his heart away so long ago. As Nicholas wondered what Marie was doing at this very minute, he heard his son's voice.

"Why does Mamma listen to them all, but not you?"

He laughed, looking down. "I don't know."

"Is Rasputin as bad as everyone says?"

"He helped save your life."

"Oh yes; I forgot."

"Poor Rasputin," the emperor said, thinking of the letter in his pocket. "He's a lost soul confused by his faith. Some day, he shall find his way. Until then, we must be patient." He lightly tossed the apple. "Now, what should we do with this? The old smelly woman told your mother that if we eat it, the war would soon be over."

"But that woman's never right."

"That is true."

"Let's throw it!"

The emperor tossed the apple to his son. "My feelings exactly."

With all his might, Alexei threw the apple into the woods.

"What should we tell Mamma?"

"The truth. It was delicious."

"It was," Alexei said with a child's delight, "wasn't it?"

"And now, my little Russian bear, I am afraid we must head back. Perhaps tonight we can watch a picture show," the tsar said as he tousled with his son's hair, "One of your choosing."

The boy shouted his approval, and ran down the hill. Watching his son running, he thought: "Everything seems clearer when I am alone in the woods. It is so quiet here. One forgets all the intrigues and paltry human restlessness. My soul feels peaceful. When one is nearer to nature, one is nearer to God."

Such a moment would help him endure this evening's conference with his generals. Perhaps after dinner he could write to his wife about Father Rasputin's prophecy and the "delicious" apple. As he walked down the slope the tsar whistled a verse of the imperial anthem. In the moment, he forgot about all the doubts he had felt by Father Rasputin's dreary letter, in the distance the town's steeple bell chimed the noon hour... twelve bells.

No word of Rasputin's disappearance had yet reached Moghilev.

The British Chancellery
Off the Banks of Neva

The British Embassy was an island in St. Petersburg's sea of uncertainty. Its staunch frame, reinforced with burnt brick, expected the worst the city and the cold Saturday afternoon had to offer. There was one object that consumed its northern view. Rising up from the outlying embankment was a massive structure of stone, the Fortress of Saints Peter and Paul. In this vast fortress rested the remains of past tsars. Their gold-chiseled tombs lined the impregnable walls of the fortress's own cathedral.

Throughout the Chancery, the British knew their Russian ally's knees were buckling. A fierce battle was being waged to keep Mother Russia, and her fifteen million sons, in this war at least until spring. Through their well-informed sources, the British were aware of secret negotiations between high-ranking members of the tsar's cabinet and the German government. These negotiations only purpose was to find a noble way to get Russia out of the war. The British ambassador had been instructed at the very highest level to use every available means to sever these peace talks. If Russia were out of the war, the Kaiser could send at least sixty battle-tested divisions up against the allies. The British and French troops would be forced to retreat, and the Germans would flood the French countryside like locusts. Trapped with their backs against a wall of water that was the English Channel, the British fate would be sealed. Within weeks, the war would be over. A new dark age would sweep across the civilized world.

With this in mind, Sir George Buchanan, the British ambassador to the Russian Imperial Court, was fully aware of his patriotic duty to keep the flames of war raging in the east, at least until spring. By then, the Americans and their fresh troops should be in the war. Sir George gave his afternoon visitors a sympathetic smile as he played with the waxy tip of his large white moustache. "I take it this is important, or the both of you wouldn't have those dreadful looks on your faces. What is it?"

"Bad business, sir," Bruce Lockhart said as he entered the dark, wood-paneled room. He was a trusted intelligence gatherer. "Word on the street is that Father Rasputin was murdered last night."

"I see. Jealous husband, I hope?"

"No, Ambassador, I'm afraid not. My sources tell me that the assassins were all members of high office."

"Not royalty?"

Lockhart hesitated. "Yes, Sir George. It is believed that two of the three were nobles, Prince Felix Yusupov and Grand Duke Dmitri Pavlovich."

"Who was the third?"

"A senator, Vladimir Purishkevich."

"What do you make of this, Benjy?" the ambassador asked his second in command Benjy Bruce.

"Sir, it could be several things. One, this information is false, and Rasputin is still alive." No one in the room believed that. "Two, Rasputin is dead, and these men of their own accord removed what they believed to be an embarrassment to the crown. Three, this is the first act of a power struggle and perhaps a Russian civil war."

"Indeed. Anything else?" he asked, sensing Bruce was holding something back. He looked away from the ambassador's stern eyes, towards a badly painted portrait of *The Charge of the Light Brigade* that covered the side wall.

"Burmin was released today."

"Released? How?"

"Still uncertain."

"Watch him most closely."

"I have two of my best men on him," Lockhart added.

"Make it four."

"Yes, sir. Consider it done."

"Benjy, do see what our good Russian allies are up to, will you?"

"Of course sir," Bruce barked.

"Very well, men." The ambassador tapped his bony fingers along the side of his desk. "Find me Jones."

"Yes, Sir George," replied Benjy as he and Lockhart rose and left the office.

As the door closed, the ambassador looked out the window across the semi-frozen waters of the great Neva at the menacing stone bastions of the Fortress of Peter and Paul as he had done so every day for the past six years he had been ambassador. The sight of its rich red structure still fascinated him. He recalled the last verse of Kipling's Recessional:

For heathen heart that puts her trust
In reeking tube and iron shard,
All valiant dust that builds on dust,
And guarding, calls not Thee to guard,
for frantic boast and foolish word Thy mercy
on Thy People, Lord!

It was not turning out to be a good day for the empire. Sir George needed to buy some time. So, he called an old friend, Grand Duke Nikolai Mikhailovich.

CHAPTER 8

Grand Duke Alexander's Palace
Sandro's Study

Bathing in the fire's warm glow, Serge's heart grew strangely cold. The rich aroma of fine leather blended nicely with the fading fragrance of his childhood. As a boy, Serge spent a great deal of time in his father's study, one very much like this one, enjoying his collection of books and the lingering scent of strong Turkish tobacco embedded in his father's favorite reading chair. It was Serge's sanctuary. But his father's study had been sealed for years, since the day Serge's mother had died.

Nonetheless, it was fun to be back in Sandro's study. The dukes, Alexander and Nikolai, were more than uncles. They were his friends. Waiting for his father's return from the empire's far-off provinces, he always seemed to find himself in this mysterious place, home to one of the finest collections of rare books in all of Russia. His adventure always began by strolling through this library of wondrous possibilities, then stopping in front of one of its crammed bookcases to grab a tale that was full of dusty dreams, penned so long ago by forgotten men now long dead.

Serge loved this place. This living library was the perfect sanctuary for a lonely child to breathe in and escape the cold world, while plunging into a fascinating new one. It was a place where one could soar through the crowded streets of some Persian city on the tattered strings of a flying carpet, or smartly sail the seven seas with a boatload of buccaneers in search of hidden treasure.

During his life, Sandro had collected as many books as friends. It was rumored that this wing alone housed nearly twenty thousand rare edition books and Serge believed it. Every inch of the high walls was lined with books. So, as the fire's flames danced before him, he sat in a comfortable chair near the fireplace, watching pale, curling smoke dance upon a warm flickering flame. Closing his eyes, he again drifted away. After his confrontation with Dmitri, he had come here.

As the crackling of the fire slowly grew silent, he was home. Near his own fireplace, it appeared to be Sophia telling him to return to bed. Opening his eyes, he was rewarded by the sight of Leo, one of Sandro's trusted servants.

"Does your Excellency require anything of me?"

"Just a brief moment with Felix."

"Very good, sir. He just arrived a few minutes ago, and instructed me to tell you that he would only be a moment."

"Thank you, Leo. That will be all."

Paging through Tolstoy's *War and Peace*, Serge smiled. Oh, you righteous tale of past patriotic glory, he thought.

Then he heard hard footsteps skimming across the atrium's marble floor. He was hoping it was one of the grand duke's sons. They were supposed to be in the city this weekend. But as the large French doors swung open, Felix entered and went towards a chair next to his cousin.

"Sergei, what a pleasant surprise. Are you here to see me off, old friend?"

"What do you think?" Serge asked, annoyed.

"I think not. Is my little cousin concerned about me? How touching." He smiled as he reached out and patted Serge's knee.

Serge pushed Felix's hand aside. "What did you do?"

He yawned, "Only what had to be done."

"Don't be so melodramatic. Why did you kill him?"

"Kill who?"

"Why must you be this way?"

"And what way is that, my observant cousin?" Felix said, loving the friction gathering between the two of them.

"Why must you do everything in your power to destroy all that you are afraid to love?"

"Whatever do you mean?"

"Felix, I have known you all my life. And I have seen firsthand the ruin you inflict on the ones who fall into your tangled web. So, I ask you again. Why did you kill Father Rasputin?"

"Yes, Rasputin is dead," Felix said, yawning. "But I am not the spider."

"I think you are, and I am not alone," the prince replied, thinking of his conversation with Inspector Renko.

"Think what you must but I'm not in a fit state to talk about it. I'm dropping with fatigue, and I need to pack for I'm leaving this evening for my Crimean estate. Irina is ill. I want to spend the holidays with her until she is well."

"I am sorry to hear Irina is ill, but I am thankful you are leaving the city."

"And why is that?"

"Don't be so naïve. Do you really believe that you can escape the empress's reaction to all of this?"

"I did what had to be done. I did what men like you lack the courage to do. I saved the monarchy, and the empress and her tainted ministers can go to hell."

"You say this now, but from a dank prison cell your perspective might change."

"Please, I am the sole heir to one of the wealthiest families in Russia, a prince and married to the tsar's own niece," Felix said, rising from the chair. "Do you really see a prison cell in store for me? I think not."

"And what do you think the emperor will do?"

"The emperor?" Felix was growing angry. "The emperor will reward us for saving him from performing the gruesome task. You see, old boy, the good father was having his way with the empress. And the sovereign's true warriors ended that moral mockery which surrounded the throne! Russia has always been led by the brave acts of the bold and beautiful."

"Nice speech, Felix. Will you be able to protect the tsar from the embarrassment such a scandal would entail. But I know you better. You couldn't care less about the vows that surround the throne! All you care about is yourself. I know about your secret, a secret that didn't die with the good father."

"Secret? Don't play games Serge. You may end up getting hurt," Felix warned. "Don't you see that the powers to be are already in motion?"

"Powers to be? Please, the atrocity of Rasputin's death is all yours. His blood will forever stain your twisted fingers. You see, my eccentric one," remembering an Oxford friend, "I know all too well that you destroy the things that get too close." With a hint of jealousy, he added, "Do give Irina my love."

"Still sore, old sport?" Felix asked. He knew Irina loved Serge more than him, but she was his wife. "The better man always wins."

"Just make sure 'the better man' is on that train tonight." After Felix left, Serge wondered at how they could be related.

"God save us from men like that," whispered the prince. A rusty old voice rang down from the heavens.

"The Lord wants nothing to do with that mess," laughed a grand duke hidden among dark mahogany shelves overcrowded with books. There, in all his glory, stood the tall and rather lanky Grand Duke Alexander. He was Serge's uncle on his mother's side. "Charming boy, my son-in-law. I can't see what my daughter finds appealing in him. Perhaps his absence." The old man laughed as only a Russian could.

"Uncle Sandro!" cried Serge, rushing toward the spiral steps. "I thought you were still at the front!"

"And miss all of this?" Sandro grinned. "Someone needs to run this lunatic asylum that we once called Russia." He looked Serge over. "I'm thankful the brutal test," referring to the war, "has returned you in one piece."

With those few words, a stream of shame coursed through the man wearing only a suit. Mumbling, as he looked toward the polished parquet floors, "Sandro, I ..."

"Say no more, son. Have faith that there is still good out there."

Shaking his head, Serge said: "All the good and the brave are now buried in a place without a name."

"And the unrest grows," declared the duke. "A situation like this cannot last long. That is why I am here. I need to warn Niki before the dark forces that currently surround him cripple him completely."

"Dark forces? Do you mean Rasputin? For he's dead."

"Rasputin, that poor Siberian peasant, is nothing compared with the sinister forces that currently confront us," Sandro said. "The tsar's own government wants him dead."

"What?"

"It is true. The government is doing all it can to increase the number of malcontents, and it is succeeding admirably. We're watching an unprecedented spectacle. Revolution is coming from above, not below."

"From above?"

"Yes, from above. These puppeteers are manipulating events—food shortages in the city while mountains of wheat rot in the countryside. Factions in the military due to poor morale caused by lies of scandal in the court."

"Do you know who?"

"I believe it all stems from the changing of the ministers. None that are loyal remain."

"Protopopov?"

"Protopopov is a hysterical coward and a formal liberal turned orthodox conservative by Rasputin's magic. They present a pair extraordinarily fit for the last act of the death of a nation."

"So there is no hope."

"There is always hope," Sandro whispered. "We will fix things, for we must. If we don't, everything will crumble to dust. Now Serge," moving to lighter conversation, the duke asked, "do tell me about your beard."

Serge laughed, as he knew how ridiculous he looked. "You don't like it?"

"You look like a street beggar."

"That's exactly how I feel."

The duke nodded. "Serge, remember the time..." With that, Alexander began one of his stories.

CHAPTER 9

British Chancellery
Sir George's Study

The door to Sir George's study slowly opened as a towering young man with orange-colored hair cautiously entered the ambassador's inner sanctum. "Sir George, I was told that you needed to see me."

"Yes. Welcome, Mr. Jones, to St. Petersburg." Malachi Jones, a hardy-framed man with composed blue eyes, promptly took his seat. It wasn't often he saw the ambassador without Benjy Bruce by his side. Malachi came from one of the wealthiest and most influential families in Wales. His father, F.W. Jones, was a self-made man having earned his millions in manufacturing. Fabulously wealthy, the Jones family represented the true measuring stick of modern day quality money.

"Jones, I don't need to tell you how important it is that Russia stays in this fight, do I?"

"No, sir."

"Never since the war began have I felt so depressed about the situation here, especially with regard to the future of Anglo-Russian relations. German influence has been making headway ever since Sazonov left the foreign office." He was referring to the minister replaced under Rasputin's influence. Sazonov was the ambassador's good friend and a believer in the cause to free Europe from German domination. He continued, "The Germans have changed their tactics. They are now representing that Britain is bent on prolonging the war for her own ambitions. I am sure that you have heard all of this in Moscow. 'It is Great Britain,' they keep on repeating, 'that is forcing Russia to continue the war and forbidding her to accept the favorable terms that Germany is ready to offer, and it is Britain, therefore, that is responsible for the privations and sufferings of her people.' This insidious campaign is much more difficult to contract than the old lies about our inaction."

Malachi had no idea where the ambassador was going with this. He had been in the capital less than twenty-four hours, and most of those had been spent drinking with a friend. Just then, Sir George brought up the last thing he expected.

"Jones, you're an Oxford man, aren't you?"

"Yes, I am," Jones said, fidgeting with his championship ring. He and Serge had played rugby together. "I graduated in the class of '14."

"A difficult year."

"For all of us."

"Quite," he replied, looking at a piece of paper. "Then you were in Oxford at the same time as Prince Felix?"

"Yes. But I didn't know him personally; he graduated ahead of me, and traveled in a different circle."

"Oh, I see," he said looking down at his dossier on Jones. "How about Prince Konstantin?"

"Why, yes, the prince and I roomed together."

"Yes." The diplomat had already been fully aware of this fact. "It is not only on the battlefields of Europe that the war must be fought. The final victory must also be won over the more insidious enemy within our gates."

"Mr. Ambassador, how does this involve Prince Konstantin?"

"Your country requires a great service from you, young man. And yes, it involves your old roommate."

Sandro's Study

Darkness engulfed Sandro's study, and the clock over the mantel had just chirped six. Together, Sandro and Serge enjoyed the soothing silence.

"What are you going to tell your father?" asked the duke.

"The truth. I am not going to leave the city. Especially now when everything is swinging out of control."

"To be young again! Cherish this time, my friend. Your days shall not always be like this."

Serge thought of his wife. "Cherish?"

"Yes. Cherish time, for in the end it is the only thing that matters. The worst thing imaginable one could do is to waste it." He paused. "Have I ever told you about my American dream?"

Serge had heard this tale before but it always moved him. He lied, "No, you haven't."

This brought a broad grin to the duke's bearded face. "The young continent of democracy," Sandro said dreamily, "and the lost notion of the Americanization of Russia. Sergei, when I was just a little older than you, I sailed with the vast Imperial Navy. Sadly, most of those magnificent vessels rest peacefully at the bottom of the Pacific, lost in the sea battle of Tsushima, but that is another story, a very sad one. I was just twenty-seven on that misty morning in 1893 when *H.I.M.S. Dmitri Donskoi* dropped anchor in the Hudson River. Officially, I came to express to President Cleveland the gratitude of my imperial cousin, Tsar Alexander III, for the help extended by the American nation during the Russian famine. Unofficially, I wanted to get an advance taste of the future and have the palm of my hand read by the spirit of a virgin race." The duke removed a book from his shelf. Then, he chuckled and returned to his chair.

"The World's Fair was about to open in Chicago, and the whole country was sizzling with excitement, the visit of the Infanta Eulalie being featured as the star attraction of the fair.

Kaiser Wilhelm dispatched Germany's most famous composer Von Burlow to counterbalance the 'Spanish intrigue.' The Scottish Highlanders sounded their bagpipes in Battery Place as part of an upcoming naval review in New York harbor, and the French answered with a specially picked orchestra of the 'Garde Republicaine.' There was something tremendously significant in this spectacle of all the great powers fighting for American friendship and goodwill. On a hot June night, while driving up gaily decorated Fifth Avenue toward the residence of John Jacob Astor, and looking at the endless rows of illuminated mansions, I suddenly felt the mysterious breath of a new epoch."

"The same millionaire who died on the Titanic?"

"Yes, the very one. But that's another tale. Patience, my young prince. So," diving back into his tale, Alexander spoke, "this was the land of my dreams! It was hard to believe that only twenty-nine years earlier this very land had gone through the terrors and privations of a civil war. I thought of the tsars. They reigned over an empire that was even richer than this new country, confronting the same problems, such as an immense population of scores of nationalities and religions, tremendous distances between the industrial centers and the agricultural hinterlands, crying necessity for extensive railroad building. American liabilities were greater than ours; our assets, larger. Russia possesses gold, ore, copper, coal, iron; our soil, if properly cultivated, should have been able to feed the whole world. What was the matter with us? Why did we not follow the American way of doing things? We had no business bothering with Europe and imitating the methods befitting nations forced by their poverty to live off their wits. So, right then and there, during the remaining few minutes of my ride in 1893, I commenced working out a large plan for the Americanization of Russia," Sandro said, giving Sergei his book.

The prince had given it a quick glance.

"It was intoxicating to be alive. It was a joy to repeat over and over again that the old, bloodstained nineteenth century was drawing to a close and leaving the stage clear for the irresistible efforts of coming generations."

"What happened on your return from America? Did the tsar listen to your proposal?" But the prince already knew the answer.

"I prepared a model for a proposed constitutional monarchy centered around this principle," Sandro walked over to a document encased in glass. "This document is a copy of the Loris-Melikov Constitution of 1881, and it was my noble blue print, drafted by order of Alexander II, my father's brother. Ironically, it was to be signed the very next day before he was assassinated. Nicholas's father could not find the courage to sign it after his father's brutal death."

"What a waste."

"Yes, it was. Sergei, the main reason I am in the capital is to see to it that before the New Year, Nicholas finds the courage his father did not possess, declares a new day for the Empire, and frees his people from bondage."

"But the Manifesto of 1905 that established the Duma," asked Serge, "wasn't that the first step toward a constitution?"

"A constitution in name only. No. Currently, the tsar is being advised to close the parliament's doors. If he does that, we are finished."

"When are you to meet with him?"

"With Rasputin's disappearance, I am certain he shall soon return from the front."

"Yes. The empress will make certain of it." The duke gave the young prince a pondering look as he recalled the past.

"Sandro, did you ever go back to America?"

"Yes, three years ago. I was having a hard time with reporters who wanted to know what I had to say about the phenomenal changes that had occurred in New York since 1893. I was supposed to compliment them on the new skyline, to comment upon the progress of the suffragist movement, to shed a tear or two over the passing of historical landmarks, and to wax enthusiastic about the future of the automobile. As a matter of fact, there was one startling change which seemed to have escaped the attention of native observers. The building of the Panama Canal and the stupendous development of the

Pacific Coast had created a new form of American pioneering. Their industries had grown to the point where foreign outlets had become a sheer necessity. Their financiers who used to borrow money in London, Paris, and Amsterdam had suddenly found themselves in the position of creditors. The rustic republic of Jefferson was rapidly giving way to the empire of the Rockefellers."

"Rags to riches, the American dream," Serge said as he gazed into the fire.

"Yes. A nation is only as strong as her dreams," the duke said as he also stared into the fire's licking flames, "Imperial Russia's dreams are nearly dead. If we do nothing to correct this the century shall be America's. By all rights, it should be ours, Sergei."

Outside the study, a small commotion was transpiring, as servants prepared Felix's packs for travel.

"Leo, what's all this?" barked the duke.

"Your Excellency," his servant replied, as he lowered a suitcase to the floor, "Prince Felix is leaving on the nine o'clock."

"Very well. One less fool to worry myself about, right Leo." This brought a big smile to the servant's face.

"Is there anything you require, your grace?"

"No. We are fine."

Leo returned to his duties as Felix appeared with two of Sandro's sons.

"Nikita and Theodore, what on earth are you doing here?" spoke the voice of a concerned father. "I thought you both were at Ai-Tor?" the duke's Crimean estate.

"The three of us are heading there now," said Theodore as he embraced his father. "I thought you were with your men in Kiev?"

"I was. I just arrived back today."

"And Serge. It has been too long old friend," Nikita said as he embraced his childhood friend. "I am so sorry to hear about your wife."

"Thank you Nikita."

"Serge," Theodore said giving his beard a pull, "I can barely recognize you with this thing. May I recommend a trip to the barber?"

"Thanks Teddy, it had slipped my mind."

"Yeah." Theodore said. He felt guilty he had even joked about it. "Well, we must be going."

Serge only smiled.

"Good to see you father-in-law," Felix said as he cleared his throat. He was standing in the distance. "But I am afraid we must catch that train. Irina sent me a note that she was not feeling well."

"Really, anything serious?" the duke asked.

"No, I think she caught a bug. I just hope she is better before the holidays," Felix said as he grabbed his coat from one of the servants. "Will we see you for Christmas?"

"Afraid not," Sandro said as he eyed his son-in-law, "Rasputin's disappearance has stirred up a great many things."

"Yes I have heard. Well, Merry Christmas Alexander. I do hope to see you soon."

"Yes. There is a great deal for us to talk about. Call me when you arrive. We need to clear up a few things."

"Sure."

Nikita and Theodore said their good-byes to Serge and their father.

"Serge, would you see them off to the station?" Alexander asked.

"Of course," the prince replied.

"We would love to have you Serge," Felix said as his eyes avoided him, "But there is hardly any room."

"Make room," the duke said as he returned to his study. "Serge, make certain they make their train."

"I will."

The duke added as he walked them towards the door. "I shall call Renko to explain."

The mentioning of the inspector's name brought a chill down Felix's spine. "Very well," he said as he left, "But it's going to be tight."

"We'll survive," Serge said as he followed Felix to the car.

CHAPTER 10

The Reading Room
In the Hotel Europe

Feverishly digging through his notes, Robert Wilton attempted to confirm his story of Rasputin's disappearance before the deadline. He sat in his favorite corner of the lobby of the Hotel Europe. Wilton wanted to make sure he did not misquote the official with whom he had spoken early in the day. This story was front-page material, and he knew it. It was a great murder mystery set in Petersburg. And like all good mysteries, it would have to have a few twists. His editor at *The Times* in London would love it, and so would his readers.

Finding his quote from Colonel Rogov, he smiled. It was perfect. Some days, these things just write themselves, he thought, just as his world turned dark. The figure obstructing his light was one Malachi Jones, a tall Welshman wearing a mop of red wiry hair.

"Good afternoon, Robert."

"Malachi. I thought you were still stationed in Moscow."

He sat down. "I still am. They just brought me up for a quick check before the conference."

"I see." The stout and disheveled reporter eagerly asked, "Anything my readers should know about? Rumor on the street is that the tsar is considering the Kaiser's terms for peace." Robert loved his job—a little too much some said.

"Robert, your brilliant mind was meant for writing fiction."

"I don't know, Jones. Reality around here is much stranger than fiction—and more interesting."

"Agreed." Jones glanced at Wilton's notes. "Young princes of death? What is this?"

He shielded the notes.

"Please tell me you are not using this?"

"Of course I am. A story doesn't get any hotter than this— a man of the cloth murdered by royalty."

"Man of the cloth? Please. This is the same Rasputin who was nearly stabbed to death last spring by one of his many mistresses."

"The story plays better if he was good, and they were bad."

"Any predictions?"

"I don't know. The empress and her clique of women evidently are in charge, and the emperor is being blindly driven into acts that will sooner or later precipitate grave disorders unless there's a revolution from within the family or from the streets."

"So, how long do you think we have?"

"Unless everybody is grievously mistaken, we have only two or three months left in which to take decisive and energetic measures."

"Two or three months?" Jones replied, knowing that his friend was an optimist. Then, as he was leaving, he recalled why he was here. "Any chance you've seen Serge today?"

"No. But that boy is nearly worse off than Russia."

"That's what I have heard." Jones recalled how distant his friend had seemed the previous night.

"It's hard to lose your wife. Check the hotel bar around nine. He'll be there; he always is."

The Yacht Club for Drinks

Two dukes bearing the same family name sat in their comfortable chairs in one corner of the club and discussed Russia's problems over drinks. It was Vlad and his younger brother Andrew.

With smoke lingering over their heads like spent thoughts, they pondered the direction of many things, mainly what could have been.

In 1894, when Nicholas's father Tsar Alexander III was on his deathbed, many questions had been asked on the right of secession. Most throughout the Court supported Alexander's brother, the ambitious Grand Duke Vladimir, Vlad's father and namesake. But, before his death, Alexander told the Court that he was passing the Crown to his eldest son Nicholas instead.

At the time, Nicholas was only twenty-six years of age, and appeared to all to be too weak a candidate to rule Russia. Many disagreed with the tsar's decision. But even on his deathbed, Alexander was a man to be feared. Vladimir would never forget this insult his brother placed on him. For, he had always been jealous of his older brother's power. And, when he thought he would finally receive his just desserts, he was once again passed over. All that jealousy quickly turned to hate after Alexander's death. Now the eldest surviving son of Tsar the Liberator was required to bow down to a mere man the size of a child. So, Nicholas and his family were the heirs to his hate. And every remaining moment, he and his wife reminded their children of that hate for the royal family. Because he knew that there would be an opportunity to seize back the power that was meant for him. And, today was that day. Sadly, Vladimir the older was now dead. But, in his sons his hate lived and grew.

The Grand Duke Vladimir bearing an uncanny resemblance to the last Tsar Alexander squeezed his massive bear-like body out of his tiny chair and approached the mantelpiece.

"The 'colonel' has sat in my seat long enough," he barked with naked ambition, "That weakling has stolen what was ours!"

His younger brother nervously agreed. Since birth, Vlad had terrified him.

"First," he said as he slammed his meaty fist into his palm, "We need to win this war. A generation of young Russian boys lay butchered in fields of mud, and for what gain— nothing! Morale is down, and poor morale can kill an army worse than any enemy's bayonets. We need a plan, and a new leader to administrate it. What has happened to the noble cause of the liberation of Constantinople?" he exclaimed, addressing the fiery hearth. "We should have been there by now."

"I agree, my brother. But, we are not. Nor I fear, shall we ever be," advised Andrew as he pulled a fresh cigarette out from his case.

Feeling the need to reason, Vlad continued. "In the beginning of the war, high command begged the tsar to avoid the Prussian lines. Our fight was with the Austrians regarding the position of the Balkan Straits, mainly the control of Constantinople, and her warm watered port. The tsar's answer to the man that would have led us to victory was that we must aid our Allies the French. If we didn't attack the Germans at that point, their overwhelming forces would have easily taken Paris. And that would have forced France out of the Great Game."

"I wish the Germans had captured Paris in '14," said Andrew, the dreamer of the two. "The war in the west would have been over before it started. How many millions have been slaughtered protecting that distant city of light? Four million, five?" looking at each other, "more?"

"I couldn't care less about that front. My concern is ours, and its three thousand miles," Vlad declared, "And, with each passing day, that shifting front possesses less of the Motherland than the day before. Poland is nearly lost. To me, it's a question of sheer territory."

"Dear Brother, our problems are greater than a shrinking empire," Andrew admitted. A few days ago, he returned from an inspection tour of the front. The duke did not like what he saw. "Allow me to share with you a conversation I had with General Palitsin the other day. And I must warn you it's distributing. In fact, I cannot get his voice out of my mind. I asked him, what should the High Command do? He replied, I don't know. Then, I asked, but you have some idea?" Looking at his brother's grim face, "He responded I have an idea, a very good idea."

Anger filling his breath, Vlad snapped, "Good idea, indeed."

Agreeing, "Exactly, Brother. Next, I asked should we attack. He said," Andrew doing an excellent impression of the general, "Well, that's not possible because we must husband our strength."

"What strength?"

"So, I said 'then we should hold our lines and fight where we are?' The old man replied. 'When we take our stand we should do it in a better place.'"

"Better place," snarled Vlad, "How's about the gates of this very city?"

"This is the part that haunts me," admitted the duke, "I told him, 'then we must retreat.' Palitsin continued by saying, 'God save us. How can we retreat? Theory shows that when you retreat you lose much more than when you attack.'"

"Retreat, or attack," barked a duke feeling his brother's pain. "Is he mad? Then what should we do?"

"That's exactly what I asked him, and all he said was *I don't know but I have a very good and excellent plan*," finished the duke with these words.

Vlad shook his head, as he exclaimed. "This butchery must end. I have heard enough," declared Vlad, staring at his brother, "It is time. We Russians have two Allies in this world. Our Army and our Navy," quoting the previous tsar. "Since our Navy was completely destroyed off China's shores a decade ago that only leaves us our Army. And, in nearly three years, we have lost three million men," forced Vlad, shrugging his shoulders, "perhaps more. Such waste of fine men. We sat back in '04, and watched Nicholas and his admirals destroy our Pacific Fleet. We must ask ourselves, here and now, in the last hours of 1916 if we are going to sit back again and watch Nicholas and his generals destroy the mightiest army in all the world?"

"The hell we're not!" offered Andrew.

Nodding his agreement, "Good. Then, we must rise up from our seats and claim what is rightfully ours. For there was once a time not so long ago when the Empire was feared, and so was its Emperor. With your help brother, we can return to those times, and win back the people's trust. By spring, under new leadership, we can be victorious. Today, there's a modern day Napoleon marching through our lands."

"Each step," Andrew advised his brother," requires the same step back," recalling Napoleon's retreat from Moscow in 1812.

"I'm counting on it. Let's show them what we Russians do to those who foolishly dare to invade our lands."

The two discussed their next bold move.

CHAPTER 11

Chauffeur Driven Limo
Headed to Nicholas's Station

Who is Prince Felix? Young, complicated, and dashingly sophisticated, the prince was not yet thirty years of age and was the only surviving child of the wealthiest and most affluent family in Petersburg, the Yusupovs.

Spoiled and sheltered since his youth, the prince was struggling to find his own identity. He felt insignificant and insecure. He had been forced to live in his elder brother's shadow for most of his life. His father, General Yusupov, not known for his kindness, exhausted the little love he did possess on his first son, Nicholas. The day that Nicholas died in a duel, his father's love turned to hate—directed at Felix. With the death of the perfect one, the heavy burden of the Yusupov name shifted onto Felix's shoulders like a dead weight. Not until Oxford did that weight lighten, when Felix found himself in the scandalous scribbling of the infamous playwright, Oscar Wilde. By the time he graduated from Oxford, he was wonderfully content with himself and liberated from his past. He enjoyed all the world had to offer, especially life's sordid pleasures. He was finally free from his father and what he represented—an old world's sense of conformity.

Felix's good friend the ballerina Anna Pavlova described his personality the best when she said: "The trouble with you, Felix, is that you have God in one eye and the devil in the other." Poor Felix did have more than his fair share of demons. But what modern man didn't? It was the dawn of a new century, and he reflected on the splendor and shortfalls of modern man. His personal maxim came from Wilde's novel *The Picture of Dorian Gray*: "The only way to rid yourself of temptation is to yield to it."

His life was full of potential. He was extraordinarily rich, possessed a razor-sharp wit and, most importantly, he was beautiful. Before he had married Irina, he had been Europe's most eligible bachelor. This odd title always made him laugh. If there was anyone he loved more than himself, it was Irina. He loved Irina because she was everything he was not. Kindness and love cascaded from her heart. She was an innocent. For him, that was true love. Some in the imperial family, including Irina's father, could not understand the couple's attraction other than that they were both gorgeous. But who can explain love? Certainly not Felix.

Tonight, Felix was in a quiet mood as his automobile pulled away from his father-in-law's palace. He didn't like deceiving Dmitri. Father Rasputin was dead thanks to the smart marksmanship of the grand duke, but his friend would have never pulled the trigger. The empress and Rasputin were not really lovers as he had told the duke. When he had shown Dmitri the forged love letter Vlad had provided, Dmitri had nearly gone mad with rage. It had taken all Felix's strength to control him until last night. While he didn't know it, the duke had been firing not at the dark one, but at the heart of the old regime.

By Tuesday, it would all come out. There would be a new tsar, and Felix knew that when Dmitri learned of his treachery, their friendship would be over. For some reason, that saddened him.

His train for the Crimea was departing within the hour. Two of Sandro's sons, Theodore and Nikita, sat across from him. Shoulder to shoulder, they gazed back; Serge quietly sat beside him.

"Driver!" Felix cried. "Take me home."

"Yes, Your Grace."

Nikita nervously asked, "Felix, do we really have time for that?"

"We shall make time!"

"Make it quick," Serge said disgustedly as he gazed out the window. They drove along the Moika embankment. Peering out of his slightly frosted window, the prince could see the massive silhouette of his childhood home. He pulled out his timepiece. There was time.

"Driver, stop the car!"

"Yes, Your Grace."

"Felix, you are going to miss your train," warned Serge. He still couldn't believe what was happening. Felix had somehow drawn Sandro's sons, Theodore just eighteen, and Nikita, two years younger, into his conspiracy. If it would not have broken Irina's heart, he would have killed Felix. He had never understood what she saw in him.

Felix chose the moment to share a holiday memory: "Remember when we were boys?" Felix asked no one in particular. "We had a very good time."

The three looked at one another. Had Felix lost his mind?

Then his happiness came to an abrupt end as he thought of his father. Presently, he was the commander in chief of the Chevalier Guards, the same regiment in which Serge had served. Felix loathed the fact that it was his own father who had hung the Cross of St. George around Serge's neck. In the prince's mind, Serge was the reincarnation of the chosen one, Felix's own brother Nicholas.

"Drive on!" the prince cried.

The car remained silent until it approached the railroad station bloated with people. "What's the commotion?" Felix shouted. "Soldiers, Your Grace."

The Nicholas Station was swarming with armed soldiers checking every passenger boarding the train to Crimea. A colonel of the military police approached the vehicle. He addressed the prince in a mumbled voice, incomprehensible as he shook with fear.

"Prince Felix," he said at a near whisper.

"Speak up, Colonel. I can't hear you," the prince called out. He lit a fresh cigarette.

"By orders of Her Majesty the Empress, you are forbidden to leave the city," shouted the colonel. "You are to return to the Grand Duke Alexander's palace and stay there until further notice."

81

"I am sorry," Felix dryly replied, as he inched closer to the sweaty faced colonel and blew some smoke at him, "but that doesn't suit me at all."

The colonel coughed. Then, he nervously looked the other way. "Those are my orders."

Felix laughed, as he debated boarding the train. However, after a brief discussion with Theodore and Nikita, Felix agreed to stay in the capital. Why run? Soon he would be a celebrity he thought, and celebrities don't hide from their fans. "Give Irina my love," he said to the two of them as they boarded the train.

Serge stood next to him, watching the train pull out of the station.

"Felix, you devil, I can't believe you got them involved in this."

"Involved in what Serge?"

"You know what. I don't know what gypsy curse you placed on Irina to convince her to marry you, but I will not allow you to ruin Sandro's good name."

"Ruin? Killing Rasputin was a noble deed, worthy of a Romanov."

"Killing Rasputin changed nothing. You will soon find that fact out. Now, I am not looking forward to telling the duke about his son's involvement in this debauchery, but, trust me, I shall."

"You must do what you feel is best, boy. I must warn you it will break the duke's heart. Are you so certain you want to do that?"

"You're the one responsible," young Konstantin said. "If I have learned anything from Sandro, it is to always speak the truth, regardless of the consequences."

With this, the prince watched Felix's smile erode from his face.

"You bastard," Felix hissed, getting into his car to leave.

"You haven't seen anything yet," Serge said to Felix. He thought as he watched the car drive away. "It's time for a drink."

Hospital Train Traveling South

An hour out of the capital, Senator Vladimir Purishkevich was safe in the private compartment of his hospital train as it headed south for the front. For the first time all day, he felt safe. That sense of security increased with each passing mile. He had made it. Scratching his beard, he attempted to recall the historic events of last night. Twenty-four hours had not yet passed but he could feel it in his bones that Russia was now different. For history's sake, he wrote in his journal:

I am surrounded by the deep of the night and utter silence, while my train, gently swaying, carries me off into the distance. I cannot sleep; events of the last forty-eight hours whirl through my mind. Rasputin is no more, for he has been killed. It has pleased fate for him to fall at my hand. Thank goodness that the hands of Grand Duke Dmitri Pavlovich have not been stained with that dirty blood. The royal youth must not be guilty of any matter connected with the spilling of blood. Even if it is the blood of Rasputin, he must not be guilty.

He paused, his thoughts drifting to Felix. The constant swaying of the train comforted him, reminding him he needed a brief nap. It was only last month that they had officially met. The day after his "Dark Forces" speech to the Senate, Felix had come to his door. After a brief discussion, they had considered their limited options. "What should we do?" the old man had asked the young.

"Simple. Remove Rasputin."

"That's easy to say, but who will undertake it? There are no resolute people in Russia, and the government supports Rasputin and protects him like the apple of its eye."

"Yes, there is no counting on the government. But in Russia such people can be found."

"You think so?"

"One of them stands before you."

Purishkevich pushed aside his journal; he needed to get a little sleep for tomorrow was going to be a long day. He thought about the past and what Russia had been like before the war. With that, he fell into a child-like sleep.

CHAPTER 12

The Hotel Europe
Caviar Bar

In the posh Caviar club of the Hotel Europe, men fought for position along the long bar. A warped wake for Father Rasputin was in full progress. All were dressed in their stiff, freshly pressed uniforms. These regulars of the rear saluted one another with praising toasts of "God save Russia," "the beast is slain," and the ever clever "the dog is dead." Exchanging smiles and downing drinks, this rowdy crowd's voices grew louder and louder. As the bartenders opened bottle after bottle of Champagne, it almost sounded as if a new front were opening.

To Serge, the entire scene seemed surreal, almost as if the room were bathed in a cloud of Champagne bubbles. He had been here too long. Absorbing it all, the prince's eyes fell upon a tarnished plaque of silver that read "Land of Lincoln." It only added to the oddity of the moment. The inscription paid homage to the American behind the bar who spoke perfect Russian with a slight Southern American drawl. The presence of the black bartender from the Blue Hills of Kentucky seemed somehow appropriate in this phony place.

Leaning against the bar, Serge was miserable. He had been drinking heavily for the last hour—mostly shots of vodka. As depression set in, he reached for the bottle again. He wanted to return to the heavy fog. After his seventh glass, the fog slowly rolled in. All that had seemed so important just a short time ago was forgotten. He was happy again, or as close as a man like him could be to happiness.

Looking around the room, he was reminded of other young men in ill-fitting uniforms at the front, those whose boyish faces were covered in dried mud and fixed stares but who still managed to smile. They all had known what they were fighting for—each other.

"What'll be, Serge?" Lincoln the bartender asked.

"Ah, Lincoln," Serge said. "How did you ever find your way here? I am sure it is a fascinating tale."

"We all have them," Lincoln said, cleaning a glass.

"We all have what?"

"Sad stories. We all got 'em."

Serge raised his glass for a refill. "You're so right. What's your sad story, Lincoln?"

Smiling, Lincoln refilled Serge's glass. "That I am surrounded by too many Russian fools."

"Lincoln, you truly are," Serge said, laughing. "But for some reason I fit in. Please leave the bottle."

Lincoln set it down. "Like I said, we all have our sad stories."

"I know. But I want mine to go away."

Finishing another drink, he was thinking of friends long gone as an old Oxford roommate strolled in. A year older than Serge, Malachi Jones had been a hellion at school. In fact, he had barely passed. It wasn't that he lacked intelligence; the man was fluent in five languages. The Welshman just wasn't interested in academics. He preferred the energy of the streets. He had majored in rugby, to the point that by his third year he had become captain and led the team to victory over Cambridge. Serge still wore that old rugby ring.

With a modest bob of his big head, "Squeaks," Serge's old rugby nickname, "I have been looking for you all day. I need you to connect a few dots from last night's little get-together."

"Jones, are you sure you want to be in here?"

"What do you mean? I just wanted to know how I ended up with that blonde last night." He liberated an empty glass from behind the bar and filled it with some of Serge's vodka.

Serge pointed to a guard captain sporting a black eye. "He's wearing one of your souvenirs of last night. He was foolish enough to get between you and a certain individual."

Serge pointed to another captain. "And the blonde was with him until you walked in."

A large beer drinker of a man, Jones cherished his grandfather's coal mining roots. "Oh, how ghastly of me. Well," the redheaded Welshman said, waving to the captain, "he should have known better than to intrude." Then, he downed his drink.

Serge slapped his back. "Intrude? When he left to fetch another drink, you took his seat. Then you took his woman. Not exactly a chivalrous act for a British gentleman."

"Who said I was a gentleman?"

They both laughed as Serge poured Jones another. Last night had been tough for both of them. Recently their old rugby roster had lost a few good names, the war had stolen even the memories of their youth.

After a few heavy sips from his drink, the Welshman said as he wiped a stray curl from his face, "Serge, I need some information."

"Information? What do I know? What do you want of me, a broken-down prince?"

"Certain ministers and members of your military have created this chaos that we're currently drowning in. As we speak, your home minister, Alexander Protopopov, is in known communication with Berlin. He and his liaison are quietly laying out the final terms of a separate peace."

"The tsar will never accept a treaty as long as the Germans stand on Russian soil."

"Trust me, Squeaks. We are certain of this. We have been closely watching these events since November, when Sturmer, the man Protopopov replaced as minister, contacted Burmin personally to orchestrate Russia's removal from the war."

"If what you say is true, why doesn't Sir George share this information with His Majesty at once?"

"We have already tried that. It all fell on deaf ears."

"I'm sure it did." Serge reconsidered his question. "Sir George has been a little too friendly towards the Lenin-like liberals and the radicals whose only desire is to eliminate the tsar. I could see why Nicholas would be hesitant to listen to him."

"I know Sir George has lost the emperor's trust, but we need someone in your government to be aware of this high treason. Our sources have informed us that the proposed treaty would take effect at the Russian New Year. That's only two weeks away."

"Again, my friend, what can I do?" asked Serge as he began to slur his words. "As you can plainly see, I have my own problems."

"For starters, you need to pull yourself together. Get rid of the beard."

"What's wrong with it?" he asked, stroking it. "I am quite fond of it."

"Hell, I am half-expecting a pigeon to fly out of it. Sophia would not want this. You're killing yourself, Serge, while your country needs you the most."

"Jones, it's too late."

"No, it's not. Serge," addressing him with his given name for the first time since his visit, "your father is one of His Majesty's most trusted generals. Speak to him. Sir George would like to arrange a meeting with him as soon as possible. He will provide the necessary proof that ministers in his majesty's government are arranging a separate peace with Germany."

"This is sheer madness. Why drag me, let alone my father, into this?"

"We must, Serge. We are on the very brink of ruin, and traitors surround the Russian throne. The Monarchy is in jeopardy. Help us."

"Who's Monarchy—mine or yours?"

"Does it really matter?"

Serge paused. "No. I suppose it doesn't. I will do what I can. But, no promises."

"Deal?"

"What choice do I have?"

"None, if you don't want the Kaiser to control all of Europe." Jones grinned and rose to leave. "Thanks for the drink Squeaks. Until tomorrow."

As the shots of vodka worked their magic, Serge laughed out loud. It was comforting to know that there were still a few certainties in the world, one being Malachi's legendary cheapness, even though he was worth millions.

Lincoln brought Serge another bottle of vodka. He would need it if he planned to see his father the next day, especially since he had missed his train. As he opened his wallet to pay his tab, a wilted flower fell out of it and landed in a puddle of booze.

How ironic, the prince thought, as he carefully picked it up and returned it to his wallet. It was from a perfect morning, the last morning he had spent with his wife. He would never forget how she had removed it from a small banquet of flowers by the bed, and told him to keep it close to his heart. "Don't go," she had pleaded as they embraced. Every day, he wished he hadn't. Perhaps things would have been different. Before battle the previous July, Serge had received a message from his father. He was hoping to read if his wife had delivered a boy or a girl.

Instead, he learned that she and their child were lost due to complications. That day, he had done everything he could to join them. He had charged a German machine gun nest single-handedly, telling himself his wife was there, behind the line, held captive. The Germans, holding the bunker, could not believe their eyes as they saw the lone Russian boldly cross no man's land, screaming a woman's name. Obviously, the man was mad. Looking at one another, the Germans smiled and placed bets. His actions were suicidal, and it would be fun to see how far he would dare come. In the trenches, one would do anything to pass the time.

From the Russian lines, Serge's advance did not go unnoticed. First, it was just a few random cries. Then, the line came alive. Reviving them from yesterday's heavy losses, they cheered him on and found their own courage. How dare these German invaders squat down on their lands! As the Germans noticed this, their commander thought they had had enough fun for one day. No use rallying the Russians. "Finish it," he had said, looking at his machine gunner. Hundreds of bullets bounced toward the Russian—but none hit its mark. The German nest grew quiet. This only heightened shouts from the Russian line.

The German officer grabbed his rifle to end this game himself. But shot after shot missed. The machine gunner had trouble reloading, and the others grabbed their weapons. As the nest opened fire, Serge smiled savagely and ducked into a nearby hole. Freeing a grenade from his belt, he tossed it casually into the air.

The Germans screamed as they saw the tiny projectile. Each man dropped his rifle, trying to catch the grenade before it exploded. One did. As he tossed it from their nest, a shadow covered the hole.

As they looked up, the lone Russian stood before them. Instinctively, the Germans moved towards their weapons. One-by-one, with his rifle, Serge began picking them off. All were terrified except one.

"Kill him!" the man shouted in German but it was too late. The commander realized all the others were dead.

Then the Russian jumped into his hole with an enormous knife in hand. "Where is she?"

"You're not real," the German officer replied, reaching for his pistol.

"You had your chance," the Russian muttered. Then he grabbed the dying man by his collar, "Why didn't you kill me? Why?"

Spitting blood, the German spoke his last words: "I tried. I tried." When Serge's comrades reached him, they found him slapping the dead, yelling, "Where is she?"

They decided to continue the attack. The Germans who lined the outer trenches had seen enough. They had scampered out of their nests and returned into the safety of the woods.

A few days later, fate answered Serge's request when he again charged the enemy line. This time, he proved to be mortal. At the field hospital where he had received his medal, his badly wounded body mended, but his spirit would not. His wife had been everything to him. Without her, his soul was lost. Now, confined to his penthouse suite of the Europe, his own personal prison, he spent his days chasing down his own demons. Lincoln's rough and raw voice ripped him back to the present, "Here's your change, Serge. Do you need anything else?"

"Forgiveness," he replied as he tossed a wad of money on the bar.

"I only serve drinks."

As Serge stood up, the stuffy room began to spin. Falling, he was saved by the most unlikely person. Her dark eyes glistened; they bore a hint of sadness. The prince recalled Lincoln's remark: "We all have our sad stories."

"Serge, why do you do this to yourself?"

He breathed her in. "Because I can."

She shook her head sadly. "Not anymore. Let's get you upstairs."

CHAPTER 13

Staff Headquarters
A Meeting of Gods and Generals

The battle of the military minds in the Russian High Command had begun some hours ago. Each general's ego extended the briefing. Every one of them was blaming another, and that was worrisome to the tsar. The only thought that comforted him was the fact that soon there would hopefully be peace throughout his land. With a lasting peace, he would be able to save his kingdom, and restore the cross to a fallen Christian city. Constantinople, his childhood dream, would soon be in Russian hands. Then, a new crusade would begin. And on the very day the cross was restored to the Cathedral of St. Sophia, Nicholas would declare a constitution, the same document his grandfather was planning to sign the day that he was assassinated. It was time to forget the past, and focus on Russia's future.

Pulling himself from these pleasant thoughts, Nicholas considered his generals. They were the very best his country had to offer. Well, almost. His friend, General Alexeiev, known for his strategic brilliance, could not attend the meeting. He was not well. His nerves had suffered a great deal during this conflict.

The generals stared at their maps as they prepared for the spring offensives. They believed that they needed to throw everything they had at the Germans to bloody them until the Americans entered the war.

Leaning back in his chair, Nicholas once again thought of his only son. He had enjoyed his hike with Alexei. He was looking forward to spending more time with him as soon as he had captured Constantinople. Constantinople! Until now, it had been an unattainable dream.

At that moment, General Gourko, a short and serious fellow with a bushy white moustache, began to read his prepared statement.

"Romania's entry into the field did not take place under the circumstances we deemed best from the point of the general plan of the campaign." He glared at a Romanian general. The Romanian general reached for his water glass. He had been expecting this.

"The Romanians, ignoring the suggestions we considered..." the Russian general continued his speech on the Romanian's failure to influence the battle.

The Romanian general cleared his throat, as his face radiated an odd mixture of shame and hate.

The Russian continued. "After a few weeks we were forced to recognize that the military value of our ally did not come up either to our hopes or our to expectations due to her army's lack of training and feeble powers of resistance."

"Feeble powers!"

"Yes, your army's lack of training and feeble powers of resistance have upset our calculations."

The Romanian shrunk back into his seat. General Gourko spoke the truth. The Romanian Army was in utter disarray. It hadn't been prepared for the enemy's punch.

Only three short months ago, his country had decided to enter the war on the side her leaders believed was going to win. All they would need to do was kick the already-beaten forces of Austria and Hungary. But while dreaming about kicking and looting the Austrians, the Romanians had forgotten about the Germans. Instead of a quick victory in the east, the remains of the Romanian army were barely able to return to the protection of their own borders. Without Russian reinforcements most of his army would have been either in a prisoner of war camp or dead.

As the chamber's doors opened, the city's cathedral bells began to toll, sounding off the hours. It was getting late. Entering the room was one of His Majesty's trusted aides.

"Krakovsky, can't you see that we are in the middle of a meeting?" the tsar asked with a broad smile. He was thankful for the intrusion.

"I apologize, Your Grace," the man said, bowing, as he handed his sovereign a dispatch, "It's a cable marked most urgent, and from Her Majesty the Empress."

"Thank you, Krakovsky. You're dismissed."

A worried expression began to engulf the Tsar's face.

The cable read:

> *Our Friend has disappeared. Yesterday Anna saw Him and he told her that Felix had asked Him to come to him at night; that a motorcar, a military one, came to take Him with two civilians, and he left. Last night a great scandal at Yusupov's house—a great gathering, Dmitri, Purishkevich, etc.–all drunk. Police heard shots. Purishkevich ran screaming to the police that our Friend was killed. Felix pretends that He never came to the house, he never invited Him. It was, apparently, a trap. I shall still trust in God's mercy that one has only driven Him away somewhere. Protopopov is doing all he can... I can't and won't believe that He was killed. God have mercy... Felix came often to him lately. Come quickly.*
>
> *Kisses,*
> *Sunny*

"Your Grace, is everything all right?" Gourko asked. Nicholas had turned white. "Father Rasputin is apparently dead," he whispered as the dispatch fell to the floor.

The men around the table looked at one another. This was the first good news they had had in some time. Though, the man who saved the heir apparent was now dead. The room was silent. Uncertain how to react, eyes moved from one another to the corners of the room.

"Those evil fumes of Petersburg! One can smell them even at the front, and it is from drawing rooms and palaces that the worst emanations come. What a disgrace! Tell them to prepare my train." Thinking of Rasputin's warning, the emperor softly said: "We are all doomed."

CHAPTER 14

A Corridor Within the Home Ministry Building

Alexander Protopopov was pleased as he strolled the deserted corridors of the Ministry of the Interior. The day had gone better than he had expected. His links with Rasputin were cut. His puppeteer was now enjoying the all-healing waters of the Neva. With Rasputin gone, the empress would be forced to lean more on him for her information. His grand scheme depended on keeping her in the dark, at least for the next couple of days. After that, it was no longer his problem.

As he walked down the ministry corridor to his office, he noticed small puddles of water covering the floor. The cleaning crew was getting sloppy.

Then, out of nowhere, a large man dressed all in black and cloaked by a dark shroud ran across the corridor followed by the strong odor of the outdoors.

"How odd," he whispered. The figure disappeared down the hall leading to his outer offices. Like a beacon, he was drawn to the dark figure. Protopopov rushed toward his office. With haste, he fished out his small revolver. He swung the office door wide open to see the cloaked figure braced behind his desk.

"I am Protopopov and I shall have your head! What right do you have to sit at my desk?"

"All the right in the world," the figure said, wheezing. The tall one removed his hood revealing himself to be the bruised and battered priest with a big beard and large potato-shaped nose. "Is that any way to treat the man you owe for all of this?"

Stumbling backwards, Protopopov turned completely pale. "You're, you're dead."

"I hate to disappoint you, my dear friend, but I am very much alive."

"I was told that you were dead."

"The nobles were fools to think they could actually kill God's chosen one. If they were professionals, perhaps, they should have waited to see if I crawled out of the Neva. That's the trouble with nobles; they are too lazy to do anything of importance right."

"But the water is freezing."

"Yes, it was. But the cold brought me back. I awoke on the banks near the Blue Bridge. "

"The Blue Bridge?" Protopopov repeated what he already knew. "The Neva? They threw you in the Neva near the Blue Bridge?"

"Yes, bruised and bound but still fighting to stay alive. The good Russian river spat me back out, for it knew no Russian saint can ever drown. It is so written."

Protopopov, in shock, walked toward the phone. He wished Rasputin would stop rifling his desk. "I must call the empress. She has been grief-stricken."

"She is a good woman," he said as he found what he wanted. "Where were they last night?"

"They?"

"My security force, you idiot. Where were they?"

"Rasputin, I don't know what you are talking about. My entire force has worked all day to find you."

"Where were they last night?"

"I don't know. They did not see you leave," Protopopov lied. "Come, Grisha. What have I ever done not to earn your trust?"

Rasputin held a handful of letters from the empress. "Trust," he spat. "What are these doing here?"

Protopopov looked down at the letters he had stolen from Grigory's apartment. "I removed them for your protection."

"How considerate of you. Since I am done with them, I would like you to throw them into the fire."

98

"The fire? But Grisha, they may be … valuable."

"Now!"

The minister began throwing them into the fire. One by one they burned. Protopopov, near tears, still held the most damaging one in his breast pocket. It was the only one that really mattered. "Don't cry, Minister. We are not done yet."

"What more do you want of me?"

"Tell me everything you know. And don't you dare lie." The minister sat down and lied. He would be dead if Rasputin knew the truth.

DAY TWO

CHAPTER 15

Serge's Penthouse
The Hotel Europe

Once again, Serge was awakened from his peaceful slumber. But this morning, the intruder was the telephone.

"Hello," the prince spat, along with a few hairs from his beard.

"Good God," cried an upset voice, "it's time to rise from the ashes son." Still recovering from his recent adventures at the Caviar Bar, Serge looked at his bedside clock, and prayed that he was only dreaming. He knew the voice all too well.

"Father," he softly muttered. "It's only eight o'clock in the morning."

"Sergei, you missed your train."

"I..."

"Meet me downstairs in twenty minutes."

Before he could respond, the other end of the line went dead.

It was then that Serge realized he was not alone. Mathilda had helped him to his bed. He remembered their conversation about Sophia. At that moment, he switched off his mind and rolled over to give her a slight kiss. But she was not there. She sat in an armchair, where she had spent the night. "Who was that?"

"No one," Serge lied.

"My, aren't you mysterious," she whispered. Then, laughed.

Wanting to change the subject, he shared, "Thank you for last night."

"Young Sergei," she answered as she gave a small smile, "we all think we are immortal, at least for a time."

Thankful, he walked over to the bathroom, "I need to change."

"You need a shower." Calling out, "And a shave wouldn't hurt, either."

"No one likes my beard. It's so ..."

"Dirty," she spat.

"I prefer unruly."

"Yes, it is that," she said, giving it a tug. "I want to see your face. I remember being so fond of it."

"I must warn you, I'm hideous." Perhaps it would be a good idea to shave. It would make his visit with his father more tolerable.

"Oh, I'm certain of it," she said as she sifted through his things.

On the corner of the table was Russia's highest honor, the Cross of St. George. Mathilda picked it up and read its inscription: for valor. Then she placed it in her pocket.

From the bathroom, Serge called out, "Mathilda would you have dinner with me tonight?"

"Marie please. Mathilda makes me sound old."

"All right then, Marie," the prince said as he attacked his beard. "Will you have dinner with me?"

"It depends."

Returning from the bathroom, "Depends on what?" Serge asked, his face covered in shaving cream.

"I will tell you in a minute." Her eyes had tried not to notice the purplish-blue welts from the scar tissue that dotted his chest. The ballerina had treated enough men at Dmitri's clinic to realize that Serge had been fortunate to be alive. She smiled at her survivor.

The prince returned her smile and walked back into the bathroom. Then the shower came on. After twenty minutes, a new man emerged from the room. "Dinner?" he asked now, cleanly shaven.

"My, I forgot how handsome you are," she said without thinking.

"Is that a yes?"

"That's a yes."

"Good," he replied as he wiped his face with his towel. "I was getting a little tired of it," referring to more than his beard.

"You look good," she said, stopping before him and combing a stray hair with her finger. "I think it is time for you to once again feel good."

"Marie," he said, "I don't know if I am ready for this."

"Ready for what? Serge, I am not here to seduce you, though the thought has crossed my mind. No, I am here to tell you not to give up on life. That accomplishment will be sufficient for now."

"I don't know."

"You're a good man. I can sense it."

The prince shook his head. "I have done many things. Terrible things."

"Let them go, Serge."

"I don't know if I can."

"You can, trust me. Now, allow me to choose appropriate attire for a young gentleman returning from another world." She held up his officer's uniform. "How about this?"

"I no longer have any right to wear that."

"That is where I think you are wrong. A man who was awarded the Order of St. George wears what he wishes. My dear, it's time to stand up and be counted," she said, throwing the jacket of his uniform over him. "I shall allow you to put on your own trousers," she said, trying to lighten the conversation.

"I don't know about this."

"Luckily for you, I do," she said, as they both stood before the mirror. "Konstantin, don't wear it for me. Wear it for her."

Serge was silent.

"She would want you to return to the land of the living."

With that, they embraced.

"Just one more thing," she told him, as she slipped on his medal.

Freshly shaven and completely dressed, the troubled prince felt like a new man, a man with a possible future. But how long would that last? "Dinner?" he asked as he straightened his uniform. "I know of a place that would be perfect—No. 22 Fontanka. Be there at seven."

"I wouldn't miss it for the world."

"Good," he said, giving her a brief kiss on the cheek. Just before he left the room, he turned. "See you then Nurse Kschessinska. You do good here," the prince chuckled.

Turning toward the window, Mathilda caught her own reflection. *If only I were a little younger* thought the poor gypsy dancer. The idea alone gave her a girlish chuckle. It was good to feel alive again.

As the elevator doors opened leading to the lobby, a beam of light momentarily blinded Konstantin. The first floor was layered in an amber afterglow. It was Sunday morning.

As he entered it, he felt alive for the first time that he could remember. It was as if for the last six months he had been forced to hold his breath until this very minute. It felt good to finally exhale. Dressed in his gray officer's uniform of Her Majesty's Chevalier Guards, Serge felt like a warrior in a strange new land.

Clothed in a newly found spirit, Serge hummed one of his favorites—music from Tchaikovsky's *1812 Overture*. It had been nearly six months since he had worn his uniform. And, for some reason it seemed the stiff fabric and texture was now holding him together. For the first time in months, he was grounded. The only thing that bothered him was the decoration draped around his neck. It was a heavy burden to bear. But for the moment, it anchored him. Marching through the familiar corridor, he disregarded the ugly thoughts that entered his head. No more, he thought. Today was a new day. Shaking off those thoughts, he passed the reading room, where the early risers were reading their newspapers and sipping their coffees. It was their daily ritual. He was surprised at the banner headline: RASPUTIN MISSING AND FEARED DEAD. He was shocked the state censors had allowed the story to run. The regime was losing its grip on the situation. Then, he thought about his conversation with Jones.

A soldier wearing a tunic of amazing blue atop of an ocean of fiery red britches approached the prince. The battle badges that lined his chest were impressive. The man had quite a swagger to him. Serge had seen that walk before, usually from men who had looked death in the eye and somehow survived.

"Good morning, young Konstantin," Colonel Zurin, once his father's aide, said.

"Good morning, Colonel."

Zurin stood momentarily silent; his eyes appeared to leave reality for a moment.

"Is there anything wrong, Colonel?"

"No," the soldier said with a weary smile. "You look so much like your father. That is all."

"Really? Most people tell me I look like my mother."

"No, you're a dead ringer of your father."

The colonel turned and smartly marched through the stylish doors of the Hotel Europe's Grillroom. The fashionable restaurant was deserted. The already set tables gave one an eerie feeling. Still, the place seemed magical. Sun poured through the stained-glass windows. The only hint of the passage of time was the slightly wilted flowers in the table centerpieces. The colonel and Serge climbed the stairs to the Europe's famed private dining rooms and alcoves.

As the colonel reached a secluded alcove, he waved Serge over. Looking up, Serge was surprised to discover two of Renko's men on either side of him guarding the dining room's entrance.

"Lieutenant, your father is waiting."

He walked into the dining room, and found his own eyes looking at him. "Good morning...father?" Serge blurted. He could not believe what he saw. His father looked ill.

107

"Son," Platon said happy to see him in his Guards uniform. The two embraced. "It's so good to see you wearing that uniform."

"Are you okay?"

"May I have a moment with my son?"

Renko nodded. Then, he and the Colonel quietly left the room. As the door closed, the hidden dining room grew silent.

Platon lit a cigarette and slowly turned his eyes to his son. "I have cancer. I have known for some time now."

"Why didn't you tell me?" stammered Serge.

"I'm telling you now. Plus, I didn't want to add to your headaches." Platon coughed hard for a moment.

"But…"

"Son, I'm fine with it. I have had a wonderful life," Platon said as he exhaled, "Better than I probably deserved."

"Can't the doctors do anything?"

"Besides providing me with a comfortable bed, nothing." Looking at his Serge, "Renko told me you looked like the devil. He could not be more wrong. Your look is one of a survivor."

"It's surprising what a shave and a clean uniform can do for your confidence."

"My uniform," Platon said as he turned to look out the room's window, "at times, was the only thing that held me together. Wear it with pride son. In the end, all that remains are the people you have shared a life with." Serge sat back and watched his father talk. It was more than he had said to him in one go his entire life.

"One by one, your circle of friends passes away until one day they are all gone and you are left standing alone, the only one who remembers what it was once like." Platon paused. "Ah. The time when I was young and hurt and looked very much like you."

"When you fought at Plevna?"

"Yes. There I had my first taste of war with the Turks. This in reality is loss—human loss. Each battlefield still possesses a piece of me." Serge recalled what he had learned from these battles from books. Now, he knew the soldier's view was always closer to reality than the commander in the rear. Blood has a certain consistency and taste especially when it belonged to a friend.

"I was always less of a man when the fighting was over. I see that same look in you. Perhaps, that's why I was always away. I never wanted your mother or you to see what I had become—a survivor. There is nothing wrong with being a survivor. But we owe it to the ones that were lost to live, son. Not to ask why. But to live." With that he embraced his son.

"It's hard, Father"

"Yes it is. But there within lays courage." For the first time, he noticed his son's medal. "Courage is doing what your body and mind tell you not to do. You wear our country's greatest honor. It is not a piece of metal that drapes around your neck. No, it's in your heart and actions. If you remember anything of me, remember this. Never order others to do what you yourself would not do. With that, I must ask you a favor."

"Anything."

"No. It must be your choice."

"What do you wish of me?"

"I need your help. In two days, the tsar will sign an armistice to end the war with Germany."

"What?"

"It's true. I have helped arrange it. In a week, all the guns on our western front will grow silent."

Serge was amazed. "The war will be over?"

"On Christmas Day."

"What were the terms?"

"We regain all the territories that we lost."

"What? Impossible?"

"It's true. Or at least that's what the Kaiser's messenger has informed us."

"The Kaiser's messenger?"

"The Grand Duke of Hesse."

"Ernie?"

"Yes, Ernie. The empress's older brother."

"Is he here in Petersburg?"

"No. He's outside the city. Safe at our hunting dacha in the woods." Serge could not believe that Ernie, a German duke, was staying less than thirty minutes from the capital. It all seemed too unbelievable.

"What's the favor?"

"Tomorrow, I need you to drive out there and pick him up at dawn."

"That's it?"

"That's it. Tomorrow morning, Colonel Zurin will be waiting for you at the Blue Bridge at five o'clock. Pick him up and escort him to our dacha. That's where I have Ernie hiding out."

"I am happy to do this errand father but why me?"

"One, Ernie knows and trusts you. And two, you are one of the few that know exactly where the old service road that leads to the palace is."

He had traveled that track enough as a child when he used to have sled races with other boys his age. Serge indeed knew the path well.

"Use our sleigh. And deliver Ernie and the colonel to the palace. My men are expecting you to arrive no later than nine. They will be waiting for you at the ruins. As soon as you deliver them, I want you on the next train to the Crimean."

"The Crimean? Why?"

"Just listen to me. I am not certain how the rest of the imperial family is going to react to this armistice. Son, I will sleep better if I know you're safe at our summer home."

"But…"

"I will see you again on Christmas. As soon as this treaty is signed, I am done doing my duty. The doctors gave me some time and I intend to spend it with my son in the sun."

"Okay then if you promise me you will be with me in a week, I will do it."

"Serge, I promise you that I will be with you in a week."

"Okay. I missed you dad."

"No more than I missed you. Renko!"

"All is arranged?" the inspector asked as he and the colonel entered the room.

Platon looked to his son, "Is it?"

"Yes. I am to pick up Colonel Zurin in the morning. Five a.m. On the Blue Bridge."

"I will be on the south end," the colonel said as he stood behind the others, "Tomorrow's supposed to be cold, Serge," Zurin laughed, "So, don't be too late."

"I won't."

"Good," Platon said with a smile, "then it is all settled."

"Not quite," the prince said as he stared at the others, "The British are already aware of the separate peace and that you are mastering it."

Zurin stopped laughing. "What?"

"How do you know this?" His father asked as he combed his fingers through his hair.

"Malachi approached me last night in an effort to speak to you."

"Malachi?" Zurin asked, unfamiliar with the name.

"Malachi Jones," Renko said, "a known British agent."

"Jones is no spy. Sir George used him because we are old friends from Oxford."

"I'm afraid you're wrong," Renko said, handing Serge a dossier. "In this world, things aren't always what they appear to be. Not even friendships. Your friend Jones is a British spy."

"What did he ask you Serge?" the general interrupted.

"Jones asked me to arrange a meeting with you as soon as possible."

"Who else was to attend this meeting?"

"The British ambassador."

The general and Renko exchanged a look. "Your plan is working, general." Renko said. "The British are scared."

"They have every right to be," said Platon. "They have much to lose."

"How can Jones be a spy?" Serge said looking at his father. "He can barely tie his own shoes."

Remembering his report, Renko offered, "Jones is fluent in five languages and his family is worth millions. Who cares about his shoes."

"It's true Serge," Platon said as he placed an arm around his son's shoulder. "He like Sir George is only doing what he believes is in the best interests of his country. Just like us."

Renko added, "The British will stop at nothing to make certain a separate peace never happens. That's why what you are doing is so vital to Russia's future."

"But if the British are interested in me, is it so wise to use me?" Serge asked the obvious.

"We will make certain tomorrow that they are chasing someone else," the general laughed and the others soon followed.

"Yeah." Zurin cried, "Tomorrow they will be chasing a greedy rabbit."

"Renko, see to it that they don't catch him."

"What?" The prince was clueless.

"Nothing son." The general still had his arm around Serge. "All you need to do is to be at the bridge tomorrow morning. Zurin will handle the rest. Right?"

"Yes, general," Zurin barked. He and Serge's father went way back. "I will be there."

"Good. Now, Serge you must not mention this to anyone. Including your Uncle Sandro."

Stunned. "Sandro doesn't know of this?"

"The only ones that know of this are Their Majesties, the Kaiser and his messenger the Grand Duke of Hesse, and we three in this very room. That's it. I have been told personally by the empress that His Majesty wants to inform the imperial family himself."

"But Sandro could…"

"No. Their Majesties were quite firm with my orders." Finally, the effects of the separate peace filtered through the young prince's mind.

"A treaty with Germany would free up a million of Wilhelm's men. By spring, a million new battle-tested troops would stare down our allies in Belgium and France."

Colonel Zurin and Renko looked at one another. Serge voiced what they could not.

"With his forces finally joined on one front," Serge shared, "good old Willy would easily crush through their defenses and end the stalemate. By summer, the Germans would win the war."

The general shouted his reply to his son. "The tsar wants us out of the war! We are out!" The sole purpose for the imperial army is to obey His Majesty's orders. And I have been ordered to orchestrate a peace settlement with Germany. Serge, as a soldier, I have been ordered to do much worse."

"You're right father," Serge said as he gazed out the window into a snow-covered square. "Russia needs peace. But it comes with quite a price."

"Yes. It does."

"Is there anything else I can do?"

"No. Go to Sandro's and check on your cousin Felix. That shall suffice."

With the mere mention of him Serge reddened. "Why? My words are lost on him. "

"Just tell me who comes to visit him, son. That's all."

"Sure."

Everyone's eyes wandered out to the wintry scene captured by the windows.

CHAPTER 16

Dmitri's Palace
Overlooking the Icy Fontanka

Dmitri's palace stood at No. 41 Nevsky Prospect, a magnificent home built of blood red brick along the River Fontanka. Its facade seemed somewhat appropriate, since the previous owner had been Tsar Nicolas's uncle the Grand Duke Sergei Alexandrovich. He had been dead for nearly a decade, but some thought his wickedness remained in the halls, seeking forgiveness and speaking with the near dead. The Grand Duke Sergei had been the man many blamed for the 1896 massacre in Moscow. One of the days, the imperial family wished to forget.

In 1896, Sergei was Moscow's governor-general. It had been the year of Nicholas's coronation. Russia had used the days leading up to the coronation to show the world its greatness as dignitaries from the four corners of the globe arrived in Moscow to pay their respect to the newly crowned tsar. A million Russians came to be a part of the coronation festivities. Too many.

To celebrate Nicholas's becoming the tsar, hundreds of thousands of proud Russians gathered in a field across from the Petrovsky Palace to glimpse a piece of history. On this tiny strip of land, a carnival atmosphere surrounded the crowning. Free food and beverage stands were set up earlier in the week. Acts of magic, plays and speakers added to the spectacle of the day. And as lines of imperial carriages passed, the onlookers cheered and drank in the idea of change and a little hope. Later that afternoon, the masses were to receive their traditional coronation gift, a souvenir. This souvenir was to be a cup of pure porcelain ablaze in color and featuring the imperial symbol, the double eagle.

But the Grand Duke Sergei did not have sufficient policemen present. Rumors were passed that there were not enough souvenirs for everyone, and that there was no more beer. A human stampede began. In sight of the palace, thousands upon thousands died.

This tragedy increased animosity against Grand Duke Serge. Years later, a lone radical waited outside his palace in Moscow. When the duke's motorcar slowed to enter the gate, the assassin tossed his bomb through the car's open window. Dmitri and his sister had been playing in the palace. A decade later, he could still hear the explosion. His Aunt Ella, Grand Duke Sergei's wife and the empress's sister, never recovered. She became a recluse, spending more and more time in a convent. She gave her palace to the young duke.

Back in the present, in his private apartment, Dmitri enjoyed his Sunday paper and thought about his plans for the day. Late in the afternoon, he planned to speak with the tsar at army headquarters. He looked at the portrait of his beautiful mother, the Grand Duchess Alexandra, which hung above the marble fireplace. She was beautiful, a goddess from Greece. Her dark eyes radiated kindness and love. He had never known her; she had died while giving birth to him.

His father, the Grand Duke Paul Alexandrovich, was Nicholas's uncle. He had never recovered from the loss of his wife, and could not stand himself or Petersburg. He left the rearing of Dmitri and his sister to their relatives. He traveled to Europe's fashionable capitals and, eventually, fell in love again. However, not only was his new love not of royal blood, she also was divorced.

The grand duke did not care what society thought of him. All he knew was his heart did not hurt as much as it had before he met the woman who would become his second wife. But his brother, Alexander III, banished him from Russia for marrying a commoner, and Sergei and Ella raised his two children in Moscow.

At times, the young duke could still hear the explosion from that distant day that had killed his uncle echoing through his head. This disturbing thought brought him back to the moment.

The newspaper was still warm from ironing, and the heat felt good on the tips of his fingers. He read one of the articles on Father Rasputin's mysterious disappearance. It was no mystery to him, of course. "Let us pray the Neva holds dearly all that succumb to her," he thought as he turned the pages. Satisfied, the duke rose and walked towards a large bay window overlooking the River Fontanka's embankment. Bright beams of light bounced off its frozen shores. He was now completely relaxed. He had survived the dark thoughts of yesterday.

He was certain that today would bring change in the empire. Today, he would travel to headquarters to have a word with His Majesty. After the tsar granted his subjects a constitution, Russia's fighting spirit would return.

He closed his eyes and began thinking of Felix. He should be nearly halfway to the Crimea by now. Dmitri missed him already; no one knew him better than Felix. A draft of cold, refreshing air entered the drawing room as both doors were flung wide open.

There stood Felix.

"Felix! Why did you miss your train?"

"It seems the empress wants me to stay in Petersburg for a little while longer," he said as he began to circle the room. "My poor friend, you are a sad creature of habit. I leave for one day and you return to your daily ritual of silence." Before the duke could respond, Felix put an arm around him. "And you know how much I hate silence. So rise, up my friend, I am hungry for adventure. Allow me to share with you last night's stimulating events over some brunch."

The two friends walked down the corridor. For the time being, they were content with one other's company. However, unbeknown to them their brilliant plan was beginning to unravel itself.

CHAPTER 17

Grand Duke Alexander's Palace
Sandro's Study

Lounging comfortably in his brother's study, Grand Duke Nikolai Mikhailovich, a pudgy bald scholar with a high sense of self-worth, paged through the biography he had written of Tsar Alexander I, who had defeated Napoleon over a hundred years ago. Bonaparte and his Grand Army all believed their war with Russia was over when they seized the nearly deserted city of Moscow. Enjoying the creature comforts of one of the tsar's abandoned palaces, Napoleon and his advisors waited for Alexander's terms of surrender. They arrived of course, but nothing like the French expected.

Instead of giving in, Alexander knew the wisdom of sacrificing a city to save an entire land. Without hesitation he ordered his subjects to burn the capital to the ground. Everything was put to the torch. In the dead of winter as the capital ignited into a fiery inferno, the over-confident Napoleon was forced to flee his captured city. With his army in full retreat, legions of Cossacks charged his lines. Their attacks were no more than a nuance a cattle prod to keep the French herd moving. Bonaparte's true enemy was the Russian winter. Day by day, more and more of his men froze to death. Alexander's men put each possible haven from the cold to the torch.

The seasoned army that had defeated all of Europe had no place left to go. Like a plump cherry, the harsh winter weather consumed them. Fleeing Russia, the Grand Army was decimated. Their bodies cloaked in Bonaparte's folly were littered across Russia's frozen tundra along with their dreams of conquering the unconquerable.

Amazingly, Alexander had turned defeat into victory with one bold stroke. This thought as well as his book dropped from Nikolai's hands with a thud. As he bent over to pick it up, he wondered if it would not be kinder to the book to toss it into the fire, fine leather finish and all. He chuckled; he was like this book, a showy relic of a bygone age made brittle by the passage of time.

"My," he whispered to himself, "I am getting dramatic in my old age." Nikolai was passionate about Russia's rich history. It was his only remaining love. A very long time ago, his heart had belonged to a young princess. But because they were first cousins, they could not marry. She became the queen of Sweden, and he never married. He often wondered how their lives would have been had they listened to their hearts rather than to reason. But what was life without tears?

For most of his life, he had lived alone with his cats. His words became his children. The duke would slowly breathe life into them, nurture them and after many trials and tribulations he would set them permanently free into the world. It was as he mulled the future of that world that his younger brother Sandro, artfully disheveled in his worn out uniform, entered the study accompanied by a young guardsman. "It's good to see you, brother," Nikolai said. "So, who is this young officer of Her Majesty's Chevalier Guards?"

"Uncle Nikolai, it's me, Serge," the soldier said with a slightly stunned expression.

"Young Konstantin, is it truly you? It seems like only yesterday that I had to drag you and a certain young duchess out of my library."

"Yes," the prince replied, "but that was over six years ago."

"Oh, that's right. Though six years is but a blink of an eye. So, how was Oxford? It was Oxford, wasn't it?"

"It was everything and more that you told me it would be."

"I wonder if I still could convince you to attend the Sorbonne," said the Russian scholar. He had many friends there, and he could recall some heated discussions on the genius of Napoleon Bonaparte versus that of Tsar Alexander. By the small hours of the morning, after consuming several bottles of fine wine, his French counterparts usually accepted the tsar's greatness, at least for the time being. The short man gave a small smile. He missed those days.

"While I was abroad, I was able to spend several weeks in Paris," Serge said. "The city and its nightlife were as magnificent as you described."

"Europe! Europe! It is our eternal fatal desire to mingle with Europe," Sandro barked, "that has put us back God knows how many years."

"Sandro," his brother retorted, "don't even start with your notion about the Americanization of Russia. America is just a European byproduct."

"All right, all right," Sandro said, smiling. The scene between the brothers had been played out for decades. "Anyway, we have some more pressing matters. Perhaps in two months there will be nothing left in this country of ours to remind us our ancestors were autocrats. Tell us, Bimbo"—the family name for Nikolai—" what have you learned?"

"Rasputin is dead."

"That we already know."

"Young Dmitri Pavlovich is definitely involved. Toward the end of dinner at the club, Dmitri came in, pale as death, and sat down at another table. Trepov, our beloved minister, was arguing for everyone to hear that it was all nonsense. But Dmitri loudly declared to the others that, in his opinion, Rasputin had either gone off somewhere or been killed."

"Anything else?"

"Yes, I enjoyed a game of cards," declared the duke, smiling at his brother. "It was a game of wolf. Speaking of which, we need to prepare ourselves for the Vladimirs. They were busy as bees in the drawing room after Dmitri left for the theatre. From what I could overhear, they plan to make a regime change. No doubt, placing Vlad on the throne. An interesting change, a revival of ruthless days."

"Vlad is a brute," Sandro said. "He does not have the support of the imperial family."

"Brother, I love you, but I am afraid you have been away from the capital for too long. Vlad has grown more and more powerful thanks to the inactions of the tsar. Russia is ripe for change. Like it or not, the old regime is through."

Sandro nodded, then looked at Serge. "What do you think?"

"Yesterday, Inspector Renko woke me to see if I was involved in Rasputin's disappearance. No doubt my father sent him. Once he was satisfied I was not involved, he asked me about Felix."

They were all silent for a moment.

"Where is my beloved son-in-law?" Sandro asked Bimbo.

"He's gone."

"So much for house arrest," Serge said.

"Where?"

"Dmitri's."

"I should have guessed," Sandro said, not even attempting to hide the contempt in his voice.

"I spoke to him last night after his return from the station," Bimbo said. "He spoke of some fairy tale about shooting one of his hounds."

"Rise up, my dear brother. You need to pay them a visit," Sandro said, smiling. "Did you call him yesterday?"

"Yes. Grand Duke Paul should be arriving soon."

"Splendid news," Sandro said with a sly grin. "I am certain the young Pavlovich would love to know that his father is finally coming home."

"Sandro, sharing this information with the duke will be worth the trip alone. I will leave this very moment."

"Good," declared the duke as he purposely kicked a three-inch-thick book on the floor. He wanted his brother's full attention.

"That's my novel!" the author cried.

"Tell Felix," one brother said to the other, "I want a word with him. He has started us down a path of destruction. We must figure out a way to save him and Russia."

Nikolai knew what needed to be done. Though, he could not dare share it with his brother. It was time for a new order to things. The tsar was too weak for his liking. There were better choices out there. As he left, he called. "Good day brother, duty calls."

"Let's meet back here tonight," Sandro said but Nikolai was already out the door.

The Bath House,
In the Steam Room

As the steam rose from the hot coals, Protopopov gave a heavy sigh. How could so much change in a period of a day? The only ray of hope was that Vlad and his loyal legions would succeed tomorrow night. If that happened, he would personally finish the death of the evil one.

From the mist, "Good morning, Minister, I see you're in good spirits."

"Can't I have a moment's peace from you?"

"Not until it is done."

"Until what is done?" he asked.

Rasputin laughed. "The good deed."

"What are you talking about?"

"Protopopov," he said, emerging from the steam with a white towel draped over his head, "must you know everything?"

"Grisha, how can I accomplish what you wish when I have no idea of your plans?"

"I will let you know when the time is right. Until then, have your men ready."

"They already are. Last night, Felix was placed under house arrest."

"Good. And Dmitri?"

"That is a more difficult task," the minister said, rising to add more coals. "He is a duke."

"Nonetheless, today the empress shall order his arrest."

"Why have I not heard of this?"

"Her Majesty is wise. She is having one of her generals inform the duke that he is under house arrest."

"She doesn't have the authority."

"No matter. She is doing it."

"That's a bold move. The imperial family wouldn't like that."

"I am sure they won't. But that is what's going to happen."

"How do you know all of this?"

The prophet removed the towel that covered his face. "I see things, and not all of them good." He paused. "In three weeks, it will be my birthday. I will be forty-eight years old."

You will never live to see it, Protopopov thought.

"You're right. I won't."

"You won't what?"

"See it," he replied with a toothy grin.

Leaning closer, he saw Father Rasputin's face was swollen and bruised worse than before. It was almost to the point that he could see only out of his right eye.

"Grisha, what have they done to you?"

"All they possibly could. Be careful what you sow."

"Are you reaping your revenge today?"

"Yes," he said as he placed his towel back over his head. "The empress will be my iron sickle. This afternoon, I want you and your men to be prepared for a call. She will want your men to guard the royals. Give them the same second-rate protection you gave me."

"What? I did my best."

"Did you?"

"Yes."

"Then you have nothing to fear."

"Fear?"

"You heard me. Tonight, choose one of your men, one who is loyal. Have him assassinate the duke in his own home."

"What? How?"

"You know how."

"Everyone will blame me."

"Must I do everything? Make it look as if he was trying to escape."

"Escape? But why?"

Rasputin's voice rose. "Who cares why? Just do it."

"What about Felix?"

The prophet smiled evilly. "I will handle the good prince personally. I want to be the one administering his pain."

"As you wish."

"Just be in your office this afternoon around three," he said as the bath's vapor absorbed him. "I will handle the rest."

"Father? Father?" he whispered to the hazy room. "This is turning out to be a terrible birthday." He needed to speak to Vlad and tell him of the change in plans. The minister had a strange feeling that his own name was at the bottom of the Siberian's death list. Perhaps the good general could save him from the beast.

CHAPTER 18

The British Chancellery
The Library

Harry Williams, a man who knew the Russian people almost as well as they knew themselves, glanced over a copy of a Swahili Bible he had just received from a dear friend. Harry's faith and reading the Good Word grounded him. And today, the good doctor needed to be comforted. Dr. Williams, a specialist in foreign languages, enjoyed reading scripture in as many different texts as possible. He was fluent in more than fifty languages. Today in the British Embassy, he was reading a favorite passage, Paul's journey to Athens: "Men of Athens! I see that in every way you are very religious. For as I walked around and looked carefully at your objects of worship, I even found an altar with this inscription: TO AN UNKNOWN GOD."

Harry could easily relate to this verse. For years, he had lived in a foreign world and watched the devoted masses worship the leader of their church, the tsar.

A native New Zealander and son of a Methodist minister, Williams had come to Russia at the war's outbreak as a correspondent for *The Daily Chronicle*.

In 1914 in the first days of the war, he had accompanied sword-wielding Don Cossacks in a patrol of the empire's southern border. He witnessed these brave, but dated warriors invade a Hungarian border town. He set down his Bible and pulled a binder out of his bag. It was his Russian memoir. He came to a page that recorded that day, and reread it. "I thought last night of a little deserted chapel on the hillside in Hungary, and I thought of a little chapel on the hill under the shadow of a mountain in New Zealand. The heart of its devotion had gone out of it. It stood limp before God. That chapel in New Zealand is happy, I thought, to be spared this, happy because dairy farmers still gather there on Sunday afternoons and sing slow hymns to the accompaniment of a wheezy harmonium." He closed his journal, reflecting that the war had now reached even that barren hillside: the New Zealanders's deaths at the Dardanelles were just the beginning. A link is being forged between the Uniate Church and the New Zealand Chapel.

Williams had heard stories of the bloody banks and bluffs of the Dardanelles. Too many Australian and New Zealand troops, known as the Anzacs, had perished on those stony beachheads of the Gallipolis peninsula in a vain attempt to establish a second front near the underbelly of Constantinople, a plan conceived in the mind of a man named Winston Churchill, a member of the British War Cabinet.

Unfortunately, his bold plan had failed and so did the expedition. The Admiralty and its fourteen-inch guns did not clear the Turkish strongholds that lined the bluffs. The Turks were able to maintain the heights overlooking the beaches. As the Anzacs came ashore, they were completely exposed to the enemy's guns. Wave by wave the soldiers came, but all the new arrivals found was death. The casualty rate was appalling.

As the ambassador's study door opened, the linguist was met by a redheaded giant, wearing a heavy grin.

"Doctor Williams," said Malachi Jones, "Sir George can see you now."

"Thh-hhh-hank you," he stuttered. "I notice a Celtic undertone, Mr. Jones. Is your family from southern Wales—around Cardiff ... no, the Rhondda valley area? Perhaps, Ponty... Ponty?"

"Pontypridd."

"Yes, thank you. Am I right?"

"My father was born in Pontypridd, but I reside in London. Now, if you would follow me," said Jones as he thought how ironic that the Russia specialist had a slight stutter. It was God's own perverted sense of humor, thought the Welshman: a brilliant mind gated by a flawed tongue.

"Jones—the Welsh flag bears the image of a red dragon, does it not?" said Williams as he moved down the corridor.

"Why, yes it does."

"What's ironic about the Russians is that their word for 'red' and 'beauty' are interchangeable. So therefore, what is red is beautiful. The same could be said for crimson."

"Fascinating."

"Yes, I shall never grow tired of the study of language."

The rest of their journey passed in silence until they reached Sir George's study.

Ambassador Buchanan greeted Williams as he entered the room. "Harry, it's so good to see you again. Now, tell me what's out there."

"A certain revolution. And it doesn't matter if it comes from the top or for the bottom. The masses are ready for change."

"Indeed."

"Her Majesty the Empress isn't helping matters. The common man does not trust her."

"Why should he? She encouraged the emperor to choose his ministers more out of regard for their political opinions than for their qualifications."

"Pro, Pro, Pro-topopov?" he asked, stuttering.

Used to Harry's troubled tongue, the diplomat moved quickly on. "Yes. Never altogether normal, his unbalanced mind has been turned by his sudden rise to power. No government of which Protopopov was a member can hope to work in harmony with the Duma."

"Perhaps its president, Rodzianko can warn His Majesty about Protopopov?"

"Rumor has it that Rodzianko has already thrown his support toward a new regime, one originating from the House of Vladimir."

"How will the tsar react?"

"He will not listen," said Sir George, removing a letter from his drawer, "He doesn't even listen to his own family. A month ago, the Grand Duke Nikolai Mikhailovich sent this letter to His Majesty: 'So long as your method of selecting ministers [with the aid of Rasputin] was known to a limited circle, affairs went on somehow. But from the moment that this method became generally known, it was impossible to govern Russia in that way. Repeatedly you have told me that you could trust no one, that you were being deceived.'" With those words, Sir George paused and looked at Williams.

Ambassador Buchanan continued: "'If that is true, then the same must be true of your wife who loves you dearly, but is led astray by the evil circle that surrounds her. You trust Alexandra Feodorovna, which is easy to understand, but that which comes out of her mouth is the result of clever fabrication and is not the truth. If you are not strong enough to remove these influences from her, at least guard yourself against this steady and systematic interference by those who act through your beloved wife. If you should succeed in removing this continuous invasion of the dark forces, the rebirth of Russia would take place at once, and the confidence of the great majority of your subjects would return to you. All other matters would soon settle themselves. You could find people who under different conditions would be willing to work under your personal leadership.'"

"I learned long ago anything is possible. Especially here."

"Indeed," he said as he drew the paper closer. "It closes with: 'You are at the beginning of a new era of disturbances; I will go further and say at the beginning of an era of attempts at assassination. Believe me that in trying to loosen you from the chains that bind you, I do it from no motives of personal interest, and of this you and Her Majesty are convinced, but in the hope and in the expectation of saving you, your throne, and our dear country from the most serious and irreparable consequences.'" He placed the paper on his desk. "Why does he not listen?"

"They never do."

"His stubbornness may be the end of him. His subjects are losing their faith in their sovereign. Even his loyal followers are second-guessing him."

"That's not good. In their mind, the tsar is an immortal being," Harry shared, "incapable of making m-m-mi-mistakes. What happens when you lose faith in your God, Sir George?"

"You simply find another."

"Indeed. Choose your gods wisely."

The Scot added as he remembered one of Kipling's famous remarks, "A leader is a dealer in hope. Someone needs to tell Nicholas that and quickly."

The Nevsky Prospect, Outside Dmitri's Palace

Once, there was a path of narrow earth named the Great Perspective. This old roadway sliced northward through what became Petersburg. But before it bore that name, wolves inhabited the densely wooded area. Ravenous and roaming, these wolves preyed on rogue travelers who made the deadly mistake of straying too far from the path.

Now, magnificent palaces of polished stone lined that old bloody trail. The wolves were still there—just older and wiser and hidden behind polished glass.

At No. 41 Nevsky Prospect stood a particularly dark, forbidding lair. It was as bold and beautiful as its possessor, the Grand Duke Dmitri Pavlovich, the grandson of a tsar. One of the young wolves of the pack, the duke had just had his first taste of sacrificial blood. Standing at the front door, a wise, old wolf rang the buzzer. Nikolai was escorted through the makeshift hospital to the duke's formal dining room. It was a mammoth room covered in magnificently framed portraits of dead faces. These frozen faces on dusty canvases stared from every direction. They were determined men with confident features. They were all Romanovs.

"Good morning, gentlemen assassins," Nikolai said as he stared at the two royals enjoying their breakfast.

"Nikolai, not you, too," replied Dmitri as he set down his fork. "Would you care for something to eat?"

"No, thank you," he said as he sat at the other end of the table. "I have no appetite for blood."

"Too bad," Felix said. "It's delicious."

Dmitri tried to defuse the situation. "Nikolai, the soufflés are delicious. Felix made them himself."

"I must admit I am talented," Felix said as he picked up his juice glass.

"Modesty was never your strong point, was it, son?"

"Confidence is a noble gift," the prince said, smiling. "You should know. Nikolai, you surprise me, a man of your age being caught up in all of this trivial gossip. It doesn't suit you."

"I am a man of facts. And sadly, it's a reality that both of you are involved in this madness," Bimbo said. "The only question I have is to what degree?"

"How can you be so certain?" asked Dmitri. "Rasputin is most likely recovering from one of his drunken orgies at the Villa Rode."

"No. I am no fool. Too many people have been looking for him. After all this time, he is most certainly dead."

"This whole business is a series of misunderstandings," Dmitri said. "We are completely innocent."

"Completely? I know every detail, even the names of the ladies who were at your party."

With this, the two young men glanced at one another. "Then you know everything," Felix said mockingly. "Then you know we are innocent. You can save us both from a great embarrassment and tell the empress to look elsewhere."

"Embarrassment?" the old one barked, "Ask my brother about what an embarrassment you are to our family. Or, for that matter, your own!" Luckily for Felix and Dmitri, a servant emerged from the shadows at that moment. As he whispered into his master's ear, the duke's eyes lit up. Then, he said, "let him in." Felix took another bite of his soufflé. Dmitri rose from his chair and turned toward the door. At that moment, Nikolai whispered in the prince's ear: "Does Dmitri know about your arrangement with Vlad?"

Felix began to choke, his blue eyes radiating fear mixed with hate. The servant returned to the dining room accompanied by General Maximovich, the emperor's aide-de-camp. He stood at attention. "Her Majesty the Empress requests Grand Duke Dmitri not to leave his palace," sounded the general.

"Are you saying that I am under arrest by the order of the empress?" asked the duke in disbelief. "You realize that she has no right to issue such an order? Only the emperor holds the authority to arrest a grand duke."

"No," the general replied defiantly, "you are not under arrest. Her Majesty insists that you do not leave your palace for your own safety."

"I consider this to be tantamount to an arrest. Tell Her Majesty the Empress that I will obey her wish," he said as he soberly saluted the general.

With a click of his heels, the general returned the salute and turned for the door.

"Interesting morning," Nikolai offered as he licked his lips. "Young Pavlovich, don't fret. I bring wonderful news."

"Good. I need to hear some."

"Yesterday, I contacted your father. He is extremely concerned," he announced as he watched Dmitri's eyes fill with dread. "He should be home soon. Tuesday—at the latest."

"Soon," the duke breathed out. "That's wonderful news."

Nikolai looked at the deflated prince. "Felix, I changed my mind. If your soufflés are to die for, I must try some."

"Nikolai, you're getting too much pleasure out of all of this," Felix whined.

With a satisfied snarl, the gray wolf showed his old fangs as he devoured his soufflé. It was delicious. Almost as good as watching the young wolves suffer. He put down his fork.

Felix noticed this, "Not to your liking?"

"A little overcooked for my taste."

Rising, Felix threw his napkin on the table and left the room. Looking up from the table, the quiet one asked, "Is my father really coming?"

"I am afraid so son. I am certain he is only coming to help."

Leaning in his chair, "Certainly. Why else would he come?" asked a son born of sorrow. His birth had snuffed out his mother's life, a fact he and his father could never forget.

CHAPTER 19

Alexander's Palace
The Mauve Room

Awaiting the arrival of Her Majesty the Empress, Alexander Protopopov paced up and down the worn pistachio colored carpeting of the Mauve Room in the Alexander Palace's northwest corner. This was the empress's favorite place. Here, she conducted her business of ruling Russia. With its worn-out furnishings and outdated fabric encircled by lavender colored walls, the room seemed a shrine to an unfashionable dynasty clinging to the past. Staring out towards the vast palatial grounds layered with a retreating fog, the minister thought about this morning's conversation with Father Rasputin. Protopopov could tell the Siberian was in great pain, but how could Felix and Dmitri have failed? The minister had practically handed the good father over to them on a silver platter. No matter. The opportunity shall arise again. But in the meantime, he needed to sever his ties with Felix and Dmitri, permanently. That would be arranged soon. He couldn't imagine what the empress would do to him if she found out about his involvement in this assassination attempt. He stared at the road that led to the palace. An old Latin adage popped into his head: *"Mille vie duthingy per secula ad Roman—* a thousand roads lead men forever to Rome. In Russia, he thought, all roads lead here, to a dated room of lavender and lime green. Turning from the window, the minister was greeted by a frail looking woman with pale features wearing a dress of mourning. It was the empress.

Once a beautiful German princess, Alexandra now resembles a bitterly broken woman struggling to maintain her husband's authority. She had ruled beside her husband for over twenty years now. Most recently, Nicholas had allowed her to handle the day-to-day operations of his government. With the tsar's attention completely focused on the war, Alexandra felt the need for change. Leaning heavily on the advice of her spiritual counselor Father Grigory Rasputin, Alexandra rearranged the tsar's ministers more to her liking.

"Beautiful, isn't it?" she said, smiling.

"Yes, it is Your Grace," he said. "I see why this room is your favorite."

"It's hopelessly outdated I know, but it is my home. I cherish this room."

Still standing at attention, Protopopov thought to himself, "She doesn't realize that she is already dead."

Settling in her chair, Alexandra was done with the small talk. "Is Father Grigory truly dead?" She could hardly bear to know.

Warned by the Siberian not to inform the empress yet of his survival, he said, "We don't yet know. But I have not yet lost hope."

"It's been over twenty-four hours since we have last spoke. My hope is fleeting. What have you learned?"

"Purishkevich has fled the city aboard his hospital train. My men shall have him in custody by the end of the day."

"Forget about him. I shall settle that matter myself. What about Dmitri's involvement?"

"I have not had an opportunity to question him personally. But as you know, he and Felix are under house arrest. It is just a matter of time until we get to the bottom of this."

"That's it? That's all you have to report? I want to know everything about this matter—now! What of the imperial family?"

"My agents have reported of mysterious meetings held at the Grand Duchess Maria Pavlovna's palace. Yesterday, the French Ambassador Paléologue and later Duma's president were seen leaving her palace. And, there have been sightings of Grand Duke Alexander in the capital." All this was a lie.

"Sandro? What is he doing in the capital? He should be at the front with his troops."

"This morning I contacted his regiment to confirm his whereabouts," another lie, "and I was informed that he was still in Kiev but could not be reached at the moment."

"I don't like this," she said as she rose from her chair. "Are they coiling for the strike?"

"It looks that way, Your Majesty. Would you like my men to place them all under house arrest until the emperor returns?"

"No. I don't want to alarm the entire world."

"Yes, Your Grace."

"Better yet, have your men ready for me tomorrow afternoon," she said, smiling. "I must pay a visit to Petersburg. Arrange it. If they are preparing to strike at my husband, make certain that there is sufficient security force to counter it. Understand, Loyalist Minister Protopopov?"

"Yes, Your Majesty."

With that, the meeting was done. The empress gathered herself and strolled out of the room.

So Protopopov left for his car. Inside he was greeted by the madness of Rasputin. "How's Mama?"

"Not well, I'm afraid," the minister said. "Your apparent demise has shaken her. She wants me to turn the world upside down to find you."

The car left the palace and traveled down the broad but bumping road that sliced through the snow-covered palatal grounds. To the minister's right stood the Catherine Palace, a massive blue and white structure in the style of the Russian Baroque. Wide, snow-white columns lead to a roof topped with a handful of golden domes. It was beautiful but like everything in Tsarskoe it was completely overdressed.

Laughing, "Shaken her? No, she is as firm as Russia is vast. For her safety alone, I must remain dead. At least until her enemies have been dealt with."

"Why don't you just share what you already know with her?"

"Not yet. I will tell you of my plans on our drive back to Petersburg."

"Very well," the minister irritably replied.

"Anything else wrong, Minister?"

"No. I am just like the rest," he said playing with his moustache, "taking the news of your disappearance extremely hard." He almost laughed.

Rasputin smiled, showing his crooked teeth. "Minister Protopopov, at times I think you would have preferred that I had died." With that, the Siberian went into a deep laugh—until his ribs began to hurt. "My good friend, are you trying to kill me?" He began laughing again. "Or are you done playing games?"

"Grisha," he said, not sure if Rasputin was joking. "I—"

"It is rare to find a politician lost for words, no?" replied the bearded one, smacking the minister on the back. "At least the empress still cares, bless her heart. Her grief shall not last. Anyway, she is a strong woman. What we are doing is for her own good."

The minister gave him a look.

"You don't believe me? Then you are like the rest. For they have always thought her to be weak, and me to be corrupt. But now you know better."

"Trust me, I know she is strong. She nearly tore my head off yesterday as I was giving my report."

"Really?"

"Yes, she was quite upset."

"I can imagine. You were personally responsible for my protection."

"Father Rasputin, I told you to stay in. And you assured me that you would. You lied to me."

Rasputin considered the fact that the security detail didn't follow him to the palace: "Perhaps I am not the only one here who has lied?"

"What do you mean by that? Am I not doing all that you ask?"

"You should, for you know who holds your leash."

The minister reddened with anger. "What tricks would you like to see performed next by your obedient dog?"

"That's the spirit, Protopopov. I like hearing your wounded pride thick with sarcasm. It's time to play fetch. I want your men who are currently guarding Dmitri to bring him to me."

"And if the duke resists?"

"I'm planning on it. Have it look like a failed escape." Protopopov wished the duke had been more thorough with Rasputin. However, he wanted Felix and Dmitri dead as much as the good father did. They were the only ones who could tie him to the assassination attempt. "Should my men handle Felix too?"

"No," Rasputin said, his voice full of hatred. "I already told you not to touch him. As much as I'm sure you would like to quiet them both, I shall handle the matter myself."

"As you wish." Protopopov leaned back to catch a nap. But he would not be so lucky.

"Now," Rasputin said, "tell me all you know about your buddy Vlad."

York Cottage, England
The Woods

The sound from the hounds ravaging through the wetlands lessened as an old sailor laid down his shotgun against the stump of a fallen tree. He was a world away from the crowded streets of London but still needed a moment's rest to catch his breathe. Perhaps he needed to return to York Cottage.

"Your Majesty, are you all right?" asked his friend Stevens from the War Cabinet.

"Yes, of course. It's just this damn hip of mine."

Early in the war, the king and queen had traveled to the front to inspire the troops. The visit was a great success. But during it, King George's horse stumbled on a rock, and the beast rolled over him in front of his men. His pelvis was broken and it still ached constantly. "Would you prefer to return to the car?"

"Damn waste, but I can barely keep up." The two began their journey back.

"Stevens, what do you think of this American note?" A little over a week ago, the British government had received a letter from the American president, Woodrow Wilson, regarding a possible conference to broker out peace between the warring nations. He had sent the same letter to all the countries engaged in battle. It received a lukewarm welcome in England.

"He's living up to his campaign promises of keeping them out of the war."

"German submarines are sinking our ships full of American goods, and he does nothing."

"He's no fool," Stevens shared, "He will wait until a time of his own choosing to enter this war."

"Yes. When the outcome is already decided," His Grace said. Nearly one hundred and fifty years after their revolution, and the Americans were still harassing a king named George.

"We have invested too much in this war to allow the Americans to waltz in and save the day. We can't stand another summer like the last one. It was far too bloody." The king didn't want to even imagine what would happen if Germany signed a separate peace with his Russian allies. By spring, his troops would be facing nearly a million more men, and an additional three thousand heavy guns. He could not allow that to happen, at least not until the Americans entered the war.

As they reached their sedan, another staff car was parked near them. In it was General Wilcox of the War Ministry.

Stepping from his car, he exclaimed. "Your Majesty."

"General Wilcox," he laughed, "What the hell are you doing here?" George could thank the Royal Navy for this colorful language. When he was young, he had been a British sailor. That was before his older brother's death, which had made him the heir apparent. "You're late if you were planning on the hunt."

"Perhaps not," the white-haired man replied. "Your Majesty, may I have a moment of your time?"

"Of course," he said, handing Stevens his shotgun. "What is it? My leg is killing me, Wilcox, and this bloody bog is not helping matters."

He handed the king a note. "This might mend your leg for a bit. My men intercepted this from Berlin this morning. It was sent to the German Embassy in Istanbul."

"Read it." He read the letter below.

From: German High Command

HIGH IMPORTANCE

Before the first of January, Russian style, we intend to sign a separate peace agreement with Russia. In spite of this, it is our intention to stay loyal to our promise of protecting Istanbul.

We propose an alliance on the following basis with the Sultan of Turkey and the Ottoman

Empire: that we make war together and together we shall make peace. Due to the proposed agreement, officially we must turn our back to the Eastern Front.

Unofficially, we shall give general financial support, and it is understood that Turkey is to re-conquer the lost territory it lost to Russia and Romania. The details are left to you for settlement.

You are instructed to inform the Turkish Minister of War Enver Pasha of the above information in the greatest confidence as soon as it is certain that there will be a separate peace with the Russian Empire. Afterwards, expect the Russians to push southwards. Tsar Nicholas's sole objective is the liberation of Istanbul. Publicly, we will be unable to offer our aid.

Please call to the attention of the Sultan Mohammed V of Turkey that the employment of an additional million men to our west lines will counter our current stalemate. With Russia out, America's involvement in the war is now irrelevant. In spring, the war will be over.

After that successful conclusion, the German Empire plans to return to the Eastern Theatre in full force. The Sultan needs only to hold on until the German Army, as a whole, marches on to Moscow. With the tsar's regiments engaged in the south, His Imperial Majesty the Kaiser will negotiate a new peace treaty with the Russians, a treaty more favorable in the eyes of the Sultan of Turkey and his Ottoman Empire.

Zimmerman

"Compel England to make peace!" the king said. "Over my dead body."

"Poor Russia. I almost feel sorry for them."

"That's what happens when you make a deal with the devil. So, Niki could not wait for Constantinople, even though

142

we assured him that the city would be his at the conclusion of the war."

"Well, I am certain the failure of the Admiralty and the Dardanelles expedition didn't help matters." Wilcox left it at that. He knew His Majesty's battleships never had a chance to clear those bluffs. But what did it matter? The allies would never have granted Russia Constantinople and the straits anyway. The British and the French had already decided how the world would look after the war, and Russian interests were not included in that arrangement. King George would never give Russia a foothold so close to India. The general surmised that the tsar realized that.

"Make certain my German cousin's greed is known to my Russian brethren," said the King.

"I shall make certain Ambassador Buchanan has this in his hands as soon as possible." They walked back to their vehicles with smiles on their faces.

King George didn't even notice his own limp. "The new year is looking better already," the king said. "Come spring, Germany will still be fighting a two-front war."

CHAPTER 20

Vlad's Palace
Seven Days Ago

"Will it work?" the prince asked as he gazed out towards the river. It was snowing.

"It better," the grand duke warned Felix, "Or both of us are not long for this earth."

They were in the duke's study overlooking the Neva.

"True," he agreed as he took another sip of his drink. "Don't worry Felix, my plan is perfect. His home is surrounded by regiments loyal to me, and our cause."

The prince exclaimed. "And the Cossacks?"

"I will handle them," the duke countered.

"You better."

At that point, two of the duke's dogs as black as a moonless night entered the room. "Come here, my boys," he said, petting them.

Not understanding why Vlad was so calm, Felix shared the obvious. "I am risking a great deal."

Still petting his dogs, the duke replied, "Who isn't?"

"I know." Felix could not hide his fear. "But how certain are you that your officers are completely loyal. All it would take is one traitor to stop us within your faction and we are finished."

"Relax," Vlad stopped petting his dogs. "I hand picked these men for this exact assignment. They are loyal."

"Okay," Felix said, not completely satisfied but he did not want Vlad to think he was weak. "Then, your trap is sprung. So all you need now is our beloved leader's return."

"That's your part."

"Yes, I am in charge of preparing the cheese."

Again, Vlad played with his dogs as he played with the prince's own ego. "Precisely. Without you, a new Russia is not possible."

"How are you certain that Rasputin's demise will force the tsar's return to Petersburg?"

"The empress will demand it," Vlad said as he tossed one of the dog's toys across the room. Both of them chased after it. Within seconds the larger dog dropped the toy back at Vladimir's feet. The other dog was no longer in sight. "Good boy. You see, Felix, Nicholas is like a simple puppy dog to her demands."

"We shall see."

"You worry too much. Soon, Russia will have a leader worthy to the task. And he will be extremely kind to those who helped establish the new regime. Extremely kind." As he played roughly with his dogs, he added. "Sasha, it's time to find you a new home."

"Vladimir, do you have one already in mind?"

"Felix, you know I do."

"All right then," he said as he went to pour himself another drink. "The Siberian will be dead by the end of the week."

"And his security?"

"The new Minister of the Interior has been most generous."

"I suppose he would be," replied the duke, as he eyed his new kingdom. "Protopopov wants Rasputin out of the picture more than anyone else. He's afraid the staret is turning on him."

"So, poor Grisha is losing all his friends. Playing politics can be lethal."

"Yes, indeed," the prince declared as he filled two glasses. "Then, let's toast to the evil one's apparent death." Handing the glass over, he said, "*Nastrovya!*""

"Nastrovya!" With the sound of crystal still humming throughout the room, "Just make certain his death is known to the empress. My plan depends on it."

"Do you expect me to escort the authorities to his corpse?" he laughed.

"Exactly. Whatever it takes. The sooner the empress knows, the sooner she will call for the tsar's return."

"But Vlad, what good is it to drag my name into all of this?"

"Soon, in the new regime, your name will ring with that of a true patriot. Prince Felix, your destiny awaits you, but before that you must dispose of a mere peasant."

Knowing he was meant to accomplish great things, Felix replied. "Consider it done."

"Good. Let's have another drink and you can share with me your plans." The two of them wandered into an adjoining room. All that remained was the passage of time. This morning, the tsar had released his new manifesto supporting the war effort. Today was Monday. By Friday, Rasputin would be dead. His death would force His Majesty to return to the capital. The empress would insist. After that, Nicholas would be doomed.

Back to the present, Vlad was wandering the halls of the Ministry of War when he ran into a familiar face.

"Grand Duke Vladimir, what a surprise to see you in the city." The duke was a large brute but Platon's over six-foot frame allowed him the privilege of looking Vlad dead in the eyes. Platon asked, "What's the occasion?"

"Konstantin, so good to see you're still with us," the duke smiled, avoiding Platon's question.

The two of them had always hated one another since their time together in Manchuria. To Vlad, Platon was just an obedient dog doing Nicholas's tricks. And to Platon, Vlad was a man corrupted by an unquenchable thirst for power.

"Why are you here?" General Konstantin asked, not hiding his contempt.

"Oh, me? Just catching up with some old friends."

"I see. They need your help?"

"It wouldn't hurt," Vladimir said as he eyed his old nemesis. "The current direction of the war—is bleak at best."

"So, what would you do differently?"

"Me? You know me Platon, I am one to always take the offensive."

"Yes, you were always the first one to charge up the hill," Platon declared as he moved closer to him. "Though, you never did understand fully the reason why."

"I shall remember that, General Konstantin. There may come a day when you must kneel before me."

"That day will never come Vlad."

"We shall see. Good day, general."

"Good day."

CHAPTER 21

Financial District
Outside Burmin's Apartment

As Burmin emerged from his building, two towering men wearing heavy greatcoats flanked him and they were not the guards Renko had given him. One of the men pointed a gun in the spy's back and said in perfect German, "It is a pleasant day for a drive, Herr Burmin."

It was Jones.

That was when Peter noticed his bodyguards laying unconscious on the ground. "What is this?" he asked as he stared down at their still bodies.

"Don't worry," Jones said, "Your boys aren't dead. Just sleeping. It's you we want."

They eased him into a waiting car. Sir George was inside. As soon as the door closed, they were off.

"Mr. Ambassador, what is this?"

"Greetings, Mr. Burmin," the British ambassador said as the car picked up speed. "It is such a pleasure to finally meet with you."

"I am a Russian, living in Petersburg. And you, a foreigner, dare to do this to me?"

"Relax, Peter," Sir George said jovially. "It will only be a moment of your valuable time."

"I have powerful friends," Burmin said.

"As do I."

"Good." He loosened his collar. "Then we have come to an agreement."

"And what is that?"

"That you are going to let me out, now, and all of this will be forgotten."

"Herr Burmin," Sir George said, banging his cane squarely on the floor. It was a signal to his driver that he wanted to stop, "This is just a warning. Treat it as such. We know that you are the German conduit the tsar and General Konstantin are using to deliver their demands to the Kaiser."

"What? Perhaps, you haven't heard that I was cleared of all those charges?"

"How convenient," the ambassador said dryly as the vehicle came to a stop along the boulevard.

Quickly, Jones leapt out to allow Burmin his freedom. "I appreciate the ride, Sir George. Be thankful that I am not going to report this to the authorities."

"Be thankful you can," Buchanan said as Jones stood over him.

"Please," his confidence restored, Burmin smiled as wide as he could, "a separate peace—what would be the odds?"

Looking harshly at the gambler, the diplomat coldly returned his own confident and arrogant glare. "I wouldn't bet on it." Jones dipped his hat, and walked toward the passenger's seat.

Peter awkwardly lit a cigarette. "Really?"

"Yes, really."

"And why is that?" he asked, blowing the smoke toward Sir George's face. Sir George was still smiling. "Bad bet," he said as the car pulled out into traffic.

As Burmin watched the ambassador's car travel down the Nevsky he thought how he needed to give Renko a call. The Brits were on to their scheme.

Tracks to St. Petersburg,
A Sleepy Station

Chaos engulfed the usually sleepy station as the tsar's train prepared to depart. Walking along the narrow platform dusted with snow was His Imperial Majesty, lost in thought. He had just sent his wife a telegram informing her of his plans. Rasputin's apparent death was the last thing he needed. What disturbed him the most was his favorite nephew's involvement in the plot. Dmitri was like a son. He couldn't understand why the little boy with whom he had played billiards would do this to him and the family who loved him dearly.

As the tsar stepped onto the train, the conductor gave out a shout. Within moments, the train jolted and began to pick up speed. His Majesty wanted to be in Petersburg by morning, and he would be.

Reaching the salon car, Nicholas's mood brightened when he witnessed his son playing in the corner with his toy soldiers.

"Bang! Take that you greedy Germans," he cried as he used his fists as tommy-guns, "and take that you dirty Turks!" He stopped when he noticed his father had entered the room. "Papa, are you all right?"

"Yes, for the time being," the tsar replied, wanting to change the subject. "Are we winning or losing?" he asked, patting the boy's head.

Alexei laughed. "Father, we always win. It is our duty."

Nicholas fell into a nearby chair, exhausted. He removed his black leather gloves, revealing a massive blue sapphire ring given to him by Alexandra. "Oh yes," he said looking at his son. Then whispered to himself: "I forgot. We Russians always win, for duty knows no pain."

Ministry of the Interior, Protopopov's Office

Minister Protopopov was growing tired of Rasputin's constant presence. As he settled behind his desk, his phone rang. It was his secretary in the next room.

"Send him in," he replied to the caller.

Father Rasputin quickly moved to a chair located at the back of the room. As he sat down, the door opened. Captain Zubov walked toward the minister and saluted.

Protopopov barely looked up from the report on his desk. "Is everything in place?"

"Yes, sir. Tonight, the Grand Duke Dmitri will be shot attempting to escape from his palace."

"Most excellent work, Captain."

"Thank you, sir."

"During the 'attempt,' make sure one of your men is killed."

"Sir?"

"It will make it a more believable story if one of your men is killed with him—someone of your choosing, of course."

"Yes sir!"

"One more thing, Captain—make certain no harm comes to Prince Felix."

"Yes, sir! No harm shall come to him."

"Not yet," thought Rasputin.

After the captain had left, Rasputin spoke from the darkened corner. "Can you trust him?"

"Never underestimate an ambitious man."

The Siberian burst into uncontrollable laughter. "Protopopov, this may be the first honest thing that has slipped from your lying lips."

With that, the two discussed their plans for Felix.

CHAPTER 22

Dmitri's Palace
Hospital Ward

To Mathilda, the boy looked too much like Serge. The only difference was that he was missing a leg—discarded, in some distant field. As his medication took hold, he was thankful. He had made it. Not in one piece. But who was he to complain? The majority of his friends from his village were gone. As he thought this, guilt crept over his handsome face. Realizing this, she gave him a small hug.

"It's okay to hurt," she said. "We all hurt. But the important thing is to start living again."

Rising to her feet, she softly tucked the blanket around him as he drifted off.

"How touching, Mademoiselle Kschessinska," Felix said. "You are truly a sister of mercy."

"We all need mercy, Felix," she said with a sly grin, "some more than others."

"*Touché*," he replied. He had to admit, even in her forties, she was dazzling. It was hard for him to keep his eyes off of her. It wasn't that he was attracted to her. Rather, he envied her and her self-confidence. In a strange way, the ballerina reminded him of his mother.

"*Mademoiselle*, do you know my mother?"

"Of course." The prince's mother, Zenaide, was a great believer in the arts. "We've talked many times after my performances and at other social soirées. She's a rare woman—both beautiful and kind."

"Yes she is. A man once told me I was much like her. Do you believe that?"

"Yes, I do."

"Of course, he meant it as an insult. But that was the nicest thing anyone has ever said to me. You see my mother, who had already had three sons, two of whom had died in infancy, was so certain I would be a girl that she had ordered a pink layette for me. To make up for her disappointment, she dressed me as a girl until I was five years old. Far from making me feel ashamed, it made me very vain. I used to call out to passers-by in the street: 'Look, isn't Baby pretty?'" The two of them sat down on a vacant bed. He needed to be heard.

"Is there something you would like to tell me, Felix? It could be our secret."

Felix grimaced. "Our secret." The prince was growing tired of secrets. "You think I am a horrible beast, don't you?"

"I don't know you well enough to have an opinion."

He smiled. "*Spasibo*. You are most kind then. For I am not a horrible beast, just a prankster."

"It was a hell of a prank you played the other night."

"Friday night was harmless," he said. "Let me tell you about a night that has become ugly. It was when I was very young and my brother Nicholas was still alive." Nine years earlier, Felix's older brother Nicholas had been killed during a duel with a jealous husband of a woman he was having an affair with.

"At that time, fancy dress balls were the rage in St. Petersburg. I owned a collection of very beautiful costumes, both men and women's. That evening, an officer in the Guards who was a famous Don Juan courted me assiduously. The officer and three of his friends offered to take me to supper at The Bear. I accepted in spite of the risk, or rather because of the risk. Seeing that my brother was flirting with a masked lady, I seized the opportunity to slip away."

"I arrived at The Bear escorted by my four officers, who engaged a private room. Gypsies were sent for to create the right atmosphere; and under the influence of the music and the champagne, my companions became very enterprising. I was holding them off as best I could, when the boldest of them crept up behind me and tore off my mask. Realizing that disaster was imminent, I seized a bottle of champagne and hurled it at a mirror, which was smashed to pieces. Taking advantage of the general shock caused by what I had done, I leapt to the door, switched off the lights, and fled."

Like a worried mother, Mathilda just listened and hid her emotion.

"My pranks could not be concealed indefinitely from my parents. My father sent for me one day. He was livid with rage and his voice shook. He called me a guttersnipe and a scoundrel, adding that people like me were not fit to breathe the same air as honest folk. He declared that I was a disgrace to the family and that my place was not in his house but in a Siberian convict settlement. Finally he sent me out of his room. The door banged so violently that a picture on the wall crashed to the ground."

"Then what happened?"

"I stood still for a moment, aghast at this outburst. Then I went to my brother. Seeing me so depressed, Nicholas tried to cheer me up. I took advantage of this to unburden my heart, and reminded him how vainly I had several times sought his support and advice. I also reminded him that it was he who had first thought of disguising me as a woman for his own amusement, and that this had been the beginning of my 'double life.' Nicholas had to admit that I was right."

"It sounds as if he cared deeply for you."

"In his own strange way, I suppose he did. Later on, when I was old enough to take an interest in women, life became even more complicated. Although I felt much attracted to them, my affairs never lasted long because, being accustomed to adulation, I quickly tired of doing the courting and cared for no one but myself. The truth is I was a horrible little beast. I liked to be a star surrounded by admirers. It was all great fun, but I did enjoy being the center of attention and doing whatever I liked. I thought it quite natural to take my pleasure wherever I found it, without worrying about what others might think."

Leaning in, the caregiver caressed his hand as she listened to young Yusupov continue his story.

"I have often been accused of disliking women. Nothing is further from the truth. I like them when they are nice. A few among them have played an important part in my life, and especially the one to whom I owe my happiness. But I must admit that I have met very few who answered to my ideal of womanhood. Generally speaking, I have found among men the loyalty and disinterestedness which I think most women lack."

"What about Irina?"

"My wife," he said, fearing to pull back too much of his curtain, "is the best thing that ever happened to me. As I just mentioned, she is my happiness. In all things, she's good and innocent. I do not know what she sees in me."

"Perhaps someone who needed to be loved?"

He gave her a strange look. "Perhaps."

"And what about Dmitri?"

"Dmitri," he replied with a mixed tone, "Dmitri is extremely attractive."

"Is that it?"

"No, he is my friend. Above all else."

"Good."

The prince massaged his temples. "Sometimes, the terrible things that I have done keep replaying themselves in my head."

"You should try to forget such things. Trust me, I know."

Just then another nurse approached.

"Duty calls. Take care of yourself, Felix—and your friends," she said, walking away from him.

"Nurse Kschessinska. You are too good for this world."

"You can be too."

"No, it's too late for me…"

"No it's not. It's never too late." With that, Mathilda smiled, then hurried to join the other nurse. Turning around, "Though, each day you must choose Felix whether to be good, or bad."

Ministry of War,
Platon's Office

The general was listening to Renko, but he did not like what he was hearing.

"Right now," the inspector warned, "Protopopov's men are guarding the duke."

"The hell they are," the old man barked. "I want you to correct this situation. Immediately. Tomorrow will be too late. For every one of the minister's men I want a shadow. We don't see any reason for this matter to escalate."

"Consider it done, General."

"I also need you to keep a close eye on Vlad and his men," he added as he rose from his seat. "We are spreading ourselves pretty thin. Do we need more men?"

"I think we are okay for the moment," the inspector admitted. "We should know more from Zurin tonight."

"Very well. We shall wait. Though I don't like the fact that we are allowing him to get this close."

"General, currently we have no proof."

"Proof!"

"Yes, proof. He is a grand duke. A Romanov and like it or not the rest of the imperial family would love to use anything they can against His Majesty, especially now."

Platon smiled like a proud teacher at his prized pupil, "Let us find that proof before it is too late."

"We will."

"Now, regarding Dmitri's and Felix's protection," he said, opening his safe. "On second thought, I don't want Protopopov's men anywhere near the royals. In fact, I don't want him involved in any way."

Konstantin handed him a small card with some scribbling. Renko had heard of the document but had never before seen one: an imperial license.

"Now, you have the authority to get them the hell out of there."

"Yes, General."

"Anything else of interest?"

"The French Ambassador and his aide paid a visit to Vladimir Palace today. They're acting like a court in waiting."

"Well, let us make certain that it is a long wait."

"And the French?"

"We will deal with them later. Renko, if there is one certainty in international affairs, it is that one can always count on the French to preserve their own interests." He thought of Sir George. "That goes for the British too."

"The ambassadors are getting bold. Perhaps too bold."

"They are desperate."

"Yes, is it wise to leave Burmin out there? I only have two men guarding him and he knows about the treaty."

Too much was at risk: "Pay him a visit," Platon said as Renko gathered his things. "I believe the British have chased Burmin long enough."

"Very well general," the inspector said as he turned towards the door, "I will handle the matter myself."

"Good."

After Renko left, Platon rested his head in his hands. There was so much going on that he was afraid he was losing control. He picked up the phone and tried to get hold of Zurin to no avail. Frustrated, he grabbed the receiver again and was greeted by his secretary's voice.

"Sir?"

"No interruptions for the next half hour."

"Yes, general. No interruptions."

According to Ernie, all was now in order for Nicholas to sign the treaty. At least Rasputin's death had saved him from making a trip to army headquarters, a place that would no longer exist in two weeks. It was all coming to an end, and not the way in which he had imagined it at the very beginning.

As he heard his door open slowly, he did not have to wait to know who had arrived. "Sandro," he cried, "It can only be you."

"Yes, Platon. It is I."

"I am tired. What do you want of me?"

"An answer. How long have you been in negotiations with the Germans?"

"Since late October," he said as he reached for his cigarettes.

"Platon, you should know better."

"About dealing with the Germans or smoking?" he laughed as he coughed.

"Both."

"I know, my friend. I know. But I am just a simple soldier following orders."

"I know you are," the duke declared as he reached for one of Konstantin's cigarettes. "But you're making a mistake following Nicholas's orders."

"A Russian duke wants me to counter an imperial order? Where is the honor in that, Sandro?"

"Honor? Where's the honor in a separate peace?"

"Peace," he said as he started to gag once again, "is honorable, no matter the price. It took me too long in my life to realize that fact."

"This price just happens to be Russia's future. Platon, finally my squadrons of planes are ready for the fight. We have two factories producing them more quickly than we have men trained to fly them. Trust me. They will make the difference come spring."

"What you have done with the limited resources the War Ministry has given you is astounding. Alexander, you have every right to be proud of the Imperial Air Force that you have helped create. But the decision has already been made."

Sandro fell back in his chair. "So it is done?"

"All that is required is the tsar's signature, and that shall come tomorrow night. In less than two weeks, it will all be over. My recommendation to you is to speak to him tomorrow before my meeting. But I must warn you, I already have tried."

"Directly?"

"No always through Her Majesty."

"Darn her German roots!"

"So it's pretty much pointless, Sandro."

"Who else knows?

"Only a handful."

"I still can't believe this is all happening."

"Believe me, you think I want to end my career like this? No. But peace is peace."

At that moment, Sandro realized what General Konstantin was willing to offer his commander—his legacy as a soldier. In two weeks, Platon would take full responsibility for the treaty. According to his doctors, by early spring he would be dead.

In some circles the general would remain a hero, but in the circles in which the power really existed, he would be despised as the coward the tsar forced to broker a peace with the Germans. "Platon, I never thought of how much you will lose," the duke said. "That is one more reason not to do this."

"No, it is not my decision to make. Alexander—no more. I don't have the energy for this. I'm tired."

Thinking of a way to restore him, Alexander said, "Do you remember what it feels like to be innocent of all this?"

Laughing, "No." Then his thoughts traveled back in time. "There was this time, right after Serge was born. It was late. Your sister Tatiana was fast asleep. He and I were alone in the darkness, and I was his sole protector. I felt utter peace."

"Childhood innocence is more precious than gold," the duke conferred.

"I agree. So what about you, my friend?" he said in the sort of way that he already knew the answer. But he asked the question anyway.

"For me it was when I traveled to Brazil."

"Share it with me. You are such a gifted storyteller."

The duke smiled. "Of course I will. Clean out the dullness from your ears, my friend, and brace yourself. Thirty years ago and thousands of miles from St. Petersburg there was a heavenly place called Rio de Janeiro. On Christmas Eve 1886, nearly to this day, His Royal Majesty's Ship *Rynda* under the combined power of steam and sails entered the territorial waters of Brazil."

"Standing on the bridge— the Southern Cross blinking between the disjointed clouds—I breathed deeply the fragrance of the tropical woods."

Platon adjusted his collar. The room had some how grown warmer, and it felt wonderful to his old aching bones.

Lifting up one finger for each remark, Sandro said as he began to count, "A harbor challenging the haughty claims of Sydney, San Francisco, and Vancouver. A white-bearded emperor discussing the imminent triumph of democracy. A jungle preserving the atmosphere of the first week of creation. A narrow-waisted girl dancing to the strains of 'La Paloma.' These four images," he said, waving his four fingers, "will forever be associated in my mind with the word," pausing, "Brazil."

"He who has tasted the water of Beykos shall return to Istanbul, maintained the Turks," Platon said.

The mention of Constantinople pulled Sandro from his dream.

"I doubt it. I have had my fill of that glorified water, and yet I feel no desire whatsoever to revisit the city of European vices and Asiatic comforts. But I would pay almost any price to live once more through the thrill of being overcome by the spectacle of beautiful Rio."

Platon had had few opportunities to enjoy a friendly port. But that was the life he had chosen. He longed to be young again, and to know what he knew now.

Sandro continued: "A cablegram from St. Petersburg awaited me, instructing me to pay a visit to Emperor Don Pedro. January being the hottest month below the equator, he was staying in his summer residence of Petropolis, high in the mountains. An old-fashioned funicular, zigzagging over the slope of the high hill, presented the only means of transportation. The jungle was upon us while we were still admiring the harbor. Far below, crystal streams were running at the bottom of precipices, but the gigantic trees and the plants crowding around the funicular made them look like spots of silver. The palms, the lianas, and all other twining colossi seemed interwoven with each other and were fighting for a breath of air and a ray of sunshine." Platon pictured being swallowed by a dense jungle that lacked light, and wondered if death was similar to that, engulfed by coolness instead of warmth. He would find out soon enough, he imagined.

"Our miniature train crept ahead, breaking branches, pushing its way through the treetops, and brushing the tall poisonous grass against our faces. The parrots yelled; the snakes crawled; the birds circled in packs; the large butterflies, colored to resemble the leaves, flew high above as if happy to remain in safety."

Leaning comfortably back in his seat, Konstantin envisioned the raw and luscious backdrop. Momentarily he was there, feeling the swaying of the small train, engulfed in pure beauty. He heard Mother Nature's heart beating.

"The voyage lasted for three hours. It was awesome. Not one iota did the jungle change for three hours. It spoke of the millions of centuries of chaos bent on maintaining chaos. I trembled from head to foot."

"My champions—two young lieutenants of the *Rynda*—made the sign of the cross," he said, laughing, "when on reaching the top of the mountain, we saw Mr. Ionin, the Russian ambassador to Brazil. By that time, we had begun to doubt the existence of human beings in this spot of the world."

"One sat out of the fringe of a mystical garden. As he peered through the dense foliage, the lieutenant told me he saw faces of friends long departed. With smiles, they greeted him and waved him in. Soon, he thought as he asked his old friends to be patient. He would be with them very soon."

"Emperor Don Pedro—his long, white beard and gold-rimmed glasses giving him the appearance of an old university professor—listened sympathetically to my description of the jungle. The absence of political disputes and even of vital contacts between Russia and Brazil permitted him to converse freely," Sandro said as he stopped to stare at his friend. Platon seemed to have slipped away into the warm confines of the jungle.

"Don Pedro told me: 'Europeans talk so often about the so-called youth of the South American countries. Not one of them realizes that we are hopelessly old. We are older than the world. Nothing is left, or at least nothing has been discovered so far pertaining to the peoples who inhabited this continent thousands of centuries ago. There is just one thing that will always remain in South America: the spirit of restless hatred. It comes from the jungle. It preys on our minds. The political ideas of today are connected with those of yesterday by no other link except that perpetual desire for change.'"

Sandro began to pace up and down. "A few years later, Brazil became a republic. Don Pedro did just as he promised: he abdicated voluntarily and cheerfully. His memory is cherished still in Brazil." He wondered if Nicholas would ever do the same, and was quiet until Platon asked him to continue.

"I liked Don Pedro immensely, and as he was in no particular hurry, we stayed for over two hours in his study. We spoke French. His very distant, grammatically correct though slightly uncertain phrasing added a touch of friendly shyness to this meeting. When we were ready to go, he pinned the cross of the Great Order of Brazil on my breast. I appreciated the honor, but admitted my preference for the Order of the Rose, a nine-pointed star in a crown of roses. Don Pedro laughed: 'The Order of the Rose is one of our humblest decorations. Practically everyone has it.' Even so," Sandro said with a smile, "it fit better my idea of Brazil."

"Sandro," the fellow general declared, "I love your narratives. You should have written books like your brother, not just collected them."

"Platon, thank you. But I have never before shared the rest of this story with you."

"The remaining days were spent by me in an atmosphere of enchanted laziness, on the fazenda of a Russian coffee merchant, married to a very rich native woman."

"You dog," he teased.

"It's not what you think."

"Then lie to me," he replied.

They shared a laugh.

"Each morning, we rode to inspect his plantations spread over several miles, and an improvised orchestra of slaves played for our enjoyment."

"The music surrounded me, then it entered me. In the evening, immediately after dinner, we sat on the balcony listening to the sharp screams of the jungle interrupting the monotonous beating of the tom-toms. We never lit the lamps; myriads of night beetles and firebugs provided plentiful illumination. The wife of our host had two nieces living with her on the fazenda. Both," he paused, taking his time to describe them accurately, "young, tall, slim, dark-haired, narrow-waisted."

"I thought you said you were not a dog."

"I lied."

Once again they both laughed. "To be young again!"

"I succumbed to the charms of the elder niece, voluntarily and eagerly. Possibly she liked me; possibly she wanted to ascertain how Brazil affects a Russian grand duke. Nothing could have been more innocent than that adolescent romance of awkward tenderness." Sandro whispered: "If she is still alive, she must be forty-eight. I hope she remembers our January evenings of 1887 with the same feeling of gratitude that I do."

Sandro looked at the old man behind the desk. Platon had closed his eyes again. Sandro softly closed the door. *"Dasvidania,* my friend." (Good-bye). When he entered the next room, he found several men waiting to see Platon.

"He is not to be disturbed," Sandro said.

"But, general—" a daring captain began. "Colonel Zurin …"

"Shhh. It can wait," Sandro warned as he left the room. "It can all wait."

164

CHAPTER 23

No. 22 Fontanka
Serge's Childhood Home

As her cab approached No. 22 Fontanka, Mathilda Kschessinska once again looked at the piece of paper in her hands.

The driver shared her concern. "Madame, are you certain it's No. 22?"

"Yes," she said, looking at the neglected townhouse. At that moment, the front gates swung open, revealing Serge.

"Welcome," he said. Then, he gave her a slight kiss on the cheek. "Thank you for coming."

"I would not miss it for the world."

Serge handed the driver a wad of money. "That will be all. I will take care of her from here."

Mathilda surveyed the townhouse. All the shutters were weathered and closed. The home appeared to have been closed up for sometime. "Was it your mother's?"

"Yes, it was. This was where I grew up. My father closed it the day after her death more than four years ago. He could not bear to go back in there."

"Such a waste."

"Yes, it is. But its true beauty is within," he said as he escorted her to the front door.

Brilliantly colored stain glass covered the inner doors. The room was full of light. Rich, warm candlelight coated the walls of the room. The soothing aroma of freshly cut flowers overtook her. The room to her right was full from top to bottom with white roses.

"They're beautiful," she said, bending over to smell one. "I haven't seen so many flowers since my last performance."

Laughing, "And I was attempting to avoid the ordinary."

"Well, I do appreciate the effort."

He pulled out her chair. "They are all for you in appreciation of you taking care of me last night."

"You did not have to do this, though I am glad you did," she said as she sat down. "You have been a busy boy." She looked at the meal. It smells delicious. You can cook too?"

He shook his head. "It would be blasphemy for me to take credit for this. I ordered it from The Bear."

As time passed, the only thing better than the meal was their conversation. Serge told about his youth and how his father was always away, and Mathilda spoke about her performances. "I have traveled the world over, but tonight I am so happy to be here."

He raised his glass, adding: "*Nastrovya*, (Cheers)! For I share your happiness."

"Serge, I wish I could take you back in time with me, and see me perform. When I was your age, I floated across the stage. I haven't floated in some time."

"I saw you perform before the war in London. You played Columbine in Fokine's Carnival."

She grimaced. "London? Not my best performance. One of the critics there called me 'a competent dancer of the stereotyped kind, extraordinarily skillful but often displaying quite unlovely gymnastics.'"

"You forgot 'fat and passé, not on the same plane with either Karsavina or Pavlova,'" he said as he covered his face, expecting a slap.

"Well, what can I say?" she admitted with a coy smile. "Pavlova has the look of a ballerina."

He reached for her hand. "I fell in love with you that evening. A boyish kind of love that's deep, though misunderstood."

She gave him a small kiss on the cheek. "Thank you, Sergei."

With that, the two of them rose from the table.

"What's next?" she asked.

"A tour of my childhood home, though it is a mere shadow of what it was when my mother was alive."

"Tell me about her. We met briefly after one of my performances. I remember she was beautiful. But that was so long ago."

"I was also there that night."

"Really?"

"It was a performance of Sleeping Beauty."

"I am afraid to ask. How old were you?"

"I don't recall."

"I met your mother early in the winter season of '04, so, let me see you were ten years old!"

"Eleven!"

She laughed. "You were a pudgy little boy hiding behind your mother's legs."

"I grew late," he said defensively.

Mathilda was still laughing. "I'm robbing the cradle."

"This is only dinner."

She bent over and smelled another rose, "We will see," she teased.

He took her hand as he had a few sultry thoughts. "Now, it's time to view the rest of the house."

Ministry of War,
Platon's Office

As the general glanced over the armistice, he heard a knock at the door.

It was Colonel Karsten Zurin.

"General Konstantin, you wished to see me?"

"Yes Karsten, please come in and take a seat." Zurin was an old friend a soldier he had served with in Russia's war with imperial Japan.

"General," the colonel asked as he strolled towards the fire. It was a long walk from the train station. "Do you mind if I warm myself first by your fire?"

Smiling, "It is cold today," he said, reflecting, as the flames danced along his blue eyes. "Do you ever miss the heat?"

"You mean the jungle, General? Never." As he moved away from the fire, "Not even on a day like this, my old friend. We Russians are not made for the heat."

"The heat was not too bad, it was the humidity that nearly drained me."

"That mixed in with a two hundred kilometer hike through the worst terrain imaginable—that was Manchuria."

"Tall mountains and deep jungles I remember. The conditions caused more casualties than the enemy. And when I say the enemy, I mean Vlad." Platon laughed.

"Yes. He was so ambitious then, and so cruel to his men."

"I saw him today—wandering the halls."

"Really."

"Yes. He said he was stopping in to see some old friends."

"More like gathering support."

"Yes. Are we making a mistake by giving him this much room?"

"No. We have time. He wants to strike after Christmas."

"Okay, call me tomorrow when you and Ernie reach the palace."

"I will."

"What do we know so far?"

"He's rapidly gaining support within the royal family." Zurin read off a list of names.

"I see," Platon replied as he scuffled through some papers atop his desk. "The list seems to be getting longer."

"It is."

"And their plans?" The general asked without hiding his concerns.

Zurin was to meet the other members of Vlad's faction. "I will find out more tonight." His meeting was less than two hours away.

"Call as soon as you can."

"I will. I plan on staying at the Europe this evening. At least until Serge picks me up tomorrow morning."

"My son is also staying at the Europe. It may be best if you meet him there."

"What is his room number?"

"He has the penthouse," Platon painfully admitted.

"The penthouse?"

"His mother's money."

"I see." Karsten dropped the subject. "I will handle it."

"Good. I will meet you then tomorrow at the palace. Make certain Ernie is sober," Platon laughed. "Well, at least not drunk."

"No promises there general." They both laughed as they recalled some old memories and old friends long gone.

After about twenty minutes of reminiscing, Platon rose from his seat and walked over to the dying fire. "It's time for me to give you a gift, Karsten," he said as he removed the samurai sword from its holder.

"No general," Zurin pleaded. "The sword is yours."

"Not anymore, colonel. Hush. This is how I want it. From one crusty old soldier to another—thank you my dear friend for trying to lighten my spirits." He handed Zurin the sword.

The colonel gave his old commander a big bear hug. "You know, sir. I would follow you anywhere, even to the gates of hell."

The general smiled. "Let's hope that's not necessary."

Vlad's Palace, An Unexpected Visitor

The interior minister's arrival did not please Vlad. Especially, since his meeting with his men was only an hour away. "What are you doing here?" he spat at Protopopov.

"There has been a change in plans."

"Are you insane? Tomorrow at this time, we strike."

"I don't know if that is wise."

"Enlighten me," the duke said.

"Rasputin is still alive."

"Nonsense. Felix told me they dumped his body in the Neva."

"They did. But the beast later crawled out."

"Impossible! I was told the peasant was shot four times, once in the head. Felix is arrogant beyond belief, but he is not foolish enough to lie to me."

"Maybe—or maybe not. Dmitri is gathering the imperial family's support."

"What?"

"It is true. They find him more polished than the incumbent, but not as harsh or shallow as you."

"Minister, the rumors regarding your mental faculties appear to be true," he said with a hearty laugh. "You are truly insane."

"How does one measure sanity Vlad? Everyone knows there is a fine line between genius and madness. Some may see that those who oppose a weak sovereign as are geniuses, while others see—"

"Madness. Protopopov, I get your point. But what makes you so certain the Siberian is still alive?"

"I have seen him face-to-face."

"Where?"

"In my office, at the club, and" pausing for effect, "at the palace."

"At the palace! When?"

"I saw him there this very afternoon. It is so good to have your attention now. When I returned to my office last night, he was there."

Not entirely believing him, Vlad asked, "What did he look like?"

"Felix and Dmitri did a splendid job on him. He looks like the walking dead. Banged up and bruised to a pulp but sadly very much alive."

Vlad began to pace. "What did he want?"

"Answers."

"And what did you tell him?"

"Nothing he didn't already know," the politician replied as he began playing with his moustache. "Mainly he wanted to settle the score with his attempted assassins."

Vlad smiled. "The prince and the duke, not to mention one crooked politician."

"Well, he does need to deal with the good senator, if that's what you're talking about. But Grisha wants to deal with the nobles first. It must be a question of breeding."

Vlad was clearly shaken. "What do you want of me? If he is truly alive, why doesn't he just go to the empress—or has he?"

"No, not yet. He wants to stay in the shadows for the time being."

"Obviously there is a reason you are telling me all this."

"Today, I have been ordered by the empress to guard the grand duke. Rasputin wants me to kill him."

"What! The empress doesn't have the authority to do that. Only the tsar himself can give such an order," Vlad spat. He was so mad that he did not hear the minister second remark.

"No matter. It is done, just as Rasputin wants the duke dead. It soon shall be done."

"Don't be a fool, Protopopov. The imperial family will tear you to pieces for murdering Dmitri. You must know that. You're not that bold."

"You're right. I am not, but Rasputin is," he said. "You see, he wants my men to make his death look like a foiled escape attempt."

"What do you want from me?"

"A deal."

Vlad was growing tired of all of this. "A deal? What deal?"

"Tonight, I shall help you become tsar—if you take care of, once and for all, the Evil One." The minister knew it was just a matter of time before the Siberian traced him to the murder attempt on his life.

"Not likely. You want me to turn my back as you assassinate a member of my family, a fellow Romanov?"

"Precisely."

"What's in it for me?" he asked, playing the game.

"Everything." The minister handed Vlad a letter. "Read it and see," the politician advised.

The letter was not what Vlad had expected. It was one of Alexandra's love letters, but it was addressed to her own husband. It began with the normal pleasantries but then the words grew lethal.

Alexandra wrote:

> *"I had a long dear letter from Ernie.... He wishes for a way out of this dilemma—that someone ought to begin to make a bridge for*

*discussion. So he had an idea of quite privately
sending a man of confidence to Stockholm, who
should meet a gentlemen sent by you....*

"How did you get this?"

"From a dear friend. You see, Vlad, I was that gentleman.
And if I'm not mistaken, the empress and her brother Ernie are
brokering a separate peace."

"Protopopov," Vlad, laughed, slapping the minister across
his back, "you may not be mad after all."

"As I said, it's a fine line."

A Duke's Palace,
View from the Street

Two trucks loaded with men quickly approached the
gates of a palace on the Nevsky. Turning in, the drivers
switched off their lights. As they screeched to a stop, men
poured out of the two vehicles. Watching the unannounced
visitors, the two men guarding the outer door grabbed their
weapon in arms.

"What's this?" they shouted as they raised their rifles.
Slowly, one of the truck's passenger doors opened. Inspector
Renko was going to enjoy this.

"Lower your weapons!" he commanded.

"On whose authority?" the more daring guard asked.

Some of the nurses emerged from the ward to witness the
disturbance.

"Mine!"

At that moment, Renko's men stormed the palace, one
group through the front, and the other through the back. The
two guards could not believe their eyes. They were overcome
before they knew it. Securing the vestibule, Renko's agents ran
into little opposition until they came across a police captain.
Then, both opposing groups raised their weapons.

"What is this, inspector?" Zubov asked. "My men have been ordered by Minister Protopopov to protect the Grand Duke Dmitri and Prince Felix. You are not helping matters."

"Noted," the inspector said to Protopopov's crony. "Tell your men to lower their weapons."

"How can I, inspector? For all I know, you have been sent to assassinate the same members of nobility we are here to protect."

Laughing at Zubov's choice of words, "Your orders have been countermanded. Now, tell your men to lower their weapons while they still have the ability to do so."

"Not until I have a written order stating your intent," replied Zubov. The captain was not planning on failing his mission because of some cocky inspector. "Run off and get your written directive and we will be here waiting for you."

Renko handed over a small card. "Compliments of General Konstantin."

"The general has no authority over us." Zubov read the card: 'By order of the Emperor. I, Tsar Nicholas, order you to obey the carrier of this note. Signed, Your Emperor,' I don't understand."

Renko took back the imperial license. "Captain, you don't need to. Men, by order of the tsar, you are officially relieved of duty. My men will handle the duke's personal protection from now on."

At that moment, from the second floor sounded a single gunshot. The familiar face of one of Renko's trusted lieutenants emerged over the banister.

"Is everyone all right?" asked Renko.

"Second floor secure, Inspector."

"What was that shot?"

"One of Protopopov's men shot at us as we secured the duke's apartment."

"What of the duke?" the captain asked. Perhaps his man had been able to complete his mission.

"Yes, captain," Renko's man replied, then began to laugh. "Though one of your men just fainted. He was the one who fired the shot."

"I see. Well then, the palace is officially yours, Inspector."

"Thank you, Captain. Make sure all your men leave at once."

"Certainly. I shall place this all in my report."

"I am sure you will."

Then the captain thought that perhaps this change of plans would work out better. If one of his men hid there until tonight, he could still complete his assignment.

It was as if Renko was reading his mind. "Captain, if any of your men are found on the palace grounds after," he said as he glanced as his watch and counted off ten minutes, "let's say, nine o'clock, they shall be shot on sight. Understood?"

"Understood. But you know this isn't over."

Renko laughed. "It is for you."

CHAPTER 24

Vlad's Palace
Game Room

Vlad stood tall among the men all huddled around a billiard table, the empress's letter secure within his uniform. He was in his favorite room, his trophy room, lined with the souvenirs of past kills and past adventures. Some privately thought it was morbid to see the collage of fur and feathers nailed and exhibited on the room's walls, not to mention the glassy eyes of the antlered heads. Through puckered lips, they seemed to smile. Perhaps they knew something the men in this room didn't. Vlad laughed out loud as he slapped the back of one of his trusted colonels. Seven commanders of the imperial regiments whose loyalty was only to him lined his view. They would help him bring down and bag the game he had been chasing all of his life—the imperial crown.

Monday night, they would march on the imperial palace and demand the tsar's abdication. If Nicholas resisted, he would die. It was that simple, Vlad thought. He was too close to possessing it all to play games. Another obstacle was the empress. She would never let go of her power. That was why they would strike at her first. She was a beast to be feared, but, thanks to Minister Protopopov, that problem should be solved with an assassin's bullet. All for Russia's greater good—at least that was the consensus of the men in this room.

Wearing uniforms—some black some green—the men stared at the paper spread out on the billiard table. It was a detailed map of Tsarskoe Selo which included a layout of the Alexander Palace grounds. Preparations for the strike at Nicholas were set. Tuesday morning would be an historic moment, if their ambitious plan worked. It had to work. If not, their heads too would be mounted on a wall.

One of the commanders fetched a crystal decanter filled with brandy; another secured some glasses; a third distributed fine cigars. Their plan was flawless and now in motion. Therefore, it was time for a brief celebration.

Five of the seven officers commanded garrisons of His Majesty's Life Guards. Their regiments would converge on the Alexander Palace and demand Tsar Nicholas to abdicate his throne to Vlad. It was that simple. Or, at least that was what everyone in this room hoped.

One member of the group was not as confident about the proposed strike as the others. Vlad sensed concern coming from an officer of the Horse Guards, Colonel Karsten Zurin. Zurin was wearing the samurai sword given to him earlier this evening.

"Colonel Zurin," the duke declared, "I admire your sword. A souvenir from Manchuria?"

Looking down, "Why yes," he said as he removed it from its sleeve and inspected it, "a remembrance of Port Arthur." The colonel wished he had left it at his hotel.

In 1904, Vlad and a small company from his regiment had accompanied Zurin in a failed effort to save that besieged city. "Yes what a wasteful war. Yet another glaring example of Niki's mis-management." The duke left it at that as his attention moved back to the present.

Zurin returned his sword to its sleeve as Vlad revealed his secret to the others.

"Change of plans men. We strike tomorrow night."

'What?' the men could not believe the news.

"So soon." One added, "Less than twenty-four hours away?" Others seemed already privileged to this information. Until now, the plan was to strike the morning of December 26th, the same day as the rebellion of 1825.

"Tomorrow night at ten o'clock?" one of the officers declared. "Is that enough time?"

"It will have to be," Vlad replied, "because that is when my rebel army will march on the palace grounds." After that, the duke discussed his plans. Zurin couldn't believe his ears. In the course of an hour, the officers were fully briefed.

Looking at his favorite, "Captain, I want you and your men to lead the assault on the palace."

"Your Grace," Belarus said, beaming, "It would be an honor. The palace will fall. I promise that, General. I shall not fail!"

"Good," the duke said, looking at his loyal recruits and smiling. "These men are here to see to it that you don't. Right?"

"Yes, General!"

Zurin was a little late in adding his voice to the crowd's. It was noticed.

"It looks like Colonel Zurin has seen a ghost. Colonel, the worst thing that could happen to us is that we are all dead by Tuesday morning." General Vlad and the others all laughed.

"To a new tsar worthy of his people!" an officer offered a toast.

Another fanned out more cigars. "May he restore Russia to her former greatness."

After a brief celebration, the men gathered their belongings. Zurin grew numb. There has to be a mistake, he thought, as he watched the others walk out of the room. He quickly joined them.

Zurin was halfway down the stairs when he heard Vlad calling to him. "Colonel, may I have a word with you? I need your opinion on tomorrow night's timetable." The duke walked into his study with one of his aides. "I need to bring you up to speed."

"Of course, general," Zurin replied, averting his eyes as he slowly climbed the steps and worked his way to the study door. He needed to get a message to Konstantin any way he could. "I am at your service."

Captain Belarus and another one of Vlad's men, entered the room behind him and quietly closed the door.

With a cruel smirk, Vlad said: "Colonel, I have my doubts," turning towards Zurin.

As Zurin instantly reached for his revolver, a gunshot rang out in the room. Vlad's aide missed. The colonel didn't. The man besides Belarus fell to the floor. Vladimir jumped out of the way as his aide moved behind some furniture.

Belarus removed his own weapon as Zurin dove behind the study's massive desk. "Karsten, lay down your weapon and you may live," Belarus lied.

The colonel removed his sword.

Vladimir took a deer rifle off the wall and made sure that it was loaded. "Zurin I have seen that sword before. In the hands of Konstantin."

"Really," the colonel replied as he crouched behind the desk. "Well, you're going to see it soon in use."

Looking at Belarus, Vlad motioned to him to flank the desk. "I knew you would never betray Konstantin. It was foolish of me to even try to persuade you."

As they inched towards the desk, Belarus and Vladimir let out a cry of surprise as the colonel leapt onto the desk.

"You want me Vlad? Come and get me." Zurin fired two shots. Both missed.

At that moment two guards in black entered the room. They were greeted with Zurin's lead. Behind a chair, Belarus fired a few rounds at the desk. This wasn't going as planned.

Jumping off the desk, Zurin made it towards an adjacent door.

Vlad yelled. "Don't let him get away!"

Fleeing out of the room, Zurin ran into two more men. Quickly, he leveled them with his sword. Others emerged from the second story rooms. As they appraised the situation, they fired at the colonel as he ran down the center steps.

With bullets bouncing off the walls, the colonel had one man to beat. Coming up the steps with a confused look on his face was Andrew.

"Colonel," the younger Vladimir exclaimed in a stunned tone, "what in God's name is going on."

Brushing by the stunned duke, "Time for me to go home son." Zurin crossed the foyer with one last man left in his path. That was when Vlad leveled his deer rifle. From the second floor, he had a perfect shot. With a squeeze of the trigger, Zurin's body slammed into the door.

Vlad lowered his weapon, yelling down to his men to secure him.

Andrew ran to Zurin. The colonel was covered in blood. Applying pressure to his wound, "It was not supposed to be like this."

"Remove your hands from me, traitor," Zurin managed before he passed out.

Andrew didn't.

As Vlad hovered over them, he sneered. "Let him bleed," as he picked up Zurin's sword. "Do you honestly believe I would not recognize Konstantin's sword?" His words were wasted. Zurin was already dead.

"General, if Zurin betrayed us, we are not safe," declared an officer wearing green.

"Nonsense. Zurin thought we were striking on the 26th. This changes nothing."

One of Vlad's men asked, "What should we do with the body?"

"Dispose of it," the general said as he strode out of the room.

Andrew was staring at his bloodstained hands. "Vlad!"

"Shut-up Andrew," his older brother shouted from the other room. "I need to think."

Alexander Palace,
Somber Grounds

Sandro was on the way to see the empress when four imperial bodyguards encircled him within the Alexander Palace's foyer. Their greedy eyes were glued to his holster and pistol.

"Your Excellency, may we temporarily liberate you of your firearm?" asked one of them.

"Son," he laughed, "if only it were that simple." He removed his revolver and handed it to the youngest guard. "But realize what you ask—for a soldier to surrender his revolver is an act of submission," the duke said as he walked between the two of them. Before he entered a drawing room, he added, "Try not to hurt yourself with it."

Chairs lined the room leading to a large marble fireplace. The entire room was finely decorated for the holidays with wintergreens. Near the fireplace, Sandro saw his four nieces were rolling bandages for the nearby veteran hospital. Alix and Niki may have failed at many things but they were masterful parents. Huddled together, the girls appeared as angels, seemingly unaware of the mounting problems facing their parents.

At least, that was what the duke believed until the youngest, Anastasia, spoke. "Uncle Sandro," she said, her cheeks aglow from the fire, "is it true that Father Grigory is dead?"

"Anastasia," he asked as he kneeled beside her, "who has told you such a thing?"

Looking at Olga her eldest sister, she merely replied, "A friend."

"Perhaps your friend shouldn't worry you about Petersburg gossip," he said jokingly as he patted her head.

"Uncle Sandro," Olga said, "I have heard it from other sources. Not to mention that Anna and Mother have been crying all day."

"And they won't tell us why," added Tatiana, the second oldest.

"I am sure everything will be all right. Father Rasputin will turn up."

"Is Dmitri somehow involved?" Olga asked. They all loved him as a brother, perhaps a little more.

"It is too early to tell who if anyone is involved."

"I bet Felix put him up to it," Tatiana said. "He's mischievous."

"I know he's married to Irina but I don't trust him. And, the two of them have been spending a great deal of time together," Olga added, jealously.

"That's true, but," he scanned the room, hoping to buy some time, "where's Alexei?"

"He's with father. They should be both home in the morning."

"That soon," the duke was thankful. "Good."

"Uncle Sandro," one of the girls asked, "what about Felix?"

The duke was saved by the arrival of a tall servant dressed to perfection. He stated in a dry tone, "Her Majesty shall see you now."

"Young ladies, if you would please excuse me, I must speak with your mother," he said. "We can continue this in the morning."

"Good evening Uncle," Olga said as she gave him a hug, then whispered, "Be kind to her. She is not well."

"I shall do my best," the duke said.

Walking into the corridor, he turned back and glanced into the room as the children returned to their rolling of bandages. He had an unsettling feeling that he would never see any of them again. He shook these dark thoughts off as he walked down the hall.

Entering the Mauve Room, Sandro saw the empress coiled on her divan and poised for an attack. In an effort to disarm her, the duke moved to kiss her hand.

"No further!" she warned. Two armed guards appeared from the shadows.

"Really Alix, is this necessary?" Sandro began to discuss the previous day's events and the growing concern about the monarchy in the Petersburg's streets. But it landed on deaf ears.

"It is not true," she screamed. "The nation is still loyal to my husband. Only the treacherous Duma and Petersburg society are our enemies."

"There is nothing more dangerous, Alix, than a half-truth," he said, meeting her steely eyes. "The nation is loyal to its tsar, but the nation is likewise indignant over the influence that has been exercised by Rasputin."

With the mention of his name, her eyes moistened as she thought of her poor son.

"Nobody knows better than I your love and devotion for Niki, and yet I must confess that your interference in affairs of state is causing harm both to Niki's prestige and to the popular conception of a sovereign. I have been your faithful friend, Alix, for twenty-four years. I am still your faithful friend, and as a friend I point out to you that all classes of the population are opposed to your policies. You have a beautiful family of children. Why can you not concentrate on matters promising peace and harmony? Please, Alix, leave the cares of the state to your husband."

She pulled out a cigarette and lit it. "The imperial family strikes out at me and my husband, and you, my 'faithful friend,' want me to sit back and watch them annihilate my family. Are you insane?"

"Please Alix, do not let your thirst for revenge dominate your better judgment. A radical change of our policies would provide an outlet for the nation's wrath. Do not let that wrath reach explosion point."

"All this talk of yours is ridiculous. Niki is an autocrat. How could he share his divine rights with a parliament?"

"You are very much mistaken, Alix. Your husband ceased to be an autocrat on October 17th, 1905. That was the moment to think of his divine rights. It is too late now. Perhaps in two months there will be nothing left in this country of ours to remind us that we ever had autocrats sitting on the throne of our ancestors."

"Traitor," she sneered.

"Remember, Alix, I have remained silent for thirty months! For thirty months I have never said as much as a word to you about the disgraceful goings-on in our government, better to say in your government! I realize that you are willing to perish and that your husband feels the same way, but what about us? Must we all suffer for your blind stubbornness? No, Alix, you have no right to drag your relatives down a precipice with you! You are incredibly selfish!"

She looked at her nervous bodyguards. "I refuse to continue this dispute. You are exaggerating the danger. Some day, when you are less excited, you will admit that I know better."

He bowed. "As you wish. I shall speak to the emperor as soon as he returns."

"Until tomorrow then," she said as a smile returned to her face. "We shall deal with it tomorrow." She thought of the treaty. After peace is declared, all will be put right.

The duke turned and stormed out of the room. So upset that be forgot to discuss the topic of a separate peace. Instead he grabbed a large vase off a pedestal and smashed it against the floor.

The two sentries at the door did not know what to do. They had never seen the duke so angered.

The duke collected himself. "I feel better now." He approached the stunned guards, and gave out his best smile. "I am thankful you had my gun," he said as he reached out for his weapon. "I don't know whom I wanted to shoot more—the empress or myself."

Sandro marched out of the palace to his waiting vehicle. As he looked back, out of the first-floor window he saw a face of pink pressed against the cold glass. It was Anastasia. She waved at him. As he waved back he forced a smile. But she was already gone.

Trinity Bridge,
Petersburg by Night

Walking across the Trinity Bridge, Serge and Mathilda both wearing brown fur hats gazed upon the lights of the fortress located on the opposite bank. From the direction of the waterfront, its bastions were always in full view. It anchored the city like a massive rock.

The blowing wind burnt their cheeks like fine desert sand. They stopped for a moment to enjoy the view. It was then that Mathilda spoke. "What do you want out of life?"

"I want what I had."

"You know that's not possible."

"Then what's the point?" He felt guilty about the last few days.

"The point is this," she said as she looked into his sad eyes, "*You* did not die—they did."

Tearing up inside, Serge's eyes moved down to the frozen river.

Only silence answered her.

"At least you had a chance to know love, even briefly."

They both pondered this as Serge spoke. "Do you often think of him?" referring to the emperor. They had spoken much of him earlier.

"Yes, I do. Nearly every day as I rise from my bed, I search for him."

"Searching but never finding" he said, as he knew the image of his wife would never leave him.

"It was," she whispered to the passing wind, "the winter of 1893. The season began, as usual, at the beginning of September. My repertoire already included three ballets. But if I was happy on the stage, it was quite a different matter in my private life. My heart was heavy and constrained, and I had a foreboding of some terrible, imminent sorrow. January 12,

1894, saw the expected announcement of the engagement between the Grand Duchess Xenia Alexandrovna and the Grand Duke Mikhailovich. The tsar and the tsaritsa had always encouraged this union. We also celebrated the event at home with the tsarevich. We sat on the ground and drank champagne."

She smiled. "Then came another event, something which I could not celebrate as I should have liked and ought to have done as a Russian, for all it brought to me, to my heart, was desolation and despair. On April 7 was announced the engagement of the tsarevich and Princess Alix of Hesse-Darmstadt. It was something which I had foreseen, expected, known must happen. Nonetheless it brought me inconsolable sorrow."

Serge pulled her closer to him.

"At the beginning of the same year, alarming rumors had begun to circulate about the emperor's state of health. The famous Professor Zacharyn had been summoned from Moscow. Nobody knew just how serious the tsar's illness was."

"This, I realized, could only hasten the tsarevich's engagement to Princess Alix. And it did. He and I had often spoken of his imminent marriage leading to our inevitable separation. He had not concealed that from me, aware of his duty which called upon him to marry, he considered Princess Alix the most likely of all the fiancées proposed to him, and that he felt a growing attraction to her." She turned toward Serge.

"I wrote him for the last time after his marriage. He replied in these moving lines, which I shall never forget: 'whatever happens to my life, my days spent with you will ever remain the happiest memories of my youth.' I cherish that letter to this day."

"I am sure you do."

"After his engagement, the tsarevich begged me to fix a time and a place for our last meeting. We agreed to meet on the Volkhonsky highway, near the barn and some way off the road. I came from the town by carriage; he rode there from the camp. As always when there is too much to say, tears tighten one's throat and stop one finding the words one would like to utter. When the tsarevich departed for the camp, I remained by the barn and watched him go until he was no longer in sight. He kept on turning back. I did not weep, but I weep now. I was profoundly unhappy, torn, and my pain went on increasing as Niki drew farther away. Then I returned home, to the house that seemed so empty. I felt that my life was over, that no more happiness would ever come to me, that henceforth I would know nothing but sorrow, great sorrow."

They approached her block. The snow was beginning to pick up. "I knew that some would pity me, but others would derive pleasure from my grief. I did not want compassion, but I would need courage to face the others. But all that only occurred to me much later. For the moment there was nothing but terrible boundless suffering, the wrench of losing my Niki! No words can describe what I felt later when I knew that he was with his fiancée. My youth's happy springtime was over." They both stood before her mansion on Kronversky Prospect. Its lights reached out into the night.

"My home," she said proudly.

"It's beautiful." Her house dwarfed some palaces in Petersburg.

"Yes," she said, looking around. "Let's get inside. I'm getting cold."

The ballerina pulled out her latchkey. Her thoughts drifted away from her, replaced by hope. While she opened the door, she laughed out loud.

"What's so funny?"

"You," she cried, flinging open the door. "You're making me feel like a child again, and it feels wonderful."

Serge just grinned. He was happy to see her smile again. They removed their jackets and crossed a grand entrance hall of polished marble. Matching columns climbed the walls until they reached the arch of a domed skylight. It was a magnificent first impression.

Looking around the house, "No servants tonight?"

"Not tonight," she said with a mischievous smile. "Do we need any?"

Smartly avoiding the topic, he decided to explore one of the rooms. Walking through her home filled with souvenirs of a splendid career, the prince stopped in front of a framed portrait. "Who's that?"

"That's Petipa, Marius Petipa."

"I am afraid that I am unfamiliar with his name."

"He was before your time. He was a brilliant choreographer, a kind man, and friend."

Serge's eyes moved from one performance poster to another, all with great reviews stamped upon them: "She danced her variations with lightness and her own brilliance and polish"; "Full of vitality and fire"; "She lights the stage"; "She was like a sudden flash of light."

"Your home is wonderful and warm." His eyes fell upon a picture that piqued his interest. "Who's this pretty little girl with flowers in her hair?"

She blushed. "That was me … a lifetime ago."

"I still see in the both of you that hint of trouble."

"Trouble?" She picked up a small pillow to throw at him. "I was eight years old when that picture was taken. What did I know of trouble?"

"That same flicker still comes out of those beautiful eyes of yours, especially when you're mad."

Then he passed a framed poster from 1911, honoring her twentieth year in the Imperial Ballet. With this, Serge realized that she had been part of that theatre longer than he had been alive.

She watched him looking at the poster. "Yes," she said, laughing, "I am older than the empire."

"No. You're beautiful and kind."

"You know you should never believe your critics," she said, eyeing him. "If you give them the power to build you up, you also give them the power to tear you down."

Then why did you frame their kind words, he thought of asking but didn't. He had learned to choose his battles better than that. Then his eyes landed on a portrait of her only son Vova sitting on the lap of his father, Grand Duke Andrew.

Looking for a diversion, the prince saw a piano in a corner, "Do you mind?"

She was genuinely surprised. "You play?"

"A little. My mother taught me, though I am afraid that I may be a little rusty."

As he sat, she could tell that he was no stranger to it. He seemed quite at peace as beautiful music began to pour from his fingertips. He was quite good. So good, in fact, that she fought the urge to dance. "You play well."

His hands traveled up and down the keyboard. "It's a fun escape."

"Play me something to dance to."

"Any preference?"

"None whatsoever."

"Let's see? Oh yes." An enchanting melody snuck into the room. The ballerina's moves were as graceful as an angel dancing across a cloud. As Serge played, she continued to dance as if her feet were actually fed by each delicious note. At this moment in time, no other world existed—just this beautiful one, created by them—and it lasted until dawn.

DAY THREE

CHAPTER 25

A Dacha in the Woods

As Serge's car slipped through the woods it was the first time he missed his beard. Inside the car was so cold he could barely feel his face or fingertips. At least the pain pulled his thoughts from her. The last time he had been here was the autumn of '14. The leaves were turning and he had spent a long weekend with his wife here. The weekend had been perfect, both the weather and the company. The two newlyweds put the war out of their minds as they explored the nearby woods.

At lunchtime, they made love on a patch of grass and watched the deer race through the woods. At night, they sat before a well-fed fireplace and discussed what they both wanted out of life. It wasn't much—just each other. The following week the prince reported for duty and they put their life on hold. That was over two years ago. What a waste. The prince's thoughts shifted back to the present. It had been an hour since he had left Mathilda's house and hurried to meet Zurin. However, the colonel had never showed. There had been some police activity by the bridge—but no colonel.

His face, at least a portion of it, was captured by the rear view mirror. For moment, he felt the guilt again of being alive and his night spent with Marie. But that passed as he smelled the distinct smell of burning wood.

Approaching the crest of the hill, Serge saw a sea of white dusted fir trees. Above them was a tall cloud of smoke coming from his family's cabin.

Some secrecy, he whispered. Within a few moments he was there.

Walking from his car, the cabin's door flew open. In its large frame stood the Duke of Hesse. The German was of average height and build but his face radiated hope and his eyes still held the gleam of a child. "Serge! You devil. You're all grown up!"

"Ernie, I hope you haven't."

"Wouldn't dream of it," the duke said with his trademark smile. Ernie never took life too seriously. It was one of the things Serge loved about him.

"Why does it not surprise me to find you here?"

"Tell me about it," the duke said as they embraced, "My dear sister has done it again."

"What's that?"

"Dragged me into a sticky situation."

"I heard the empress was good at that."

Laughing out loud, "She most definitely is."

"Is that why Willy chose you?" said Serge, referring to the German Kaiser.

"Why else?" the duke shared. "Certainly not for my political expertise. Though, I would like to think it's for my flair for intrigue."

The two laughed at that. German or not, the duke had a wonderful sense of humor. The good duke for a brief time had been married. That marriage had not lasted. The duke's tastes were diverse, and his wife had not appreciated sharing him. Now, he was a reborn bachelor and declared he would be for the rest of his days.

"Well, we'd better move inside. This place is positively frigid. I don't know how you Russians do it."

"We Russians love the cold as much as we do war."

"The war? What a morbid topic." The duke was not one for such deep thoughts. So he changed the subject and said, "I heard the Petersburg's nightlife is getting wilder?"

"Yes. And trust me you don't want one part of it. Those in Russian society high or low are using any and all methods to escape the borders of their own minds. Some permanently."

"The last tango of the night?"

"Something like that. People find death appealing."

"Do they? How sad. This war is such a waste for both sides."

"Yes, a terrible waste."

"That's why I am here," the duke offered. "To do my small part for history. Though your father's choice of accommodations has much to be desired. A log cabin in the middle of winter; I nearly froze to death last night."

"War is hell."

"Yes it is," he laughed. Ernie slapped Serge on the back. "How's your father?"

"You haven't seen him yet?"

"No, a man named Renko drove me here from the station. Why?"

"We need to talk." The two of them walked towards the warm confines of the Konstantin cabin.

"Hey? Why are you all alone? Renko told me a colonel would be arriving with you. What happened?"

"That's one of the things we need to talk about."

The Embankment, Senate Square

Wearing a troubled face, Alexander hurried down the stone steps leading away from Platon's office. Moments earlier, he had been informed that the general was enjoying his daily walk. The weather was a bit frigid, but the duke could understand the wish to escape.

General Konstantin saw his friend approaching from across the square.

"What a glorious day, Sandro!"

"It is all-beautiful but cold," was the response.

This made the general stop in the middle of his stride. Alexander was always an optimist. "Sandro, what's wrong?"

"I still can't quite believe it myself, but I'm afraid my Niki and Theodore are somehow involved in this dreadful affair. I just found out this morning."

"From who?"

"Niki called me this morning." It was how the day had greeted him.

"I see. Why are you telling me this?"

"For your investigation of course. I sent someone to fetch them from the Crimea at once."

"Who else knows?"

"No one."

"Good. Keep it that way." He fished papers from his jacket and handed them to the duke. The papers were a three-page summary on Rasputin's murder. Sandro's sons were not mentioned.

"Platon, you don't have to do this. You substituted the two women for my sons, didn't you?"

"Perhaps."

"You mustn't do that. The tsar needs to know. Niki as supreme protector of justice is duty bound to punish the assassins, particularly as they are members of his family."

"Duty?" the general spat. "Sandro, you have always been the righteous one, but the decision had already been made. They were never there."

"Why are you doing this?"

"Sandro, your boys are sixteen and eighteen."

"But they are guilty."

"They are guilty of being young and foolish, but they are innocent of the crime. We both know that Felix is entirely responsible for all of this. And I assure you that I will use every means to see that he is brought to justice and fully punished."

"Okay, but...?"

"No buts, my friend." The general stopped to look over the Neva and thought of his dead wife. "Sandro, your family name holds a dear place in my heart."

"Tatiana?"

The general nodded.

"I miss her."

"As do I. She was your wife, but she was also my sister."

"Sandro," Platon grasped the duke's hand. "Pray with me."

"When did you get so religious?" Sandro, near tears, asked.

"Just recently," replied the dying man.

They both laughed at this. Then they prayed for lost loves, dear friends and Mother Russia. Finally, Sandro looked at his friend. "I am going to miss you."

"I know," Platon replied, wanting to say more.

Their eyes moved from one another back to the Great Neva. The wind howled.

As they neared the general's office, they saw Renko rush down the stone steps. "What is it?" the general asked as he braced himself. They knew they had just found him.

"They have just fished a corpse out of the Little Neva," the inspector said. "It appears to be Rasputin."

"Inspector, take the father's remains to the Veterans Hospital at Tsarskoe. Get Dr. Lusiten to examine the body as soon as possible. We need to be certain."

"It may be a while. They told me the body was completely frozen."

"Then as soon as it thaws."

"Inspector Renko, would you mind if I came along?" Sandro asked.

Renko looked at his boss. "General, would that be appropriate?"

"What could it hurt?"

"In that case, General Mikhailovich, please follow me. I have a car waiting for us."

Sandro shook Konstantin's hand. "Thank you, Platon. I feel I must."

"I understand," he said. He watched Sandro hurry toward the awaiting car.

Then he whispered to the wind, "I am going to miss you too, my friend."

CHAPTER 26

Dmitri's Palace
A Duke's Bedchamber

Sunday evening inevitably faded into Monday morning at No. 41 Nevsky Prospect, and the crimson-colored palace greeted the new day with a dirty grin. Dmitri's door slowly began to open.

"Who's there?" he mumbled into his pillow.

No one answered. It must have been a draft, he thought as he tried to return to sleep.

Then, a firm voice said: "Get up."

Hovering over his bed was a blurry image of a tall, good-looking man wearing a general's uniform. "Get up, son. What have you been up to?" The Grand Duke Paul Alexandrovich yanked his son out of bed.

"Why are you here?" Dmitri weakly asked.

"Don't play me for a fool!"

Still in his pajamas, his father harshly escorted him down the hall. They entered a darkened room, and the father reached for his dead wife's Bible.

"You swear to me," Paul almost shouted, placing his son's hand on the black leather, "that you had nothing to do with this madness."

Staring at his mother's portrait on the wall, Dmitri said: "Father, I am innocent of murder."

He pressed his son's flesh against the Bible. "You swear?"

"I swear it."

"I don't need to know anything more about the tragedy," Paul said, smiling for the first time since his arrival and giving his son a hug. "I knew it couldn't be true, not my precious son, not my Dmitri."

Still within his grasp, he whispered, "Father, you have been misinformed."

"That I now know. And soon, so will my nephew," he said. "I will fix this." With that, Dmitri's father turned and marched out of the room.

Fear and guilt consumed the son. He had lied. Hell of a wake-up call, he thought. He hated Felix for involving him in this mess, but, in truth, he hated himself more.

Ashamed, Dmitri fell to his knees before the portrait of his mother. "Lord, give me a chance to redeem myself. Please," he pleaded, "For my father's sake."

Dmitri still sat on the floor as Felix strolled in. "Felix, what have we done?" he asked.

"What's done is done, my friend," the prince said. "There will be a time, many years from now, when you will be thankful you had the courage to rise up and save Russia, to slay the Siberian peasant who threatened to ruin it all."

"I am not so sure. Here I am, lying on the floor because my father dragged me here to swear on my mother's Bible that I was innocent of Rasputin's murder."

"What? I thought he wasn't due back until Tuesday."

"He must have caught an earlier train. Nonetheless, I lied to him about my involvement."

Just one more day, Felix thought to himself. Just one more day, then Vlad will be in power and all this ugliness shall fade away.

"Felix, are you listening to me? I swore on my honor that I was not involved. My sacred honor."

"Yes, yes. I know. Trust me, Dmitri. We just need to survive the day, and all will be put right. By the end of this week, we shall all be heroes."

"Heroes don't lie," Dmitri muttered.

Felix just shook his head. "Some heroes do."

Outside Petersburg,
Nearly Home

The swaying of the train hypnotized the tsar as he stared into the deepening darkness. He looked down at his son, resting upon his chest. He could not put into words the amount of love he held for his child. The little one's innocence was truly contagious. He could not wait to be surrounded by his family today and tell them the splendid news—the war will soon be over. Just thinking about it sent chills down his spine. The new offensive in the spring would be glorious.

He looked out the window; they were leaving the plains and entering the woods and would soon be home. Nicholas recalled a past conversation with the prophet. He had asked Rasputin, "When will the war end?" The starets had replied, "When you take Constantinople, that will be the end of it." He spoke the truth. Why is my sole purpose for this war the liberating of that forgotten Christian city?" he asked himself. As he eyelids grew heavy, he knew the answer all too well. He was the one chosen to restore the cross to the altar of St. Sophia. Resting his head against the window, he remembered Professor Konstantin Pobyedonostzev, his private tutor. The professor had other titles—priest, law professor, and judge—but the most important one was that he was a believer. Pobyedonostzev was the same man who had taught Nicholas's father, Alexander III, to believe and to rule Russia with an iron grip. As the train rocked Nicholas to sleep, he could once again hear that energetic, nasal voice.

"In 324 AD, rounded by water, a quiet place stood firm against the harsh winds of time," the professor once whispered, "Generation after generation defiantly passed as the city basked in the warm summer's sun, as its inhabitants spent their mornings staring outward – toward the glimmering sea and its horizon. Each morning, they rose as one, as always, and performed their daily rituals. Gazing out towards the rolling waves that slowly rippled in they wept. They knew that some day this humble place might change."

"Before their teary eyes was the mighty River Bosphorus, and its broad banks dividing two worlds, that of the West from that of the East. From their differing vantage points, high above the bluffs, each scene looked heavenly. Below them, the contrasting masts of small vessels lined the sandy beaches of this safe harbor. Their white weathered sails merged sweetly with the rising and falling backdrop of a turquoise sea. The tranquility of the entire scene pleased the eye."

"That is, until one fine day. As the dawn broke against the tiny village's shores, the peasants woke to find something unusual competing for their attention—two pillars of dust had developed to their West. What had the prevailing winds brought them? In their field of vision, they witnessed two armies gathering along a narrow and winding road. As the day grew longer, the thunderous clamor of tens of thousands of feet marching towards each other could be heard.

The combined footsteps seemed sinister, but enchanting, like the delicious first bite of a forbidden fruit. In the surrounding hills, they were witnessing a battle being waged between two opposing gods for the sole control of the Holy Roman Empire. Licinius Augustus of the East fought his brother-in-law, Konstantin Augustus the Emperor of the West. It was a battle of faith between a Christian and a pagan."

"Konstantin the Great!" the tsarevich said in a boyish glee.

"Yes, Your Grace."

"The Great. Just like Peter the Great. I would like to one day be known as the Great. Yes, Nicholas the Great. I like the ring of it."

Settling the young man back to his tale, "I am certain one day you will, as long as you continue with your studies. This skirmish between living gods from Rome played itself out above the surrounding heights of this seaside village, the midpoint of the empire. As the faithful soldiers of the two Roman legions engaged, the ground shook."

"After some time and much blood, one imperial banner stood tall amongst the heaped dead. It was the banner of the West whose mighty men had defeated Licinius's legions. In doing so, Konstantin had reunified the Roman Empire. No longer would there be opposing legions of the East and West. From now on, they would all bow down to one deity, the Christian God."

"Still covered in mud and blood, Konstantin gave thanks to the supreme being. Haunted by the moment, his eyes full of grief could bear no more. So, he found hope within the gloom as he turned his head and looked down the jagged coast, where he saw an enchanting city by the sea with the mystifying name of Byzantium. At that moment, a familiar voice entered him. 'There.' Facing a small village that lay on the tiny tip of the Golden Horn, he smiled," as the professor showed him on the map. "As one of his men approached, he breathed in fresh sea air. Pointing down, he exhaled and said, 'There! In the distance, that precious place shall be the New Rome!'"

"The New Rome?" the child asked. "Wasn't St. Petersburg also to be the New Rome?"

"Yes. And it is," replied the tutor, as he added, "Peter the Great did the same thing when he moved the capital from Moscow. He pointed to a barren wasteland, on the northern frontier, and told his subjects, 'There.' And that is where the city stands today."

The professor returned to his story. "With the passage of time, the city grew and flourished. Emperors like Konstantin had their noble agents scavenge the vast empire in search of precious antiquities, mainly religious, especially those linked to the last days that Jesus Christ walked the Earth. The emperors also commissioned artists to create great objects of art praising the Christian faith. The most famous and some say the most beautiful were the holy icons of Byzantine art, the mosaics. These masterpieces of blue and gold adorned the walls of the massive cathedral the Great Church of St. Sophia. And, for more than a millennium, one faith reigned over Constantinople. In that time, it became nearly as impregnable as the heavens above. With its high-ridged walls, which circled the city, it appeared to be a fortified island. Constantinople never fell. Assault after assault, the Cross above the copper-topped church stood firm."

"But centuries later, the empire was no longer respected or feared. Time, neglect, and countless crusades had left their mark. By the middle ages, the city was an eyesore, and a cause of grief to the civilized western world. So, as a rogue wind from the east howled, the gate creaked open. And through that opening entered an opportunistic man. Named Mohammad II, he was a young sultan of the Ottoman Empire and a devoted disciple of Islam, and as ruthless as he was brilliant. The sultan decided the Christian stronghold was ripe for the taking. But there was a Christian man in his way, a soldier with a powerful and noble name. He was Konstantin XI, the Roman emperor, and he didn't want to be the last. When he heard that the forces of Mohammad II were massing, he pleaded with Europe to send more troops and ships."

"Did any come?"

"Shh, you shall soon find out. Konstantin gathered his few men and prepared for a siege. He realized his people's only hope was for reinforcements to arrive. So, each day as he rose, he looked out to the sea. But, all he could see were the countless ships that peppered the sea like massive whitecaps rolling toward his shores. Sadly, they all flew the flag of the crescent moon, the imperial flag of the Ottoman Empire. Standing on a high tower, he looked through an eerie fog at what his men of less than ten thousand stood against: Mohammad's army totaled more than seventy-five thousand strong. They had cut him off and encircled the city. The Turkish navy controlled the surrounding sea.

"Enormous elephants dragged heavy guns and canons nearer. Each morning, he prayed he would wake to see Europe's vast armadas appearing over the horizon. But no one came."

"Then, one Monday night, the moon's bright beams of pale iridescent light became dull as they were eclipsed by a crescent shaped sphere, a bad omen to the evil that was to come. The night sky that once bore the cross appeared to change alliances, as it now resembled the crimson crescent of the Ottoman Empire. With this revelation, the invaders knew their god would give them this once-impregnable Christian city of Constantinople. As dawn broke, they chanted: 'The city is ours!'"

"As the sultan's guns chipped away at the city's outer defenses, Konstantin realized he was to be the last Roman emperor."

"That day, the sultan's endless supply of men finally breached the outer wall, and began scaling the city's second wall. At that moment, the Emperor Konstantin removed his imperial purple and pulled out his sword. One last time he looked back at the dome of the great church as his bodyguards urged him to escape. His only response, 'I will stay with my men!'"

The tsarevich was getting scared. He hoped he never had to make such a decision.

"With that, he and his remaining men charged toward the breach, but it was too late. They were quickly overwhelmed as the Janissaries's heavy blades crashed down upon them."

"Janissaries?"

"Warriors, almost as furious as our Don Cossacks. The enemy was now within the inner gates. The city was doomed. In the great church, Constantinople's last citizens, baptized in shining sunlight, attended one last mass. Behind the barred doors of the ancient cathedral, children wept, as their terrified mothers wondered if their husbands were still alive. Soon, rumors of the emperor's heroic death were passed. As they prayed out loud, their words of hope did not comfort. Tears and desperation covered their faces. Their time had run out. With this, everyone in the church huddled as one. Like the Apostle Paul, they were all prepared to die for their Faith.

"Then, an explosion jolted the building. Amid the falling debris came the sultan's sword-wielding Janissaries. They mercilessly cut through the remaining men, and then turned their stained blades toward the women and children. With the chamber secured, the sultan's personal entourage cloaked in flowing robes entered the bloody cathedral. A single Turk walked through the broken door. Wearing a crimson-colored robe, he came to claim his ultimate prize, and approached the altar of God. Walking down the center aisle, he nearly slipped on Christian blood. Unrattled, he gave a small chuckle."

"He placed his head to the stone floor, and began a prayer directed at the God of Islam, the prophet Mohammed. And with that single prayer, the Great Church was converted from a Christian Church to a Turkish mosque. A lord of a different name now resided within this mighty house in the city that now bore a new name—Istanbul."

"Istanbul?"

"Yes, Istanbul. Almost five centuries have passed since the Turkish conquest, and many Christian crusaders during the years have attempted to restore the cross to Constantinople, but they have all failed to reach the altar of St. Sophia. But deep within the bowels of the forgotten city, the ghosts of the slain men cry out: 'Reclaim this city of Christ!' Imagine the greatness God would grant to the man, the noble man, who would restore His church to the true Faith."

"So, young Nicholas, you wish to be great? Then give back to God what is rightly His—liberate Constantinople from the heathens." The tsarevich could only imagine doing so. What a legacy it would be!

Another young tsarevich shook him, "Papa, we're home," Alexei said.

"So we are." He gave his son's head a quick pat. "Did you sleep well?"

"Always when I am next to you."

"Good. Now remember, we must not tell mama about our walks. She worries so."

"It will be our secret."

As they walked to the adjoining car to clean up for their arrival, Nicholas remembered that it was the professor's poor advice that had led him and his country into the last war and the 1905 revolution. For over twenty years, he, like the Christian Job, had seen much that he loved and cherished torn from his grip. Could it be that he was making a mistake? No, he told himself; by spring, the city should be ours. He smiled. It was good to be home.

CHAPTER 27

Back Road
To the Ruins

It was a pleasant ride to the ruins besides the gloomy December day, thanks to the bottle Ernie and Serge shared in the cabin. As they neared the outskirts, two stone towers separated by a bridge, they both noticed that they were no longer alone.

From both flanks, within the white-covered shrubbery, a group of riders approached kicking up snow. One of the riders cried as a misty cloud emerged from his horse's nostrils, "Halt!"

Serge and Ernie looked at one another as they pulled their horses to a stop.

The officer in charge was one of Zurin's men. Circling them, he questioned, "Where's the colonel?"

"Never showed," Serge replied, not liking the officer's tone.

"What?" the officer asked, his worried face said it all. He knew Zurin would be here if he had a choice. "Okay. We will take it from here." Looking to one of the other men, "Make certain the prince reaches his train. I need to report the colonel's disappearance at once."

"I am not going anywhere!" Serge could not believe this was it.

"Afraid so sir. Kicking or screaming, you're catching the first train back to Petersburg," the officer said smiling. "Blame your father, Prince Sergei. His orders were quite firm on the matter."

The German spoke for the first time. "Serge, your job is now done. This is not a game. Colonel Zurin is missing for a reason."

The young officer agreed.

The duke added, "These fine men will escort me to my sister. The best place for you is back in the city."

As if he had a choice. "All right Ernie, it was good to see you again."

"Yes, it was. Until next time Serge."

"Your Excellency, we need to go. For we are not the only ones in these woods."

"Fine, captain. As you wish," Ernie replied as he gave his horse a quick kick. He was familiar with these woods. "*Auf Wiedersehen,* my friend. Give my regards to your father." The other guards followed him.

With that, all but one of the soldiers was gone. The others were riding further south towards the palace.

"What next?" the prince asked the remaining man.

"Time for me to drop you off at the station," the lieutenant said as he began to turn away.

"I see."

In twenty minutes, they arrived at Tsarskoe station. Their ride was uneventful.

St. Petersburg, The Blue Bridge

Renko shouted something to the policemen who encircled the body at the Blue Bridge, and it wasn't a compliment. The bundled-up vultures with cigarettes dripping from their beaks were hungry for souvenirs. The inspector ordered his men to secure the corpse by wrapping it in wool blankets.

"Renko, what would it hurt to have a few pictures taken?" a police captain asked.

"Take all the pictures you want, Captain. But I am leaving and so is the body in five minutes."

Sandro could not believe the condition of the body. It appeared the Siberian had put up a good fight. His hands were untied, and he gave the impression of gazing upward. If that was true, Rasputin had not died from the brutal beatings; he had drowned. Not a good sign, the duke thought. It's the Orthodox Church's belief that possible saints cannot perish by water.

"General Mikhailovich, we are finishing up here," Renko shouted. "Would you like one of my men to drive you home?"

"I would appreciate it, inspector."

As a crew hoisted the corpse from the river, Sandro could not believe that two of his sons had been involved in this sickening endeavor. At this point, he could kill his son-in-law. Still watching the removal, a freak wind caught the wool blanket that covered the body. Like a tiny sail, the blanket moved back and forth, revealing Rasputin's torso and face. His face screamed out a tale of agony worthy of a Greek tragedy.

Finally, the body was placed in the ambulance. As the doors closed, a driver approached Sandro and told him he was at his service. "Take me to Grand Duke Dmitri's palace," the duke said, sickened by this morning's events.

"As you wish, General."

"Thank you, son. That is exactly what I wish."

The White Tower,
View of the Palace Grounds

From atop a tall, whitewashed tower which overlooked the palace grounds, Vlad had a somewhat imperfect view of his future kingdom. Fog engulfed much of the park, though it had spared the palace. Like a present wrapped in paper and bows, all that he surveyed was soon to be his. What a wonderful Christmas gift to himself. At that moment, from the corner of his eye, he saw a motorcar race from the direction of the Arsenal toward the palace. The car's speed alarmed him. Was the driver en route to warn the tsar of his fate? Vlad and his four men peered over the edge to get a better view of the driver. The vehicle slammed to a halt as a cloud of exhaust and dirt engulfed the imperial guards that stood before the palace's main entrance. Emerging from the car was the Grand Duke Paul, the only living brother of Nicholas's father, Tsar Alexander III.

They all exhaled at once.

"Poor old Paul, noble as ever, protecting his only son's valor," Vlad said with a laugh. Having Prince Felix's actions draw the emperor into his trap was the masterstroke of his plan. He pitied his uncle; doubtless, he was bringing news of Dmitri's death.

"I would hate to be Niki now. Paul will blame him for it all," Vlad said to his underlings.

"Perhaps Paul shall settle matters for us today," one captain said, laughing. Another said: "I must admit the old man has some flair."

"Yes, he does," admitted the duke. "He remembers what it is to be a Russian duke."

"I hate to see the grand duke get all worked up for nothing," boasted the regimental commander wearing the unforgettable green uniforms of His Majesty's Preobrazhenski Guards. "Dmitri shall be freed by morning."

"Indeed," another said. "There needs to be a place in the new order for young men like Dmitri."

"Yes, men, there shall always be a place for young men like him," Vlad said, unsettled by their fondness for Dmitri. "Releasing him from custody shall be my first official act," he lied. Protopopov's men should have finished their business. If so, it would be an excellent reason to seize the minister and have him taken to the fortress for questioning—where he too could die trying to escape. This thought made the duke laugh out loud.

Then, Vlad's greedy eyes looked toward the Arsenal located on the wooded heights directly above the Alexander

Palace. This octagonal fortress housing the tsar's personal collection of weaponry was an ideal launching point for the invasion.

He turned toward his men. "Ten o'clock."

"Ten o'clock, Your Majesty," they said in unison.

"I like the ring of that," the duke said, smiling. "We will gather our forces at the base of the tower. Captain Xavier, I want your cavalry stationed here." He pointed to the tower's grounds. "It shall be your responsibility to cut off any possible escape routes. Gentlemen, I don't need to remind you what will happen if Nicholas escapes." They all knew. The hunters would become the hunted. They all knew that Colonel Zurin's regiments were no longer involved in the conspiracy. His units believed Vlad was going to strike on the day after Christmas.

Vlad stared at a seasoned officer with a stern face. "Now, Michael. I want your men to seal the palace gates. No one in, no one out."

"I shall handle the matter personally, General."

"General," asked a major with a worried face, "what of reinforcements from the north and south? The Horse Guards are quartered just beyond the palace." Major Fedorov added, "Our flank shall be exposed by a regiment of His Imperial Majesty's Escort, the Cossacks. They will fight us to the death."

The officers grew silent at the mention of the Cossacks. There was nothing on this world like a squadron of Don Cossacks charging you with their sabers slicing through the air.

"I have handled that matter personally," Vlad said. "This afternoon, wagons filled with cases of the best wines and liquors shall be delivered to their barracks along with some questionable women, all compliments of His Majesty for the celebration of the coming of Christmas. Trust me, we have nothing to fear from them. When they awaken tomorrow, they shall be under my complete authority. Tonight, Nicholas will abdicate his throne." He thought, but did not add—even if he must die.

"Yes, Your Majesty," they chorused, while wondering if that would be enough. Drunken Cossacks killed just as effectively as sober ones. But no one was willing to voice the thought.

"Remember, men. We shall have control of the palace communications, along with the palace's power station. The barracks that are not participating in this historic night shall be cut off from the world." He pointed to an adjacent hill. "There, we shall have artillery support covering our flank and rear. From that position, our guns shall have complete control of the field."

Vlad turned to the battery's commanding officer. "See to it."

"Yes, general," the soldier replied, "My guns shall rain down death on all those foolish enough to get in our way." Nonetheless, he still wished he had Zurin's machine gunners to reinforce his battery. But there was no time to recruit them.

Vlad brought up his binoculars for one more look. At the back of the palace, near one of the colonnades, he saw a bundled-up figure attempting to light a cigarette. The smoker's identity surprised him—Alexandra's brother, the grand duke of Hesse-Darmstadt.

The rumors of a separate peace must be true. By capturing Ernie, Vlad's job of legitimizing his regime would be complete. He could see the banner headline now:

"German house guest found in Palace." That was such good news; especially when that house guest was the empress's own brother and, no doubt, the Kaiser's messenger. "Now, what the hell are you doing here?" he whispered. "What luck."

"General, is there something wrong?"

"No, all is fine. We have thought of everything," he said as he turned his back on his future kingdom. "As Tsarskoe grows silent, we will take the palace. Gentlemen, remind your men that the tsar belongs to me."

The remark about the tsar worried the others in the group. Their mission was to force him to abdicate, not to assassinate him. It also was troubling that four thousand men who swore their allegiance to Nicholas were stationed within five miles, and two thousand mounted cavalry were not much farther away. Fedorov, the young strategist, calculated that their mixed legions of mutineers totaled about three light regiments. That was only twenty-five hundred men.

Vlad looked at him. "Major Fedorov, stop it."

"General, stop what?"

"Worrying," he said as he continued towards the stairs. "You need to relax. The worst thing that can happen to us is that we will all be dead by tomorrow at this time." Vlad did not fear death, only failure. He was the only one of the group.

Alexander Palace, Within the Rotunda

Leaping from his motorcar like a man half his age, the Grand Duke Paul made his way to the palace's main entrance. His son's denial burned within him.

Always fearful of the old guard, the two soldiers protecting the grand entrance slowly advanced toward the gray-haired man. "Your Imp—" was all they were allowed to say.

"Out of my way!" the duke ordered as he passed them.

"Yes, sir!" They followed him into the palace.

The inner bodyguards patrolling the foyer were accustomed to irate dukes. With rifles ready, the leader of the House Guard demonstrated, "Your Imperial Highness, we cannot allow you into the palace without a permit from Minister Protopopov. I am sure as a general you understand the importance of following an order."

The duke continued on his way.

"It's for Their Majesties's security."

He kept walking.

The guard now shouted: "General, those are our orders! Halt!"

Paul removed his service pistol. "This is the only permit I have on my person."

The bodyguards looked toward their leader, who shook his head. "As you wish, General. We are only doing what is asked of us."

"Son, I realize that. That's the only reason you're still standing." With gun in hand, he entered the empress's chamber.

"How did you get here?" she shouted, radiating hate. "My guards shall be punished for having disregarded my orders and allowed you to enter the royal palace."

Flamboyantly bowing, the old man replied: "Madame, truly your servants are faithful, but a loaded revolver is like a bewitching feminine beauty: it has great powers of persuasion."

Nicholas sat in the corner smoking. Seeing his uncle surrounded by the palace guards, he laughed out loud as he stood to greet him. "If only my father were alive to see this," he thought. "All of Russia would have seen him roll with laughter." He smiled at his uncle. "Guards, please leave us."

Following the guards, the empress rose and gave the grand duke a fixed stare as she moved towards the windows.

The emperor clapped his hands and offered the grand duke his seat. "Now that the little theatrical has ended, what are the wishes of Friend Paul?"

"You must tell me why Dmitri was arrested."

"Your son was arrested for the murder of Rasputin."

"He is innocent. I swear to you by my honor, Dmitri is innocent of murder." Paul slammed his fist into his hand. "You shall liberate him at once!"

The tsar spoke, "You wish for me to order his release? So you are quite certain of Dmitri's innocence?"

It was then that the empress began pacing the room and gazed upon her husband like a wounded dove.

"Uncle Paul," Alix hissed, "your recent intimate relationship with a certain element in Petersburg and

214

elsewhere has repeatedly been called to my attention. Your hospitality to the elements that are plotting against our dynasty indicates ill of you."

"Halt, Madame!" he yelled at the top of his voice. Alix took a step back. Paul cooled a bit, and then gave a small bow. "The son of Alexander the Second," he said sharply, "was taught to regard the fatherland more sacred than the dynasty."

At this point, Nicholas closed his eyes and waited for the empress's reaction. As she paced near the windows, she kept repeating the word "treason" over and over again. At the end, it became a tiny whisper. He loved his uncle dearly, but enough was enough. "My dear uncle," the emperor said as he rose from his chair, "the investigation of the murder is not yet completed. For that reason, I am unable to order Dmitri's release. I'm sorry."

"But...?"

"I have already given an explicit order that the investigations regarding the murder are hurried up and that your son be accorded special considerations. All these are sad events. I am afraid, according to the initial reports, Dmitri was involved."

For the first time, Paul looked his fifty-six years. The son of a tsar was told no. What was happening to Russia?

Guiding Paul toward the door, the tsar said, "I pray to God that Dmitri will be found innocent."

As the door closed, the empress began to say something, and then a look from her husband stopped her.

The tsar truly felt sorry for his uncle. He wondered what the new regime his uncle had hinted at would do differently. He did not know. He did know he wished he were back at the front, where it was clear who the enemy was.

CHAPTER 28

Hotel Europe
The Stairwell

Platon observed the airy ambiance that was the Europe. He was never one for plush surroundings, but he had to admit that his son had chosen wisely his current home. Somehow, the revolving doors kept all the war's ugliness out, he noticed as he climbed down the Hotel Europe's main stairway.

The general had gone up to Zurin's room, to no avail. It was empty. Platon received a call from the palace stating that Ernie had arrived an hour ago but without Colonel Zurin. So, where was Zurin?

He pondered this as he reached the mezzanine level. Looking across the crowded lobby floor, the general saw someone he knew.

With a fatherly hint of disapproval, Platon stopped and said, "Mr. Jones, how do you do?"

"General," Malachi Jones replied, looking up, "so good to see you." Those words trailed off as he noticed the older man's changed appearance. What had happened to the robust man he remembered from only a few years ago?

"Have you seen Serge?" asked the general.

"Not in his room?"

"No. I just tried." Platon lied.

"Some things don't change," Malachi said with a grin.

"Sadly, no," the Russian said, laughing.

Finding his courage, "General Konstantin you are a man of honor, a man of your word. Why are you bartering a deal for peace with…?"

Cutting him off, "Young Jones, don't believe everything Sir George tells you."

"It's not just Sir George. Look for yourself on page four, sir," Jones said, handing the general his folded newspaper.

It was a small article headlined: "Peace by Christmas? We Shall See." The general was surprised the censors had allowed it to run.

"General Konstantin, everyone who wants to know realizes that you are the one brokering the peace. Your son once shared with me that you believe a man is known by the sum of his actions. Sir, I have taken that advice to heart, and recommend you do the same. We as a civilized world cannot allow the Kaiser to control Europe. It would be the beginning of another dark age. Russia must stay in the fight."

"Son, I am a soldier. And when I am given an order, it is my *duty* to fulfill that task to the best of my ability. I may not agree with the order, but that is absolutely irrelevant. I am but a tool in the service of His Royal Highness the Tsar."

"Sir," Jones replied as he grabbed his jacket and quoted from Disraeli: "*Duty cannot exist without faith.*" He disappeared toward the doors.

The general was not accustomed to verbal lashings, especially from a youth. But in his heart, he knew that Jones was right. As he walked outside and waved for his driver, Platon thought that the chains of service that bound him were growing too tight. He was so tired of the heavy price of doing his duty.

Jumping into his vehicle, he said curtly, "Driver, take me to the British Embassy at once."

Dmitri's Palace,
The Drawing Room

It was unlike Dmitri to show so much emotion. His father really must have gotten to him, Felix thought. Nonetheless, everything would be put right when Vlad took over. Everyone would find out Father Rasputin's dirty little secrets—except the one that involved Felix. By the end of the week, he and Dmitri would be national heroes for killing the beast. Walking into his room, he noticed smoke pouring out from a chair that faced his balcony.

"Who's there?" he said with disgust.

An uncomfortable silence returned his call. As he walked toward the chair, he feared that Dmitri's father was there. For some reason, the grand duke had always scared him. It was as if the old man's cool eyes could penetrate his lies.

"Enough games."

A feeling of dread engulfed him. What if it was Rasputin, back from the dead? Not possible, he told himself. He reached the chair. "Bimbo, what are you doing here?"

"You're right, son. Enough games. I want to know everything about the other night."

"I have already told you," Felix arrogantly replied. "I wasn't involved."

Bimbo eased back in the chair. "Really? Not involved, you say? Not involved in Vlad's plot to overthrow the tsar? I know it all, young Yusupov. So don't lie. I know that Vlad recruited you. And you recruited Purishkevich and Dmitri to assassinate Rasputin."

"You're insane."

"Am I? Vlad needed Nicholas to return from the protection of the front. In the last two months, he has replaced the commanders of the Imperial Guards with his cronies. Minister Protopopov has spoon-fed the empress false reports that everything was all right. And you tell me that I am insane."

The prince had a dumbfounded look on his face.

"And tonight, at ten o'clock, there will be an assault on the palace," Bimbo continued as he took another puff from his cigarette, "to liberate Russia from the ironclad grips of a fool."

"How do you know all of this?"

"I know much, but I want to know more. Tell me about Friday night."

"Everything?"

"Everything."

"All right, we shall have it your way." For the next twenty minutes, Felix shared all the gruesome details of Rasputin's final moments on earth with the duke.

When the prince finally finished, Bimbo repeated slowly the names of all who were involved. "The Grand Duke Dmitri, Senator Purishkevich, the princes Theodore and Nikita Mikhailovich, and a few others," he paused, "and of course, you." He knew Felix was not lying. "You bastard," he said as he rose from his seat and grabbed the prince by the lapels of his uniform. "How dare you involve my nephews in this!"

"They wanted to come."

"Shut up!"

"But Bimbo, you wanted to know. Perhaps you should focus more on your own family history," Felix said, smirking.

With an extraordinary amount of self-control, Nikolai said: "My family history is your family history, and for some reason, my niece Irina has given her heart to you. I would hate to be the one to tell her that her husband was guilty of having an affair." He enjoyed seeing the agony enter Felix's face.

"You wouldn't dare."

"Don't test me on this, son. The worst thing about it is that I think she would somehow understand—if you had been having it with another woman."

"Now we both know we can hold a secret."

"Yes, for the sake of my brother your secret is safe," Bimbo said. "But if there is any mention of my two nephews's involvement in all of this, your secret will be known, and to more than just my niece. Understood?"

"Understood."

As the door slammed closed, Felix whispered to himself, "Just survive the day." That might be harder than he had earlier thought.

Dmitri's Palace,
The Entryway

Still recovering from the lashings of one Mikhailovich, Felix nearly fainted when he saw Sandro climbing the steps. "Grand Duke Alexander," he said, attempting to grasp the situation, "what a pleasant surprise."

"Save your play acting for my daughter," the duke said, grabbing Felix by the arm. "I need a few moments with you."

"Sandro, please. I can explain everything."

"Oh, I am most certain you can explain. But I am only interested in the truth. I want to know why you thought it was in the best interest of my sons," he screamed as he held Felix by his lapels, "to involve them in this madness?"

Felix pulled free. "I warned them you wouldn't like it, but they did what the older generation only talks about—disposed of a beast that was tearing the country in two."

"You fool. Before he was just a drunkard with his hand out. Now, he is a martyr. By killing him, you gave him the power that he always wanted."

Felix's confidence eroded as he began to realize everything his father-in-law was saying was true. "But," he weakly offered, "we just wanted to save the empire."

"Felix, you are young and foolish. You know nothing of matters of state. If I were you, I would pray for the tsar to be lenient."

"I am a hero!"

"You're anything but," Sandro said, preparing to leave. "I will try to explain your actions to His Majesty."

As he left the palace, Sandro felt no better. Felix was a fool. Fabulously rich but still a fool. What worried the duke now was that his older brother's automobile was leaving the palace as he arrived. What was Bimbo up to?

The British Chancellery
Entrance Hall

The Russian general was greeted as if he were the German Kaiser himself until he reached the inner corridor of the British Embassy—until he found Benjy Bruce. "General Konstantin, we are honored," Benjy said before he was cut off.

"Take me to your master."

"As you wish, general. Follow me."

Walking through the corridor, the general reminded himself why he hated all things British. Every time the Russian army marched south toward Constantinople, the Brits fought them, claiming they needed to protect India from Russia.

Bruce attempted to cool the situation. "General, I read your book on your war in Manchuria. Fascinating tale. I am amazed you reached Port Arthur in one piece. A courageous feat that you must be extremely proud of."

"It was your war too, Bruce. Don't forget who sold the Japanese their battleships and big guns. With their new toys, they bombarded our outpost with deathly precision until all that was left was rubble."

"General, you don't believe the British government had anything to do with that, do you?"

Catching sight of Sir George in his study, he pushed past the young man, "Bruce, I have already answered that."

Seeing General Konstantin charging into his office, the ambassador thought to himself, be careful what you wish for, because it may be delivered to your door. Buchanan gave the general a toothy smile. He was perfectly calm; he had to be.

"General Konstantin, so good to see you," the diplomat said, attempting—and failing—to disarm Konstantin. He looked at Benjy. "Mr. Bruce, I think it may be best that I speak to our friend and trusted ally alone."

His aide gone, the Scot offered the general a seat. Platon just shook his head. His blood was up, and beginning to boil.

"Sir George, if you ever use my son again to meddle in affairs of state, you will be sorry, deathly sorry."

"General, accept my sincerest apologies. I knew of no other way. Call me an ultra pessimist, but I believe you Russians are trying to get out of this war," the old man said, completely composed. "Cigarette?"

"Mister Ambassador, as a Russian soldier, I have grown tired of Europe always standing in our way. My grandfather fought the French at Borodino, my father fought you and the French at Alma and Balaclava, and I was at Sha Ho River."

"Sha Ho River? I know in your mind you blame us, but we only provided Japan with arms to protect herself."

"You think I am a fool. Besides arming them with heavy guns, diplomats very like you warned the world not to come to our aid."

"General, please."

"Our entire Pacific fleet now lies at the bottom of the ocean just the way your government wanted it."

Buchanan knew Platon spoke the truth. Unofficially, the British had blockaded Admiral Rozhedstvensky's Baltic fleet by threatening the powers of the world not to offer port or passage to his grand armada. The British threatened the Germans with war if Germany provided the Russian convoy with coal. But the Kaiser told the British to go to hell and, somehow, the flotilla reached its goal.

"The riches of the Far East are still yours… for the moment. But someday, Sir George, those same heavy guns may rain down on you."

"Perhaps, general. But politicians are such-short term thinkers. This time, dear fellow, we have been placed on the same team."

"Really?" his voice said it all. "I have my doubts."

"The same team your son fought on until he was wounded."

"My son? Yes. You are right," he said with an icy glare. "I did not come here to discuss matters of current policy. On the contrary, I came here as a father. And if you wish to speak to me in the future on matters of policy, call my office. Understood?"

"Understood, general. I am thankful you are here. I needed some way to get a word with you."

"Still, that does not explain why you involved my son."

"That was a mistake, and it shall not happen again." He paused. "General, our two nations have had their differences, but today we are allies. Please treat us as such. If we must fight the Germans alone, we shall do so."

"That day may come, Ambassador."

"Not if you don't want it to."

"Ah, it is so simple for you British. You only give lip service to loyalty, to honor, but…" Platon stopped. "Good day, Mr. Ambassador. Remember what I said."

"I shall," Sir George replied with an icy stare, "And you do the same." As the door slammed in front of him, Sir George turned toward his window to once again look upon the Neva. Exhaling a cloud of smoke, he said, "Things could have gone better."

Bruce entered the room.

"Bruce—what did you think of the general's appearance?"

"He doesn't look good. But he remains intimidating."

"Yes he does. Do inquire about the good general's health. I would find it disturbing if the tsar selected General Konstantin, a Russian war hero, to negotiate the dishonorable terms of a separate peace if he were dying."

Bruce agreed. "I can call Grand Duke Nikolai?"

"No. Let's be a little more discreet. Try your friends at the hospital."

"Of course, Sir George."

"It appears Russia's going to hell and we with her."

With that, Sir George turned to stare out his window. What was happening here?

CHAPTER 29

Alexander's Palace
The Empress's Bedchamber

The empress needed to lie down after Grand Duke Paul's visit. It appeared to her that the entire royal family was attacking her. As she tossed and turned with in her bed, Alix could not get the thought of Rasputin's death out of her mind. It was as if she were plagued by the misery to come. Her friend and Russia's savior was gone. What would happen to Alexei? Who would restore him from the dead?

She sobbed into her pillow. "Why Lord, why?"

"Mama," a voice from her dreams answered, "it is not ours to ask."

"What?" she nervously asked as she rose from her bed, "Who's there?"

"Don't be afraid. I am not here to harm you," she heard as a ghostly image of Father Rasputin emerged from behind the curtains. "Just to warn you."

She fell to her knees. "No," she whimpered, "You cannot be gone."

He smiled. "Good woman, I am not."

"What? I don't understand."

"I know. And for now I must keep it that way."

"But why?"

"For your own safety. There is evilness that encircles you like a bad dream."

"I know. I can feel its hands around my throat, suffocating me."

"As can I," he declared with a grin. "Have courage, Mama, for the vultures are preparing to strike."

"Do you know who they are?"

"Members of the nobility. For one, Grand Duke Dmitri."

"But why?"

"He was tricked by Prince Felix to kill me. He was innocent. But now his hands too are stained with my blood."

"Felix is like all Petersburg," she hissed, "rich, ruthless, and incapable of anything decent."

"Sadly, the city has the same effect on the poor."

"What do you mean?" Rasputin was referring to his acts of drunkenness, extortion, and even rape. Alix had heard rumors of this side of Rasputin. But she did not want to believe it to be true.

"Yes, those reports were all true," he said, reading her mind. "Those, and much worse. I am a devil. I am a demon. I am sinful, whereas before I was holy, I was pure."

"Let light shine out of darkness,'" she said, quoting scripture.

"Even now, when the entire world sees the ugliness that is me, you somehow see the good. You amaze me." He walked toward the door. "Thank you for your kindness, even though I was not worthy of it."

"Priest, turn around," the empress commanded. "This I know, the light always devours the darkness. Stay faithful."

He bowed. "I am finding my way, Your Majesty."

As she awakened from her dream, she saw Anastasia hovering over her.

"Mama, why are you crying?" the daughter asked. "Papa's home."

"Tears of joy," she replied. "Tears of joy. Where's Papa?"

"Down the hall," Anastasia said, smiling. "He and Alexei are telling war stories."

"I see. Well then, let's go find them."

Ministry of the Interior, Protopopov's Office

Alexander Protopopov could not believe the morning report that was on his desk. Why had his men left the palace without more of a fight? But first, he wanted to give a certain general a piece of his mind.

He picked up the receiver. "Get me General Konstantin at once!"

After a moment, he heard: "This is General Konstantin speaking."

Platon had just got back from the British Embassy and his blood was still up.

"How dare you counter my direct orders!" the Minister barked.

"Good day Alexander. So good to hear from you," the general said as if he was greeting an old friend.

"I am Protopopov, the Minister of the Interior and technically your commander. You should address me as such."

"I know to whom I am speaking." The general's tone soured. "And, technically, Special Branch only answers to His Majesty."

"Now I know that is not true."

"Minister, do you really want to push this matter? The prince and duke are both secure and under my protection. That burden has been removed from you."

"That's the entire reason for this call."

"Minister Protopopov, I know the real reason for this call. If anything happens to either one of them under my custody, I shall hold you alone responsible."

"What? That's insane. I just don't like you stepping on my toes. That's all."

"Believe me, Minister. When I decide to step on your toes, you will feel it."

A troubling thought popped out of his mouth before he could stop it. "How is Rasputin going to respond to this?"

"What?" Platon asked, gathering his own thoughts, "Trust me Rasputin doesn't care."

"What?"

"He's dead. My men dragged his body out of the Neva this morning."

"Dead? Impossible."

"Yes, the last person you and your men had under your protection was found floating below the ice this morning near the Blue Bridge. It appears he was shot."

"But how is that possible? I spoke to him last night."

"Alexander, it's easy to get lost in an imaginary world, isn't it?"

"I," the minister stumbled with his words, "I...must go, General."

"Protopopov," Platon said feeling some sympathy for a man that was once a brilliant politician, "I will have one of my men drop off what I currently have within the hour. You need rest. Check yourself into the hospital...before you hurt yourself."

"Goodbye general." Protopopov already had tried the hospitals. "I appreciate your advice." As he ended the call, he began to cry. It had all seemed so real. Just then, he felt a cold and clammy hand on his shoulder followed by a strong scent of decay. Startled, he was too scared to scream. It was Rasputin. Who else would it be?

"My dear minister, you now know the truth and more importantly, so do I. You were the only one that held the power to demise my security detail."

"I—"

"Don't bother lying. I know it all now. I was a fool to trust you."

"Grisha, please don't hurt me."

Rasputin smiled, revealing black and broken teeth. "I won't. I will leave that to others."

"Then why torture me?"

"I couldn't resist," he said, walking toward the closet door.

"Where are you going?"

"Away from here. Though I will see you soon—sooner, than you think," the Siberian said as he broke into an amusing little laugh.

"But when?" he pleaded to the dead air drifting toward his coat closet. He understood that none of this was real. But he had to make sure. Grasping the doorknob with his trembling fingers, he prayed, "Please be in there. Please, be in there—for you must. Grisha?"

The door opened. The closet was empty except for a few articles of clothing. The minister was slipping into madness.

As he fell upon his knees, he cried out, "I am growing so tired of it all!" He was in over his head. His hand reached for his moustache. He began to rock back and forth on his knees. He was running out of time. The poor minister was losing his mind.

CHAPTER 30

Mathilda's Mansion
The Entrance Hall

As Mathilda descended her staircase, her thoughts drifted toward Serge. What was she doing? The boy was nearly half her age. But still, she was falling for him. It was more than his looks; last night she had danced again, not for others but for herself, and she could not recall the last time that had occurred. Certainly not in the last ten years, and because of that, this morning of mornings, she felt young. It had been a very long time since love had entered her heart. She had been the Grand Duke Andrew Vladimirovich's mistress for more years than she cared to count, but being with Serge brought back the joyful days she had spent with another young officer—one named Nicholas.

"Oh, to be his again," she whispered. The doorbell rang. Thinking it might be Sergei, she hurried down the steps to answer it herself. It was Grand Duke Andrew. He looked terrible.

"What's the occasion?" she asked as she escorted him into her drawing room, lighting a cigarette as they walked. Then she noted the alarm in his face. "Is something wrong with Vova?"

"No, our son is fine. My dear, for once the problem is not mine to fix," he said.

"It's too early in the day to speak in riddles. Just tell me what's the matter."

"I have wandered the streets all night."

"You look it. What's wrong?"

"Niki is in trouble," he said as he removed his greatcoat and tossed it on the floor. Andrew was still wearing his uniform from last night.

"What? The tsar has men to handle his problems."

"Not this one," the duke said. "Vlad is raising an army against him."

"That doesn't surprise me. Luckily, Nicholas is at headquarters surrounded by his most loyal legions. From there he will crush any rebellion."

"The tsar is in the capital."

"What?" questioned Mathilda, fear filling her voice.

"Yes. Rasputin was killed because my brother knew his death would force the emperor to return to the city."

"He's just declared the Manifesto earlier this week, Andrew. So, I am certain he is still at the front. Don't scare me like that."

"No, he arrived from headquarters early this morning. The empress requested him to return at once when Rasputin disappeared. She's scared. She thinks she's next."

"Wouldn't that be lovely," the ballerina dreamed. "Doesn't she realize that he is safest at the front?"

"This I know," the duke declared. "Rasputin was killed for this reason only. My brother knew the Siberian's death would force His Majesty to return to the city."

"But why?"

"The men loyal to him are all at the front. The imperial guards surrounding the palace are watered-down replacements. These replacement troops are all led by commanders loyal to Vlad. And, tonight, my brother plans on using those troops to storm the palace."

"Tonight. Impossible. His Majesty's personal envoy, the Cossacks, would never betray the tsar."

True, the duke thought, but he was sure Vlad had a plan for them. He always did. "I don't know, but we must warn the tsar as soon as possible."

"I will call him at once."

"I don't trust anyone around him. Not now. That's why we must go to the palace and warn him ourselves. That's why I'm here. He might not believe me, but he has always believed you."

Noticing his uniform for the first time, "Is that blood?" she asked.

"Yes. Last night, I watched Vlad kill a man."

"I don't understand."

"We don't have time for this. I will explain on the way to the palace." The duke grabbed his coat. "My car is parked outside. We must stop this madness from becoming reality."

Not dressed to travel, Mathilda said, "Give me five minutes."

"Okay, I will be waiting in the car."

Three minutes later, she emerged from the house wearing a mink. She saw Andrew's head through the back window of his car.

Stepping into the car, "Driver, take us to the Alexander Palace, at once."

"My apologies, ballerina absoluta, but this car is heading to Vladimir's Palace," said an ugly man wearing a black uniform. Belarus waved his service revolver at her to frighten her.

"What's this? Get that gun out of my face, boy." Mathilda managed as she pushed her weight towards the door. Opening it.

The lieutenant guarding Andrew responded by giving the ballerina a hard slap across the face. "Close the door."

As she grabbed her face, "Bastard."

"You idiot!" Belarus shouted back at his man, "Was that necessary? The general said don't harm her," as he looked at her bruised face he handed her his handkerchief that she refused. He tossed it to the floor. Then, nodded to his driver to move on. From the front rear mirror, "Lieutenant, you better pray that the general does not notice your handy work. I will leave it entirely to you to explain your actions."

In the backseat, Mathilda looked at Andrew. He was unconscious. She cried, "What did you do to him?"

"He's all right," the captain assured her, "though he is going to wake up with one hell of a bump on his head. Now," he added, glaring at Mathilda, "to the palace and no more tricks."

Veteran's Hospital, The Morgue

Sakulina, the nurse who stood before the thawing corpse, knew the ruined man lying on the table. He was a friend. Yes, Father Rasputin had sinned. She could recall the numerous times her quick feet had avoided his forceful passes, but what was different about that? Half the men wearing the cloth had done the same to her at one time or the other. But how could the state of the body before her be justified?

Father Rasputin's arms were pointing upward. She tried to move them down, but they were still frozen. She took a wet cloth and attempted to sponge his bloated and beaten face. But that did no good. The blood was as thick as dried mud, and debris from the river had engulfed his unruly hair and beard.

"Who do they think they are? Gods?" the nurse cried out as the doctor entered the room.

"In Russia, they are gods." The doctor saw that the body needed at least a day to thaw before the autopsy. "Sister, what's done is done. Let's worry about the ones we can save."

After the doctor left the room, she went back to wiping Rasputin's face. That was when she noticed his crucifix nearly welded to his chest. It carried an inscription: to save and to protect.

Bending over him, she recalled a comforting verse. "The cords of death entangled me, the anguish of the grave came upon me, and I was overcome by trouble and sorrow. Then I called on the name of the Lord, save me!" As she turned off the light, she called out, "Lord save us all." At that moment she bumped into a tall man fiddling with his moustache. "I am sorry. No one is allowed back here."

"I know. So leave us," he said.

Vlad's Palace, View Overlooking the Neva

Sitting in the luxurious confines of the Vladimir Palace, Andrew and the mother of his child stared out the window. How could this possibly be happening, they both wondered.

In the other room, they heard voices arguing. "This is all getting a little too melodramatic for my taste," cried the voice of an older man.

"This changes nothing, Nikolai. They shall be released tomorrow, at the latest—after Niki's abdication."

"Much can happen in a period of a day."

"Yes. There is much to do before then, my friend. Much indeed," Vlad replied, "but I am doing it."

"All right, all right. What of tonight?"

"All is set in place. My commanders are aware what they must do. And they shall not fail us."

"Make certain of it. There is still time to gather more forces. I know of other regiments that would be open to revolt. Two more days and it could be arranged."

"We have a sufficient force to handle the palace guards."

"My only concern is His Majesty's Cossacks. Perhaps we can order them on maneuvers for the evening," Bimbo said. "We can use the upcoming conference as a ploy to check security in the city."

"No," replied Vlad. "That will only increase suspicion." He whispered in Bimbo's ear, "I have my men liberating Andrew's wine cellar. Late this afternoon, truckloads filled with the finest cases of wine and vodka will be delivered to the Cossack's barracks, compliments of the tsar, for services rendered."

"Andrew is going to kill you when he finds out."

235

"I know. But by then, I shall be the new tsar. What kind of host would I be if I didn't provide my men with wine and women?"

"Women?"

"Questionable women."

"Those are the best ones," laughed the historian.

"They will arrive after dark. I even commissioned a small gypsy band to perform in their barracks. Trust me. When they wake up in the morning with their heads near their knees, they shall be swearing their loyalty to a new tsar."

"It seems you have thought of everything."

"I have," Vlad boasted, thinking of his third wave.

"Good," the historian replied. "Sir George assures me that King George will back any government willing to stay in the fight."

"Now, we just need more local support," said Vlad, "I have most of St. Petersburg's key officials falling in with us."

"More good news… though, I still believe we need more men to secure the palace." Nikolai knew the entire plan counted on capturing the tsar at the palace.

"Nonsense. We shall strike the palace like lightning. Two full regiments will be enough. Anymore and I would be afraid of leaks."

"Very well. What about your brother Andrew and Mademoiselle Kschessinska?"

"That is disappointing," Vladimir said. "Unfortunately, he went to tell his mistress of our little plot."

"Are you certain that he has told no one else?"

"Yes, quite. I have had my men follow him constantly since Saturday."

"Good. Then no harm done." But as the pair went into the next room, Bimbo noticed the ballerina's black eye. "Vlad, was this necessary?"

Vlad noticed the injury for the first time and became enraged. "Who did this?" An underling jumped to attention, quivering.

"Your Excellency, she gave me no choice. Mademoiselle Kschessinska attempted to escape."

"Come here!"

Vladimir slapped him hard with the back of his hand. It took all the lieutenant's strength to stay on his feet.

"Sir," he said, blood trickling down his cheek, "it shall never happen again."

"Of course, she attempted to escape, you fool. She's a fighter." With that, he gently brushed her hair away from her face. "But she is also a lady. I shall not warn you again. She is my guest. I apologize, Mademoiselle. A famous ballerina of the Imperial Theatre is a national treasure and should be treated that way."

"Vlad, how can you be your father's son?" she said coldly. The Grand Duke Vladimir had been a champion of the arts. "Your father was a gentleman. Sadly, I cannot say the same for you."

He laughed. "Mademoiselle Kschessinska, if I were not a gentleman," he whispered into her ear, "you would not be here." It would have been much easier to eliminate her, but he could not kill the mother of Andrew's bastard child.

"Bimbo," the ballerina said, "I am shocked at your involvement. I thought you were smarter than that."

"Mademoiselle, you're a lady of the stage, and no stranger to drama," he replied. "I have grown tired of watching the empire that my grandfather helped create being ripped to pieces by the incapable hands of a buffoon. As a Russian, it is my duty to free him of that responsibility."

"Is your brother aware of your treason?"

"Sandro has his own problems," Vlad interrupted. The unexpected involvement of the duke's sons in Rasputin's death had already become a hard point, but that would be over tomorrow.

Vlad then removed his brother's gag. "Why, Andrew? Why did you try to betray me? Your own brother. The empire is crumbling before us. I am the only man left who can save it. Can't you see that?"

"No, brother, I can't. You have always been a bully, and Russia does not need any more bullies."

"Your opinion is noted," Nikolai said.

"So, brother," Andrew said, "what shall you do with me?"

"What I have always done. I shall keep both eyes firmly on you," the duke said as he walked toward the captain of the guards. "Take them both to the cottage. And make certain nothing happens to them, or this time it will be your head."

Bimbo and Vlad moved to the adjacent room. It had a splendid view of the river. "Wouldn't it be wiser to leave them in the palace under lock and key?" Nikolai asked.

"No. If anything goes wrong, my brother's mistress would be an excellent bargaining chip."

"If anything goes wrong, we are dead."

"Niki would never let anything happen to his first love. He still loves her, and always has."

Nikolai nodded. "Just make sure she doesn't escape. Andrew's cottage is in Nicholas's backyard."

"Don't worry. This time tomorrow, everything will be put straight."

"Or, this time tomorrow we shall both be dead," Bimbo said, stealing Vlad's favorite line. "Remember, Vlad," Bimbo repeated what Vlad had said the other night, "to rule Russia, you must be ruthless. And today, you must be ruthless."

The general nodded. "This I already know."

CHAPTER 31

Alexander's Palace
The Mauve Room

The minister played with the points of his moustache as he paced the room, waiting for the empress. It had taken him a while to recover from seeing Rasputin's corpse, but a liter of vodka seemed to help. Like a raging storm, the empress entered the room.

"So, you failed."

"Yes, Your Majesty," he humbly replied. "Father Rasputin's corpse was found early this morning in the Little Neva."

"Are you certain?"

"His daughters identified the body."

"Where is he?"

"Close. General Konstantin's men took the father's remains to the Tchesma Veterans Hospital. We can plan a visit for tomorrow, if you wish." He hoped Vlad would put her next to Rasputin that evening.

"Today. Arrange it."

"Of course, Your Majesty. As you wish."

"What of the grand dukes?"

"Nothing new, Your Grace. Prince Felix and the Grand Duke Dmitri are still under house arrest."

"And Vlad?"

"No word yet, Your Majesty. My men are working on it."

"Really? Protopopov, look at me as you lie to me."

"Lie? I would never do such a thing. On my sacred honor, I am your most loyal subject." Vlad now was his only chance of survival, and he couldn't even trust him.

"Coming from a twisted politician that means a great deal. No matter. I suppose that will have to do until I find out their involvement myself," she said, plopping down into her chair.

He whispered to himself as he was escorted out of the room. "You will find out sooner than you hoped. Pleasant dreams, Your Majesty." Perhaps, it would be wise of him to stay nearby this evening. He could pay a visit to an old friend, one who was good and dead.

Alexander's Palace, The Inner Chamber

It was only mid-afternoon, but it had already been a long day for the emperor. As he walked down the hallway toward his private study, he heard a woman crying. As he slowly opened the door, he saw his wife sitting in the Mauve Room in her favorite easy chair.

The Minister of the Interior had just left.

Nicholas pondered if she truly loved him anymore. At the front, he had heard rumors of an alleged affair between his wife and Rasputin, but he had not believed it possible until now.

"Would you weep for me?"

The empress noticed her husband for the first time. "What?"

"Would you weep for me as deeply?"

"He's dead!"

"Yes, he is," he said, grabbing her. "Why are you crying? Are the rumors true? Would you have preferred that it was me? Were the two of you having an affair?"

"Why are you saying such things?" A look of disbelief passed over her face. "Not you too! I cannot bear that."

"Then, tell me," he pleaded, kneeling at her feet, "Please. I beg you."

Patting his head, she gave a motherly smile. "It is not how you think. At least, not what others would like you to think."

"Then what? I must know."

"It's hard to put into words."

"Did you love him?"

"I did."

"More than me?"

"No, my dear. How could that be?"

"But you said you loved him."

"And I answered you honestly," she said, staring into his kind eyes. "I loved Grigory because he is a man of God, a holy man. Through his Grace, the Lord saved our son."

She paused for a moment to gather her thoughts.

"Do you remember your hunting trip at Yalta?"

How could he ever forget that awful summer? "The time when Alexei fell ill."

"Everyone thought he would not survive the week."

"Yes," he said, somberly, "I remember." He had sat before his son's bed and watched him slowly fade away. He had never felt so powerless in his life.

"I shall always remember that night when our little boy asked me, 'Momma when I'm dead, will there be no more pain?' That night nearly broke me. But instead, I began to pray. I prayed for the Lord to save my baby. The following day Father Grigory told me all would be all right and to have faith, for he was the Lord's noble messenger. Do you understand?"

"No."

"When you asked me if I loved him, I do," she paused. "I did. The love I hold for him is of a mother whose child he saved. Nothing more."

Guilt began to replace the hate in him. How could he have been so foolish? For deep within him, he held the same love for the Siberian.

She continued: "For over twenty years, I have been a stranger here, a person no one trusted or loved. The only love I found in this cold, dreary place was yours, and the family we made."

"I am so sorry, Sunny," he said.

"Shhh." She put her finger to his lips. "My one and only love, don't allow them to take your love from me. They can despise me all they want, for my heart has grown cold. But don't allow them to strip away our love, for what am I without you?"

"Please forgive me for ever doubting you. I am so tired of this. I feel so old. I never wanted to be tsar."

"I know. But a tsar you are."

He grinned. "Wouldn't it be nice to return to our quiet little life?"

"The war has robbed it from us." She almost shared her plan for peace with him, but for some reason, she didn't. Later, with Ernie's help, they would return to those pleasant days before the war.

The Financial District, Burmin's Apartment

Renko sat alone in a dark room, enjoying a few minutes of silence, before he heard a key enter the lock. He was in Burmin's stately apartment located near Petersburg's financial district.

Burmin entered shouldered by two other men, who had been running his errands all day long. "You guys are worthless. Your laziness could have jeopardized my mission." The German spy was still complaining about yesterday's encounter with the Brits. Noticing the inspector, "Renko, what are you doing here?"

"Leave us."

The agents immediately shut the door.

"What's going on? I thought we were supposed to meet later?"

"Plans have changed."

"Really, how so?" Nervously, he lit his cigarette, "The tsar hasn't changed his mind?"

"No. There will be a treaty."

"Good," Peter said as he exhaled a large cloud of smoke. "You scared me for a moment."

"Part of my nature," Renko said as he rose from his seat. "Grab your things. You are no longer safe here."

"So, you have heard about Sir George?"

"Yes, that's why I'm here. The British are getting too close."

"They are scared," the gambler said as he walked towards his desk.

"They should be."

"Renko, that arrogant bastard is going to crap his pants when he finds out." Peter began stuffing a bag with money and his personal papers. "I only wish I could see his smug face when he learns..." That's when he noticed Renko raise his revolver.

"I'm afraid that's impossible." With that, he fired two shots into Peter's chest. The force threw him hard against the study's wall.

Stunned, all he could manage was, "Why?" as he coughed up blood.

"You are no longer needed."

The inspector felt no guilt. Peter played too close to the flame. Instantly, the agents stationed outside came through the door with their firearms in hand. They saw Burmin lying dead on the floor. They weren't surprised or sad.

"Inspector, is everything all right?"

"Yes. Just one less traitor to deal with," the inspector declared as he stood over the spy's lifeless body. "Make certain no one ever finds him."

"Yes sir."

Renko wandered out the front door of Peter's apartment. Across the street Jones and two other men sat in a parked car.

Jones didn't like it. "Who's that?" They were too far away to have heard the shots a minute ago but he sensed that something was up.

"Renko. He's a member of the tsar's secret police," replied the English agent sitting in the passenger seat, as they saw him walk towards his car. "Damn, he knows we are here," he said, as he pushed his hat over his face.

Jones rolled down his window and stuck out his melon-sized head. "Why is a member of His Majesty's Secret Police protecting a known German spy?" the Welshman asked in Russian.

"Perhaps you have not noticed. This is not London Mr. Jones," he said in textbook English as the inspector took the time to light a cigarette. "Petersburg is a cold place especially for tourists. Good day."

With that, he disappeared as he turned the corner. "Splendid," whispered the agent from the backseat. "Renko handles all General Konstantin's dirty work. If we see Burmin again, it would be a bloody miracle."

CHAPTER 32

Dmitri's Palace
The Ward

After wandering through St. Petersburg's crowded streets, Serge found himself in a large ballroom transformed long ago into a hospital ward. To him, it was an odd sight. The brass beds filled with bandaged and wounded men that lined the room were not what bothered him. It was far too late in the war not to realize that it was a bloody business. No, what seemed to him surreal was the location, the grand ballroom of Dmitri's palace. Underneath two massive chandeliers of glittering light lay the fallen, rows upon rows of them. For many, it would be their first and last glimpse into the lifestyle of the privileged.

He had looked for Mathilda all day and called her home obsessively. But her housekeeper responded with the same statement each time: "I am sorry, Prince Konstantin, but Mademoiselle Kschessinska is not presently in."

Now he asked one of the nurses, and received roughly the same answer. He had waited to check the hospital until last. He had a good reason for that decision, and it was now approaching him.

"Felix. I was hoping not to run into you."

"But why? My mere presence makes you more interesting," he teased.

Serge was in no mood for banter. "Have you seen Mathilda?"

"Mathilda?" he asked, his grin widening. "What do you want with her?"

"Why must you be this way?"

"It's obvious. I despise you."

"But why?"

"That uniform," he paused. "You look just like my father when he was young. He too was a member of the elite Chevalier Guards. Hell, he's the one who draped that ridiculous piece of metal on you. And don't give me that look. I have seen that look all my life."

"What?"

"The loathing look one gives out of pity. So you can just go to hell."

"Felix, I just want to know if—"

"I have not seen Andy's whore." Inside, he told himself that she was too good for the likes of Serge or, for that matter, himself.

Serge grabbed him by his jacket's lapels. "She is not anyone's whore!"

Once again, Felix's eyes fell upon his cousin's medal, particularly the image of St. George slaying the dragon. "Pretty. What dragons did you have to slay to receive this piece of tin?"

Serge shook his head. "You never fought. So, you would not understand. Why are you so full of hate? You have everything a man could ever wish for."

"Not everything, Serge."

"What do you lack, Felix?"

"Poor Serge, you don't realize that we live in a place where the dragons always win," he chuckled.

Tired of Felix's games, Serge turned and said, "*Dasvidania,* (Good bye), cousin."

Well out of earshot, Felix recalled his earlier conversation with Bimbo and whispered, "Poor Serge, you're about to be devoured by a dragon, and you don't even know it."

The Palace Grounds,
Vlad's Cottage

Bound back to back, the duke and the ballerina pondered their situation.

They were in a cellar surrounded by cases of wine.

"Any idea where we are?" Mathilda asked.

"Yes. We are in my cottage's wine cellar."

"What! We are within the palace grounds," she said.

"Just east of the stables," the duke somberly replied, "a few minutes ride from the palace." They were both quiet for a moment with their own thoughts. That was until the duke asked. "What time do you think it is?"

"I haven't a clue." The cellar's windows were covered in dust but it was obvious the hour was growing late.

"It must be after four. The sun's already set," Andrew said, trying to loosen his binds without much luck. "It's pretty bold of them to bring us here." He thought of his brother's plan. "Tonight, within the palace gates, Vlad will amass an army three to four thousand strong, all members of His Majesty's Imperial Life Guards." At that moment, a key was placed in the locked door. Heavy steps echo down the cobblestone floor.

"Thanks for your hospitality, brother," Grand Duke Vladimir said, pointing to his men which cases they should take.

"A little early for a celebration party, brother."

"Oh, they're not for me," he replied as he rested his boot on the edge of a neighboring box. "I would have chosen a better vintage. How are your restraints?"

"Now Vlad," Mathilda cried. "There is still time to avoid all of this."

"Mademoiselle, you are beautiful, but not very bright. I have waited my entire life for this moment. I am willing to sacrifice anything for it."

"Even your very life?" she asked.

"*Da*," he said, turning back toward the door. "You should be happy, Andrew. By tomorrow, you will be one of my new provincial governors in a place far away from here."

"You're not the tsar yet."

"I will be soon," Vlad said as he headed up the steps.

"God speed brother!" Andrew shouted as his brother reached the top of the stairs. "I am certain you have a most *excellent* plan!"

Vlad felt his face redden with anger as he closed the door behind him. Andrew always knew what to say to get under his skin.

To the guard he said, "Make certain Mademoiselle Kschessinska is prepared to travel by nine o'clock."

"And your brother, General?"

"No harm must come to him, understand. He will feel better about all this in the morning."

With that the cellar door closed, followed by the heavy sound of a bolt falling into place.

Alexander's Palace, The Dining Room

The dining room was too quiet as the emperor entered. "Where are the children?" he asked.

"They have already eaten," Alexandra said.

"Already eaten? But it's my first night home." At first he thought she was being romantic, then he noticed the table was set for three. "Who is this mystery guest? My dear mother?" he asked as he began to laugh.

"No, Your Majesty," the grand duke of Hesse-Darmstadt said as he entered the room and gave a formal bow. "I am afraid you are going to have to settle for me."

Dumbfounded, "Ernie, what in God's name are you doing here?" the tsar asked, looking at his wife.

"I am on a diplomatic mission of incredible importance," he said, chuckling nervously. "I am afraid my dear sister has, without your authority, begun negotiations with our cousin Willy."

"What?"

The empress turned beet red. "It is an offer of peace."

"Lies!" the tsar cried out.

"No, Your Majesty," Ernie said. "Right or wrong, my sister has proposed terms for a separate peace that she never thought Willy would accept."

Nicholas reached for his wine glass. "Well, only for the sake of being a good host, let's hear them."

"All currently occupied land, including Poland, returned to Russia."

"All of Poland?" he asked, giving strength to the word all.

"It is true," the empress said. "I saw the message myself."

"What else?" The tsar was irked by his wife's involvement.

"The Kaiser knows that the French and the British will never allow you the possession of Constantinople, even though publicly they have promised it. Within these terms of a separate peace, the Kaiser offers you the ability to finally liberate the fallen Christian city."

"How is that?"

"A separate peace with Germany will allow your army to march south. The battle for Europe was never meant to be your concern. His Majesty respects you, and wants to give you the opportunity to choose your own fate."

"And when does my cousin plan this armistice to take effect?"

"The sooner the better."

The tsar laughed. "Of course. With a stroke of a pen, his eastern front would grow silent, freeing up over a million of his crack troops."

"*Ja*. That is true." Ernie knew what was next.

"By spring, those forces would reinforce the western front, upsetting the current stalemate."

"*Ja*, but what have your allies done for you? One of their ambassadors, Sir George, is currently mingling with revolutionaries. Niki, these are generous terms. They will allow you to recapture a city that you have always dreamed of. They give you a reprieve, time to get your *own* house in order." Ernie thought of what his sources had told him about Vlad.

"I shall think about it," the tsar said. "Thank you, Ernie. It seems, however, I have lost my appetite."

He looked at his wife. She rushed to him.

"Niki," Alix almost squeaked, "it is the only way out of this dilemma. They long for peace, just like us. I wanted to get it all in place before your return as I knew it would be unpleasant for you."

"Unpleasant? What I find so unpleasant is your involvement in all of this."

"Ernie," she pleaded. "Tell him."

"Alix, I think it is best for the two of you to be alone," he said, heading for the door.

"Thank you, Ernie," the emperor said. "Your terms are generous, and I shall consider them. You shall have my answer in the morning."

The grand duke bowed and made his exit.

As the door closed, he could hear his sister cry, "I'm sorry."

"Who knows of this?"

"Just General Konstantin, he helped arrange everything."

"Konstantin, he is a man of honor and would never…" the tsar stopped there. From her expression, he knew he had been deceived. "Alix what have you done?"

Sandro's Palace,
The Study

In the safe confines of his brother's palace, the Grand Duke Nikolai Mikhailovich was in a reflective mood. His heart was heavy with the involvement of his two nephews in the Rasputin affair. It was a night to forget, he thought, until his brother entered the room. "Sandro, my dear brother! Sit with me this evening and we can recall the sun-filled days of our youths," the historian said as he gazed out of a nearby window.

"I wish I could," he said, smiling as he removed something from one of his cases. "Perhaps tomorrow." He wanted to know about his brother's visit with Felix, but other matters were more pressing, especially his coming audience with the tsar. Anyway, Nikolai appeared half-drunk already. He would be asleep within the hour.

"No, tonight. Stay with me. I liberated a fine brandy from your cellar, and I must admit it is divine. I am thinking about fetching another."

"What is mine," he said, rolling up a large document, "is yours, Nikolai. Enjoy your brandy and your evening. I must go speak with the tsar."

"Niki?" A sick feeling overcame Bimbo. "You can't go to the palace tonight!"

"I am afraid I must. You are free to come if you wish."

"Go tomorrow," he said, the liquor already clouding his thinking. "The fog is too heavy."

"If I wait for the weather to improve," gathering the last of his things, "I will be here until summer. Brother, come with me, but make certain you bring that bottle. I might need it after I speak with our cousin."

"I can't. I have grown tired of warning the weak." The statement took Sandro aback.

"Brother, what! Would you prefer to let the events unfold as they are? To not even try to correct them?"

"They are beyond correction, my dear brother," he said, taking another swig from his glass. "Russia needs a shot of good old-fashioned ruthlessness."

"Vlad?"

"Why are you being so difficult? He is the spitting image of Tsar Alexander III, the same emperor you have always praised. He is the only one who can lead us away from the abyss."

"Away from—dear brother, he is the abyss. He will return Russia to the dark ages."

"Perhaps that is exactly what is required," Bimbo said as he finished his drink.

"Brother, you're drunk. We will begin this discussion again tomorrow. And, I shall show you that there is still hope for Niki."

"There is only one way—the use of sheer, unbridled power."

"Perhaps in the past," Sandro said, holding his scroll tightly. "But modern Russia shall be free to choose her own course."

Nikolai laughed. "Sandro, you are such a wonderful dreamer. Good luck. Give the tsar my regards."

"I haven't given up on you, brother," Sandro called out as he left. "We will continue this discussion in the morning."

"By then, only hatred will replace the love you felt for me," Nikolai whispered as he refilled his glass. "Be careful, brother, for you have no idea what awaits you."

Alexander Palace,
The Rotunda

As Platon emerged from his staff car, he noticed someone moving to the far left of him, near the palace's west wing. His instincts told him to follow him, which of course he did. He hoped it was Zurin, but he somehow knew it wasn't.

The four guardsmen at the entryway watched the general quickly disappear into a lingering fog that covered the palace grounds. One by one they looked at one another. They knew better than to ask why.

Quickly, the old soldier gained on the cloaked figure, as he appeared to stop to light a smoke. As the match ignited the stranger's face, Konstantin wasn't shocked at who it was.

"Ernie, enjoying your stay?"

"What?" the German duke searched until he found the person attached to the mysterious voice.

Seeing him materialize from the fog, "General Konstantin, how good of you to join me."

"Well, I suppose tonight is a historic night."

"We shall see." The German was doubtful after his recent visit with Nicholas.

"What do you mean?"

Looking down to hide his displeasure, the German spoke of his sister's deception. "I am afraid my darling little sister orchestrated this 'historic night' without her husband's approval."

"What!" The general was dumbfounded. "But everything I received had His Majesty's signature?"

"Forged, most likely."

"Forged?" he did not want to believe it. Then, it all seemed to make sense. "What have I done?"

"Only what you were told."

"Yes, like a trained dog."

"General, I just want to assure you that I knew nothing of this. In fact, I was there when my brother-in-law found out."

"And?"

"I have never seen him so hurt."

"What was she thinking?"

"I know. It's horrible."

"It's worse than that," he said thinking of Burmin.

"I suppose we are all thinking of a way to end this madness. Peace is possible. The Kaiser's terms are genuine."

Giving him a hard look, "Yes, and too generous."

"I agree. But his fight was never with you." Rationalizing it, "Blame the British for boxing us in."

Platon sighed. "The British, the universal enemy. What next?"

"Nicholas wants us to discuss it after his meeting with Alexander. I figured I would take advantage of the fog, and go for a walk."

"Don't wander off too far. You are liable to get yourself lost."

"I know. It wouldn't be good for me to wander into any Petersburg bar."

"No, it wouldn't."

Laughing as he thought of his earlier conversation with Serge, "Well then, tomorrow I leave for home. And tonight, the tsar holds the hopes of peace by a very fine thread."

Together, they looked upon one another and hoped for the best. Platon glanced over at the palace's beckoning light, "Enjoy your walk Ernie."

"I shall."

With that, the German disappeared into a curtain of fog.

CHAPTER 33

Sandro's Palace
The Study

As Serge entered Sandro's study, he noticed Bimbo slouched over in his chair.

"Bimbo, are you all right?"

The historian stirred, slurring his words. "Of course I am all right. A better question would be, are you?" He looked at the young man and laughed. "You're so young and honorable, Sergei."

"No, I am not. And I haven't been for some time now."

Nikolai continued to chuckle until he started to choke.

"Bimbo, what's so funny?" Serge asked.

Then, the duke stopped his giggling and said, "You're funny."

"Me? How so?"

"Because," he said, reaching to grasp Serge's medal, "the Order of St. George Cross is given only to the brave."

"Yes." Serge was a little defensive about his award, especially since Felix pawed at it.

Nikolai fingered the medal like a cheap piece of tin. "For service and valor. Valor. Young Konstantin, do you realize how ironic it is that you wear that cross?"

"I received this honor in battle. Not only because I am my father's son."

"An act of bravery all its own, young Konstantin."

"Nikolai, what can you tell me? I am waiting and willing to be enlightened by your historical perspective."

"Oh Serge," fishing out his watch, "in due time. I am fully confident that I shall impress you. Though at the very worst it shall help us pass the time. That's one of the great benefits of being a historian; you know so very much but accomplish so very little."

Serge grabbed the bottle. "You're drunk."

The grand duke returned the timepiece to his pocket. "And you are a fool! Don't!" he hissed. "I will tell you, child, when I have had enough. That's the trouble with men of your age. They believe they know it all. In reality, they know so very little, but God shows his twisted humor by rewarding their arrogance and utter weakness of mind with sound bodies. Don't you find that ironic?"

Serge grabbed Bimbo's arm. "Perhaps, it's time to call it a night."

"Let go of me. I don't deserve your pity."

"Have it your way uncle," the prince replied as he brought his fingers toward his medal. "Tell me about the significance of the cross."

"The cross," Bimbo said, clearing his throat, "is a symbol of good conquering evil."

"That I already knew."

Bimbo chuckled. "As I was saying, you are too young to know anything at all. I advise you to just shut up and listen, and perhaps you may learn something, and actually comprehend its meaning. The emblem at the center is St. George slaying the great dragon."

Serge wasn't in any mood for a lecture.

"It first appeared in Russia over three hundred years ago, and it is even older than that. Throughout the years the dragon was many things but he always represented evil. What I find so ironic, Sergei, is that the great dragon after all these years has become us. A noble idea transformed into a brutal reality."

"What?" he replied, thinking of the discussion he had had the other day with Dmitri. "Bimbo, sadly I am not nearly as drunk as I need to be for this conversation. Thanks for the talk but I have got to go." He patted the old man on his bald scalp as if he were a baby boy getting ready for bed. "You just tell Sandro that I was here."

"You don't understand." Bimbo viciously slammed down his drink. "My dear brother Sandro won't be coming back."

"What? Where did he go? Not back to the front?"

"The front? Yes, he left for the front," he said as he pulled out his pocket watch once again, "a little more than an hour ago."

"How can that be? He said he was staying in the capital until he had an opportunity to speak to the tsar."

"I told you, he went to the front," Nikolai said. He still could not believe he had let his own brother go to the palace. But what other option did he have?

"I don't understand."

"You wouldn't. You see, at this point in time, the Russian empire has two choices: a revolution from above," he said as he pointed toward the ceiling, "or—" as he pointed to the floor.

Serge could not believe his ears. Was his uncle talking about a palace coup? Could he somehow be supporting Vlad? "What are you talking about?"

"My gallant dreamer. Can't you already see what is already laid so plainly in front of you? For once, look beyond the tip of your own nose. Can't you see that history is being made this evening?"

"History?"

"Yes, tonight Russia will finally be freed from the chains of mediocrity."

"What? Vlad's troops are striking tonight?"

"Yes."

Serge rose. "I must warn His Majesty."

"It's too late. Too late for them both."

He grabbed Bimbo. "Where's Sandro?"

"At the palace—surrounded by three of Vlad's crack regiments."

"No! You did not let him go there. Not when you knew that he was walking into a trap."

"Yes. The continuous invasion from the dark forces must be stopped! At all costs, even my own brother. The rebirth of Russia depends on it."

"You're a traitor to everything that you once believed in. I can't believe you once wore this same uniform. Remember the Imperial Guard's motto: faith, honor, and loyalty. Are they but words to you?"

"*Da*, just meaningless words. I have lost my faith in the current cause. I am too old to be honorable, too wise to be loyal. But I shouldn't be so hard on myself. Look at you, part of an obedient generation of great martyrs like St. George."

The prince no longer listened. He was heading for the door.

"You ever wonder what the tsar wears around his throat?" Bimbo screamed. "Your youth!" As he did, he fell out of his chair like a white albatross falling into a deep sea of blue. Serge was already gone, headed for the only man he thought could help him—his father.

A Silent Night No More—Sixty Hours Ago

L eft for dead, Father Grigory Rasputin, a Siberian priest yet never ordained, slowly worked his way out of tiny back exit that bordered the outer barrier of the Moika Palace, the regal home of one of Russia's most influential families the Yusupovs. For the moment, he was free. Though, Rasputin knew if he did not move faster away from his captors, mainly Prince Felix, his freedom would be short lived.

So, disheveled by a day of drinking, Rasputin pressed on as he slid his slouched over frame down the snow-covered steps. The steps lead to a gated courtyard facing the iced over

River Moika, one of the many canals that geometrically sliced up the Venice-inspired capital of St. Petersburg. As the priest traveled through a patch of light pouring out of a tall nearby window, he thought he heard music coming from within. Someone was playing the phonograph quite loudly. Something odd and in English, the canned noise referred to *a Yankee Doodle Dandy*. The strange tune only added to strangeness of the moment.

Peering up towards its source, Rasputin felt the palace lights beckoned him in. He resisted its pull and pushed on, inspecting the house once more with a backward glance. The soft beam flickered off his large, doll-like eyes now void of mercy. Cold and coatless he passed through the patch of snow capturing his full look: black velvet trousers tucked into his knee-high matching leather boots, a torn silk tunic smeared in blood, and held together by a raspberry-color slash. His savagely long black beard and black hair mixed poorly with the costly garments and gave him the twisted appearance of a madman attempting to flee an asylum by wearing his doctor's discarded clothes.

At forty-seven, Father Rasputin remained many things—a liar, a mystic, a drunkard, a womanizer yet still he thought of himself only as a generous healer. And that was the only reason he had the empress's ear. Years ago, he had been the only one in the eyes of Her Majesty who was able to save her son Alexei from what seemed to be a certain death. Since then, the 'good father' has been incapable of doing a wrong. Though, his close ties to Empress Alexandra enraged the Russian Royal Court and resulted in the steady flow of blood presently dripping down his back.

Looking up from freshly fallen snow, the father's infamously large, lifeless eyes had scanned the surrounding grounds for the easiest possible route of escape—in was a five-foot high black metal gate. He smiled revealing from his bearded lips, dark, jaded teeth. Rasputin was a hard man to kill.

An earlier evening storm coated everything in his view with a fine white powder. As the crunching of snow filled his head, he thought how beautifully it all had appeared once.

St. Petersburg had been willed into existence by the grandiose outlook of one tsar who wanted a possible future for this poor, backward country. That past tsar was Russia's Peter the Great. Tsar Peter had wished to build a glimmering new capital, to be the envy of all things large and beautiful, for his empire may have been poor but it was vast, covering nearly one-sixth of the globe.

It was to be Peter's showpiece city to the world. The only problem was Peter chose a most inhabitable place to put it. The climate was terrible. At frozen northern exposure of Tsar Peter's empire, the city nestled on the chilly banks of the Gulf of Finland. It was home of marshes, and sink-pools in the summer, and bitter cold winter and bad weather for the majority of the year.

Militarily, and in theory, it was a brilliant move, forever severing Sweden's complete control of the Baltic Sea by establishing a capital fortress touching the outreached hands of Sweden's Charles the XII.

Significantly closer to the north pole than Moscow, St. Petersburg was a place of onion-shaped domes topping red-stone cathedrals, mammoth pastel-colored palaces of marble and rare rocks, large bronze monuments of Russia's great soldiers and conquerors, its waterways resemble those of Venice, rich-looking government buildings commissioned by former tsars and empresses, in all, architecture to be envied. This backdrop dotted the landscape of a handful of inserting islands. Thoroughly planned out and crafted, it was a place for the heart of an expanding empire.

So, where else would a vulgar priest from Siberia come to roam in the pursuit of wealth and power? For every conceived notion, good or bad, could be fulfilled here. Though, being new to all this no one told the 'good' father how tightly the old cling to all that's precious and new.

"Stupid me," a frozen cold of steam escaped from his wine-stained lips. "This is what I get for thinking with my penis."

After this remark, as if, on queue, a tidal wave of brilliant light flooded the courtyard when a roly-poly man waving a revolver emerged through the blinding light. It was the Senator Vladimir Purishkevich a religious extremist only a year younger than Father Rasputin. The senator considered Tsar Nicholas as 'God's Emissary' to the Russian Orthodox Church, the same church Rasputin was currently making a mockery of with his crude acts of behavior.

Senator Purishkevich, obviously inebriated, waddled into the open courtyard, stopped, aimed his piece through fogged glasses and fired two shots into the night. They both missed their mark.

Father Rasputin, still hunched over, continued to struggle through the dark until he finally reached his objective, the courtyard's iron gate. He could feel the wonderful cold metal within his grasp. It felt to him like freedom.

Another figure emerged from the doorway. It was Grand Duke Dmitri Pavelovich—the tsar's favorite nephew. An Olympian athlete and model soldier, the duke currently served as an officer in His Majesty's Horse Guards, the imperial forces elite. Rumored to be the man Their Majesties wish their eldest daughter Olga to marry. He was a friend and confidant to Prince Felix and known hater of Father Rasputin's growing relationship with the royal family.

The duke coldly removed his Browning service revolver from its holster and carefully aimed the weapon as a stray moonbeam reflected off its steely frame. "Good-night, my dear father."

"Dmitri, no!" shouted Rasputin with all his remaining strength, "I will tell it all to the empress!" The fiery orange flash from Dmitri's revolver answered Rasputin's cry and the round of bullets quickly found its target.

The bullets's sheer force turned the priest completely around. Now, facing the lighted palace, the fallen saint began to pray out loud. The blood-soaked snow became his altar. Kneeling before his God, he begged for forgiveness. The cold, soothing snow blanketed his brown, tangled body. His famous steely eyes glared toward the illuminated doorway that had once represented his artery of freedom. "Why now?"

Rasputin could not believe it had come to this. He saw the duke from across the snow-covered court. Dmitri coldly stared at Rasputin as he aimed his firearm once again at Rasputin's chest.

The fourth shot of the night sealed Rasputin's fate, and the courtyard grew quiet.

In the pale palace light stood the beaming Prince Felix. He looked almost god-like. He emerged from the light of the palace. Blond, bold, and beautiful, the decadent prince was dressed to kill. Wearing his cadet uniform of the Imperial Corps of Pages with high Pershing collar and white leather belt, his costume was complete—except that the friend and lover he had betrayed had torn off one of his shoulder epaulettes.

Hours ago in the palace's basement Rasputin had been Felix's dinner guest. The Siberian was enjoying himself. The prince played sad gipsy songs on his guitar after dinner. As Rasputin got up and wandered the room, the music stopped. Admiring a piece of art that hung from the cellar's wall, Rasputin asked Felix why he had stopped. Before he could turn, a force threw him to the floor. After that his world became blurry. That was, until he saw Felix kneeling over him, Rasputin could not believe his ears; as he drifted into semi-consciousness he learned from Felix that the royal family was preparing a coup. Rasputin had dreamt of this very thing earlier that week. When he awoke from his dream he wrote a letter to warn the tsar of this possibility. The Siberian had hoped it was just a dream, but it had felt too real. In detail, the prince told the dying priest how he and the others planned to murder the tsar.

Not long after the prince's attempt on Rasputin's life, following an hour's celebration with his friends upstairs, Felix had returned to the basement. He wanted to make certain Rasputin was still dead. Instead, he found him slowly clawing his way up the basement stairs.

After a brief confrontation on the steps, Rasputin quickly overtook Felix. Even with a bullet lodged in his back, the Siberian was more than the prince could handle. Choking the life out of Felix, Rasputin felt a moment of mercy. Instead, he tore off one of Felix's epaulettes. As he pushed him down the stairs he told the prince he was unworthy to wear a Russian uniform. Somehow, the prince knew it to be true.

But that was ten minutes ago.

Three men, a senator, a duke, and a prince, now crossed the snow-covered courtyard. Their evening's murderous business was nearly complete.

Spitting out blood, Rasputin hoarsely asked, "Why, Felix?"

"Tell me, my clairvoyant friend," Felix said to Rasputin, entertaining his conspirators, "how could you not foresee all this? Are you *not* a mystic?"

The priest, struggling to breath, had no answer to their hate. He had been wise to mail his letter to the tsar. "Lord," the holy man prayed, "I am in your hands now. Do with me what you wish."

The three circled the fallen one like birds of prey.

"Patience good father," Felix taunted. "You will see him soon enough."

With the fresh gypsy ballads sung earlier by Felix still ringing softly through his head, Rasputin looked toward the iron gate. He was so close. Now, his freedom was out of reach. "Why?" he asked.

"Scum," Dmitri yelled. "You know perfectly well why!"

But the priest did not.

"Surely you must know?" said Senator Purishkevich, his overweight frame gasping for air, as he wiped the fog away his glasses.

"Did you think no one was watching?" Dmitri asked.

"Watching?"

"Yes—watching! Watching you taint Her Majesty with your filthiness. I despise everything you represent."

"An affair?" Rasputin managed. "Me—and the empress?"

"Yes," Duke Dmitri replied, "and you dare call yourself a man of God."

Felix hissed, "I think not."

"What?" Rasputin laughed, "Me and the empress?" Poor Dmitri, he thought, as he looked into his fierce eyes. You're being tricked too. He began to grow faint.

"Our Siberian friend has been indulging himself too much in drink these days," the senator laughed. "No use denying it. We already know what you have done. Bastard."

"Senator," the priest gasped, "who made you judge and jury?"

"Hush now," Felix said with an actor's flamboyant flair, "it is I, Grigory, and I have come for you." Felix raised Dmitri's revolver. "Your influence over the House of Romanov has ended."

"That's what you think, Felix," Rasputin said with a bloody smile as he stared at the duke. "Poor Russia. What has it done to deserve this?"

"What?" the duke asked.

"Now, do what you must," Rasputin said and closed his eyes.

With a pull of the trigger, Felix sealed his and Russia's destinies. The shot rang throughout the frozen embankment's grounds. It echoed along the tranquil banks of the Moika and nearby Neva rivers, bouncing off the high bastions of Fortress

Peter and Paul. Felix attempted to control his trembling hand. In his mind, he compared the incident to putting down one of his hounds. It was only a dog's death, the prince told himself. Nothing more. Rasputin deserved it, didn't he? He had threatened to tell Dmitri of their affair. Now, he would reveal nothing.

"Well done, Felix," spoke the senator as he spat on the peasant priest.

Dmitri simply stood there. It was finally done, but it did not seem real. Not yet. As if in some play, he was waiting for the actor to get up.

Placidly, Felix handed him back his revolver. It seemed heavier.

"Now," said the senator looking down at the Siberian's corpse. "We have a little more work to do", referring to the disposing of the body.

"Yes, mission completed," the prince said. "The only thing that remains is the tossing of the rubbish. Grab a leg, gentlemen."

Much has happened in a short time.

Ministry of War, Platon's Office

Serge entered his father's office out of breath.

The clerk behind the desk recognized him, "Prince Konstantin, how can I help you?"

"Is my father in?"

"No, he left some time ago for the palace."

"I see. What about Inspector Renko?"

"He's with his men guarding the grand duke, I believe."

It was then that the office door flew open with a loud bang.

265

"Where's the general?" barked a colonel of the Imperial Guard.

"He's out." The clerk was not one for such excitement. "May I help you?" he asked in a librarian tone.

"The Petersburg police just found Colonel Zurin's body near the palace embankment."

"What? When?" Colonel Gorvin of the general's staff demanded, having emerged from his office in time to hear the news.

"An hour ago."

"Are we certain it is him?" another asked.

"I am afraid so. I was just at the morgue."

"Call the palace at once. They are striking now! Tell the Household Guards that His Majesty is in danger."

Another officer came into the room. "What's going on?"

"Zurin's dead. His body was found an hour ago outside Vladimir's Palace," the intruder replied.

"Alert the guards! I want my men ready to move in twenty minutes!" barked the most senior man in the room.

The receptionist picked up the phone. "We need to tell General Konstantin too. Yes, operator. Connect me to the palace. What do you mean the line is being checked? Try again—this call is most urgent. Keep trying until it goes through."

They all looked at one another. "Call the barracks. We need to warn them of the threat."

Once again the clerk picked up the phone. "Connect me with General Dubrovsky," he said in a most un-librarian voice. Pausing, "What do you mean, that line is also being checked? The line is dead," he said to the group. He tried again. "Get me General Rohr at the Winter Palace." At last, a call went through. "I need the general."

An officer grabbed the receiver. "Zurin is dead and we have lost communication with the palace."

"What?" Rohr asked, sitting at his desk. "Where's General Konstantin?"

"At the palace."

"Rally my men!" the officer heard him declare to another. "Find me Renko!"

It was then that one of the officers noticed Serge had left.

Tracks North of Tsarskoe

A little after nine, a conductor pulled a lever and applied the brakes to a southbound train. Plowing through the newly fallen snow, it grounded to a halt just outside the town of Tsarskoe Selo. With the iron stick still in his meaty hand, the engineer admired the simple beauty of the surrounding woods.

Aboard the iron beast were two companies of cavalry from the Preobrazhenski Regiment, His Majesty's Elite Guard.

With steam still pouring out from underneath the train, the doors of three cars suddenly opened. Groups of armed men dressed in green jumped out. They lowered wooden planks from the cars to the forest's floor. Each group made certain the planks were secured before they called out: "All clear!"

Then, they raised their hands and waved their brethren forth. The darkened hollows of the cars came alive as soldiers on horseback raced out into the night. Their mounts's frozen breath mixed with the fog and cold night air. The old Guard bore one hope—that their departure from the capital was as yet unnoticed.

"Men, to the tower!" an officer shouted out as soon as the train was fully emptied. Every rider dashed towards the security of the woods. The train then jolted forward to its next stop—blocking the line to the city in hopes of cutting off reinforcements from Petersburg.

Dmitri's Palace,
The Drawing Room

Felix knew Serge was not bearing good news as he walked into the parlor. Minutes ago, most of the men guarding the palace fled out into the night. So, he new it was time to take the offensive.

"It's too late, Serge. What's done is done," Felix said as he lit his cigarette.

Renko was nowhere to be found.

"Why did you kill Rasputin?"

"Because I could," said Felix, exhaling smoke.

"No, that's not the reason. You killed him to lure the emperor away from the front."

Felix turned away. "Nonsense."

"Really? After all this secrecy surrounding the days leading up to the event, and you suddenly decide to share everything with the authorities."

"Define 'everything.'"

"You wanted the empress to find out."

Dmitri had entered the room unnoticed. So far, he didn't like what he was hearing.

"Pure fiction. I did no such thing," Felix responded. "We killed Rasputin to safeguard the state. I told the police nothing."

"Nothing? What about the blood?"

"I told them it was from one of my hounds."

"So, you didn't tell them you murdered Rasputin on the spot."

"I am not a fool, cousin."

"I have my doubts," Serge countered as he saw Dmitri standing near the door. "Inspector Renko tells me differently. The inspector says that when he arrived at your palace on Saturday morning, you escorted him to the basement."

"Please," Felix sighed, "I did no such thing."

"You brought him and his men downstairs to show him the exact spot of the crime."

"No, I didn't."

"No use lying anymore. We already know the truth. You laughed at Inspector Renko as you showed him the rug drenched in Rasputin's blood. The same rug you wrapped him up in."

The prince's eyes moved towards the room's fire.

Serge continued, "Then, when he asked you where the body was, you told him."

"I said that it was where it belongs!"

"This morning, the Neva gave your gift back."

With that, Dmitri made his presence known to all. "What's going on here?"

"He's lying," Felix eyes turned to the duke.

Dmitri looked stunned. Serge spoke: "Dmitri, we don't have time for this. We need to warn the tsar. Vlad and his men plan to strike tonight. Don't they Felix?"

"What?" This was too much for Dmitri to handle all at once. "Felix, what do you know about this?"

An odd silence followed. Finally, Felix said, "Rasputin was going to tell the empress about our—." He stopped and stared at Serge. "I shall always hate you."

"So, the truth finally comes out. You told me he was having an affair with the empress."

"He was."

"I don't know what to believe any more, except that my involvement in it sickens me," the duke said as he picked up the phone.

"Dmitri don't!" Felix said, rushing toward him. "Vlad's now our only hope."

"Connect me to Tsarskoe immediately." Then, after a moment, "This is the Grand Duke Dmitri. Get me His Majesty at once." More silence. "Impossible." He turned to the other men. "The line is currently being checked for repairs."

Serge said, "More lies."

Dmitri picked up the receiver again. "I know. This whole mess stinks of treachery," he said. "And Felix, you couldn't resist it, could you?"

Felix turned away as Oscar Wilde's words popped into his head. "The only way to beat temptation is to succumb to it," he said as he walked to the door. "Good night, gentlemen."

Dmitri shouted into the receiver: "Operator! Connect me with Pavlovski Palace."

CHAPTER 34

Alexander's Palace
The Tsar's Private Study

The British ambassador's audience with Tsar Nicholas was going on longer than expected, especially given that the conversation was a little one-sided. "Your Majesty, if I may be permitted to say so, you have but one safe course open, namely, to break down the barrier that separates you from your people and to regain their confidence."

Nicholas gave him a fixed stare. "Do you mean that I am to regain the confidence of my people, or that they are to regain my confidence?"

Without missing a beat, the diplomat answered, "Both, sir, for without such mutual confidence Russia will never win this war. Your Majesty was admirably inspired when you went to the Duma last February. Will you not go there again? Will you not speak to your people? Will you not tell them that Your Majesty, who is the father of your people, wishes to work with them to win the war? You have, sir, but to lift up your little finger, and they will once more kneel at your feet as I saw them kneel after the outbreak of the war in Moscow."

Nicholas, chain-smoking, was too furious to respond.

"Your Majesty, I call your attention to the attempts being made by the Germans not only to create dissension between the allies, but to estrange you from your people. Their agents are everywhere at work. They are pulling the strings, and are using as their unconscious tools those who are in the habit of advising Your Majesty as to the choice of ministers. They are indirectly influencing the empress through her entourage, with the result that, instead of being loved as she ought to be, Her Majesty is discredited and is accused of working in German interests."

The tsar tried to control his anger and responded with a lie amid a cloud of smoke: "I choose my ministers myself and do not allow anyone to influence my choice."

"How then does Your Majesty select them?" the Scot was treading down a dangerous path, but he could not stop. Not now. "There is, for example, Protopopov, who, if Your Majesty will forgive my saying, is bringing Russia to the verge of ruin. So long as he remains Minister of the Interior, there cannot be that collaboration between the government and the Duma that is essential for victory."

Nicholas was outraged. "I chose Protopopov from the very ranks of the Duma in order to be agreeable to them—and this is my reward!"

"But, sir, the Duma can hardly place confidence in a man who has betrayed his honor for office, who has had an interview with a German agent in Stockholm, and who is suspected of working for an armistice based on Germany's evacuation of Poland and Russia's acquisition of Constantinople."

"No such offer would carry any weight," Nicholas said, thinking of his last appointment of the night. Ernie was going to receive a no.

"Your Majesty, England only wants to protect her current allies. You may be interested in this." The British ambassador tossed the Zimmerman telegraph on his desk.

"My, Sir George, aren't you growing desperate?" he said as he picked up the paper and read it quickly. He knew it was genuine. The Kaiser had lied.

"Your Majesty, if you want Constantinople, you must stay with us," Sir George said as he gathered his things to leave.

"How did you get this?"

"Does it truly matter?"

Nicholas began brushing his beard with the back of his hand. Everyone had lied to him, even his own wife.

"Your Majesty must realize that in the event of revolution, only a small portion of the army can be counted on to defend the dynasty."

"Carry on."

"As Ambassador, I am well aware that I have no right to speak to you in this way. I can say only that my boldness is because of my feelings of devotion for Your Majesty and the empress. If I were to see a friend walking through the woods on a dark night along a path which I knew ended in a precipice, would it not be my duty, sir, to warn Your Majesty of the abyss that lay ahead of you? You have, sir, come to the parting of the ways. One path will lead you to victory and a glorious peace, the other to revolution and disaster. Let me implore Your Majesty to choose the former."

"Thank you, Sir George. The Russian people have no better ally than Great Britain. Tell my cousin the king that I remain firm and faithful." Within those few words, a tiny piece of him died.

Alexander Palace, The Anteroom

As Sandro waited in the vestibule for Niki, he saw Sir George emerge from the darkened corridor wearing a typical British smirk. All Sir George needed was an umbrella to complete the stereotype. "Sir George, it appears you're in a fine mood."

"Grand Duke Alexander," he chirped, still wearing his smile, "it is so good to see you. I was just having a word with the emperor regarding the war. He assured me that the Russian Army remains firm and faithful."

"Splendid," Sandro said holding a scroll and a tiny box under his arm.

"How's your air squadron? You did receive the shipment of new airplanes last month?"

"Yes, and they are greatly appreciated. Sir George, now tell me. Your government couldn't care less about the great puppeteer behind the curtain as the legions continue to be led toward the front. Alexander III would have thrown an ambassador of your species out of Russia without even the ceremony of handing you back your credentials."

"Too bad he is not here today. I am certain he was not one to back down from a fight."

"We will see, Ambassador. Perhaps our troops should not stop at Berlin?"

"First you must get there."

Platon appeared from the corner room, wearing a broad smile and clapping his hands. "Gentlemen, gentlemen," he said, "now I'm getting a little too old to separate you two."

The three men shared a laugh, and then Sir George put on his hat. "General Konstantin, I think we all are getting a little too old and tired for this."

"Good night, Mr. Ambassador."

"General Konstantin," Sir George said, the Berlin dispatch on his mind, "may I have a moment of your time tomorrow?"

Platon laughed. "Yes, Mr. Ambassador, you may. Just arrange with my secretary, not my son."

At that Sir George smiled and gave a slight salute. "I shall. Good evening gentlemen."

Watching Sir George's exit, Konstantin handed Sandro a package. "I wouldn't worry about Sir George. It's the load that he must bear for being British."

"What's that?"

"Arrogance. They wear it as proudly as their own king's crown."

"Well then, here's to uncrowned kings."

"Speaking of which, His Majesty knew nothing about the separate peace I have been arranging for the last two months with Germany." This news stopped Sandro in his tracks.

"What?"

"The empress arranged it all without his knowledge."

"Alix alone? How is that possible?"

"I falsely assumed all the directives were coming from him not her."

"That foolish woman. What is Nicholas going to do?"

"I don't know? I am attending a meeting with the tsar and the empress's brother Ernie to discuss that matter later this evening."

"The duke is here?"

"In this very palace," Platon said as they nearly reached the tsar's outer chamber. "May I suggest you stay around to attend our meeting?"

Shocked, "I wouldn't miss it for the world."

With that, Sandro was escorted through the door.

Tsarskoe, The Encirclement

At the corner of Mariaya and Srednaya stood the imposing complex that provided all the electrical power to the Alexander Palace and its surrounding parks. It was just outside the park's outer gates near the new Veterans Hospital, a stone's throw away from the station.

It was a silent but unusual night. Boris Dvortsky, the chief electrical engineer, was never here this late. Tonight, a new tsar would take the place of the old, and Boris had a role to play in this grand drama. One of Vlad's men had visited him this morning with a big bag of money just to flip a switch—a simple task for an engineer to do. By tomorrow, Boris would retire a very rich man.

Sitting behind his desk, he extinguished his cigarette. It was time.

"Misha, I just got a call from the hospital—it's Anna," he said as he entered the control room. Anna was Misha's expecting wife.

"The baby isn't due for three more months."

"You worry too much," Boris said as he handed him his coat. "The doctor said it's not serious, just fatigue. But you should go to her anyway. If only for the sake of the little one."

Misha looked down at all the gauges. "But?"

"Don't worry, my friend," he said calmly, though he wanted to scream. The money he had received was not worth seeing his colleague tormented by his lies. "I will watch the grids until your return. All night if necessary."

Misha embraced his friend, "Thank you, Boris. You are a true friend."

"Get out of here. Your wife needs you more than I."

"I will be back."

"Nothing ever happens here."

As Misha left the control booth, Boris secured the door. There was no turning back now. He hoped his friend would understand. If not, he could buy some new ones. Not as good, of course, but they would do. Picking up the phone he asked for the hospital. To the other voice on the phone he warned, "He's coming."

A Few Blocks Away From the Exchange

Similar regrets were being felt a few blocks down in the basement of the lyceum, Tsarskoe's telephone exchange. For nearly twenty minutes, communication between the palace and the outside world had been severed, thanks to the two operators in this room. All callers attempting to reach the palace were told the line was being repaired. The call a few minutes ago from Grand Duke Dmitri had greatly disturbed one of the operators. "I hate lying to nobility," the younger man said, "for at times, I think they can actually read your mind."

"Nonsense," his associate said. "The duke has his own problems. Remember, he is currently under house arrest. This thing will be over before you know it."

Just then the phone rang. Neither one wanted to answer it. Finally, on the fourth ring, the older operator grabbed his headset.

"Operator." The call was coming from the Petersburg station. "Connect me with the palace," spoke a harsh voice on the other end.

"I am afraid the line is being checked, sir. I can connect you as soon as it is restored."

Inspector Renko shouted into the phone, "Soldier, in twenty minutes, I will be at the exchange to check the line myself. And if it works, the flash of my revolver will be the last thing you will ever see."

"It's the line," the operator nervously replied. "You can check for yourself when you get here."

"Don't lie to me! Connect me with the palace—NOW!"

"One minute, sir. I will try to connect you." Even though the room was freezing, the man was sweating profusely. He pulled the plug to break the connection.

"What should we do?" the younger one asked the older. "I don't know about you, but I'm not going to be here when that man reaches Tsarskoe."

The two grabbed their jackets and headed for the door. "Vlad, don't fail us," prayed one of them as they walked out the door. "Let's get a drink."

St. Petersburg Station

At Petersburg station, General Rohr stopped shouting out orders when he saw the inspector hang up the phone.

"The line just went dead," Renko somberly replied. "All communication with the palace has been cut. We have to assume the palace may be surrounded."

Looking at his men boarding the train, General Rohr shouted, "Tell the conductor we are leaving now!"

"General," his second in command protested, "we need a few more minutes for all of the men to board. The train isn't fully loaded."

"Then they will have to walk! Colonel Smirnov, if this train is not off this platform in sixty seconds, it's your head!"

"Move! Move!" the colonel cried as he fought his way to the engineer. "Get this thing moving!"

With the release of the brakes, the train leapt ahead. Soldiers scrambled aboard, abandoning some of their equipment. The last one to board was Inspector Renko. In an awkward silence, the train hurried down the tracks and quickly was consumed in a syrupy fog.

The Hour Grows Near

It had been fifteen minutes since Serge had helped Dmitri escape.

Now, Serge was leaning out the window of Dmitri's Mercedes attempting to see. It was pointless. The fog covered everything in sight. "It would be nice to arrive in one piece," Serge shouted over the noisy motor.

"We have to assume that they have cut the lines. Hopefully the call I made will make a difference."

After his conversation with the palace operator, Dmitri had called a regimental commander at Pavlovski, a palace located less than twenty minutes from the Alexander Palace. The loyalty of Colonel Tushkin and his Imperial Dragoons was without question. Dmitri knew that Vlad would not dare approach Tushkin with his little scheme.

"Dmitri, we are but two men against God knows how many."

"Have faith, Serge. For tonight, we shall make a difference."

Staring at the three hunting rifles on the backseat, Serge wasn't so sure. A few minutes later, they approached the palace's outer gates. All seemed normal. Small squads of soldiers were guarding the gate as Dmitri's car ground to a halt.

"By order of His Imperial Majesty the Tsar, there shall be no visitors to the palace this evening," the commander said. His men had their hands on their rifles as their eyes shifted from one man to another. They were ready for anything.

"Good evening, Lieutenant. Actually, I am here to see the new tsar," Dmitri said coolly. "Prince Konstantin and I are here on Tsar Vladimir's orders."

"What? I was not informed of this."

"Lieutenant, I will hold you personally accountable if I am late."

The lieutenant wavered. He had told his commander they would not let anyone pass. But the duke was one of the conspirators in the plot to kill Father Rasputin. He had to be on their side. Tsar Nicholas would not have placed him under house arrest if he wasn't. Right? "Your Excellency, I apologize for the delay," he said as he waved to his men to open the gates, "Give His Majesty my regards."

Dmitri restarted the car's engine. "I shall, Lieutenant, I shall. Your loyalty shall be rewarded."

As they passed the outer gates, Serge said, "How did you know they had turned?"

"Their green uniforms. They wore the Preobrazhenski regimental colors. The soldiers at that gate should have borne the colors of His Majesty's Imperial Life-Guards."

"So, it was a matter of color."

Dmitri nodded. "I hope we are not too late." Soon, they would be at the inner gate to the palace grounds. Dmitri knew that more competent men would be guarding that gate.

Alexander Palace Grounds, Second Checkpoint

Dmitri was right. At the second barrier, a much more stern-looking man waved them to a halt. He was wearing a black uniform. This time, the duke left the car running and in gear.

"Good evening," the officer said as he peered into the vehicle. "They should have told you at the first gate that His Majesty is not seeing anyone this evening."

"What about General Vladimir?" Serge asked.

"What are you talking about?" The officer waved to his men to encircle the vehicle.

"We wouldn't miss this historic night," Dmitri said. "Not on your life."

"This evening is no different than any other, sir."

"That's where you are wrong, captain," the duke said with a broad, toothy grin. "I am here on General Vladimir's orders."

"Sorry. I have my orders."

"As do I, so open the damn gate!"

"Not tonight."

"What?"

The officer leaned into the car. "You heard me."

"I am the Grand Duke Dmitri," he barked, "and this is Prince Konstantin. We are already late, so raise that gate soldier!"

"Your Excellency, I recognized you when you pulled up. But as I said, I have my orders, and they do not include raising that gate, not even if the ghost of Peter the Great rose from his tomb and wished it. You of all people should understand the meaning of NONE SHALL PASS!"

"None shall pass – please!" spat out Serge. "To whom do you think you are speaking, soldier? Now raise that gate before I lose my temper."

The officer simply said, "No." He didn't see Serge as much of a threat.

"Prince Konstantin, relax," Dmitri said. "The captain is just doing his job."

"His job?"

"Yes, his job," the duke replied. "Well then, it looks like we must wait to celebrate until tomorrow."

"Your Excellencies," the captain of the guard stated as he gave a textbook salute, "thank you for your understanding. I apologize that it was a wasted trip, but an order is an order."

"Thank you, captain for reminding us of that," Dmitri said as he had taken his foot off the brake. "You shall see us both again in the morning. Until then, we shall just turn around and be on our way."

Vlad's men moved back toward the warmth of a small fire.

Dmitri took his time turning the car around, giving the impression that he wasn't a good driver. The men guarding the gate turned around and covered their faces as they laughed.

Placing the car in neutral, Dmitri trod on the gas. The German machine roared. The soldiers began to laugh out loud at the duke. Then Dmitri slammed the car into the proper gear. It leapt forward as it came to life. The captain did not even bother to run. He already knew that he was dead. His body bounced off the Mercedes's hood with a loud thud—crashing through the gate.

"Was that necessary?" Serge asked as they sped away through the broken gate.

"Most definitely."

Slowly recovering from the loss of their leader, the soldiers guarding the gate moved from the fire and raised their rifles. But they were too late. The Mercedes was already out of range. Before they knew it, the car had disappeared into the night.

"I thought Felix was the crazy one!" Serge said.

"You thought wrong."

Gaining speed, the outlining trees became a blur as the car headed into the woods. Soon, the vehicle approached a massive stone wall; it missed the wall by mere inches as he had taken a hard left.

"Remember what I said about one piece?"

"I remember."

They raced along the inner wall that bordered the palace grounds. To their left were the woods and to their right was the wall. In front of them was a small canal.

"What are you doing?"

"Watch." The duke slammed on his brakes, forcing the car to slide. Its back end fishtailed onto the frozen stream. Without missing a beat, he gave the car more gas. They were heading directly toward the wall. Then Serge saw the large archway to the bridge that covered the canal. Driving underneath it, they were now on the palace grounds. Rushing toward them was another, much smaller bridge.

"Dmitri?"

"I see it," he said as he attempted to turn the speeding car from the ice.

The wheel would not turn.

"What are we to do?"

"Jump!" he said, opening his door.

The two scrambled out of the vehicle just moments before it crashed into the bridge.

They both stared at what was left of the vehicle. Smoke and fire poured out, followed by an explosion.

"We need to move," Dmitri said briskly. "At the end of this road, there are some barracks a few minutes further down. They should have heard this."

"But are they friend or foe?"

"The end of this road leads to His Majesty's Personal Convoy."

"The Cossacks!"

"Yes."

"Good. We needed a change of luck."

A top the old Arsenal, nestled between two of his men, Vlad looked out toward the darkened palace and laughed. He slapped the men on their backs. "Poor Niki. You have nowhere left to run. That goes for you too, Ernie." Earlier in the day, Vlad had told his men of the importance of capturing the German duke alive.

"General, the men are mounted and ready," one of his underlings declared.

"Good, for our destiny awaits."

Precisely at that moment a huge explosion rocked the woods directly behind them. "What the hell was that?" one of the men shouted.

"Captain, send a patrol to investigate. On second thoughts, "don't bother," the duke said as he walked toward the door. "Our future is in front of us. I want every available man with us to storm the palace. If there is resistance, I shall deal with it later."

"As you wish, general."

"Well then, gentlemen," he said as he looked over his commanders, wearing uniforms of black and green, "until we meet in the Throne Room."

"We will save you a seat," one officer joked.

"Please do," Vladimir said, giving a slight bow.

CHAPTER 35

Tracks to Tsarskoe

Ten minutes after leaving the station, the train came to a screeching halt. As all the men fell upon each other, Renko moved toward the engine.

"What is it?" he yelled.

"Sir, there's an unscheduled train blocking the tracks."

"What would happen if we just rammed it?"

"Ram it?" The engineer scratched his head. He was paid to avoid such situations. "Well, technically, we could attach ourselves to it and push it back to Tsarskoe. We have sufficient power."

"Then make it so."

"Just one problem, sir. If we ram it, and it has its brakes applied, it's going to get ugly."

"Ugly? You just said that we could hook up with it."

"We can't if their brakes are locked."

"Why?"

"Traveling at our current speed, it would derail us. It would be like us trying to plow through a brick wall if we were riding a bike."

"Then we are going to have to make certain the brakes are no longer applied. Get as close as you can."

Renko returned to the coach car. "Men, terrorists have blocked our path to Tsarskoe. They stand between our worthy sovereign and us. Therefore we shall storm the train before us. Then we shall press on. These men are traitors to His Majesty. Show no mercy to them. Not tonight! Not ever!"

"Yes, sir," they shouted as they leapt off the train, "Faith, honor, and LOYALTY!"

However, the inspector felt some pity for these misguided fools in the train before them.

As their train slowed, Renko could easily tell the one in front was deserted. They were too late. Their enemy was elsewhere. But where?

Renko could easily guess.

The Tsar's Private Study

Shadowed by a giant Cossack, Sandro entered the tsar's private study. Nicholas, sitting behind his desk, noticed the scroll and packages. "A little early to exchange presents," the tsar said as he motioned his brother-in-law to take a seat.

The duke gave a formal bow. He replied, "Your Majesty, I prefer to stand."

Sandro's formality surprised Nicholas. "As you wish," he said as he braced himself for the second lecture of the night. "It appears I have been to the front too long."

"Me too, Your Majesty." At full attention, the general gave his report. "We are going through the most dangerous moment in the history of Russia. The question is: shall Russia be a great state, free, and capable of developing and growing strong, or shall she submit to the iron German fist? Every one feels this, and this is the reason everyone, with the exception of the cowards and the enemies of this country, offers up their lives and all their possessions."

The tsar sat back and smiled. He had grown accustomed to dukes telling him what to do. His mind was on the document delivered to him by Sir George. His dream was now on hold until the spring.

"And at this solemn time, when we are being tested as men, in the highest sense—as Christians—certain forces within Russia are leading you, and, consequently, Russia, to inevitable ruin. I say you and Russia, because Russia cannot exist without a tsar, but the tsar alone cannot govern a country like Russia. It is absolutely indispensable that the ministries and the legislative chambers work together. The existing situation, with the whole responsibility resting on you and you alone, is untenable." He paused.

The tsar inspected his fingernails. He was growing tired of being coached.

"Disaffection is spreading very fast and the gulf between you and your people is growing wider. They need assurances."

"Who are 'they'—the small or the great, cousin?" He thought of the royal family's recent treachery.

"Both."

"A very nice speech, Sandro," said the man behind the desk. "You are aware, however, that nobody has the right to kill, be it a grand duke or a peasant," referring to Rasputin's murder.

"Niki, our problem is bigger than my son-in-law's involvement in this foolishness."

"Foolishness?" he said as his hand slapped down onto the desk. "A man is dead. The man who nursed my son from the grip of death was murdered by members of my own family, and you dare come here to lecture me on mortality!"

"You want to talk about murder, Niki?" Sandro yelled. "What about the millions of young men who shall never return from the front?"

"You think I don't think about those brave boys every waking moment. Inspecting a line one day, and the next, it is half the size. And me on my horse confidently passing by as their young eyes burn their hate into me. Damn it, Sandro, I too have seen their faces."

"Admittedly, you have a difficult job, your grace."

"Made more difficult by the constant lies," Niki said as he stared at a portrait of his wife, "Even from my own family."

Sensing it, "I already know about Ernie and his offer of peace."

"You seem to know more than I. But what is new."

"Now is the time. You must take the initiative and grant your people a Constitution."

"A Constitution—in due time I shall."

"You have no time left. A dishonorable escape from the war will not help save you. Too much has already been lost to just walk away."

"What? You think I would turn my back on the war?" he barely whispered it, "Not you too?"

"No. It is others not me."

"I see," he said calmly. "Destroy three hundred years of Romanov rule with a stroke of a pen?"

"Not destroy—save. You could in a few bold words give the country what she really wants: a ministry of confidence. If you were to do that, the Duma would become your ally, and this war would be won."

"And what then would become of me? There would not be much need of tsar."

"You would die old and full of days. You would be Nicholas the Liberator, the tsar who gave Russia her true freedom."

"Freedom? I am not so certain."

"Niki, long ago you asked me for help. Do you remember?"

He thought back to a conversation they had had when his father died. "I told you that I was not ready to be a tsar."

"Over twenty years have passed since that moment. This evening, you have the ability to lead Russia forward or return to the past. The decision is yours alone. I brought you two Christmas presents." He laid flat the constitution prepared for Alexander II before his death. "This brings new hope to Russia, and liberates an empire." Then he unwrapped a tiny cup of gold and blue. "This reminds us of the errors of our past."

The tsar recognized it—one of the coronation cups given to the masses moments before the stampede.

Setting it on the tsar's desk, Sandro said, "We must not go back. You have an inner strength your father never possessed. Trust your subjects, and offer them their freedom based on the model written down here—a constitutional monarchy."

"Sandro, I am the tsar, the autocrat, and I am in full control!" Before the duke could respond, the lights flittered for a moment. Then, the power to the palace went out.

From the dark, Sandro snickered, "You were saying, Your Majesty?"

"Do shut-up, Sandro."

CHAPTER 36

The Hospital

Protopopov sat in a warm, comfortable corner near the hospital's front desk. Even after two hours, the image of Rasputin's mangled corpse was burned into his frail mind. He no longer knew what was real and what was merely a hallucination. He had a strange feeling he had not seen the last of Rasputin. The minister had had Captain Zubov and his men secure the entire basement including the morgue. He was not taking any more chances.

Looking at his watch, he knew that Vlad was assembling his army nearby. In a couple of hours, it would all be over. But, he had one last thing to do.

A man walked up to the desk, asking for his wife. The woman at the desk told him that no one had been admitted during her shift.

"Do you mind if I look?"

"Be my guest."

Protopopov got up, "Misha?"

"Do I know you?" the engineer replied.

"No," Protopopov said with a sleazy grin, "but your wife does."

"Is she okay?"

"Yes, just tired."

"But the woman at the desk said…" the engineer stated as he pointed to her.

"Don't worry about her, she's an idiot." The minister said as he waved to her with a smile.

"Oh."

"Your wife is sleeping comfortably upstairs." Protopopov lead the way up the stairs.

"I see," Misha said as he climbed the steps, "And how do you know my wife?" Through the windows you could make out the lit palace. Just then, the distant lights began to flicker. "What is this?"

Turning back, "What is what my good man?"

"The palace lights are out."

"Nonsense," Protopopov replied as he reached slowly for his pistol. "Your wife is in the first room up the stairs."

Misha pressed his face against the window, "No, they are out."

"Perhaps it's a drill of some sort."

"No. I would have known of it. I am an engineer at the power plant."

"Bad generator?" Protopopov had his firearm pressed against his leg. He just needed to get to the second floor to use it. Then, he noticed a soldier looking at him.

"The generators are in perfect order," declared the engineer. "Guard, come down here."

"What is it?" the soldier asked as he left his post. Quickly, he brushed by the minister.

"The palace lights are out."

"What do you mean the palace ..." but his words trailed off. As he looked to where the palace should be all he saw was darkness.

Protopopov was about to bring up his pistol but it was too late.

The private reached for his whistle. Instantly, the noise from it echoed throughout the halls.

As the private and Misha hurried down the steps, Protopopov thought it was a good time to catch some fresh air.

A few minutes later, the minister was on the roof playing with his moustache. The roof was a splendid vantage point to the palace grounds. In the streets below, a small group of men were moving towards the palace gates. He felt a chill creeping up on him. Turning, a man he knew to be dead greeted him. It was Rasputin.

"So much for surprise."

"You're not real," the minister shrieked as he closed his eyes.

The Siberian laughed. "Just because my body lays three floors below, doesn't mean that I no longer exist."

The minister turned away from the priest's stare, but he could still feel Grisha's presence.

Then he heard a harsh whisper: "Time to pay for past sins."

The minister summoned his politician's charm and declared to the sprawling sight before him, "Sins? What sins? My dear priest, you forget that I am an atheist." Bursting into uncontrollable laughter, Protopopov knew then that he had lost the battle for possession of his own mind. He walked across the roof, in search of a door, all the while mumbling, "How can this be?"

Not Far Away

Sitting high on his mount, Vlad would have held an excellent view of the battlefield if only a velvet cloud was not covering the woodland. Moments earlier, he had heard an explosion coming from within the palace grounds. But he could no longer wait. He would reach his destiny or cease to exist. "Gentlemen," he yelled, "IN LIFE, a soldier is asked only TWO TASKS. They are TO LIVE, and they are TO DIE. Tonight, we live so, tomorrow, RUSSIA SHALL NOT DIE!"

In that moment, his entire regiment, aglow in the thousands of handheld torchlight, removed their sabers from their sheaths. As they cheered, they waved their weapons wildly in the air. Removing his own saber, their commander added, "Let's seize what is ours—GLORY!"

The men screamed in unison, "The GLORY shall be ours!" Vlad spurred his heels deeply into his horse and steered him toward his new home. It was time to take back what was rightfully his.

The Barracks

Stumbling into the woods, a Cossack cautiously set down his bottle of wine and tried to adjust his hat. A few minutes earlier, he thought he had heard an explosion coming from the woods, but it had to have been just a falling tree. Speaking of trees, he thought, it was time to relieve himself of some of the wine.

He set his rifle down. As he went about his business, he heard steps crashing through the woods. He quickly buttoned up and picked up his rifle. Perhaps his friends had sent him a woman? That would be too much to expect. Most likely it was only a deer. He lifted his rifle and waited. It wasn't a deer; it was a Russian duke. "Halt!"

Dmitri stopped dead in his tracks. As he raised his hands, Serge bumped into the back of him.

"What are you doing in the woods at this hour?"

"Take us to your commander at once," Serge said.

"First, I want to know why you're here." The guard knew better than to lead two strangers back to the barracks without some idea of their intentions.

"We don't have time for this," Dmitri said as he walked slowly toward him.

The Cossack again raised his rifle.

"Move no closer," he warned. He was starting to feel the effects of all the wine he had drunk. "Where are your papers?"

"Papers? Take us to your captain, you fool."

The soldier was thankful that these two would soon be his captain's problem. Taking them to the captain also would let him return to the party. He thought of what he was missing.

"You idiot! The palace lights are out!" the duke declared, pointing.

The Cossack looked. He couldn't believe it. He repeated, "The palace lights are out!" He stood still as the two men ran to the barracks. He could only repeat, over and over, "How can this be?"

Within the Cossacks's Barracks

Through a cloud of gritty smoke, circle-dancers moved as they clapped as gypsies sang and musicians played their tiny instruments to a feverish beat. This is what awaited Serge and Dmitri as the Cossack guarding the front door escorted them into the large wood framed barracks of His Majesty's Personal Guard.

Snaking through the crowd of tall bald men clinging on to big bosomed women, they were led to the Cossack's captain, who towered two feet over them. The bearded man wore a bright red tunic covered with shiny ornaments and shells. His intense eyes drilled into the two intruders.

As the royals strode through the scene, the flamboyant kicks from the folk dancers slowly ceased and the music and noise died out as all turned to look at them.

The led Cossack attempted to explain but his captain brushed him away like an annoying fly.

Dmitri looked up at the imposing man and announced, "Captain, the palace is under siege."

"What do you mean? Under siege, by whom?"

"If you don't believe us," the prince advised, "then look for yourself."

"I shall. And for both your sakes you had better hope that—" He stopped in mid-sentence. Through the window he could see that the park lights had been extinguished and there was nothing but darkness out there.

As he rushed outside, he saw several of his men standing in the middle of the yard. He called out for them to prepare the horses. An aide brought him his jacket and hat.

"Captain, General Vladimir is attempting to storm the palace and take control. He may already have two or three regiments in the woods northwest of the palace," Dmitri warned.

"So?" the Cossack captain said smiling, his blood rising, "They shall all be dead by morning."

More men poured out of the barracks. "Captain, what's going on?"

"Guards and brothers!" he yelled out, "Grab your rifles. The Great Don is in need of us to ride. Our good sovereign's very life is in jeopardy. Like fools, we have allowed enemies to enter within the palace gates."

One of his men brought over three horses.

Climbing up on his mount, the Cossack captain signaled to Dmitri and Serge to do the same. "Tonight we will drink glory or death! His Majesty is under attack. All who are loyal, to the palace at once! And annihilate all who dare to stand in our path!"

CHAPTER 37

The Tsar's Private Study

Four men entered the tsar's private study, holding large gas lamps. One was Chekhov, the other was Ernie.

"Your Majesty, are you all right?"

"Yes. What happened?"

"The power has been cut and there are reports of enemy forces within the palace gates," a soldier said.

"It's Vlad," Ernie said, a little winded. "I saw his forces gathering to our north, ten minutes ago."

"Hell of a walk, Ernie," General Konstantin dryly replied.

"Tell me about it. I nearly messed myself."

The tsar wasn't amused.

"A few of my men have already confronted a hostile force to the west of us," the captain of the guards reported. "I believe they were just scouts. All of them bore the pure black uniforms of the Vladimir Regiment."

"Captain Gogal, have your men bar all the doors," General Konstantin said calmly, removing a shotgun from a nearby cabinet. Colonel Zurin must be dead. "If they want us, they will have to come and get us."

"Platon, we have no idea what's going on out there," replied Sandro. "For all we know, it could be the entire Guard that has turned."

"Impossible," he said, loading his weapon. "His Majesty's Life-Guards would never turn." He said it with more confidence than he actually felt. "It could only be a few platoons of the Preobrazhenski Regiment mixed with Vlad's men. The Cossacks shall soon wipe them out."

Then, another officer of the Guard entered the room. He nervously reported, "I have sent riders to the Cossacks's barracks, but no one has yet returned."

"Anything else?"

"Yes. Their lights are still on."

Like a closing fist, silence choked the room. That was until the emperor spoke.

"Well then," Nicholas said pounding his hand down on the table, "if they want a fight, then that is what they're going to get." He removed a revolver from his desk. As he checked to make certain it was loaded, he said, "Captain, get my horse!"

Sandro and Platon looked at one another. Perhaps there was a little bit of his father in Nicholas after all.

"Sire," Sandro said, "we respect your bravery, but we mustn't jeopardize the regime. And you are the regime."

"Alexander," the tsar said as he fastened his sword to him, "for two-and-a-half years I have been forced to listen to these fools while millions of my subjects perished. You have seen firsthand the results. For once in my life, I feel empowered to do something about it."

Another officer marched into the study, surrounded by sentries. "Your Majesty, there is a great force north of us near the old Arsenal," he said out of breath, "I saw it with my own eyes less than five minutes ago."

"How large?" Konstantin asked.

"Three, perhaps four, regiments, all on horseback."

"Three to four thousand men," muttered Sandro, "within the palace grounds?"

"Yes, general. When I saw them, they were preparing to mount."

"What about His Majesty's Cossacks?"

The man offered, "I don't know."

"Very good," the tsar responded, "Gather my family, commander. You will be in charge of their personal protection.

Grab as many men as you need and take them to the cellar. See to it that nothing happens to them."

"Your Majesty," Platon said, walking towards the door, "with the entire palace guard, I believe we can make our escape to the east. We can penetrate this doom that is encircling us, but we must act quickly!"

Nicholas shook his head as he walked towards his horse. "Vlad is no fool. The roads leading to the east will now be guarded just as well as those leading west. He knows that if I escape his trap, his head would be mine. No, our only hope is to confront his troops."

Moving outside through the colonnade, the tsar looked at one of his waiters holding a deer rifle and smiled. "Let's bring the fight to Vlad. For those who throw the seed of trouble shall reap a whirlwind."

In the distance, through the fog, a large mass moved.

"They are coming. I can feel it," Platon said as they mounted their horses.

Sandro shook his head. "I don't know. I hope we see the Cossacks soon, or this is going to be a short ride."

As he rode into the darkness, the tsar prayed, "Lord, please give me the strength to do mighty things."

Just then, they heard canon fire resonating from the hills. Lightning sparked atop of a small hill, followed by the sound of thunder. It appeared the gods were angry.

"Ride with me tonight, O Lord. Ride in me," the tsar prayed.

The Heights above the Palace

Smoking a cigarette to calm his nerves, Major Fedorov told himself that it would all soon be over. From his vantage point from a hilltop high above the palace, all looked in order. The combined ranks of Vladimir's Regiment and the

Preobrazhenski Guards should already be mounted. In twenty minutes, the palace would be theirs.

The fog was beginning to lift, ensuring his battery a splendid view of the field. By tomorrow, he would be a major general. Not bad for a thirty-four-year-old. Not bad at all.

Walking in front of his guns pointed toward the woods, he thought he heard something, a sort of sickly howl. His men nervously stared at one another, their gooseflesh rose then, their large white eyes moved together toward the woods. The dark refuge hinted at nothing but the swelling noise of men on horseback traveling quickly through the undergrowth. This wasn't part of the evening's plans. This wasn't supposed to happen. Below and across the frozen marsh, another cry came from the woods. It was a battle cry.

The major's men quickly aligned their guns. They all knew that nothing good was coming from those woods. All the men loyal to Vlad were now at the steps of the old Arsenal. Below them, the clambering continued. It had to be the tsar's personal envoy, Don Cossacks, whose barracks were located on the other side of the mound. The gunners made certain their weapons were loaded and ranged in. Hopefully, the guns would make a short order of them.

The cannons barked down the line one by one—BOOM–BOOM–BOOM—each puffy cloud obscuring the major's view a wee bit more.

The Cossacks exploded through the woods. All their horses were in full gallop. Like black ants fleeing a trampled anthill, they emerged from the dark woods and devoured the white meadow. It was a ghostly image made real when the riders screamed out their fiery rallying cry: "To the death!" The men atop the hill, all looked at their leader as he told them to commence firing at will. They wasted no time. The artillery sailed over the Cossacks heads and landed in the woods behind them. Harmlessly, timber began to explode, causing a glorious fire show. The Cossacks unaffected from the first volley pressed on.

The second salvo was better aimed. This time, a few of the men on horseback fell. With this, the Cossacks separated into two groups. One rode in the direction of the palace, and the other headed directly toward the battery of guns.

The major could not believe his eyes. How could this be? He had at least two more chances to save himself.

Undaunted by the canon fire, the riders approached as clouds of smoke filled the skies.

The third volley landed, but the band of screaming Cossacks continued. As they charged the hill, they all lowered their lances.

"Steady men, steady," the major warned, but some of his men were already beginning to turn and run. "Fire!"

With a flash of light, the fourth salvo barked as the first riders reached the hillcrest. There was a problem. Fedorov had no machine gunners to support his heavy guns, thanks to Zurin.

"Damn you, Zurin! I will see you in hell!"

As his men scattered down the hill, the major ran for his horse. When he had nearly reached it, he turned back and saw the hilltop littered with men.

From their horses, the Cossacks with their long sabers were chopping at anything that moved. Then, one of them closer than the rest lined up with his lance and charged at him. He watched the one shot he managed to get off miss.

Falling to his knees, he whispered, "So be it?"

The advancing rider showed no mercy.

Vlad's men stopped. Their prize lay just ahead of them. Then they heard the canon fire coming from the direction of their flank. Vlad knew what that meant—the Cossacks were coming, and soon.

Within a Herd of Charging Cossacks

Serge and Dmitri eyed one another in silent thought: how in the hell had they got here?

They had been under fire since breaking the tree line. As they paused to collect themselves, they saw the lancers closing in on the heavy guns. At that moment, the field in front of them exploded into a dark murky cloud. Serge braced himself for the worst, but as he rode through the falling snow and dirt, he saw Dmitri's horse.

The duke, covered in wet snow, smiled. "Hell of a night! You okay?"

Serge yelled, "Never better!"

"Good," the duke declared as he tightened his reins. "Tally-ho!" The duke's "tally" was much more convincing than his "ho," for as they reached the crest, he witnessed the size and strength of the enemy. Aglow by a thousand torches, Vlad's army was in motion. Below them came an opposing army two or three thousand strong of Russia's elite soldiers, all on horseback. They appeared invincible. Nonetheless, the Cossack captain wasted no time. Like a moth to a hot flame, he led his six hundred men straight toward them.

In full gallop, Serge attempted to get Dmitri's attention. But the duke was as fixated as the captain on stopping the rebellion. Then Serge caught sight of a man who nearly dwarfed his horse. It had to be Vlad. The prince hoped that Nicholas was no longer in the palace, for it would soon be overrun.

Looking over his shoulder, Vlad saw cavalry approaching from the west. They could only be the Cossacks. Damn waste of fine wine!

"General, would you like me to lead a charge against them?" one of his commanders asked.

"Why bother?" he shouted as he spurred his horse. "The prize is in front of us, not behind." Then he muttered to himself, "What's happening to my excellent plan?"

The palace was getting closer. Then Vlad noticed a small squadron of men riding toward him.

Belarus saw them too. "Palace guards. Not a threat."

"Doing their duty to die for their emperor," Vlad grinned. "See to it personally that we are accommodating."

The fog was gone now, and the night had become crystal clear. There was a pale crescent moon. Now, the only uncertainty that lay before them was the outcome.

General Konstantin, with a shotgun still in his hand, shouted at the top of his lungs to Sandro: "The doctor said I had months to live. I am beginning to have my doubts."

Sandro was too busy laughing to reply. Then, they noticed the tsar's white charger bolting ahead of the pack of horses.

As the distance closed, Vlad realized it was no ordinary squad approaching—it was the tsar himself. Good, he thought, rushing to the lead.

Belarus cleared his throat. "General, I believe— "

"I already know. Nicholas is approaching. Your orders are the same. Form a line and finish him!"

Vlad's men were within a hundred yards when the emperor brought his horse to a halt. His Majesty's Life Guard slowed their horses and moved to surround him. The tsar's bodyguard Chekhov urged his horse closer to the sovereign, holding his saber in his hand as he eyed the traitors.

When Sandro and Platon reached Nicholas and his guard, the four of them and the rest of the palace guard were encircled by friend and foe.

Vlad and Belarus arrived shortly before the Cossacks, who were dumbfounded by this odd sight. All lowered their lances, and reached for their sabers. Nicholas spoke. He looked magnificent on top of his mount, as if he was truly his father's son.

"Gentlemen, you wanted to pay me a visit," declared the tsar. "I am before you. What is it that you ask?"

Silence greeted him.

Again the tsar spoke as his steed, causing an eerie cloud of vapor, traveled in tiny circles. "I say, what fool brought you all out on a night like this?" There were a few snickers. "Gentlemen, before we all freeze to death, I ask you once more—what do you wish of me?"

"Just your death," Vlad growled, moving his horse closer to the tsar's mount.

"Yours first!" Platon said, pointing his shotgun at Vlad's chest. The general noticed the handle of his old sword.

"General Konstantin, please lower your shotgun," Nicholas ordered.

Reluctantly, the soldier obeyed.

"And my glorious Cossacks, please lower your weapons. You too, Chekhov."

"You don't understand, Nicholas. You are no longer giving the orders," Grand Duke Vlad said imperiously.

"Really? Is that true, my brave men? Am I no longer worthy of your trust?"

One of Vlad's men spoke. "Your Majesty, the war has turned the world upside down. Grand Duke Vladimir would be a better choice for restoring our ranks to proper order."

"I see."

"Nicholas, as you plainly must realize, you have two choices: live or die," Vlad said tersely. "You decide."

The ground began to shake as a mass of riders approached. They all looked to the south, where the combined regiments of the Horse Guards and the Dragoons from Pavlovski Palace were emerging.

The tsar spoke: "My dear cousin, there's one more choice that you have not mentioned." He unsheathed his sword. "And that is for you to get out of my way!"

"So be it," Vlad said, freeing his own sword.

CHAPTER 38

What Remained

At that moment, as Vlad had moved towards the tsar, he knew all was lost. Most of his men had never seen the tsar appear so godly. So they fought half-heartedly. It hadn't helped matters that General Konstantin's shotgun had decapitated the brave but foolish Captain Belarus as he pushed his commander out of the way. All this tallied up to ruin.

When the Cossacks started wielding their sabers, and their cry combined with the enormous cavalry charge from the south, he knew it was really over. Two-thirds of his men scattered like guilty thieves into the nearby woods.

"It's over, Vlad," General Konstantin said as he raised his saber. "You must realize it by now."

"I feel that I have lost a battle, but not the war," he challenged as he turned his stallion toward Konstantin. "By tomorrow, I will have another army under me!"

"By tomorrow you will be dead!" Konstantin replied as his saber fell upon Vlad's sword.

As Vlad's retaliating blows crashed down on him, Konstantin was barely able to protect himself. Sandro, from a distance, aimed his pistol at the giant attacking his friend. Vlad, through luck or misfortune, turned just in the nick of time. The bullet grazed his shoulder. That was when Serge first saw his father from the other end of the field.

Weakened, Konstantin would not give up. The general knew that all he needed to do was to keep Vlad engaged until the dragoons arrived. "Looks like you're running out of options," Platon shouted.

"So are you, old man!" Vlad sneered and, with lightning speed, his sword drew blood. The duke took out his frustrations on an old foe. "Platon, it should not have been like this."

Seeing this, Serge crossed the field in full gallop. He yelled, "No!" With one last swing, Platon fell from his horse shocked that he had not won.

"Father!" Serge cried as he reined in his horse. Reaching his father, he quickly dismounted.

Platon looked at his son. "Sergei," he gasped, "I tried." The old general smiled and closed his eyes.

Sandro arrived and checked his pulse. "It's weak, but steady."

Serge asked. "Where's Vlad headed?"

From across the frozen meadow, Vlad's large horse moved towards the protection of the nearby woods.

"Escaping to the north," Sandro said as he placed pressure on Platon's wounds. "He must be heading to his brother's cottage across the woods. If you hurry, you can cut him off at the ruins. And if you catch him—finish him."

Serge nodded. He knew the ruins well. He had played there often as a child. Serge brought his saber's blade to his face in a salute to his father. With that, the prince rode off in the direction of the ruins.

The tsar, seeing all of this, dismounted from his horse. "How is he?" Sandro's eyes and his tunic covered with the general's blood stated the obvious. Konstantin was going to die.

Nicholas moved closer and cradled the general's head. "Platon, my most loyal friend," he said as tears filled his eyes. "You have always done what was asked of you." With that Platon slipped into unconsciousness but the tsar kept speaking. Crying out, "I did not know, Platon. For God's sake, please believe me. The separate peace was all Alix's doing!"

Sandro answered for his friend, "Platon already knew."

This news only worsened how the tsar felt.

The Way to the Ruins

Nikolai was right, Vlad thought, as he fled the field. We should have waited and recruited more men. As cries of pain and death filled the night, he looked down at his saber still in his hand and felt sorrow for only one. He believed General Konstantin deserved a better death.

Vlad was able to regroup with a few of his men. "Almost," he said to them as they headed quickly toward the cottage. He had one chance of escape, but he needed the pretty little ballerina as a bargaining chip for his safe passage to the south.

"The battle is not over yet, general. Our men can still fight," one of his remaining officers said. He was too much of an optimist. They had dared greatness and failed.

As they neared the cottage, Vlad wished for the return of the night's earlier fog, but it had all lifted. No hiding anymore. They were being chased by a small group of Cossacks whose horses were closing in on them quickly.

"General, we must split up if we are to have any chance of surviving."

Vlad, covered in blood, nodded in agreement. "Do what you can, son."

The officer turned his horse. "See you in hell, General!"

Vlad smiled. "Save me a seat."

What soldiers were left followed their commander to a certain death. The other half followed the duke. When Vladimir reached the security of the trees, he looked back as he heard a voice scream, "Long live Tsar Vladimir! Long live Russia!"

It was a gallant act, but a costly one. The rebels were cut down quickly. The Cossacks were taking no prisoners, and Vlad's men felt their vengeance with every slicing blow.

Vlad did not look back again. He could not afford to. He had underestimated his cousin. In the south, he could recruit more men. He could once again try to overthrow Nicholas. He thought of the new battles to come and smiled. He was five minutes away from the stables. With Kschessinska by his side, he could flee the capital and head south. Then, he heard a horse above him on the top of the ridge.

Vlad hurried down the hill, but his horse stumbled and threw him. He was lucky the horse did not roll over him in the fall. Grabbing his revolver and sword, he walked out of the woods as the brightness of the crescent moon blinded him. As he closed his eyes, he heard his pursuer slicing through the woods.

"Give me your horse! I will make certain you are saved." Vlad commanded in a vague hope that the horseman was on his side.

"Not tonight, General," Serge said as he came into the light. "As far as I am concerned, you are already dead!"

Nearby were the ruins, an old fort made up of two towers connected by an arched bridge. What an ideal spot to finish it.

"You want me, Serge," the general said, "then come and get me."

"You killed my father," the prince said as he leapt from his horse and unsheathed his sword. "And now I am going to kill you."

Vlad began testing his new sword. "Do what you must boy. I need a horse." He paused. "And yours will do."

Serge looked at his mount. "Here she is—your freedom. Now, all you must do is get past me."

Young Konstantin possessed an eerie confidence. Vlad had seen this look before. The boy wanted to prove something to the world. "Serge, let me pass," he said in a charming tone, "and I will let you live."

"Vlad," he coolly replied, "you can't kill what is already dead." With those words, the prince rushed across the narrow bridge. The duke raised his sword in a salute, "Your last chance, Serge. Join me or die."

Striking his first blow, he cried, "Never."

From the distance, their silhouettes danced across the slivered moon. It was a timeless struggle of pain and pride played against a Gothic backdrop of earth and stone.

Back and forth, creeping over the bridge, the two men exchanged blow after blow. It appeared to be a stalemate. Vlad was nearly twice as big, but Sergei was fierce and quick, and fighting for revenge.

"You're quite a swordsman," Vlad shouted with a toothy grin. "It is a pity all that shall soon go to waste."

"If you can, then do it," Serge replied with one more powerful blow, one that drew blood.

Vlad was startled. Never before had he been cut in battle. He brought his sword up one last time, and saluted the younger man. "The day is yours," he said, still wearing his grin. "But I am afraid your horse is mine."

Serge rushed him. "Not quite."

"Quite," Vlad said, raising his revolver and pulling the trigger. He aimed low, at Serge's leg; the shot took him off the bridge. Serge fell hard, but he did not scream. He was too mad to scream. Vlad looked down at him. "You, my boy, are worthy of the Konstantin name. Remember that."

The duke knew the shot would not go unnoticed. He quickly leaped onto Serge's horse. "Young Konstantin, you're a good fighter. But sometimes that is not enough."

Holding his leg, Serge didn't bother to pull out his own empty revolver.

"You can't escape, Vlad! Now, you can never escape."

"We will see. Your new girlfriend will be my ticket out, and she is just over the ridge. Goodbye, Serge. I am certain our paths shall cross again."

Just then, like some medieval knight, Dmitri emerged from the tree line, holding a lance. He raised it, yelling "Traitor!" Then he charged directly at his uncle.

Vlad's confident smile disappeared from his face. "Long live Russia!" the general countered. "Long live the House of Vladimir!"

Then, Dmitri's lance found its mark. The giant fell in one pass. Serge recalled a piece of Scripture: with one swing, the dragon was cast down along with all his angels.

Dmitri reached Serge with a look of redemption on his face. "Are you okay?"

"Yes, I'm good."

"The Lord offered me a second chance, Serge."

"And you made the most of it, my friend. Let's make sure this is finished."

Returning to the spot where Vlad had fallen, Serge half-expected the duke's body to be gone. But it wasn't.

The dragon was not dead, but Serge had seen enough dying people to know he would be soon.

"You came close, Vlad," Serge said as he grabbed his father's sword. "But Nicholas is tsar."

"Not for long," he said, as blood spat from the corners of his mouth.

"For long enough."

Vlad grew quiet and still. He was gone.

Dmitri searched the dead man's pockets to shed light on the names of those involved. But all he found was a map, and a letter. The duke recognized the handwriting. It was Alexandra's.

"What's that?"

"I don't even want to know," he said, setting the letter ablaze. "Serge, where were you a week ago?"

On the Steps of the Ruins

The tsar and a small army of men reached the place a few minutes later.

"Where is he?" the emperor shouted.

Serge pointed to the ground. "Here."

The field became still. Then the tsar shouted, "Bring him back to the palace."

"Wait. What about Mathilda?"

"Mathilda?" the emperor stopped dead in his tracks, "What has Vlad done?"

"He told me that she was just beyond the ridge."

"The cottage?"

"Your Highness," declared an officer on horseback, "I just came from there. We found the Grand Duke Andrew tied up in the cellar. The rest of the house was empty."

"Major, take a few men to guard the duke's body. The rest of us will search the imperial stables near the cottage."

They found her in a stall, bound and gagged. The tsar told his men to wait outside. He slid open the door. "Marie!" his pet name for her when they were young. He was so thankful she was safe that he had some fun as he untied her. "How do you get yourself into these things?" Then he noticed her black eye. He traced his fingers along it, and whispered, "Bastard!"

"I am all right. Is he dead?"

"I assure you he shall never harm anyone again."

Then it was her turn to tease. "Niki finally you came back!"

"Yes, it took longer than I expected." He gently caressed her bruised face as they both rested upon a bale of hay. They quickly embraced, melting into one another. It was only a moment, but for the two of them it felt like a lifetime. "I am sorry I ever left." He said these words in a tone reserved for lovers.

"Your forgiven," she laughed as she brushed the dirt from his face. "What did I miss?"

"Vlad's dead and a lot of my men are dead or wounded, including my friend Konstantin."

"Not Sergei!"

"No, his father, Platon." At that, the tsar lost his words.

"But why did they do this?"

"They thought I was weak."

"They were wrong."

"Were they?" He said, picking her up off from the ground.

Sandro stood alone on the porch aglow in torchlight. Hovering above him was the palace of yellow and white. There, within its walls, he had just laid his good friend down to an eternal sleep.

"Where's Platon?" the tsar asked as he and Serge rode up. His men had taken Marie back to Andrew's cottage, where she would be safe. Sandro looked at Serge. "He passed away in my arms five minutes ago. His last words were, 'Take care of my son.'"

Grief encircled Serge. He remembered the missed years of not speaking and then he felt his stomach drop. Falling to his knees, he felt no pain from his wound, just a longing to speak to his father one last time.

"Sergei, like all great generals he left us in the midst of battle," Sandro said. "I think he would have wanted it that way."

Behind them, thousands of men with torches searched for Vladimir's remaining men. Those hidden in the woods were doomed. There would be no mercy for them. There could not be. An example needed to be set. Bursts of gunfire and cries of pain were muffled by the passing wind.

The tsar handed his horse's reins to a servant. "Let's go in."

Ernie stood at the palace entrance along with the empress. He was covered in blood. He had fought bravely this evening.

"What should we do with him?" Sandro asked. "He knows too much about tonight."

As if reading their thoughts, "Niki," Ernie said, trying to wipe blood from his own hands, "I don't know what happened tonight but it is no concern of mine."

"Ernie," the tsar said, "German or not, you're my brother-in-law. I appreciate you picking up a sword for me. I..." The tsar had trouble finding the words.

Ernest slowly nodded.

"Now," Nicholas asked as he raised his revolver, "will you swear to me that you will tell no one of this?"

He bowed. "I swear it, on my own sister's good name."

"I guess that will have to do," Sandro said. The comment brought laughter to the awkward moment. Alexandra turned and went inside.

"Ernie," the tsar said as he put his arm around him.

"I know. The Kaiser's terms of peace?"

"They were never real. Tell him come spring, the Russians will be ready for him, not basking in the sun."

"But why the change of heart?"

"Blame Zimmerman's telegraph to the sultan."

"The sultan...I don't understand."

"It doesn't matter, Ernie. Willy was never planning on giving me Constantinople. Therefore, I must take it."

With that, His Majesty entered the palace, with the others behind him. The lights that lined the palace's long driveway came on, one by one. "We have power," a guard said.

"Yes, but for how long?" Sandro thought to himself. "Tonight was just the beginning."

CHAPTER 39

A Father's Funeral

Surrounded by friends and loved ones, a bandaged Serge looked down upon his father's casket draped with the imperial flag. It appeared that his world was unraveling before his very eyes. Then, his attention was drawn to the large concrete box that bore his family's name—KONSTANTIN. He had never felt so alone.

The prince found it difficult to believe that he would never see his father's face again. Like a whirlwind, the events of the last few days replayed themselves in his head. As he looked to his left, he saw Marie holding hands with Andrew. It appeared that perhaps they were together again, which was good. To the right was Jones, deep in thought, wearing a dark heavy coat with fur at the collar. Malachi had told Serge about the argument he and Platon had had regarding the dishonor of signing a separate peace. Jones now felt terrible about it. Especially when Serge told him what the empress had done.

The Welshman and the Russian exchanged a glance. Jones slightly bobbed his head and gave his old friend an awkward smile. As the old priest continued his prayer, Serge's eyes moved to Sandro. From the prince's perspective, the duke had aged a great deal this week. The creases around his eyes had deepened and he had lost the brisk bounce in his step. The loss of Platon had cut deep.

Still, Grand Duke Alexander managed to give Serge a half-hearted smile as the clergyman concluded with words from the book of Isaiah. "Though your sins are like scarlet, I will make them white as snow, though as red as crimson, I will make them as white as wool. Oh Lord, open your gates and receive this righteous soldier back into your glorious fold. Amen."

One by one, the guests departed.

After which, Marie and Andrew approached Serge. "It is a shame Niki could not be here ..." she hesitated, allowing Andrew to finish.

"But Rasputin's burial is today," the duke said sheepishly. "His is a private affair."

In some way, it made sense to Serge that the tsar had made this decision. Looking out into the park-like setting except for all the snow-covered grave stones, he absorbed this news and the grayness that came with it.

Andrew added, "I am deeply sorry, Sergei. We never thought it would come to this."

"We both grieve," the prince declared, "I for a father, you for a brother."

"You would not be grieving if it weren't for my brother."

Sergei smiled, "Loss is loss."

Andrew nodded his thanks, then left, giving Marie and Serge a minute alone.

"Your father is now beside his beloved," she said.

"Somehow, that fact alone makes it somewhat bearable." He paused. "So, you are back together?"

"Yes. For the moment."

"Good," he said halfheartedly.

"Do I detect a little jealousy, my young prince?" she teased.

"No. Maybe." He was now completely alone. All his family was dead and buried.

"Maybe?" She held his hands as she bit her lower lip. "Remember that you have your entire life before you. So, no more looking back," she smiled. "You see, I have wasted too much of the present retracing the days of my youth."

"With Nicholas?"

She watched him return to his dark thoughts. "Don't, Serge. Your life is ahead of you, full of promise."

"Promise? But what should I do?"

"Everything," she said as she gave him a peck on the cheek. "In ten years from now, I shall only be a fading but pleasant memory."

"That will never happen."

"Trust me, dear one. You shall see that I am right. One day we shall pass on the street with only fuzzy memories of this day."

"Until then," he said as he pulled her closer, "I shall miss you."

"You better," she whispered in his ear. Then she turned and walked away.

Only Sandro and Jones remained.

"Good sermon," the duke offered. "Your father would have liked it."

Serge stared at the draped coffin. "How so?"

"It was short." All three burst out laughing. Sandro was the first one to collect himself. "Let's get out of here."

"What's next, Sandro?" Sergei asked as he walked with the aid of a cane.

"I don't know," the duke said, eyeing Jones. Malachi took the hint and headed back toward the car. He had heard how much the duke despised all things British.

"Squeaks," Jones said, "I will see you back at the hotel."

The prince gave Jones an appreciative glance.

In the distance, nearly shielded by headstones, was Renko, alone as usual. Jones and the inspector shared a professional nod as they passed one another. Today they were once again allies.

The duke and the prince slowly walked through an area of waist high headstones with the high stone pillars of Cathedral of the Lady of Kazan looming behind them. Serge leaned heavily on his cane.

"Tuesday, the tsar officially severed communication with the Kaiser," Sandro said when they were alone. "There will no longer be a separate peace brokered by the hands of the empress. The French and British are pleased, but we have no idea how involved they both were in the coup."

"And the others?"

"I think he wants this all to be swept under the rug. Ernie left empty-handed and my precious son-in-law was ordered to his country estate."

"I have heard. But why did he send Dmitri all the way to Persia? Without his help, Vlad may have succeeded in his coup."

"Nicholas gave me his word that it was only for the time being. I am sure it was a compromise he had to make with the empress."

"What is Nicholas going to do with her?"

"The empress is the empress. I wish the tsar would just send her off to a nunnery and be done with it, but that will never happen. Her past sins have already been forgiven."

"I haven't heard a word of this on the Petersburg streets, nor in the papers," said Serge.

"And you won't. It apparently never happened. The papers fell in and reported that Vlad died in his sleep at his palace of a heart attack. This weekend, his name is to be added to the honored dead."

"Amazing" He was afraid to ask, but was compelled to do so. "And Uncle Bimbo?"

"My brother was ordered to his country estate for the time being." His eyes drifted away from Serge, utterly ashamed.

"Will there be a constitution?"

"Nicholas sees the logic of it, but would rather wait until spring and declare it from a position of power. He says he will consider it after our first offensive victory."

"The spring is a long way off."

"I know. But he does not want it to appear that he's being forced into it." Sandro paused. "Well, I must be getting back to Kiev and my men. Sergei, what are your plans?"

"I'm heading back to the front."

"When?"

"As soon as my father's affairs are settled."

"Good," Sandro said as he patted him on the shoulder. "We definitely need you, now more than ever." He paused, smiling at his nephew. Hope had entered him again. "Son, have you ever flown before?"

"No," Serge admitted as he looked up at his only remaining friend.

"I have a strange feeling you would be most excellent at it."

"Me—a pilot?"

"Why not?"

Staring down at his feet, "Perhaps after the war. Until then, I shall forgo the delight."

The duke smiled. "Why wait?"

Amongst countless monuments to the dead, the prince agreed, "Why indeed."

As the wind picked up, Sandro began another story: "Serge, have I ever told you about the time your father and I..."

The two wandered back to their waiting car.

CHAPTER 40

The Station
St. Petersburg

Days later, Serge was on a train headed toward Kiev. He was going there to see a man who planned to teach him to fly. Sandro was right. He needed a new beginning, another chance. As he entered his train compartment, he was surprised to find an envelope lying flat on the seat. Nervously, he fanned his fingertips through his hair.

Mustering his courage, Serge took his seat and grabbed the manila envelope. With one glance, he knew it was from Renko. Breaching it, he could feel his palms begin to sweat. At that exact moment, a piece of paper freed itself and floated slowly to the floor.

> *Serge,*
>
> *All the beautiful words are from others. I can offer you these: FAITH, HONOR, and LOYALTY. Your father was molded by these three words. What else is there to say? On Saturday, he asked me to give this letter to you before you left the city. When you didn't leave, I decided to hold on to it for safekeeping. I am thankful I did. I don't know what he wrote. Regardless, never doubt the fact that he truly loved you. He did. So take care, and live your life.*
>
> *Renko*

Serge's hands were now numb as he gazed upon his father's handwriting. He read it painfully. It was more than he probably deserved.

Sergei

What warmth and tender thoughts your name brings to me as I write this. You are the legacy of the love your Mother and I shared. Remember that always.

My dear son, you cannot imagine how many farewell letters I have written during my lifetime, far too many. In my youth, I was far too eager to shed my blood for the glory of others. I wasted so many precious moments in the outskirts of the empire when I should have been home with you and your mother. I can only blame myself for the distance between us.

You see, I missed so many firsts in your life. The first time you ever laughed, the first time you lost a tooth, or for that matter the first time you attempted to walk. How can I call myself a father when I was never there?

Though allow me this one moment. I am not certain you will remember it. I do, as if it only occurred last night. I was between assignments and you were so scared of your room. I think you thought you had monsters living under your bed. Ha! Even then, you had such a splendid imagination. It is such a gift. That night, a thunderstorm passed through Petersburg and it got the best of you.

To this day, I can hear you running through the darkness, your tiny feet scampering down the hall as you called out 'Papa, make 'm stop.' How easily I scooped you up to safety then, and within a few moments your weary head fell upon my shoulder in a deep sleep. There, at that moment in my life, I knew what it was to be a father. Someone you could run to. Your mother just sat back in happy astonishment and observed us.

I now know that she wanted to record that one moment, to replay it over and over when I was gone. And, sadly, I always seemed to be gone. There is no forgiveness for neglecting those who you love and who love you. I realize that now. I have always known that my darling Tatiana deserved a better man than me. But since she placed her beautifully stubborn eyes on me, she saw a man that needed to be loved. She was and is my darling Angel.

As you might already know, I am dying. The one thing that makes my passing bearable is that I will soon be returning to your Mother. She was the one who somehow kept our family together and strong. She always focused firmly on what mattered—the three of us. I see so much of her in you. Her goodness. Her will. You have the same pureness of nature, and that is a true blessing. I pray the war has not worked out all the good.

I trust the Lord to keep you well, son. Please don't return to Petersburg, I don't want you to remember me like this. Instead, keep this letter in memory of me, and at times, pull it out and recall a stormy night when you were scared, little, and running blindly through the dark and I was there. From now on, living in spirit and memory, I always will be.

So, follow your heart, son. Lay down the heavy name that we both bear and choose your own path. Do what you love. I know you will make me proud, Sergei you always have. Never doubt my love for you.

> *Your devoted father in the dark,*
> *P. Konstantin, Petersburg,*
> *Winter of '16*

As Serge finished, he placed the letter on his lap and wept. As the train began to pull away from the station, he saw Renko standing at the end of the platform, bundled up against the cold.

Waving at him, Serge mouthed, "Thank you."

Waving back, Renko replied, "You're welcome."

Then, he was gone, replaced by the sight of weathered warehouses. A faded advertisement plastered to the side of one of the buildings caught the prince's eye. Somehow, it seemed appropriate. It was an old war poster. It reminded him that he was now beginning his journey from who he was to who he wanted to be.

Dragging himself away from it, he eased back in his seat and closed his tired eyes and remembered an honorable man wearing an easy smile. Right then and there, in that precious moment, he knew that his father had truly loved him. And in the end, that's all he really needed to know.

What Happened Next?

"Sometimes—history needs a push."
Vladimir Lenin

The Romanov Family

As the war raged on and on in no apparent direction, support for Nicholas's regime faded until it reached an all-time low in late February of 1917; then His Majesty under enormous strain was forced to relent his full authority to a new Provisional Government. This government formed and supported by those loyal to the empire sought to right the Russian ship currently adrift.

They failed. Leaving the door wide open for Lenin and the Bolsheviks (financially backed by the German Kaiser) to overthrow the Provisional Government creating a bloody civil war.

Those loyal to the old ways, the Whites, fought hard to oppose the forces of the new formed Soviet government, the Reds. During this power struggle, Nicholas had been held against his will, first by the members of the Provisional Government than those of the Soviet.

In the summer of 1918, General Alexeiev, one of Tsar Nicholas's most loyal generals, led a fraction of the White Army towards the industrial city of Yekaterinburg—a territory on the southern steppes of the Ural Mountains in Siberia held at the time by the Red Army and where the Soviet regime headed by Vladimir Lenin decided to detain Their Majesties and their five children.

On the early morning of July 17, 1918, as General Alexeiev's forces big guns pulverized the Red Army protecting the city, the last Tsar of Russia had been awakened in the wee hours of the morning and informed of his fate. Pavel Medvedev, a soldier of the Red Army, witnessed Tsar Nicholas's murder firsthand wrote. Quoted from Robert Wilton's *the Last Days of the Romanovs*. Wilton was *the Times* reporter Jones bumped into at the Hotel Europe when he was searching for Serge.

I am Pavel Spiridonovich Medvedev, 31 years of age, and belong to the Orthodox Church; able to read and write; born a peasant of the Sissert factory of the Yekaterinburg district...we entered the lower floor of the house. After entering the corner room, adjoining the storeroom with a sealed door, Yurovsky [Lenin's agent and the captain of the guards] *ordered chairs to be brought. His assistant brought three chairs. One chair was given to the emperor, one to the empress, and a third to the heir.*

The empress sat by a window, near the rear column of the arch. Behind her stood three of her daughters... the heir and the emperor sat side by side, almost in the middle of the room. Dr. Botkin stood behind the heir. The maid, a tall woman, stood by the left post of the door leading to the storeroom. By her side stood one of the tsar's daughters (the fourth)... It looked as if all of them guessed their fate, but not a single sound was uttered. Eleven men walked into the room at the same time [began firing]: *Yurovsky, his assistant, the two from the extraordinary commission, the Cheka, and seven Latvians.*

I saw all the members of the tsar's family lying on the floor, with many wounds in their bodies. The blood was gushing. The doctor, the maid and the servants had also been shot... the heir was still alive, and moaning. Yurovsky walked over to him and shot him two or three more times. The heir fell still.

Such was the final moments spent of Tsar Nicholas II, Empress Alexandra, their five children and a few loyal servants.

Eight days after the executions, the town of Yekaterinburg was captured by the White Army.

Schastleevo, St. Petersburg!

The Others...

Grand Duke Alexander Mikhailovich—Sandro, authored three books on Imperial Russia before his death in the French Alps in 1933.

Grand Duke Nikolai Mikhailovich—Uncle Bimbo, older brother to Sandro, shot by the Bolsheviks January 28, 1919 at the Fortress of Sts. Peter and Paul. Was told before his death by Lenin, *"the revolution does not need any historians."*

Grand Duke Paul Alexandrovich—Nicholas's uncle, shot by the Bolsheviks in the same courtyard of the Fortress of Sts. Peter and Paul that Bimbo found his death, January 30, 1919.

Grand Duke Dmitri Pavelovich—the tsar's favorite nephew. Married an American heiress from Cincinnati, Ohio. Died in 1942.

Grand Duke Andrew Vladimirovich—Nicholas's cousin. Married Mathilda-Marie Kchessinska (prima ballerina) in Paris in 1921. Died 1956.

Senator Vladimir Purishkevich—religious extremist. Died during the Russian Civil War fighting for the Whites, the anti-Bolshevik movement.

Alexander Protopopov—Minister of the Interior. Executed by the Bolsheviks January 1, 1918.

Sir George Buchanan—British Envoy to Russia until 1918. After the Russian Revolution, he returned to Britain to finish his memoir, *My Mission to Russia and Other Diplomatic Memories*. Died 1924.

Mathilda-Marie Kchessinska—Prima Ballerina Assoluta of His Majesty's Imperial Ballet. She married Grand Duke Andrew in 1921. Lived in Paris as a ballet instructor until her death in 1971.

Prince Felix Yusupov—sole heir to Russia's wealthiest family lost everything during the Revolution. Died practically penniless in Paris 1967.

What happened to Prince Sergei Konstantin?

Find out in David Shone's next novel *Champagne Haze*. Set in Paris, it is a story of the 'Lost Generation' trying to find themselves.

Here's an excerpt.

"In the spring of '27, something bright and alien flashed across the sky. A young Minnesotan who seemed to have nothing to do with his generation did a heroic thing, and for a moment people set down their glasses in country clubs and speakeasies and thought their old best dreams."

F. Scott Fitzgerald
Echoes of the Jazz Age

The Hotel Majestic, Paris
Penthouse Suite

A new day's sun danced atop a booze-soaked floor littered with shards of broken glass. Within this wreckage, a group of five old friends sat and laughed as their eyes descended on what remained of their room. Their little soirée had lasted until dawn. At its peak, in the wee hours of the morning, the piano played at a feverish beat. Like a drug, it pushed them and the night on.

That was about five hours ago—when this room had been packed wall to wall with people—a fiery mix of parasite-like beings they picked up from the various nightclubs in the Left Bank they had stumbled into last night. Most of them they had found in the trendy bars that lined the Quarter—Paris's own version of sin—warmed over.

As the first rays of light crept in, the piano slowly grew silent as their party guests vanished like ghosts, running off to spook less fortunate of places.

Now, in the embers, the five still wearing what was left of their tuxedos from the night before took an inventory of the last twelve hours. One by one, they smiled at one another, smoking and joking. They were bone tired but it was worth it. Even in their early thirties, these boys could pack a punch. It was a talent the five had for squeezing the most out of a moment. And last night was no exception.

Yesterday, they had arrived here from various ends of the world—New York, London, Berlin. Two lived near here.

These boys's common quality is the love of a sport that they can no longer play—at least not to their former level of greatness. That sport is rugby. To them, it is much more than a game, it is a state of mind, a passion taught to them in their mud-covered youth at Oxford. But that had been fifteen long years ago.

Now, these relics of a team dubbed the Immortals are in Paris for the weekend to host a stag party for their former captain, Jones. You know Jones. He too, is like them—rich and irresistible. These men are no warriors of Great Causes anymore. No. These guys are here to enjoy one another's company as they rape and pillage Paris.

So here, all too tall and too handsome for their own good, are the remnants of that old Oxford team in no particular order.

Prince Serge Konstantin, their back, is a wealthy drifter now living in Paris. Serge is Jones's best man and the one that arranged for this stag weekend to occur. At Oxford, his team nickname had been 'Squeaks' because Serge never made mistakes on the field. The same could not be said for the prince's personal life. A decade after the Russian Revolution and the fall of the Old Regime, nothing really mattered anymore—especially worthless titles. The Russian's claim to fame, he is the great grandson of Tsar Alexander I, the emperor that beat Napoleon's Grand Army when they invaded Moscow.

Richard Killingsworth, cold and devastatingly charming bachelor and aristocrat, is the shiny penny and hated hero of the group. He is the winger who scored the winning 'try' versus Cambridge. Richard lives a very charmed life— a choice title, old money, and a stable full of beautiful girls in his life. The future British lord reeks of confidence and is being groomed by his demanding father for greatness. Everyone wants to be Richard. Even Richard. The rugby reunion is not the main reason for his trip to Paris. No. His motive is more complicated than that.

Lars von Eberwine, their forward, is a reckless German who enjoys a good fight as much as he loves the ladies. His lifestyle is fast and furious. Lars's likes to drink, but his main vice is women. The handsome German has an uncanny knack of attracting the worst ones. It isn't that Lars is a bad guy. On the contrary, he is generous and loyal to a fault. Though, something in the German is broken. The rest of the guys can't see it. To them, he is the wild one with wild blonde hair that rests like a shiny mane on his shoulders. Lars makes each night out unique and entertaining. But if you look closely, one can tell there is much sorrow buried in his deep blue eyes.

Jules de Vouge is the team's hooker. A sophisticated but distasteful clotheshorse, Jules is a bit too decadent and too young for this group. He was so good at rugby that he joined the varsity team during his freshman year, which gave him a nickname that suited him perfectly— Rookie. His family owns one of the finest and oldest wine labels in France, though you would never guess it by his actions. Jules is the sole Frenchman on the team and much beloved smart ass of the group. He is the one slouched in his chair with the cigarette clinched perfectly between his lips. He looks right at home in a room of ruin.

Taggart Sullivan a big ol' Yank from New York, is their center. Taggart is the one holding the champagne bottle squarely in his meaty hands. They all call him Tag. And, for a Yank, they don't come better. Though, his sharp wit normally gives Eberwine a run for his money as the team clown. His politician's charm is a gift from his father, the three-term senator from New York. Of course, Tag's humor comes in quite handy on Wall Street. He closes million dollar deals over jokes and drinks.

As Eberwine repeated last night's tale again of him pissing in the Luxembourg fountain, the room's telephone rang once, the signal from the front desk that the bachelor Jones and his fiancé have arrived.

"Pull the curtains," Richard barked to the others, "The Neanderthal is finally here."

"Got it," said Serge. Bouncing up, the former prince walked with a slight limp to the large terrace window capturing a postcard perfect view of the city. He gave the tall drapes a yank. Instantly, the room was in complete darkness. *Au revoir*, Paris! Until we meet again.

Bibliography

Alexander, Grand Duke of Russia. *Once a Grand Duke.* New York, New York: Farrar & Rinehart, 1932.

Buchanan, Sir George. *My Mission to Russia.* London, England, 1923. Cassell PLC, a division of The Orion Publishing Group (London) as the Publishers. All attempts at tracing the copyright holder of *My Mission to Russia and Other Diplomatic Memories* by Sir George Buchanan were unsuccessful.

Hynes, Vulliamy. *The Letters of the Tsar to the Tsaritsa, 1914-1917. Journal of the Royal Institute of International Affairs,* May, 1929. Vol. 8, No. 3, p. 285.

Kchessinska, Mathilda. *Dancing in Petersburg.* London, England: Victor Gollancz ©, a division of The Orion Publishing Group, 1960. Used with Permission.

Nicholas II. *The Secret Letters of the Last Tsar: The Confidential Correspondence between Nicholas and His Mother, Dowager Empress Maria Feodorovna.* New York, New York: Edward J. Bing, 1938.

Paul, Grand Duke of Russia. *The San Francisco Chronicle,* Sunday, September 17, 1917, p. 8.

Simanovich, Aron. *Rasputin, der Allmachtige Bauer.* Berlin, Germany, 1922.

Whitman, Robert. *The Last Days of the Romanovs.* New York, New York: George H. Doran, 1920.

Youssoupoff, Prince Felix. *Lost Splendor.* AVANT L'EXIL © Librairie Plon, 1952. Used with Permission.

Dedicated to my children, Aalijah and Aaniyah. You've always been my motivation.